THE QUEEN'S GAMBLE

GAME OF GODS BOOK 2

NICOLE SANCHEZ

First paperback edition March 2023

Edited by Tashya Wilson

Proofread by Amanda Iles

Cover Art by Karen Dimmick / ArcaneCovers.com

Header and Page Break art by Leigh Cover Designs

 Created with Vellum

For my sister, for honing my love of mythology

AUTHOR'S NOTE

As an author, it is important to me that all my readers to feel safe when reading my books. Some elements of this story may be upsetting to some readers. If you're not interested in learning more, please feel free to turn the page. If you have concerns, please see the list below:

Attempted sexual assault, pregnancy, miscarriage (past), animal death (on page).

If you need further clarity or are concerned about an unmentioned trigger, please feel free to email me at author.nicolesanchez@gmail.com

1

The endless buzzing will haunt my dreams. After twenty-three hours of hearing it, feeling it reverberate through my soul as it embeds itself in my DNA, I'm certain the sound will ring in my ears for the rest of eternity.

I check my watch and shift around, trying to find a more comfortable position. The stone throne I am sitting on has not warmed during the hours I've been occupying it. It's cleaved directly from the stone of the Underworld—my own domain—but it doesn't soften, not even for me, its queen. This seat is largely ceremonial, and I can only consider that having me use it is another way to punish me. Always tit for tat.

Posey was the one who *insisted* that if I'm going to cling to the idea that I'm still Queen of the Underworld, then I should sit on my throne. She also did *not* want me to wear my crown.

Another power play among the unending ones that Posey and I tussle over on a daily basis. She said if the challenge was to be held in Solarem proper then, as its queen, she should be the only one to wear a crown.

She didn't like it very much when I pointed out that she always wears a crown in my realm.

I'll give it to Helene for picking this as Galen's first challenge in the Trials. Each member of the Council—Xavier, Posey, Helene, Kai, Finn, and Dion—was required to submit a challenge. Finn and Dion are sitting in for the spots held by Essos and Galen. Apparently, after my death was announced to the Kingdom of Solarem, it was agreed that my Council seat would remain vacant until there was a new Queen of the Underworld.

Until the end of the Trials, I'm in an odd limbo. Queen of the Underworld, but not. Citizens still address me as the queen I was, but Posey is adamant that until I am wed to Galen, I am not actually queen.

When I proposed the Trials, I thought I was buying myself and Essos time to find a way out of this situation I was manipulated into, but we're only one month past the Calling Ball, and I'm regretting asking for six months. The situation hangs over me like an anvil, with no guaranteed way out.

When the details of the Trials were first discussed, I pushed back...

"If Galen should fail to win a majority of the Trials, I believe the vote of no confidence should be canceled," I argue.

Posey elected herself head planner for the Trials without resistance. Helene is already mad at me for having to play referee between Galen and me on a daily basis. Xavier didn't say it, but clearly, he is leaving the planning of this event in the hands of the women. He also didn't say he thought planning was a woman's job, but his actions—or lack thereof—heavily implied it.

I have my best friends by my side, and I feel stronger for it. Cat and Zara are learning so much more now about how Solarem operates than they did during the Calling. I insist on having them by my side when-

ever possible so they can learn the intricacies of the culture. Often, they're only observing, but right now, just having them in the same room makes me feel like I can actually survive this mess.

"These two events are not related, despite what Daphne might think. If she wants me to win the Trials to prove I belong in her bed, fine, but the vote of no confidence applies only to ruling the Underworld and cannot be rescinded."

"And you can't take control of the Underworld without our marriage," I hiss. *"When I married Essos, we made a blood exchange during our vows. The blood of the king runs through my veins. "Until Essos abdicates or you and I wed, you have the power to make decisions, but you won't have the powers of the Underworld. If I have my way, you never will."*

Galen doesn't reach for me but rather around me as he steps against me. It takes me a second to realize what he's doing, and it's not until I hear the garbled sounds of Cat choking that I realize he's got one hand around her throat.

"Submit," he snarls, our noses nearly touching.

Fuck. Fuck. Fuck.

I feel him raise his arm, and I know he's lifting Cat. He's backed me into a corner. We all know it, and I want to kill Posey for watching us like it's a fucking polo match.

"Yes, fine. I submit. Let her go." I hate that I'm giving in to him, but for Cat, I will drop to my knees right now if it means that he'll put her down.

"Since threatening you doesn't seem to work, know this: If you insist on stepping out of line, I will take your defiance out on Cat and Zara. You claim to need their support? Let's see how long they support you if you're being an insubordinate cow." Galen releases Cat, and I listen to her gasp for air as Zara moves to her side.

Gods forgive me for this. *I laugh in his face. "You had a fifty-fifty shot there of picking the one I actually care about. You got lucky that time."*

"What is that supposed to mean?"

Forget the Gods. Zara, please forgive me. *"Do you think I'm keeping Zara around for anything more than a lesson on what happens when someone crosses me? She thought she could push me toward you and take Essos for herself. She fooled around with my husband."*

Galen grabs my cheeks and kisses me hard. *"Don't forget, dearest, I'm going to be your husband."*

"Win the Trials and prove it."

"WOULD YOU STOP SQUIRMING?" Finn hisses, pulling me from my memory. His golden-eyed gaze slides over me as I shift again. My ass went numb an hour into the trial, and no amount of squirming has returned feeling to it. Not even the short walk I took was enough for me to regain feeling.

"I can't help it," I whisper, crossing and uncrossing my legs, trying something, *anything*, to get comfortable. My heel gets caught in one of the underlayers of my skirt, leaving me stuck. Of all the bad actors on the stage today, this dress is not one of them, and it feels unfair to take out my frustration on the gown.

"You need to." Finn's voice is firm as he grabs my wrist and squeezes gently.

"Focus on this." I snatch my hand out of his and hit him in his midsection. I'm satisfied when I hear a grunt.

I still don't know the full extent of my strength and powers. Some days, I'm strong enough to punch through a cement wall, and others, I can't even open my dresser drawers without feeling exhausted. My powers are returning, slowly. Nothing like my reincarnation has ever happened before, so no one—not the healers nor my so-called family—has any answers. On the upside, it means I can lash out with my powers and no one can blame me for it, thanks to their unpredictability. Breaking Xavier's nose last week was a bonus, even though it was unin-

4

tended. The flip side is that using my powers leaves me feeling drained.

That's why, when it comes to Galen, I already stepped back from being truly adversarial, even when he wasn't holding Cat and Zara over my head. For the first two weeks after the Calling Ball, I barely left my room, stepping out only to show myself in the house and make sure things were running smoothly. After I turned the kitchen into a veritable rainforest, Estelle firmly suggested that I take time to allow my body to adjust to its new circumstances.

I turn my eyes back to the pit below.

I zero in on Galen, who is sitting in a glass box. His legs are crossed and his eyes are closed as hundreds of bees buzz around him. For the first hour of the challenge, he stared at me as if he expected me to stop this trial from going forward. I could still stop it, but that would mean giving up on Essos and giving in to Galen. I might let him think I'm getting soft where he's concerned, but I'm not going to give in.

The warehouse in Solarem that is housing this challenge looks like it's home to an illegal fighting ring. Galen is in the center of the ground floor, and three stories of spectators are seated above him, with screens all around streaming the trial. Members of the press speak in hushed tones, like they're at a golf event, commenting on how good Galen is at sitting there and doing nothing. As if that isn't the most accurate description of him that I've heard.

The Council and I are on the highest level, part of the select few who are allowed here, along with, most unfortunately, the press. They keep casting curious gazes at where I sit, flanked by Zara and Catalina. Finn came over to stretch his legs, but none of us want to miss a moment in case that's the one when Galen cracks.

"Your Majesty." In front of me, a young woman drops to one

5

knee with her fist over her heart and her head bent. My gaze flicks to Posey, who is watching us, lips pursed.

"Please stand up. What is it that you want?" I don't mean to be rude, but Sybil told me that the press has been reaching out to get my statement on the events of the ball and how exactly I came back.

The cover story—that I was killed after giving up my immortality to spend a year as a mortal—can stretch only so far, and everyone knows that I'm not the most willing to stick to that lie, so Posey won't let me speak with anyone.

"My name is Celestina. I'm a harpy reporter for the *Solarem Sun*. I would love to ask you a few questions." She flashes me a genuine smile, and I study her. Ashy grey wings are tucked tightly against her body, and there is a sharpness to her yellow eyes that I don't like very much. In case I don't believe her, she offers me her press badge.

The *Solarem Sun* is a gossip rag, and I'm not interested in adding to their drivel. The logo of the paper is one I'm familiar with; it features a sun rising over the cityscape crown that is the emblem of Solarem. Their tagline, *Shining light on the dark, dirty secrets of the Solarem Elite,* is a crock of shit. Just seeing it brings forth a memory that I try to suppress, to no avail.

"HAVE YOU SEEN THIS?" *I ask, outraged, dropping the paper on Essos's lap. I didn't see the puppy he's holding, and the grey beast lets out a yip.*

"She didn't mean it, Dave," Essos coos, scratching behind the dog's ears. I kneel in front of him to see the puppy properly. He's all awkward limbs and too large paws, with a cheery disposition. Immediately, he starts to lick my face.

"No, Mommy did not mean it, but she's very mad at the mean newspapers." I use the puppy voice I swore I would never use. "Are we sure he's going to bond with the other two?"

"Yes, he will." Essos snorts, and I look up to see he's finally reading the headline. We're still two weeks away from our wedding, and I'm a bundle of nerves. "So, who is the daddy?" he asks, flashing me a glimpse of the inside article. I've already read it—twice—and nearly tore the whole thing to shreds. It's a photo of me and Xavier, outside after getting lunch to talk about what I should get Essos as a wedding gift. The angle makes it look like his hand is resting on my stomach, because we'd just broken off from a hug and he'd twisted to see who'd called his name. My stomach barely looks bloated, but apparently it was bloated enough to call for a bump watch.

I grab the paper from Essos and roll it up so I can smack him in the arm with it gently. "That is not funny," I tell him, getting to my feet.

Essos laughs and pulls me onto his lap, displacing Dave for a fraction of a second before the pup shifts onto my lap and gives both Essos and I licks.

"It's hilarious. Who cares what they print about us? The only thing that matters is that, in two weeks, I get to formally make you my queen, and I plan to make love to you in nothing but your new crown."

"Do we have to wait?" I ask with a mischievous grin.

"I don't see why we should."

"No." It's a complete sentence, and I look past Celestina, clearly dismissing her.

"So, I should print 'no comment' as the Queen of the Underworld's response for why she felt it was worth risking her life to play at being mortal for a year, leaving her realm in chaos after her death, when her people needed her?"

If only they realized how true that "play at being mortal" would become.

"I believe I said no questions."

She doesn't look the least bit chagrined. "If you change your mind, you can have Sybil contact me. They have my number.

Welcome back." Celestina bobs a short curtsey before backing away.

Maybe someday I'll be allowed to tell my story, but it won't be to the *Solarem Sun*.

One level below us, I can see gods and goddesses growing frustrated at the lack of excitement surrounding the event. A nymph throws her glass at the box, probably hoping to agitate the bees. She succeeds only in pissing off Posey, who turns her into a puddle on the spot. The poor nymph drips off the upper level and down into the pit before dissolving into nothing.

Behind me, Zara gasps. She's had a lot of adjusting to do since the Calling ended. Our lessons didn't cover nearly enough information to prepare anyone for life in Solarem, so I've been trying to fill her and Cat in where I can, and where I can't, I point them in the direction of my library. The most important lesson they've learned is that only gods and goddesses are truly immortal. The other beings of our realm are gifted with long life that verges on immortality, but they're still susceptible to illness and catastrophic injury —such as being turned into a puddle—which can lead to death.

The gods are as capricious as we're painted to be in the mortal realms. The cover story might have been that I was going to the mortal realm to research life as a mortal, but now that I've actually been there, there's enough truth in that story to make me think about how Solarem operates and how we can do better.

My gaze flicks to the clock, which counts down how much longer Galen needs to be in the glass box. The large red numbers are getting uncomfortably close to the twenty-four-hour mark. I don't want to see him win. It would be cheating, but I wish I could nudge the bees closer to him so we can end this. I can't stomach him winning the first challenge. It would set the tone for the rest of the Trials.

The bees seem undisturbed, and so does Galen. Until one bee

skirts a little too close to Galen's neck, and he flinches. After hours of bees doing just that, he must have hit his limit. There's a change in the air that has to be caused by Galen's mood, because the bees are now agitated.

One bee swoops in and bites him, drawing blood. Helene never said just what types of bees she put in there, but I'm hoping they're the bloodthirsty kind. I don't care if it makes me look biased—I lean forward in my seat, more awake than I have been in hours. Days, even. I can hear my blood rushing through my ears as he gets stung again, and the bees are whipped into a frenzy. It's astonishing how quickly he loses control once the bees scent his blood.

I fight to maintain my composure. I can't afford to let the hungry wolves outside the box see my own excitement that Galen is losing the trial. The crowd starts cheering, just as delighted by the blood as the bees are.

Galen's blood spatters on the inside of the glass box as the bees tear at his flesh, and I smirk. Of course, Helene wouldn't pick regular bees for this challenge. No, these bees are nearly three times the size of a murder hornet, so when they dig into flesh, they really *dig in.*

When he catches my expression, Finn pinches my arm. I scowl for his benefit, and he seems pleased by this reaction.

As the bees continue to dive-bomb him, Galen loses all control and burns them alive.

When the smoke clears, Galen is alone in the box, panting, his skin glistening with blood and sweat, his blond hair askew. He faces the judges' table, where Xavier, Posey, Helene, Kai, and Dion all sit, stone-faced. Helene rises to deliver the verdict for her trial. There is absolute silence in the room as she waves a hand and makes the box he is stuck in vanish.

She looks every part the queen she is. Her long blonde hair

cascades down her back in large, rich curls, and her crown of seashells and sea glass glitters in the dim light.

The crowd sucks in a collective breath in anticipation. I've waited one month for this first trial. One agonizing month of being forced to put on a happy face for meals and couples therapy with Galen.

One month of sporadic stolen kisses with the man I love.

Posey objected to making the first trial a public spectacle, but Xavier insisted, citing increasing pressure to have the masses attend. My announcement at the Calling that Galen would participate in the Trials to prove his love to me had made all of Solarem titter with anticipation. It was the most exciting thing to happen in centuries.

For those who couldn't score an invite, there is the livestream. The whole of Solarem just watched the God of War lose a battle with bees. So much for having patience on the battlefield. *Good.* I wanted him humiliated the way he humiliated me...the way he humiliated Essos.

I bury the thought of my husband and turn my attention back to the proceedings, focusing on how furious my sister-in-law looks.

Posey's little mouth is twisted into an angry sneer. She is committed to supporting Galen in his attempts to overthrow Essos and take over the Underworld. She was a committee of one when it came to planning the Trials, right down to objecting to Helene and I wearing crowns so people wouldn't be confused as to who was *the* Queen of Gods. Posey managed to object to everything, including the menu—she was aghast when Helene suggested it consist entirely of honey-centric items. It got to the point where Helene and I were shooting for shock value in everything we said to her.

I turn my attention to Galen. He doesn't look at either of his siblings, just me, his expression a silent promise to make me pay. I am his prize at the end of this, but he's tiring of my resistance to him. I haven't defied him publicly, not like I did the night I proclaimed the Trials. Since he voiced his threat to Cat and Zara, I've played the good girl. Let him think he's wooing me with breakfast in bed when I'm too weak to rise. I need him to think I'm on his side.

I should look disappointed he's lost. After all, I did choose him over my husband.

Then I found out it was Galen who murdered me and left my body for my husband—his brother—to find. What a twisted little web I'm stuck in.

"Galen has failed this trial. The task was to remain still for a period of four and twenty hours while surrounded by four hundred murder hornets. By being stung, you failed." Helene is trying—and failing—to keep the delight from her voice.

Xavier reaches for the large wooden gavel and cracks it on the table. The crowd erupts in a deafening cheer.

Across the room, I catch Helene's eye, and I smile.

2

After getting cleaned up for the ball that will follow the first trial, Galen approaches me.

We have done our best to dance around one another since the end of the Calling. The morning after the Calling Ball, he was apologetic, trying to sway me with flowers and pancakes. I had worn a simple tank top that morning so he could see the bruises I bore on my throat from his hands. When I wilted the flowers on sight, he chose to give me some space. He tried to be the boy who'd wooed me when he'd first arrived at the mansion. But the sight of him during that first week after the Calling Ball never failed to drive me to nausea.

I desperately needed that space, even if it was mostly spent asleep with dreams chasing me. It was space for me to remember some of the life I had before, space to learn what I had missed, and space to sort through the tidal wave of emotions that assaulted me daily.

Today was a good day, other than the numbness that stretched from my lower back and down my legs from that fucking throne.

Around the room, debts are being settled. The odds were heavily in Galen's favor. Once the first trial was revealed, bets had ranged from how long he would last, to how many bees would sting him, to whether I would kiss him at the ball. Finn and Helene had lost their bet with me, and I knew I was going to have to chase them both for a payout. The credits and favors I won mean little in the grand scheme of things. I took the bet only to prove a point. I know my betrothed too well. They'd doubted Galen would make it to twelve hours, let alone twenty-three and change.

Galen drops into a deep bow before offering me his hand. I tip my head in his direction, mindful of the black onyx crown on my head, and slip my hand into his. My crown was never part of my usual wardrobe. I used to pull it out only for events like balls or when doing public work, but I've made it a point to wear mine every damn day as a reminder of who I am, not just for Galen, but for me. There are moments when Daphne the college girl prevails and I have to remind myself I am no longer that naïve, direction-less girl. I'm Daphne, Goddess of Spring, Queen of the Underworld.

"You look lovely," Galen offers, hope in his voice. His features are schooled into complacency, but I can feel the anger humming through his veins like a hundred bees. My gown is a deep purple and bares almost as much skin as the one I wore the night of the Calling Ball. I have a message to send, not just to Galen, but to the people of Solarem. The Queen of the Underworld has returned, and I might have been the Goddess of Spring, but I was also the Goddess of the Dead, right alongside my now-missing husband.

The top of my dress consists of two pieces of thin satin fabric that barely contain my breasts. The fabric connects to my skirt in a series of complicated drapes and chains. My midriff is exposed, and my skirt sweeps the floor as I move. Galen's hand on my back gives me a chill, but I don't let it show. *Conceal, don't feel.*

"Thank you. You cleaned up nicely after the trial. I'm glad to see you're doing well after all those stings," I remark. He lets me spin away from him, my skirt creating a safe distance around me before I'm pulled back against him, tighter this time. It appears that his control is snapping.

His muscles are taut under his tuxedo, and I try not to think about how deadly he is. If I focus on taking things one day at a time and not provoking him, maybe I can survive.

"How goes the wedding planning?" His voice is soft, but I hear a hard note under it. A reminder of the control he continues to flex over me. A reminder that I belong to him in no uncertain terms. I've found one reason or another to avoid the wedding planning sessions. I'll meet with Posey for five minutes, ten max, during which time she will scold me for avoiding her, and then Zara or Sybil will approach me with something important I absolutely *must* do that *cannot* wait. Rarely will I put Cat in direct contact with Posey, after the level of contempt she's shown my best friend. In fact, after the trial, I sent Zara and Cat to their rooms, knowing that the party could be a lot. Gods and humans are a dangerous mix. After seeing that nymph turned to water, Cat and Zara gave no objection.

"As can be expected. My vision of what the day should look like clashes with Posey's." I don't say that my vision doesn't have Galen in it. I don't need to say it—as convincing as I may sound, I think, deep down, he knows that I would rather anyone else be at the end of that aisle.

"I, for one, cannot wait to see you walk down the aisle and pledge yourself to me. I hope my brother is able to make it. Have you heard from him lately?" He is watching my expression carefully.

I keep my mask on, pleasant and unruffled. "You expect your brother to reach out to me after I chose you in front of everyone? I expect he's off enjoying his newfound freedom. No wife or king-dom. I'm sure he's a new god because of it."

Galen dips his face into the crook of my neck and scrapes his teeth against my skin. I fight the urge to shudder. If he were bloodthirsty, I wouldn't put it past him to rip my throat out right here, but I know better. To take the crown, he needs me alive and compliant. No one wants to test whether I'm more susceptible to death now that I've experienced it once.

I let out a sharp breath, letting him think that it's not dread I feel at his touch, but arousal. I feel his mouth lift into a smile then kiss me there this time, soothing the skin. Before I can react, we're interrupted by Dion and Finn, who are all smiles.

Galen takes in the sight of them, his lips twisting with disgust, his body tense. Dion was away during the Calling, but after the ball, he returned to his boyfriend's side and hasn't left since. Neither of them has made it a secret that they are standing by *my* side in this battle of wills. For all the posturing of the Council being impartial, these two are happy to buck the system.

It's easy to tell where everyone allies themselves, which is why it's shocking that I'm being forced to follow through with what happened at the ball. If anyone has the power to undo the vote of no-confidence, it's the Council. Yet, every time I directly broach the subject with one of them, they get confused and insist that this is how things are meant to be before abruptly changing the subject. Posey is unafraid to voice her support for Galen, even if it leaves her on an island all alone while everyone else is verbally on my side, even though they don't vote that way. The only wild card is Xavier, who insists that his will is the law. I hope that maybe he will tire of these games, release me from this ill-conceived arrangement, and let Essos return.

"Phineas." Galen sneers.

"Wow, with such a warm welcome, you should try to steal

Xavier's seat instead." Dion doesn't miss a beat. "At least his wife is interested in you."

I have to bite my cheeks to keep from grinning.

"My betrothed and I were in the middle of something."

"The queen must play hostess. Can't have you stealing her away like you did for the last one thousand seventeen years."

My heart aches, hearing Finn spell out just how long Essos was alone. For us, for gods, that's equivalent to fifty mortal years, give or take. I'm sure Essos felt every minute of it. I know, because I feel every second that we are apart now. Every little reminder of my husband breaks my heart just a little more.

Because he *is* still my husband, regardless of what Xavier and Galen and anyone else say about it. My vow to Essos was for not only our endless lives, but my entire existence.

"Excuse me, my lord," I say demurely, tilting my head to Galen.

Galen moves back, allowing Finn and Dion to steal me away. I slip my arms into theirs as we make our way across the vast room. I don't know how much more kissing up to Galen I can take.

A few gods who were not in attendance at the Calling approach, each offering me a white lily of support. Finn was kind enough to fill me in on the significance. Following my death, the white lily became my unofficial symbol. People wore it or presented it to Essos to show him how sorry they were for his loss, and lilies have been sent to the house off and on since the end of the ball. As we cross the room, we accumulate more and more of them.

I hold on to Dion a beat longer than necessary, rubbing the sleeve of his purple velvet coat. It grounds me for a moment before I let myself disassociate from everything.

"Tell me this is almost over. Give me a sleeping draught and let me sleep until everything is decided," I plead before sitting down on a lounge chair by the pool with a flourish. Dion and Finn flank me in their own chairs. They hand me the collected flowers, nearly three dozen this time.

"People were impressed by him today," Finn remarks.

I scowl at him and check my nails, annoyed by the reminder. People were supposed to be bored by Galen today, but instead, he showed them that, contrary to what everyone thought, he has the patience needed to lead.

"My challenge should change some of that," Dion assures me.

"You can't tell me what it is, and you know that. The last thing we want is for him to cry foul, and then I have to marry him tomorrow. Speaking of—" I look at Finn "—*where is my husband?*"

Finn stares back. He's the only one who's been able to leave and go to wherever Essos is hiding out, but he won't tell me. As the Messenger God, Finn has free rein to meet with people who otherwise are persona non grata. If Galen's questions are any indication, he suspects what Finn is doing, but he doesn't have the level of control over Finn that he does me. Fucking with his brother's wife and her friends is different than fucking with his other brother's favorite son, and messing with Dion is the only real way to control Finn.

"He's coming up with a plan to fix this mess." Finn's voice is pointed, and I know he hasn't forgiven me for my role in landing us where we are now. There has been no shortage of back-and-forth discussing how we could have done things differently, but at the end of the day, Finn is still angry that I didn't listen to him, and I'm angry that he didn't find a way around the Calling rules the way Galen did.

Although, if I'm being honest, I don't blame him. I haven't been able to forgive *myself*.

I was a fool, naïve, to let Galen mess with my head during the Calling. He took advantage, manipulating me into doing what he wanted, into thinking that he loved me, that Essos was the one who murdered me. While Essos played by the rules carefully laid out by the Council, Galen hopped, skipped, and jumped through every loophole there was. It makes me want to run him through with the same dagger he used on me, but the blade hasn't been seen or heard of in centuries. Presumably, Posey knows where it is —after all, she was the one who released my soul from it so that I could be born again. But I don't think Xavier would let such a dangerous weapon float around freely, so I have to trust that his sense of self-preservation has not allowed him to leave its location to chance.

"There is no need for that," Dion chides. His guilt at not being around during the Calling weighs on him. As Xavier's firstborn son, he sat on the Council as first alternate while I was dead, and he knew the loopholes just as well as Galen and Posey did. If he had been around instead of on a three-month-long wine tour of Europe, he could have stopped or circumvented the rules as well. At least, that's what he keeps telling himself. Finn and I have assured him that nothing would have changed. If anything, his presence might have made Galen take more drastic measures. I shudder to think what that might have looked like.

"When is the next trial, anyway?" Finn asks before standing and pacing. Everyone around me seems to be blaming themselves for my actions. Finn for not protecting me, Dion for not being here, Helene for not pushing to kill her brother a millennium ago when the chance was there.

The guilt is mine and mine alone, and it weighs heavily on me.

"We're having one trial a month, the idea being that we have one month to plan for the next trial and the after-party, like the one we're having now," I tell him. It works out for me. I have time to get back on my feet, figure out my powers, and catch up on how things have changed in the Underworld.

Sybil has been helpful with that, sitting with me when I'm too exhausted to get out of bed and joining me when I do have the strength to get out and check on each level of the Underworld.

Essos stayed true to our vision of what we wanted the Afterlife to look like, and the souls appear to be thriving as best they can under the circumstances. It seems that the souls can sense the change in leadership, and I wonder, albeit selfishly, if they even knew I was gone. From what I've been told by Sybil, the souls have been restless, even in the levels of Paradise, where good souls go. On the worse end of it, the souls in the Deep have been grumbling enough that I overheard Xavier asking Sybil about security.

The only marked difference I noticed is a change in the handling of the souls in the Deep. Where once we were content to let them languish, there are now different sorts of torture created for each soul based on their transgressions in life. Every fear they had when alive is exploited, forcing them to face it day in and day out.

As much as I want to check in on my birth parents in Paradise, I loathe the idea of giving Galen more ammunition over me, so for now, I'm leaving them be. Knowing Essos, he has done what he can to protect them from Galen.

The doors open and Posey strides out, trailed by two small nymphs. I recognize the one in the green velvet gown as the nymph who spoke with me the night of the Calling Ball. I rise, as is expected of me in Posey's presence, but do not curtsey when Finn and Dion bow. Posey's thin lips press into a line, but I refuse to take the bait.

"These are your new lady's maids," she announces, the sound of her high-pitched voice grating on my every nerve. She tries to force a smile, her mouth twisting unnaturally before she gives up. Today she wears an extravagant purple dress made of feathers; the skirt and arms leave a trail behind her as she goes. She and Galen deserve each other—they really are birds of a feather.

"I am not in need of any ladies. I already have two." My tone is haughty to match hers. I don't mind the young nymph, but I don't know her well enough. I can't even recall her name.

19

"You shall have two more, as befits your station. I hardly know how you got away with having *none* previously, but this time, if you insist on being treated as a queen, then you will have five ladies-in-waiting." Posey grabs each woman by the arm and shoves them in front of her. They both dip into curtseys and wait for permission to rise.

"Honestly, Posey." I roll my eyes. "Please rise. What are your names?"

The one from the ball steps forward. "I'm Ellie, ma'am." She gives another quick curtsey but doesn't meet my eye. Something about her nags at me, but I can't place it.

The other girl, who wears a blue dress, steps forward and does the same. Her blond hair is styled in a simple French braid. "I'm Miranda." Her voice quivers, and her blue-eyed gaze darts between me and Finn and Dion. I don't trust her at all.

"I suppose you're not giving me a choice?" My words are directed at Posey, even as I continue to study the girls. No, not girls. Women. No doubt women whom Posey considers close allies. Ellie is now defiantly meeting my gaze, and Miranda can still barely look at me.

"None whatsoever," Posey confirms, and I want to smash her teeth in. Instead, I straighten my spine and look down at her. Even with her pointy stilettos, I still tower over her. Posey always hated the height difference and would do anything to one-up Helene and me because of it. It's why her crowns and hair have gotten taller and more ridiculous with every passing event.

I blow out a breath through my nose. "Fine. Starting tomorrow. Tonight, you can take care of these." I thrust the gifted flowers forward, not watching my new ladies but Posey, whose nostrils flare. "Put them in water and on the piano once it's back in place. I'm tired; I'm going to bed." In my periphery, Finn and Dion bow, and Miranda and Ellie curtsey once more. I sweep past them into the ballroom.

Galen catches sight of me and strides over. "Leaving so soon?" He pulls me onto the dance floor again.

I meet his gaze and force a smile onto my face. "I have two new lady's maids starting tomorrow, and I was hoping to get some rest so I can prepare for possibly needing to train them." The orchestra starts to play a slow song, nearly causing my eyes to roll back in my head. I hear the clinking of glasses and cheers for us to kiss, as if this were our wedding night. To the crowd around us, the Trials are about our love, or about how deep Galen's love for me goes. They don't know that they're really meant to prove he's not worthy of me or the title of king. As Galen dips me and kisses me, I'm grateful that our wedding is still months away.

I wish that marriage wasn't a requirement for him to become king, but it was Essos who made the rulers of our court share blood. It was a romantic gesture at the time, meant to share everything between us, including our powers. It means that, while I wasn't born to be the Goddess of the Dead, through our union, I received power over the souls. I can soothe them the way Essos can, and I can act without his explicit approval.

During the wedding ceremony, if we get that far, I'll be forced to mingle my blood with Galen's and share that kernel of Essos's power that lives in me. I'll have to show the realms that I want the wedding, that I want to share that power, even though doing so will kill me all over again. Pretending that I want it, that I want Galen, means maybe he won't hurt me again, physically, even as every day by his side hurts me emotionally.

I've had to make allowances and sacrifices this month to sell the charade. A kiss here, a peck there. I rationalize it isn't anything I haven't done with Galen before. I try to make it feel less like I'm selling my soul.

There is a moment, when his lips meet mine, that I can almost pretend kissing him isn't one of the worst things I've done. Then Galen does what he always will—he presses against me so that our bodies are molded together, and his tongue pushes into my mouth. What he lacks in finesse, he tries to make up for with sheer force.

My head is resting in the crook of his elbow as my ponytail touches the ground. I grab his jacket, not trusting him to not drop me. To onlookers, it must appear that I'm holding him close like a lover would, and so they cheer.

"All right, enough PDA," Xavier proclaims, and Galen lifts me into an upright position. There is a hunger in his eyes that I am doing my best to discourage. I keep pushing off the matter of him taking me to bed. He's asked once, and only once, and I put him off by explaining that all his talk at the Calling Ball about whoring me out to his friends after getting me pregnant didn't exactly incite desire. He apologized profusely, assuring me that he'd let his anger at Essos leaving get the best of him. That he wouldn't hurt me like that.

It would have been easier to believe it if I hadn't still had bruises on my neck from when he'd tried to claw back the events of the previous night.

There have been nights of debauchery with his buddies, celebrating how he's going to take over the Underworld, when he has taken a woman to bed. The morning after it happened the first time, he asked me probing questions, as if he hoped that I'd heard them and that maybe his exploits had awakened the jealous monster inside me. It doesn't matter how many women go through his room; it is me he wants there, and he won't relent until I give in. He might be giving me space now, but he was never very patient.

I dip into a curtsey and slip away as the group behind me cheers, unaware of the lengths that Galen and I will both go to come out on top.

3

I walk into the same bedroom I used for the Calling and find
Dave and Waffles snuggled together on my bed. Their
friendship had a rocky start, with the pit bull taking to the
cat much faster than Waffles took to Dave, but they finally came
to terms, and at least there is peace somewhere in this house. I
kick off my heels, thankful to sink the four inches to my normal
height. I flex my toes into the lush carpet, hoping to get feeling
back.

My senses prickle, and I tense. Vines weave down my arm,
forming a dagger that fits easily in my hand. It's obvious I'm
suspicious of whatever is in the room with me, but it doesn't
make its presence known. I stalk toward my reading chair in the
corner, holding the edge of the blade a fair distance from the back
of the chair, seemingly at thin air, but I know better.

The smell of vanilla and sandalwood and cinnamon gives
him away, and Essos appears in the chair. In his hands is the
Helmet of Invisibility, one of the ancient weapons said to have
been forged when the universe was created by the God and
Goddess Supreme. It was something he inherited when he took

over the Underworld, along with the Scepter of the Dead, though he seldom used either. It's unlikely anyone remembers they exist. Xavier, Galen, and Kai were all said to have received their own blessed gifts, but I'm not sure I ever knew what they were. Tonight, the Helmet of Invisibility is glamoured as a Yankees cap.

"You're getting better at that," he remarks with a smirk, and I want to throw myself in his arms.

I pull back my blade from where it was pointed, just below his Adam's apple. "You must be out of your mind," I hiss, the blade dissolving to ash in my hand. The fine particles drift down lazily to coat Essos's lap. If he were someone who meant to do me harm, I could have slit his throat easily. It wouldn't have killed him, but it would have made anyone think twice before coming into my space uninvited.

"Not exactly the warm welcome I was expecting," he teases but makes no move to get out of the chair.

I storm into the bathroom and run the sink. As I expect, he follows me and leans against the doorframe, watching as I brush my teeth and scour my lips. I won't kiss my husband while the taste of his brother is still in my mouth. It's that casual lean that makes me want to throw away all caution and responsibility and run away with him. His eyes rove over my exposed flesh, and it feels like a hundred tiny flames are licking my skin.

He looks so good. He's out of his usual three-piece suit, in a fitted black shirt and jeans that he wears so well. His hair is tousled and it's been days since he last shaved, if the stubble on his jaw is any evidence. I want to run my fingers through the tangles of his dark curls and taste his full lips. More than that, I want to feel him beside me when I fall asleep and be able to rise to the lazy lovemaking we once savored in the early mornings.

This isn't the first time I've seen Essos since the end of the Calling, but the animalistic need I feel for him hasn't diminished.

When we were together the night of the ball, it was pure frenzied fucking as my entire being thrummed with need for him.

I spit and rinse, then turn to look at him before launching myself into his arms. He kisses me firmly, pressing me against the doorframe, his hands roving all over my body as he struggles to find where to set them. They start on my waist before threading into my hair and pulling the hair tie loose so my dark waves cascade down my back. My hands are equally undecided, starting on his face and slipping through his hair before settling in the back pockets of his jeans. His mouth is everything I remembered and, at the same time, it's like kissing him for the first time all over again. His lips are soft and smooth, and he's insistent, but there's no brute force like when Galen kisses me. I banish the thought, focusing only on the feel of my husband against me.

"I hate that he kisses you," Essos says, sucking in air through his nose. The muscle in his jaw twitches, the only physical indication of how deep his displeasure goes. The backs of his knuckles gently trace my jaw. I don't have to question how Essos knows what's happening in our home. He always had a sixth sense for these things, but in reality, I think the dogs are tattling. They tend to mill about on the fringes of every room. It's the only explanation for how Essos knew I spilled pasta sauce on his favorite Solarem University top. Spot was watching me eat with begging eyes; it had been the ultimate betrayal when I dropped the tortellini on my shirt instead of into his mouth.

"I'm not exactly a fan either," I admit, my voice sharp.

He holds up his hands in surrender. I turn my back to him, holding my hair aside, so he can unclasp my dress. The first hook releases, and he places a tender kiss to the spot at the nape of my neck before releasing the others. I drop the dress to the ground and turn, bare before him. His gaze doesn't leave mine, not even to flick a few inches lower.

Essos places a kiss in the center of my forehead. He lets his fingertips trail up my arms to my shoulders. His touch is tender, featherlight, raising goosebumps on my skin. He slides his hands down my back and finally settles them on my hips as he steps closer to me.

I press myself against him and feel his muscles tremble. He wants me; I can feel the rigid length of him, but he won't give in. We may both want to reduce the other to a boneless heap, but the risk of being caught is too high. My husband has always been excellent at controlling himself, often to my dismay. What happened the night of the Calling Ball was a rarity for him. It reinforced to me his desperation for us.

I pull away and slip into my silk bathrobe. The tether he has on his desire is great, but I can't help but feel like each time he checks in on me, he's coming closer and closer to losing that control. If he does, it could go one of two ways; either we're both exceedingly satisfied, or Essos gets himself captured. As much as I want to see Essos, want the confirmation that he's alive and well and whole, Galen could have access to the dagger and could kill him. It's a risk I'm not okay with. I tie the robe's belt angrily, and Essos snorts in response.

"You're not supposed to be here," I repeat, settling on the bed.

He walks back to the chair and sits, placing one ankle over his knee. "You're right, but I couldn't help it. I needed to know how the trial went, and I couldn't wait for the papers to report it."

His voice is tired. For every day that I have had to put on a fake smile, he has had to worry about what Galen is doing to me and to our realm.

The first few times he stopped by to see me felt like fever dreams. He was sitting by my side when it felt like I broke through the haze of my body adjusting. After that initial torrent at the Calling Ball, my memories have kept trickling in, but my body and mind needed time to adjust to all the changes. From the return of my powers to several thousand years' worth of memories, I was overwhelmed.

We don't talk about where he is staying, much as I'm dying to know. It's a danger if I do. I'm terrified of slipping and revealing to Galen that Essos has easy access to the house.

"He lost. In spectacular fashion, right at the end. I was afraid he was going to win, and this trial was our sure thing. I would have lost faith if he had."

I'm not sure the loss matters. Posey has some hold on the Council and is determined to see her new bestie on my husband's throne. I might not have all my memories back yet, but I can say with near certainty that they were never friendly before.

Essos grabs at his heart. "You wound me fiercely when you have no faith in me."

I rise again to take off my makeup. "I have every faith in you, Es, but I cannot marry him. I won't." I meet his eyes in the bathroom mirror. He sits on the edge of the tub, the position reminiscent of nights when he would watch me get ready for bed. He would bide his time, waiting for me to be ready enough by my standards before throwing me over his shoulder and ravishing me.

"I'm not going to let it come to that," he promises. I believe he means it, but I'm not confident it's a promise he can keep. We're silent as I wash my face.

"Remind me to flay my brother's fingers and lips when the time comes. I hate that he's able to touch you and kiss you with impunity while I'm left to skulk in the shadows."

It's a wound we both share as memories from the Calling rise unbidden. He was never the instigator, but he didn't tell the women throwing themselves at him not to kiss or touch him. And how many Callings did he go through? I have so many questions, but now doesn't seem the ideal time to ask them. I might never get answers...but do I really want to know?

"I promise you, I like it a lot less." I lower the washcloth in my hand and notice how miserable Essos looks in the mirror. I turn to face him. We're a king and a queen stuck playing the part of pawns in a game we want no part of.

"I'm sorry I failed you. I'm sorry you're in this position to begin with. I haven't been able to do right by you. I made a vow to you, and I've done nothing but fall short of it. And now..." He runs his hands over his face, looking so weary. He has lines on his face that I don't remember seeing before, and I want to kiss each one of them away.

I get up, not wanting to hear more apologies. "And now we deal with it, the way we dealt with everything else that's been thrown our way. You are the one I truly chose. You're the only man who owns my heart and soul." I pause, girding myself for what I have to say next. It's the right thing to say but it doesn't make it easy. "You can't keep coming here."

His fingers find the edge of my robe and fiddle with the silk. "Daphne, I just...."

He stands abruptly, forcing me to take a few steps back. His hand presses to the nape of my neck, and he leans down to kiss me, gently, before prodding my mouth open, his tongue flicking against mine. My hands fist in his shirt as this kiss becomes the start and end of my whole world. Nothing matters but the feel of his heart beating against my own, something I never thought I would feel again. I spread out my fingers, needing the feel of him under my palms.

"I love you," he breathes, pulling away, pressing his forehead against mine. "Keep practicing; you were much faster tonight." He turns to leave, but I grab his arm.

"I still can't control my powers. I woke up bound in vines the other morning, and Waffles and Dave were not happy about it." My powers are manifesting how I feel—trapped, unable to do anything to escape. I try to hide how much it scares me.

28

"You're only going to be able to control them by trusting them and yourself. Your powers are acting out because you're simmering in fear. They aren't trapping you—they're trying to protect you from the outside world. My love, you are *so* strong. You were before all of this, and now I can feel your power running just under your skin." Essos trails a gentle finger down my arm before glancing out the window at the sentries patrolling the grounds. "I have to go. I love you. Trust yourself. Even in the past, you struggled with that, but you need to, now more than ever. You were always strong enough to fight him, but you let yourself think you weren't. *You are.*" His lips meet mine in a frenzied kiss, and then he grabs his Helmet of Invisibility. I'm still holding his hand as he does, and I watch him fade. He gives my hand one last squeeze before vanishing from sight.

I drop onto the bed hard, falling back and disturbing the dog and the cat. Both lift their heads and glare at me for disturbing their slumber.

"Oh, hush," I scold, reaching over to give each of them a scratch behind the ears, Waffles first, then Dave.

I don't believe that Essos is right about my powers. Maybe they are trying to protect me, but I'm capable of only small, precise magic. I haven't been able to turn men into trees or force anyone to choke on flowers since the night of the Calling Ball.

Only Cat, Zara, and Sybil know this. I haven't even let it slip to Finn or Helene, too afraid that the more people who know, the higher the chance of the wrong someone finding out. I'm nearly defenseless and scared to death about it. The times I've tried to push my powers to greater strength or to deliberately gain more memories, my nose bleeds, and I feel ill for hours.

Every minute I'm not actively working against Galen feels like a waste. I don't know how long he spent plotting to kill me. Long enough for a weapon capable of killing gods to be forged. Is Essos right? Was I strong enough to defeat Galen on my own? Could I have done something different at the Calling Ball? Should I have?

A copy of the *Solarem Sun* sits on my nightstand. It might be absolute drivel, but it's still interesting to see what Solarem society is gossiping about these days. Helene managed to track down a veritable library of old copies for me to look at so I could get a handle on what I missed, and I've started reading the newer releases too. This particular edition has a photo of me from the Calling Ball with the most imperious glare on my face. It's not clear who I'm looking at, but I can guess it must be Galen or Posey.

There are three additional photos of me from the same night, taken at various points in the evening. One picture is of Essos and me as my memory block was lifted. He's cradling my face as our lips touch, and a tear streaks down my cheek. I don't even remember crying. The second is of Galen and me as he sniffs my neck, and the photo looks almost loving if you completely miss how tense my body is. The last is of Xavier and me dancing, and from the angle of the camera, it looks like we're kissing. Fucking hells, will they ever give it up? Naturally, the headline accompanying this article is clever and scathing--*Queen of the Harem: How many men does it take to satisfy Queen Daphne?* The interior article has photos of Finn and Kai as well as photos from before my death. Some are innocent, at a party or a gala, but some feel too personal, like one of Essos and I during a party that Posey was hosting where he's very obviously squeezing my ass. The image was taken from behind, but his head is turned toward me, the knowing glint in his eye revealing he's aware that I'm trying *not* to react.

I toss the magazine toward the trash and focus on unmaking it so it crumbles to dust the way my weapon earlier did. This is the last thing I need to read and get in my head about. I trust that if

Essos is seeing the news elsewhere, he's not thinking twice about it.

Any articles about Essos were scrubbed from the papers before Helene brought them to me, which I both hate and understand. I should hear what my husband was up to while I was gone from him and no one else.

I take a deep breath and consider who I can ask for help. A face flashes through my mind.

Rafferty, the God of Memory. There is no one better suited. Someone should be able to track him down for me. Finn is the Messenger God; he's supposed to be able to reach any god at any time. I remember that Rafferty was a professor of history at Solarem University, but his tenure was short, and his classes were rarely held in person. I'll have to check with Helene or Finn, but if my memory isn't failing me, it was for just a semester to fill in for another professor. He wasn't at the wedding when I married Essos, and not a single one of these periodicals mention him.

Waffles stands and stretches into downward dog before walking over and climbing onto me. His lithe body circles on my stomach before he begins to knead my abdomen aggressively. I wince as his tiny claws make micro-punctures in my skin before he settles down. Dave turns and licks my face.

Downstairs, the party continues. I hear laughter and music until the early hours. I hope this means that Galen will leave me alone most of the day. He might have lost the trial, but he is still celebrating like he won a battle. I worry that this silent victory for me will embolden him to go harder next time.

4

I'm sitting in bed when a knock thumps against my door. The clock tells me that it's barely six a.m., and I want to murder the person on the other side. I glance at my pets, who show no reaction. A friend, then, but not for much longer. I didn't sleep much and was already awake, but if I had been sleeping, this visit would have been exceptionally rude.

I call for them to enter, and Cat slips into the room, followed by Shadow and Spot. She might be the only person who can get away with coming here at this hour.

"That was intense." Her voice is jittery as she walks in with a tray of breakfast foods, along with all the relevant newspapers and the *Solarem Sun*. She's done an excellent job of handling the various peculiarities of what my life entails. It's unsurprising that she's adapted well to managing press inquiries and tackling all the welcome-home mail I've received from people in Solarem. Cat took it upon herself to do her own research about what transpired after I died to better equip herself to address questions.

The papers that reported on my death were omitted from the ones Helene gave me.

A few years after my death, one paper included a small check-in with Essos. It wasn't a long article, just a snapshot of him alone at a ribbon-cutting ceremony for a community garden the souls of the Afterlife created in my memory.

Cat places the tray on my lap, pulling me from my downward spiral as she nudges Dave away from the food. Dave listens for about five seconds before twisting his head to try for the bacon again. Ever indulgent, I pat his head and leave him where he is. The puppies, as I call them, have been a bright spot in my days. They've been happy to give cuddles whenever I need, and they've been more than vocal about positioning themselves between me and the door.

My best friend has fit seamlessly into this world, understanding that, until this is over, we all have a part to play. I have to be the dutiful betrothed, while Cat and Zara fall into the role of my ladies-in-waiting. I hate it. I hate that I'm expected to treat them as below me because they were born mortals. Even before my death, I never kept ladies-in-waiting. I hate that the best way I can protect them right now is by being aloof when we're in public. It's why I've kept my distance from Zara as best I can. Galen believes I'm angry with Zara for pursuing Essos during the Calling. I let him believe that I'm a small-minded person who will walk all over my friend thanks to something neither of us could control.

"It was. You and Zara didn't have to stay for the entire trial." I take a bite of bacon and break off the extra crunchy part then slip it to the dog. Essos won't be happy that I've added yet another bad habit—eating in bed—to Dave's never-ending list of bad behaviors.

"No, but we are your attendants, so we should be present during the Trials. This is, after all, your realm. Does it not put Posey in her place to have you running around with an entourage?"

I snort, shaking my head at Cat's vindictive streak.

"Speaking of," Cat continues, "there are two women here. They allege that you agreed to take them on as ladies-in-waiting?" Concern crosses her face before she schools her features. I've been working on this bland expression with her and Zara so that when others harass them, they give nothing away. The last thing I want is for anyone to use them the way Galen used and manipulated me.

"Yes, yes, it's true. Posey foisted them on me last night. Trust neither of them." I give Dave more bacon before Shadow and Spot figure out this is an option. Shadow is Cat's constant, well, shadow, while Spot tends to trail Zara around, acting as an additional source of protection. It's exactly where I want them. I can't be everywhere at once, but they can act as my eyes and ears if there's a problem. Unless it's mealtime, at which point, they stick to Mom's side, knowing that I will share the goods.

"We'll need to be more clever with my schedule now, so if they come looking for me, we have a decent reason they can't find me. It goes without saying, but I would like to be as inaccessible as possible. I don't think Posey or Galen will approve of me training and trying to get stronger."

Cat takes a bite of my toast. "So, strike 'Plan a Coup' as a weekly meeting?" she confirms, and I nod.

There is another gentle knock at the door, and Zara enters. She has with her some papers that I know are from Sybil, who is practically running the realm without us. They haven't been booted from their position as assistant to the ruler, but I don't know if they've been assisting Galen. While I was bedridden the week after the ball, Galen petitioned that he should be the one making all the decisions. I'm still being kept from knowing what is going on in my own realm.

Sybil, who is the smartest of us all, knew what was happening during the Calling Ball as it was happening. The moment Galen demanded I kiss him, they slipped into the shadows to hide anything and everything Galen would want to get his hands on. I can only assume that the helmet and scepter were a part of the hidden bounty. The morning after, Sybil reappeared as if they had been around the whole time. I like to think that Essos and Sybil have met and discussed what needs doing, because the truth is, Sybil has been by Essos's side since my death and doesn't need my interference with the running of the Underworld.

"Now what?" I groan, my voice a little sharper than I planned. I wipe my hand on a napkin before holding it out for the papers. I render my glasses in my hand and slide them on before looking over what Zara has handed me. I flip through them, confused.

With my memories still filling in, it's taken longer than I wanted to readjust to my old life. Things that were as simple to me as smiling or breathing take effort. It's more than just my memories or my powers, which are both also lagging. I'm thankful that Sybil has picked up my slack. After Essos and I ruled the Underworld for a few thousand years together, most of our job became automated. We have departments of Solarem citizens who monitor how the souls are doing and handle security, banking, and intake of souls. Essos and I wanted to become redundant, and knowing that he succeeded in that goal brings me a level of peace I never expected. Our interference is limited to matters like adjudication and being the physical reminder that the Underworld is not to be feared.

Essos and I handled the Underworld jointly, passing judgments and monitoring the incoming tithes from souls as they passed. The Solarem economy depends on the value of each soul, and for that reason, Essos and I set the bar low for entrance into the Underworld. We wanted souls to have a place to belong without having to linger in the Inbetween. The tithe—the weight of a soul—allows Essos and I to fund social programs in Solarem that help businesses and schools to thrive. Much of what we did was simple accounting, so Xavier felt it was only natural for Essos to manage the banking system for all the gods as well. Essos was the one who tracked what Solarem funds were being used on. With Xavier's negligence and Essos's absence, Galen will have access to all of this. Out of all the brothers, my husband somehow managed to be the one doing the most work while Xavier pretended he had the most to deal with. I imagine he still does. One of these days, I would love to take him to task.

The numbers in front of me don't look right, though. As I review the tithes and where our funds sit, I gnaw on my lip, wondering where the money is going.

My bigger question is...what is Sybil handling, that they're not here delivering the news themself?

I look at Zara and see her blanch at my glare, and I mentally chide myself. None of this is her fault, and I shouldn't be treating her like this in private.

She's dressed in a chic black blouse and skinny jeans with black pumps that make her legs look a million miles long. Her black hair is pulled back and her baby bangs brush her brow line.

"These numbers are from yesterday or today?" I ask. If I'm reading them correctly, we've started to run at a deficit, something that never happened when I was alive and, as far as I know, hasn't happened in centuries. Not only that, but the number of unsorted souls is staggering.

The goal Essos and I had for the Afterlife was that, regardless of their actions, every soul would have a place, even if that place was in the Deep. We strove to provide not only those in the Underworld but also citizens of Solarem with safe spaces. We may not have been king and queen of Solarem, but that didn't stop us from caring and trying to do better for the whole of Solarem.

Zara shifts on her feet, knowing that she's bringing bad news. I haven't used my powers for violence since the night of the ball, but every so often, Zara will flinch if I move too fast.

Sybil, to an extent, blames Zara for her meddling during the Calling. She didn't seek to hurt me maliciously, but she had her sights set not only on Essos but on being queen as well. Galen said all the right things around her to ensure they made their way to me, deepening my mistrust of Essos.

I don't blame Zara at all, but I've let this misunderstanding stand. The more people think I'm on the outs with her, the safer she is.

"Sybil said the figures are from this morning," Zara confirms.

I lean back on my pillows, startling Waffles, who glares at me. "I'm going to need them to run a report to see when the tithes started to dip." As far as I know, there hasn't been a stoppage of death in the mortal realm, so there's no reason for our income to be taking a hit. "Please also have Sybil run a separate report on our gem output to the human world. That should be covering us, but it doesn't appear to be. Also, see if they have a lead on those who support Galen—perhaps there's a clever fee we can impose on their accounts to help cover this issue."

Zara turns to go, her head down.

"Oh, and Zara, there are two new ladies-in-waiting, Mitzy and Elphaba," I add.

Cat startles and turns to look at Zara. "Miranda and Ellie," she corrects.

I wave my toast, uncaring. "Fine, Ellie and Miranda. They exist outside the circle of trust. Nothing, and I mean, *nothing* gets relayed to them without my explicit say-so." My voice is firm.

Zara nods.

Before she leaves, I stop her. "I need this before my session with Luminara at nine."

Zara blanches, knowing that Sybil and Galen will be furious for different reasons—Galen because he's trying to stem the flow of information I receive, and Sybil because my asking for this so quickly is annoying. But Zara makes no comment as she closes the door behind her.

"You could be nicer to her," Cat says, walking into my closet to choose my wardrobe for the day.

"I could." I try to make sense of the papers in my hand. I should explain my actions to Cat so she knows I'm still the same person who was her bathroom buddy during frat parties and would play hangman with her when she studied for her German vocabulary tests. But Cat is in enough danger, and I can't add Zara to my list of concerns. Anything that distracts me from my goal of defeating Galen is a problem. I need to protect my friends. Cat is a vulnerability Galen won't hesitate to wield against me.

Cat steps from the closet, a red pantsuit in her hands. Her outfit selections for me are always fierce, meant as armor to protect me from the demons I face daily. I appreciate the thought she puts into her choices, using the magic closet to bring her imagination to life. Her attire has become drabber, her golden hair swept into a neat bun, as she does everything she can to fade into the background. If she becomes part of the unnoticed staff, she can hear things and learn what it is Galen is up to.

But she isn't going unnoticed by everyone. Xavier has been finding more and more reasons to be at the house, sniffing around Cat, particularly after he heard that Galen threatened her. When she and I walk into a room, his head snaps up and he finds any excuse he can to talk to her.

"That looks amazing," I say, setting the tray and papers aside before climbing into the shower.

Cat stays in my bedroom.

I shout to be heard over the water. "I think I should start training with Kai soon. Confirm with Helene that his offer is still on the table." There's no reason it wouldn't be, but I'm not going to be presumptuous. Things have cooled between Helene and me. After each sweet gaze Galen gives me, she glares at me. I suppose I shouldn't be surprised. I am the reason she's not home with her own family. Xavier wants her here to make sure Galen and I don't maim each other, but I've been as kind and caring to Galen as I can stomach.

As the water rushes over my body, I think about my need to regain control, not just over my abilities but also over my strength. I am the Goddess of Spring—I never needed to know how to fight beyond basic self-defense. Even in my defensive powers class at Solarem University, I learned the bare minimum because, if anyone was going to be attacked, it wasn't going to be me, and once I was with Essos, no one would dare try to hurt me.

Except, of course, Essos's brother.

I'd trained more in the years before Essos and I decided to have a baby. After that, I went soft. I lay around trying to make my body the perfect host to carry our child. Now, I don't have the luxury of lazing around. I'm going to war, and I need to be ready.

With my eyes closed, I remember the feel of Galen's body weighing mine down. I remember how I tried to call vines to pull him off me, how I tried to fight him and couldn't. Everyone has limits to their powers, but as a prince and a child of the God and Goddess Supreme, he had access to far more power than I ever did. The memory of feeling so helpless feeds the fire burning inside me. Stoking the flames helps keep me on task.

Outside the shower, I hear Cat let out a noise of surprise before there's a thud. I turn off the shower and grab a towel then hurry out.

Vines are snaking up her sides and squeezing her. I immediately turn them to ash and rush over to help her up.

"Still working on control, I see?" Her voice shakes, though she tries to sound calm.

"I'm so sorry. I was thinking about..." I trail off, and her green eyes focus on my hand, which is rubbing my chest where the knife hit home.

39

"You don't have to explain. While you're with Galen and Luminara, I'll confirm with Helene that Kai is still up for training you." She reaches out and squeezes my arm.

My mental list of things to do gets longer as I decide to talk to Xavier about a protective charm for Cat when I warn him off her. I'm exhausted. I don't know how to do this—how to be all things and struggle with memory and power issues all at once. Part of me rationalizes that I *can't* do it all. I can try and try and try, but ultimately, something has to give. I just don't know what to sacrifice. Sooner rather than later, if I don't make that choice, the choice will be made for me.

Cat is silent as I get ready. We've been in uncharted friend territory for a while now, and neither of us knows what to do about it. How do you console your friend who has been reincarnated following her murder by her brother-in-law whom she is now betrothed to? The whole thing makes a telenovela look like a Bible verse. And for myself, how am I supposed to help my friend, who was once my equal, into a role that places her value as less than mine?

I step into the jumpsuit and put my arms through the arm holes. Cat clips the back, and I look in the mirror at the cape that hangs from the shoulders.

"I should have peed before I got into this," I remark with a sigh.

Cat smirks. "You're telling me that gods have to use bathrooms just like the rest of us?"

I roll my eyes before closing them so she can apply my makeup. I appreciate her attempt at levity, and even if she actually does know better; it highlights how much information I still need to impart.

As Cat bullies me about keeping my eyes closed, I internally cringe. I hate having her do all these things for me, but I need to prove she is useful to me. Miranda and Ellie might be Posey's attempt to make my friends irrelevant and force me to send them to their afterlives. This is where Galen's and Posey's aims differ. Posey wants me to be as isolated as possible, while Galen will use whatever tools he can find to keep me in line.

"You're dead; don't you still eat, sleep, and pee?" I point out.

She stops what she's doing, the makeup brush tickling my cheek. "You know, I never really thought about it. What is with that?" She sits on my bed. My eyes flutter open and I turn to her.

"Well, you're still taking in food and beverages that you don't need, so your body is still processing the intake. You don't get your period anymore because your uterus isn't re-lining itself. You sleep because your brain is still functioning, and it needs that time to process. I can keep going. I still pee because I am an immortal. My body is back to functioning the way it used to, including periods, to my chagrin." Although, mine are not exactly regular yet.

I let Cat absorb this information as I put on lip gloss. I had my first cycle last month, shortly after the Calling Ball, and told no one, not even Cat. It's one piece of information that could hurt me if it got out—if someone found out, and I was forced to get knocked up. It's a sticking point for Posey now. She wants me to prove my worth and let Galen get me pregnant before the wedding. Never mind the fact that she doesn't have any children of her own, insisting she's too busy being mother to all of Solarem now that the God and Goddess Supreme are retired. Every time she makes a reference to me taking Galen to bed, a piece of me dies inside.

"You get a period? Can you get pregnant? Have you ever been pregnant?"

I freeze, thinking of the life that was just taking root when Galen murdered me. I shut that shit down immediately, because thinking about what could have been isn't going to get me anywhere. It only fuels the flames of my fury.

"Are we almost done here?" I ask.

Cat's managed to finish only one eye, so she's far from done. She springs back into action. I'm a monster for how I'm treating her, and I know it. I let that thought fester even as Cat brushes my hair into simple waves down my back then adorns my head with a ruby crown.

I don't want to think about answering her questions about pregnancy. Essos and I always wondered why my womb was such an inhospitable place. Xavier had bastards galore, but I couldn't give Essos one child.

I'm reaching for an old pair of ruby earrings when a memory slithers into my mind, inky and full of dread. I'm most prone to being hit with memories after I'm asleep, as my mind tries to catch up to my consciousness. I've learned the hard way to just let it happen. But this one surges into me with an insistence that raises the hairs on my arms.

Essos is swamped at work and can't meet me for lunch like he promised. We've been together only a few months, but during that time we've been inseparable. At least as much as we can when his work allows it. It's not the first time that's happened, as pressure from his father mounts. Essos needs to present three options for how to shape the Underworld to manage the souls from the mortal realm. For now, his father has left the souls to their own devices. The truly evil mortals are able to live alongside the purely good. Essos has told me of crimes being committed even now, and how souls are languishing in these conditions. He doesn't know I overheard his father one night in his study, asking if Essos is up to the challenge of ruling, or if he's too distracted by me to do it right. So, I've been helping him brainstorm and keeping him focused and well-fed with snacks when he's busy.

Today is no different. Even though our relationship is so new compared to our lifespan, I know him. Essos will work through lunch and dinner and will realize three days later that he still hasn't had anything to eat.

I get us both sandwiches from the vendor across from his office, and I'm nearly bouncing on my toes to get to him. Maybe if he relaxes a little, he'll be able to focus better on the task ahead. A blow job wouldn't be the most insane idea I've had, and I wouldn't be opposed to a quickie.

I've got my long hair pulled back into a ponytail to show off the ruby drop earrings that Essos gave me last week. The look is ostentatious for the office, but they match the red bra and underwear I have on.

As I walk toward his office, I notice no one's meeting my eye, and I wonder if something has happened. Essos has never been the type to yell; he's more fond of attracting bees with honey and is a firm believer that if your staff is too scared of you to come to you with a mistake, then you're doing something wrong.

Once I get to his office, I notice his assistant isn't at her desk. I decide to slip in quietly, in case he's on a call or in a meeting.

As my hand closes on the door handle, I hear it.

The sounds of grunts and moans and flesh meeting flesh. It's obscene, and in my present-day mind, I want to stop myself from opening the door. Nothing good can come from it...but I can't change something that's already happened.

So, I have to live through it again. I meet Essos's gaze as he slams his hips into another woman, but before she can lift her head, the memory ends.

"GET OUT," I snarl, sweeping my arm over my vanity, letting the coffee mug shatter on the floor along with my makeup and a vase of flowers I've been working hard to keep alive. They wilt in the face of my rage and fall to the ground along with my other things.

"Daphne?" Cat asks, placing a hand on my shoulder.

I start to shake. I can't do this. I can't deal with a betrayal that's thousands of years old and now feels as fresh as yesterday. But I have to. I need to face it, because I've just had my heart ripped open and stomped on the same way it was when I was a young goddess, a fledgling who was still learning her place in the world and with Essos. I want to reach back through my memories and shield my younger self from all that is about to go wrong in her life. She never knew how cruel the world could be until she got involved with Essos and his family, and I want to protect her from all of it, but I *can't*. I can't do it, because it already happened. She's already had her bright, shiny view of the world shattered and diminished.

"Didn't you hear me? I said *get out*." But my voice isn't as strong as it was when I first came out of the memory. Tears are slipping down my face, no doubt ruining the makeup that Cat just painstakingly applied. My body is slowly curling in on itself to shield my heart as I try to hide not only from what happened but from how I just spoke to my best friend. I silently battle the tears and try to search my memories for more context around what I just saw. Beyond remembering running home and crying alone in bed, I can't pinpoint anything stronger. By that point, most of my friends had stopped talking to me, telling me that being with Essos had changed me, and those who were still around told me his cheating was to be expected.

Cat wraps her arms around me, tugging me into her chest. "It's okay. Whatever it is, we'll figure it out," she whispers, soothing me as she strokes my hair.

Whatever I did in my past life was not enough for me to deserve a friend like Cat in this one. I cling to her like the life preserver she is and cry harder.

I need to be stronger than this. I need to focus on today, and not on something so old, I doubt anyone else even remembers it happened.

I collapse in on my friend and vow that, when we make it out of this, I'm going to give her anything and everything she asks for. I don't know how I can begin to explain what I'm going through, so I don't. I lean on Cat, absorbing all the love and support she has to give. When the pain is less fresh, I'll tell her, but right now, I just need to be held.

5

Zara bounds into the room with the paperwork I asked for, startling both Cat and me. There is no meeting Zara's eye as she hands me the papers, because she's going to ask what's wrong, and I'm going to have to not answer her, and I can't take the guilt from pushing her away. Because right now, not telling her isn't about pushing her away, it's about burying this jumble of emotions. I feel like a jack-in-the-box, except when I explode, I'm going to take everyone out with me.

I take the papers and lay them out on the bed next to the ones from the morning. Cat tries to fix my face as I survey the report. Zara, spotting the mess on the floor, moves to clean it up. I want to remind her that I have a magic house and that no mess lasts too long, but I'm too focused on what's in front of me. I stare at pages and pages of numbers, watching them align in a way I was afraid of. The paper in my hand crumples as I squeeze it, then storm out of the room. At least this is something productive I can focus my energy on.

Galen is at the foot of the stairs, welcoming Luminara. I practically fly down and push him.

"Did you shut down production in the mines?" My voice does not hide my fury. It's the first time I've lost my temper since the Calling Ball. I take a deep breath in through my nose and let it out through my mouth, but that only serves to leave me pissed off and a little lightheaded.

"Yes, I did," he confirms, as if he said he wanted milk with his coffee. There is an unapologetic glint in his eyes, like he wants me to lash out. He doesn't question why or how I know about this change. I give that deep breathing exercise another try.

Nope.

I'm still ready to shove my bare hand into his chest and rip out his heart. I've never tried to Kali Ma someone as a goddess, but there is a first time for everything.

"*Why* would you do that? Our production goes to the mortal world. Without it, they lose their precious gems, and economies collapse." I'm bewildered at his overreach, but as I say the words, the whole picture comes into focus. I'm no longer looking at just a moon; I'm looking at the entire *Starry Night,* and I'm even angrier. What the actual fuck?

"I'm the God of War. If economies collapse, there is war. When there is war, there is death, and death means that our realm flourishes." His voice is calm, as if I should want this too.

What he's lost sight of—what most gods have forgotten—is that first and foremost, gods exist *for* the mortals. They may not worship us the way they do other gods, but that is what makes us all the more important. We touch mortal lives every day without them knowing, and it's up to us to not be the cruel and capricious gods they believe us to be. We should be kind and fair and not what we actually are—ungrateful and bitter over the smallest of slights.

Luminara places a hand on my shoulder. I feel a sense of calm flood through my body as my mind tries to fight back, knowing this is wrong. She might be the Goddess of Harmony, but it doesn't give her the right to take my emotions from me. It's a gift that Essos has as well, but he's only ever used it to soothe a soul through their grief. I am not in need of soothing, nor am I mortal. I'm going to need Sybil to make it clear to their girlfriend to keep her hands off me. It's obvious that Luminara has no respect for anything that comes out of my mouth. I should tell her now, make my stance clear, but she's drained every last bit of my fight. When I tell her off, I want to bring the whole weight of my fury down on her.

Thus far, Luminara has proven herself to not be the impartial party she's meant to be. Since day one of the farce called therapy, she's tried to push me toward Galen and resolving our feelings with each other. I have no idea how this is the same woman who coyly watched me and Essos talk before our flag football game during the Calling.

"Why don't we continue this discussion in our safe space?" she asks, leading us both to her newly installed office next to mine. Galen adjusts his suit jacket.

Following the departure of his brother, Galen tried to elevate his fashion. He evolved from his usual T-shirts and jeans to wearing suit jackets, as if this lends him legitimacy. He might be trying to dress like my husband, but a rat in a suit is still a rat.

Luminara is dressed in her usual garb, a purple muumuu that's bright against her black skin and her grey hair pulled into a braid. She might be new to my ever-expanding household, but she's made herself comfortable in that short month. Even when she's not here, I can feel her influence.

Like children being walked into the principal's office, we trail her before taking our customary seats on either side of the couch. This is perhaps where I'm able to be a little more myself. Outside this room, I have to pretend I'm giving him a chance, that I *do* want him to succeed. In this room, I can be bitter and mad that he took my life. After all, that is the purpose of "therapy."

The richly-appointed space has a calming effect. The walls are white with a mellow yellow accent wall. The couch is grey and easy to sink into with colorful throw pillows. Our first session was lively, before Galen put his hands on Cat, and I was freer with expressing my anger and frustration with the situation. The first batch of throw pillows didn't survive that session, and the session after that took place two days after he choked Cat. If I could have, I would have suffocated him with each and every pillow in this house. I'm glad to have them back, plucking one up and hugging it to my chest. If I can distract myself with the pillow, maybe I won't kill Galen.

I kick off my heels and rest my feet on the Damask carpet. Luminara had a few specifications for the space, and I was happy to invest myself in making it cozy. I hoped that if I felt comfortable here, maybe I could finally feel safe. Since I'm barred from actually doing any work while I "readjust" to life, I need pet projects.

That thought alone makes me ill. I'm no bored housewife looking for something to busy myself with. I am a fucking *queen,* and if people don't start treating me like it, maybe heads should roll. It took until today for me to get my hands on real paperwork. I don't know what changed that Sybil was able to sneak it to me, but I'm not going to look the gift horse in the mouth.

"We'll circle back to what just happened outside." AKA, Luminara isn't actually interested in addressing my issues. "But first, I want to discuss going back to the beginning of your relationship. I want you to tell me what went wrong. Galen, you have indicated that you and Daphne are the ones who should have been together to begin with," Luminara prompts Galen.

His gaze travels from her to me, his eyes staring at my bare feet before they meet mine. We talked about this *once,* what feels like a million years ago. He tries to hold my gaze, but I look away.

"I was interested in Daphne first, but big brother decided he wanted her, so he pursued her." He still sounds bitter about this centuries later. He hasn't apologized to me once for murdering me or for almost choking me; he has no regret over what happened. Galen sees me as his property.

Luminara holds out her hands to both of us. "Let's visit Galen's memory, shall we?" Her serene voice makes me want to strangle her with vines. Galen places his hand in hers easily, while I hesitate. I've always hated her ability to have others relive specific moments in time. It's helpful for therapy, but that doesn't mean I want it used on me. A part of me wonders if it will even work, given that I don't have my full memories back, but I realize that means she'll focus on Galen's memories. I don't want a reminder of how this all started, even though memories of him have bled through. I wonder if that has anything to do with how strong my feelings about him are.

Luminara doesn't take her gaze off me, patiently waiting, but it's when Galen opens his mouth, probably to point out that I've proven his point, that I take her hand.

GALEN IS SITTING *at a table in the library, watching me. I'm alone, my hair in two braids on either side of my face as I chew on the end of a pen. I see myself through his eyes. It's like I'm shrouded in light. He's ignoring his reading as I check my watch and pack up my papers before running out of the library.*

We skip to another event. I'm at a party with friends and I'm smiling while taking a sip of my drink. My brown hair is pin-straight in a long ponytail that flows from the top of my head down to my waist, and I'm wearing a black leather strapless dress. Galen doesn't miss his chance to meet me this time. He crosses the room to me, shouldering people out of the way without taking his eyes off me, and places a hand on my shoulder, causing me to spin around and face him. My eyebrows shoot into my hairline, because, of course, I know who he is. I would be a fool not to know. I've caught glimpses of him around campus, surrounded by his all-female fan club and the men who would lick the bottoms of his shoes if he asked. I also know his reputation, but I'm young, and the attention of one of the three royal sons makes me grin like a fool.

"Yes?" I ask, my eyes bright. I lift my drink to my mouth, sipping through the cocktail straw.

"You know, I was feeling off today, but you've turned me on again."

I choke on my drink, looking into his light brown eyes. I contemplate rewarding this boldness. "Did you come up with that all on your own or did you read it in a book?" I ask, fighting my smile.

"Your beautiful face moved me. Are you a muse, by any chance? Because you inspire me to worship your body all night long." He holds out his hand, and my blush burns from my cheeks to my ears and down my neck. My gaze slips to his outstretched hand, and I surprise myself by taking it.

I dance with Galen, my body grinding against his until the group of girls I came with drag me away. I knew his name, but he never asked mine. I thought maybe it was a one-time thing, a night of dancing. One chance meeting, and it would never go past the party.

We kept this up, meeting and dancing, until one night I didn't show up. Later, Galen learned I'd been asked on a date by a different prince. I went on that date untethered to anyone, but, at the end of it, I found I was tethered. Tethered to a dark-haired, blue-eyed man who took me to dinner and kissed me and claimed me as his.

That memory is my own, pushing away Galen's, to remind me to whom I belong.

LUMINARA RELEASES OUR HANDS QUICKLY, as if the last memory to slip through should be forgotten, and clucks her tongue at us. She pushes her glasses up her nose and sits back in her chair. Once glace at Galen confirms he saw the way Essos looked at me and experienced how loved and treasured by him I felt.

"So, that's complicated," is Luminara's only comment, and I laugh.

"It's *complicated?*" My voice is dry.

"I loved her first." Galen's voice is hard as he says it, and I let my gaze drift to him. Those nights dancing were so few, and so long ago—I never realized he held them in such high regard. How different my life might have been if he had tried to talk to me, had bothered to ask my name, instead of only feeling me up in the darkness of the club.

"It doesn't matter if you think you loved me first. I'm a person capable of making my own choices, and I chose Essos." *Then and now* goes unspoken as I glare at Galen for forcing me to be here and maybe forcing me into so much more.

"You forgave *him* so easily when he betrayed you, but it's different when it comes to me."

The sheer fucking audacity of this man.

I study Galen, the hard set of his shoulders and his clenched teeth. His anger at having to see that final memory rolls off him in waves. I try for just a moment to see his side of it, the side of him that coveted me in those days. The idea of it is tainted by his tone, his wording. He believes that I belonged to him, that he was entitled to me because he was one of the royal sons.

"Did you two ever kiss?" Luminara asks innocently. I look down at my nails and change the color on them from the honey yellow I had for the trial to a red that matches my outfit.

I don't look at Galen, who I sense is looking at me, waiting for me to answer. Waiting for me to admit that we did.

"Should we...?" Luminara prods, offering her hand again. She knows there's something between us, something more to Galen and me. But what happened was a few millennia ago, and nothing that would make me consider choosing Galen over Essos. All the same, I don't want to talk about it.

"We kissed just last night." I'm being obtuse.

Galen snorts. "Why don't you tell Luminara about our first kiss?" he taunts.

6

I reach out and grab Luminara's hand roughly, shooting a withering glance at Galen, who gives me a smug smile as he does the same. This time, the memory is my own, one that is new to me. That's the problem with reliving several thousands of years—some memories, like the one this morning, will bitch-slap me; others nestle themselves in the back of my long-term memory until I go hunting for them.

I AM LYING in a field of wildflowers, staring at the sun and hoping it will burn my eyes out. I know it won't, but I put forth the effort anyway. My eyes are burning, but not from the sun. From the tears that are prickling behind them, threatening to overflow. I do my best to hold them back. I've already cried too much.

I hear a branch snap, and I sit up to find Galen approaching. I quickly wipe away the tears and stand to face him. He's dressed fully in his armor, carrying a spear and a shield.

"Galen. I didn't expect to run into you here," I say, gesturing at the field.

He studies me carefully before he takes another step toward me. "I have to say the same, Daphne. I thought you would be off with Essos, dreaming of ways to run his world."

I frown, trying not to think about how wrong everything with Essos has gone. Trying not to think of catching him with someone else. "You're so out of touch you don't even know your brother is on to the next new thing?"

Essos and I were together for only a few months. That's like a minute in eternity, so maybe it meant nothing to him, but it was everything to me.

Galen approaches me and wipes a tear from my cheek. His touch is gentle, almost reverent. "Is that why you're crying? Because of Essos?" he asks, not unkindly.

"I am through *crying over your stupid brother. If he wants to bury his prick in nymphs galore, he can have at it. I'm done with his bullshit." It's such a lie. I'm not done with his bullshit. But...I have to be.*

Galen laughs. "I'm glad someone else sees through his trash. Everyone is so busy kissing his and Xavier's asses that they don't see what they're really like."

"And what are they like?" I ask. I'd known the brothers were not particularly close—when I visited Essos in their palace in Solarem, Galen had separated himself from his brothers. At dinner, Galen was always seated on the other side of his mother, across from me, while his siblings sat closer to their father, lapping up his attention at the head of the table.

"They're both no better than two-bit whores, parading around town like they own the place," he says bitterly. He moves closer—we haven't been this close since we used to go dancing.

"It sounds like you're jealous that you're a prince and not the king of a realm," I challenge. "What are you doing out here, anyway? Running drills?"

Galen breaks his spear with one hand, crushing it to splinters.

"*Actually, being the God of War means something to some people,*" *he snaps.*

I shrug haughtily. "Not during peacetime. Seems like you have very little to do." I turn my back on him, which might be a mistake, but I lift a dainty shoulder at him and swish my skirts.

"*What would you know about it, flower girl? Are you even a full-fledged goddess?*" *He says it with just a hint of malice, as if trying to find a way to take me down a peg after I did the same to him.*

It's my turn to have a crack of temper. The entire field around us wilts, the greenery fading to an unnatural shade of grey. The flowers crumble to ash around our feet.

"*I am, thanks for asking,*" *I say icily. "I think you should go." I turn my back on him again and kneel. I press my fingertips into the rich soil, bringing the flowers and trees back to life.*

"*I shouldn't have said that,*" *Galen says. His hand is gentle on my shoulder.*

I turn to look up at him. The flowers are blooming under my hands, and they grow even taller this time, as if our combined power adds to the well I can draw on. "I guess I shouldn't have teased you, either. But Galen, learn to take a joke."

He takes off his armor and leathers and sets them to one side, exposing his bare chest. I cannot figure out how he's supposed to do battle dressed like that. I imagine the chafing and the way his body is exposed to injury.

"*But you're exactly right. I am the God of War and Suffering. I don't rule any realm, I ruin them. I make people suffer. I'll tell you what, though, at least I don't make people suffer the way Essos is hurting you. Do you want to talk about it?*" *Galen sits beside me.*

I'm still kneeling, infusing life back into the ground I just drained. The act of taking life and giving it back exhausts me. I'm still learning the extent of my powers and pushing my limits every day.

I sit down beside him, staring into his golden eyes. I open my mouth to say no but find the whole sordid tale flowing from my mouth. "I went to surprise your brother at your father's office and found him fucking some nymph. I don't mean to sound derogatory toward nymphs and dryads, but they're always throwing themselves at his feet.

"And maybe we hadn't clearly defined our relationship as exclusive, but I thought that, after six months together, it would have been obvious I wasn't interested in seeing anyone else."

Galen reaches forward and brushes a tear away from my cheek again.

"Now I'm crying and embarrassed."

"Can I come clean to you?" he asks, gently grabbing my chin and tilting my head so that I look at him.

A pang of guilt hits me. I shouldn't be here talking to Galen about Essos. I'm in love with his brother. But...I want someone to be on my side. When I tried to talk to them about Essos's betrayal, all my friends told me to assume this—that if I became queen, it would be my fate to have my husband stepping out on me constantly. But that's not the life I want. I've never understood why women in power are supposed to be okay with their husbands being unfaithful, but ever since Essos expressed interest in me, it's all I've heard. Their rationale is that neither Xavier nor Titus is known for fidelity, so I shouldn't expect it from Essos.

I lock eyes with Galen, ready to listen.

"About seven months ago, I spotted you in town. You were sitting in a ray of sunlight, laughing at something your friend said, wearing a green sweater. Your hair was free and long, with curls everywhere, and I wanted to run my fingers through it. I wanted to talk to you, but by the time I crossed the street and made my way to where you'd been, you were gone. When I saw you again in the library, I was too much of a coward to approach you. I thought if I interrupted your studies, you might never forgive me. When I finally saw you at the club, I was struck dumb. I couldn't even remember my name. I said the first thing that popped into my head, which was a dumb, cheesy pick-up line. I enjoyed dancing with you and was working up the nerve to ask you out. I will

admit that, when it comes to you, I was cowardly. Too afraid that you would reject me. Imagine if that got out? God of War and Suffering, afraid of a broken heart. By the time I did work up the nerve, you'd stopped coming to the club. The next time I saw you, you were on the arm of my brother, meeting the family for the first time."

I tilt my head, staring at him. I remember that first day he talked about. I'd actually noticed him across the street. I remember thinking about what a bright person he seemed to be. All eyes had been on him, but he'd seemed oblivious to the attention. I was running late to a class on the mythology of the Fates that day.

"This may seem forward, but...give me a chance. Essos is clearly too stupid to see what a great thing he had with you, but I promise you, I am not. I will never treat you the way Essos did. Give me one date. One dinner so I can show you that I'm the right brother." He cups my cheek and gently pulls me toward him until our lips meet, sweet and gentle. I think about pulling back, about resisting him, but then I ask myself, Why? My feelings didn't matter to Essos, so he shouldn't care that I'm kissing his brother.

Galen holds my face with one hand, the other sliding through my hair as the kiss deepens. But a feeling of wrongness settles over me, and I know that I don't actually want to be kissing Galen. I just want to get back at Essos and hurt him the way he hurt me.

It isn't Galen on my mind as I kiss him. It's how heartbroken Essos left me. It's thoughts of the nameless woman he had bent over his desk. It's the chastened look of pain on Essos's face when I caught them. It wasn't shock or surprise that I was there; it was resignation, like he was doing something he thought he had to.

I agree to go on the date, because I want Essos to realize that he fucked up. But as soon as I say yes, I regret it.

In this memory, I know that I would have canceled even if Helene had not intervened. It was Helene who helped to mend the bridge between Essos and me. It wasn't easy. There was so much for us to work through. But we did it. We both wanted to make our relationship work

because, by then, we'd both realized there was never going to be anyone
else. I called off the not-date with Galen and got back together with
Essos.

"So, you and Essos broke up for a period?" Luminara looks at me.

My thoughts are a whirling storm. Of *course*. Of course, the
day I get back the memory of walking in on Essos having sex with
someone else is the day I have to relive the one time I kissed
Galen to get back at Essos. I haven't even relived the worst of that
scene with Essos, flinching away from thoughts of the woman's
face, but I know it's going to come. I'm also going to remember
the fallout with Essos, and how devastated I felt after catching
him.

I know without a doubt that the memory will ruin me. I don't
want to remember any of it. Whatever happened between us
already happened; I don't need to relive it.

My stomach cramps, and beads of sweat break out on my forehead. "Yes, we did, but it doesn't matter what happened with
Galen during that time, because Essos and I got back together." I
subtly wipe my forehead as I thread my fingers through my hair to
flip it away from my face.

"Does Essos know that we kissed?" Galen probes, and I falter.

What was my indiscretion compared to his? I caught Essos
red-handed, a nymph bent over his desk with him between her
legs. A kiss with his brother was nothing—it was apples and
oranges. Still, I can't confirm anything because I don't remember
specifics, and as if that doesn't make me want to rip my hair out,
now I have to *defend* actions that I might or might not have taken.

"We agreed that what happened when we were broken up
was irrelevant. It meant nothing to me." It isn't a total lie, but I'm
not being totally honest either. I can remember my feelings from
that moment exactly. Kissing Galen had only reminded me how

much I loved his brother. I had agreed to a date, but one that never happened.

"If it meant so little to you, then why not tell Essos? Call him here now. Get it off your chest," Galen taunts.

It's a double-sided ask; calling Essos here would be calling him into a lion's den while drenched in blood. If Galen can get Essos to the house, he could force the transfer of power. What that entails, none of us really know. It's never happened, and the fact that he's trying to force it now is pure insanity.

"Enough of that, Galen. We're here to focus on your relationship with Daphne and how to better the realm. I think you two should go on that date."

I open my mouth to object, but Luminara holds up her hand, silencing me. I can't keep talking, the breath stolen from my lungs. I grip my chest and glare. After a moment, she releases her hold on my chest.

"I am excited about the prospect," Galen says, preening.

It's a victory to him, forcing my hand, forcing us together.

"Since I know you have reservations about this—" Luminara nods at me "—I'm going to temporarily wipe your memories. You were drawn together once. I think if we return you to that moment, you might find that you're still drawn together."

I gape at her, catching Galen's smug smile out of the corner of my eye. "Whose side are you on?" I'm disgusted with this entire process. I don't understand how the Goddess of Harmony can claim to be impartial when this could do serious physical *and* psychological harm.

"I am on the side of true love. I am on the side of helping fix this friction between you, if you're to be co-rulers. My job here is to help make you an effective team. We won't do it if you don't agree, but I encourage you to give it a chance. It might help you get past your hang-ups." Her voice is soft and sweet, but it doesn't make me want to kick her in the teeth any less.

"You mean my hang-up about the fact that he *murdered* me?" I demand.

Galen has the decency to look sheepish at the accusation. It's the bare minimum he can do.

"Yes. Without the circumstances that led to that, maybe things would have been different."

Her explanation is bullshit, pure and simple, but I have to remember that I'm supposed to be slowly giving in to him. I can explain away my actions the night of the Calling Ball as the madness from the rush of memories Essos and I shared, but every time I resist now is just solidifying to him that I'm against him.

I could never want to be with him, even without my memories, so I do the only thing I can do.

I agree.

7

"Do you need to invite Rafferty to block my memories?"

I think I feel the room tremble in response, but neither Galen nor Luminara appear affected. It's another piece of my dignity sacrificed to Galen, but if Rafferty comes to the house, maybe I can work with that, work with him.

"No, I can handle that on my own. As the Goddess of Harmony, I have the ability to block memories, particularly for those who have been traumatized. If you would like, I can also wipe memories of your murder."

"I'm going to have to decline that offer." I'm not going to explain myself to anyone, even if Galen looks like he wants to object.

"Okay," she agrees in that same patronizing, soothing tone she used earlier.

Luminara reaches her hand toward my forehead, but I swat it away.

Reaching down, I slip my shoes back on. "We can have the date tomorrow. I have meetings and paperwork and inconsistencies to sort out." I look pointedly at Galen, who meets my eyes and smirks.

When I married Essos, everything was about being partners. He might have been born to the throne, but I was his queen, his equal in nearly every way. To be told now that I don't have an equal right to be involved hurts, not only because I deserve to be a party to ruling my realm, but because I'm forced to watch Galen change and ruin systems that I put into place.

"Very well. I will remain on hand until after your date to restore your memories," Luminara says, giving a small dip of her head.

I rise, not waiting for someone else to declare the meeting over. Galen jumps to his feet beside me, while Luminara rises as well. At least they're still showing some signs of deference.

"If that is all, I have matters to attend to." I stride out of the room, holding my head high as I walk toward Essos's office. I'm not allowed to access information about the Underworld, so it's posturing to claim I have work to do. For the most part, I'm left alone in the sacred space that is Essos's office.

After the ball, the door to my office revealed itself, perfectly preserved beside Essos's from the last time I was there, right down to an unfinished cup of coffee and my half-burned candles. I loved the space, and the adjoining door between Essos's office and mine was always open. We never had anything to hide from each other.

Since the return of my memories, I have walked into my office only once. Just the familiar scent was overwhelming. I might not remember specific events or emotions, but the feelings are still there.

I opted instead to conduct my business in Essos's office, yearning for the reminder of him. Even the creak of his chair makes me want to tear up. I would tell anyone that I use the space for efficiency, but that's a lie.

I wish I had a way to contact Essos beyond waiting for him to appear in my room. Today I'm seething, on the verge of tears and wrath. I need his guidance, to confirm I'm making the right decisions about Galen and how I can fix the tithes situation. But I also want to rage at Essos for breaking my heart. It might have happened ages ago, but when I close my eyes, I see the curve of his bare hip as he enters the faceless woman, and I feel bile rise in my throat. I can't get comfort from Essos right now. Not in the way I need. And yet, he's the only one who could comfort me. I need him to hold me and remind me that we weathered the storm together once, and we can weather it again. Only the biggest storm we've ever faced is not one of his making, but of mine.

So, I *can't* go to him. I can't let my emotions rip me apart inside, leaving me a raw, open wound when people are counting on me. I can't let this fear, this pain, tear me open and leave me vulnerable to Galen *again*. I have to do the hardest thing, which is trust that while I *feel* unsteady in my relationship with Essos, we are *not* unsteady. I need to trust him; I need to trust us.

I close the door behind me and step into the masculine space. All around me are the touches I've added over the years—the curtains, several candles, my favorite books on his shelves. During the Calling, if I'd had an inkling of who I was, it would have been obvious. The art Essos showed us included some of my favorite pieces. The books we read were ones that I read a hundred times. The trinkets in his office are some that I picked out, including an old vase from Italy. I can't look at the couch without remembering the times we made love on it, lying entwined, each of us focused on wringing pleasure from the other before dealing with some of the more upsetting aspects of our job.

Angrily, I throw myself into his swivel chair. I turn in it the way my mind is turning with the details and gravitas of what I have done and what I am doing. I'm constantly in a position where one wrong move will topple the house of cards I've built. I don't have my full memories back; there are too many years, too much that still needs to be filled in. My powers are another wild card, acting out of turn. It's easier if I don't use them at all.

I glance to the corner of the office at the plant that I've been practicing on. I give it the half a thought I used to need to make something bloom, and nothing happens. I throw a little more juice at it, and the roots expand so rapidly that they shatter the planter.

"Fuck," I mutter, looking away from the mess I've made. What an apt metaphor. I scrub my hands over my face then lean back and stare at the ceiling, trying to sort out what needs doing.

My main focus needs to be on my people, all the souls living out their afterlives. I also need to figure out what Galen is up to.

There is a gentle knock on the door, and I stop spinning and grant them entrance.

Sybil walks in, holding a stack of papers. "Your Majesty," they say by way of greeting, head lowered demurely. Their brown eyes drift toward the plant in the corner, and they wince at the mess I've made. *They* have no problem fixing the pot, making it larger to accommodate the monster roots I just grew. I blow an annoyed huff of air out of my nose.

"You were never this formal with Essos," I chide, holding out a hand for the papers. I wish they were as comfortable with me as they are with my husband.

Sybil waits in front of my desk for me to grant them permission to sit. I do, waving my hand at the chair while I flick through the papers. I have to give credit where credit is due. They have worked hard with Essos to keep each of our systems running smoothly, and even corrected some redundancies we had in place.

"I've known Essos longer than I've known you."

My frown deepens as I look through the papers, only half-listening to Sybil. Our funds have dipped, and more and more new souls are being sent to the Deep or are lingering in the Inbetween, thanks to a change in the tithes. This isn't what Essos and I envisioned when we dreamed of how the Underworld would work.

Essos and I always tried to be fair. If a soul was truly evil, they would not be allowed to enter Paradise, the realm of the righteous. Instead, they would go to the Garden of Evil. The worst of the worst were sent to the Deep; it was a punishment we seldom used. Now that I have my memories, I know that James Blane, a man who abused a teen pop star and whose sentencing I witnessed with Essos during the Calling, is currently wasting away in the Deep. I flick my hand at my pen, adding a note to make sure his punishment is up to my standards.

We never involved ourselves in the torture of corrupt souls, but just this once, I'll make an exception.

As I look over the new information, I see why the Deep has had a sudden influx of souls. It's not because the standards were lowered, but because the entirety of the Garden of Evil has been rendered obsolete. Not only that, but more and more souls have been left wandering the Inbetween, a space too small for so many souls. They need to pass on to their appropriate afterlives. We need to free up space.

I glance up and am surprised to see Sybil still sitting there. "What is happening? *When* was the Garden of Evil closed?" I ask. The shrillness of my voice could break glass.

"We stopped accepting tithes below a certain amount, and most souls no longer have enough to pass on to the appropriate afterlife. The Garden of Evil was shuttered yesterday. All staff who worked there were also let go. Souls from the Garden are being shepherded into the Deep over the next few days."

I don't know which issue to deal with first. It takes an unbelievable number of staff not only to secure the borders of the Afterlife but also to keep souls in the Garden of Evil and the Deep from attacking each other. For the most part, souls have stayed in their designated area, but there are always malcontents with the intention of bettering their situation, even though it never gets better when they try. Dave, Spot, and Shadow always helped us enforce order, but they've been otherwise occupied, staying in the house.

This certainly explains why Sybil was able to bring me information today. With Galen and likely Xavier focused on the Garden of Evil closing, there isn't anyone to stop Sybil from filling me in.

I can't do anything about the closing of the Garden, so I switch my focus to something I can try to fix. "When was the tithe amount changed?" I need to dig into the paperwork more deeply to see when the scales tipped in the wrong direction.

I barely have access to paperwork for my own realm; I won't have access to the accounting sheets for all of Solarem. But what I *am* looking at shows that we're spending and transferring much more than we're taking in, and it's sending us toward financial ruin.

"About two weeks ago, Galen directed me to more than triple the requirement. The mortals have been gathering in the Inbetween until someone makes a decision about where these souls should go."

Of course, he did. There are so many words I have for Galen and Xavier for thinking I will let them run roughshod over me. Xavier is the one keeping me from doing my job. They're both in for it if they expect me to lie down and take this like a good girl.

I open my mouth to push further when there's another knock on my door. Sybil shoots to their feet like they don't want to be caught sitting in my presence.

"Enter!" I shout.

In walks one of the women Posey is trying to stick me with, a silver tray in her hand. A teacup rests on it, rattling as she walks. A certain defiance flashes over her face before it's gone. There's something so familiar about her, but I can't find the memory...it keeps slipping through my fingers like smoke.

"Your Grace." She places the tray on my desk.

Cat enters the office right on her heels.

The woman lifts the teakettle and pours me a cup. Her hands are shaking as she does it, her head kept low. I wish I could remember which one of them she is, but dealing with two unknowns is at the very bottom of my worries.

"She is to be addressed as 'Your Majesty,'" Sybil corrects.

I decide I'll leave this formality in place. Maybe I should try and woo this girl to my side, but something tells me I won't convince her.

"Your name, again?" I ask. I know I've been told a few times already but it just doesn't stick.

"Ellie, Your Majesty." There is a bite to her tone as she swirls a spoonful of honey into my cup.

"Ellie, thank you. You're dismissed. Cat, if you would stay."

Ellie bows lightly and walks out of the room.

"Can I get you something?" Cat asks once the door is shut.

"I want to bounce ideas off you. Es and I would do this when faced with a problem. I'm obviously not expecting you to be up to the same level of knowledge, but I could use your mind." Cat is unafraid to sit in my presence and drops into one of the two chairs across from me.

"All right, shoot," Cat says, opening her hands to me as if offering to take whatever of my burden she can.

Sybil sits too, as if realizing this isn't going to be quick. I make moss grow up the walls, my paltry attempt to dampen the sound leaving the room. It's an energy suck, but I need privacy. If anyone is listening, I don't want them to hear a thing. This is at least one skill I've been honing for the last few weeks. My first few attempts managed only to grow mold and make my walls wet.

"So, I'm going to just talk at you, and I'm sorry for that. When a being dies, they enter the Underworld and are initially held in the Inbetween until we can determine their tithe, at which point they pass into Paradise, the Garden of Evil, or the Deep. While they're in the Inbetween, souls can petition to change where they're assigned to go. We set a tithe amount to enter each level of the Afterlife, so for the most part, the transition is seamless. Currently, our tithes are down, so we're not making money from the souls coming in. The tithes convert to useable currency only once a soul passes into its appropriate Afterlife. It's a sort of trade —in exchange for their tithe, we—the royal *we*—allow them into their Afterlife. We use those tithes to run our realm, and they provide the money for Solarem to do things like maintain infrastructure and fund public projects. Without the tithes, I don't know what will happen. In the grand scheme of things, it's Xavier's job to figure out what happens as we move deeper and deeper into the red, but Solarem has no way of generating its own income. Our income comes from the dead and the precious gems in the earth."

"So, wait—dead people need to, like, come with money the way some cultures bury their dead with goods for the Afterlife?" Cat asks.

"Hardly. The tithe is the weight of someone's soul—the amount of good, or, in many cases, the amount of bad. These set amounts determine what sort of afterlife you have. Most souls go to Paradise, so we could do our best to keep families together. The weight of each soul funds so much in our realm, it's the literal gold standard. Souls back our money. Without the tithes from the souls, our economy will crumble." I cast a look at Sybil and then at Cat, who is trying her absolute best to understand what I'm telling her.

"So, what's the problem?" Cat asks.

"The tithe requirements were...altered." I let this sit for a moment before continuing.

"More and more souls are lingering in the Inbetween. The weight of their soul isn't enough for Paradise, the Deep, or the

Garden of Evil anymore. To get into Paradise now, you need to be saint-level good. For the Deep, you need to be one of the worst souls on the planet. It's virtually impossible to be sorted right now." I don't mention that the Garden of Evil is now no more; that's a whole new can of worms I'm not ready to tackle.

"So, again, I ask...what's the problem?" Cat says. She reaches up and lets her long hair loose, as if to relax the blood flow to her brain.

"The problem," I start, throwing my pen on the desk, "is that there are now millions of souls lingering in the Inbetween unable to move on, and I have to go on a date with Galen tomorrow without the memory of him stabbing me, and I've just remembered one of the worst days of my immortal life, *and* the whole of Solarem is going to be cast into financial ruin and my husband is going to be blamed for it!" I'm shouting by the end of my diatribe. I let out a sharp breath and stand.

"Okay, one problem at a time. How would you previously handle the souls in the Inbetween?"

This is why I needed Cat to stay. I need her to level me out.

"The tithe acted as a way to pre-sort souls. If a soul disagreed, that's when we had to act on it. As king and queen of the Afterlife, Essos and I would make a joint decision to move a soul on. It had to be so someone wasn't making unilateral decisions. My mother-in-law felt that this realm bore too much responsibility, but we were married before Essos took it over entirely. Before him, his father oversaw the realm, and it was pure chaos. There was no rhyme or reason to where souls were, and there was a lot of push-back from many of the souls when we did implement our system." We went through so much, trying to forge the boundaries between the different levels of the Afterlife. It's why I will not back down from people trying to minimize my role as queen. We did the work together—it's not just Essos's blood sweat and tears that went into creating harmony, but mine too.

I stride to the fireplace and brace my hands on the mantel, trying to coax the fire to life. With a small spark, it ignites and, thankfully, doesn't spread out of control, though I think that's more because of a charm cast by Essos when we were first building the house.

We were careless one night, so focused on each other that we didn't notice the fire creeping out of the fireplace until it had burned its way to the carpet we were on.

I look at the floor and see the scorch mark still there, a forever reminder. Gently, I toe the mark. It's little things like this that remind me what Essos and I had was real—that it actually happened and isn't all in my head.

"So, what you're saying is, you can't make this decision on your own?" Cat asks.

I give her a withering look. Like I needed the reminder.

I take a deep breath. She's trying to understand, and I can't fault her for that. "No, based on the quote-unquote rules set by the Council, I would need Galen to agree, and since he's the one who changed the amounts to begin with, I doubt that he's eager to do anything about it." I slump in my seat as I blow out an undignified raspberry. "Let's try changing the amounts back and see what happens. Even if he changes them again, maybe we can send a few thousand souls where they're supposed to go."

"If it's really going to cripple your economy, then why not talk to Xavier about it? Surely, he'll want to avoid that? What did Essos do in your absence, anyway?" Her voice lifts at Xavier's name, and I really, *really*, don't want to add the two of them to my list as a concern. Xavier should know better. But it might be worth a conversation.

"Stay away from Xavier," I warn, remembering the way he looked at her during the Calling Ball and the way he asks about her whenever he has a chance.

"I helped," Sybil says, in answer to Cat's question. I turn and look at them, waiting for elaboration. "Apologies, but when it became obvious that something had to be done, I stepped in. I helped to ensure the souls were moving along, Your Majesty, but Essos had to get special dispensation for that. I'm nothing more than a washed-up prophetess Essos took pity on."

I scowl at them, doubting their assessment of the situation. Essos saw something in Sybil.

They were brave and warm during the Calling, unafraid to defy Xavier or talk back to Essos. It had to have been hard on them, and everyone involved, to watch me ruin all their carefully laid plans. Though, like Finn and Essos, Sybil isn't blameless for what happened. I alluded to them that I was starting to have dreams and memories, and when they cautioned me to be silent about it, I was further inclined to accept the version of the truth that Galen was offering me.

So many times, I wonder...if I had just *asked* Essos about the dreams, would things be different?

"I sincerely doubt that. But, please, stop calling me 'Your Majesty.' I know we didn't know each other before, but I didn't like being called that then, and I hate it now. I'm still me, even if I have some holes in my memory."

"Can we backtrack to the date thing?" Cat asks, redirecting us to another issue totally out of my hands.

"*Someone's* girlfriend—" I glare at Sybil "—decided that Galen and I should go on a date we never went on from, like, a million years ago."

"I can't tell if you're hyperbolizing or being serious." Cat leans back and crosses her legs.

"Mostly, hyperbole, but also sort of serious." I pause. "Essos and I broke up briefly at the very start of our courtship." The reminder burns. I hated to tell people about this, even before I died. This one action always colors people's perception of Essos. And maybe people call me naive for forgiving him, or say I was manipulated, but Essos and I put in the work together to make us better. I don't yet remember specifics, and the whole situation is freshly raw, but I know that I wouldn't still be with him if he hadn't.

"So, you almost fucked his brother?" Cat asks, laughing.

I open my mouth to voice my rebuttal and I find I don't have one.

"Yeah. Yes. Yes, I did."

Cat keeps laughing.

"It was a different time!" I explain, trying to back out of this moral corner I was in. "They were princes still, not yet the kings they have become. Essos was different. So, so different. I was different."

"You were a ho, is what you're trying to say."

I bite my lip, thinking about her words. I was like every young goddess, enamored by the princes, wanting to find one for myself. Even Helene had a harem of men at her disposal until Kai emerged, birthed from the depths of the sea just for her.

"Yes, yes I was." I pace back toward her to sit on my desk in front of her.

"And you're going on this date?" she asks.

"I don't have much of a choice. I could very well have to marry Galen at the end of this. I'm supposed to be giving him a 'chance.'"

Sybil, who has been quiet, looks physically ill at the thought.

Same, my friend, same.

"You don't think he will..." Cat doesn't finish her sentence, worry written on her face.

"No, he's not going to hurt me, not again. I really think some part of him loves me, or did love me. He wants me alive. He wants me to love him." There is no confidence behind these words. His hands were around my throat the night of the Calling Ball; I don't doubt he'd do that again. That's why it's important I play along.

"Didn't we learn he was married?"

I look up at Cat, surprised by the question. "Yeah, we did, but Callista hasn't been seen in years. Since before I died. She never appeared anywhere with him. From my understanding, they were mostly estranged from day one. They were married shortly after Essos and I."

"Ballsy, to pursue your brother's wife while you're still married?"

I snort at Cat's words, walking over to the decanter. "You say that like Xavier didn't once corner me in a dark hallway." I take a sip of my drink.

Cat spins to look at me, a jealous glint in her eye. "I'm sorry, what?" she barely chokes out.

I hand her a glass of the whiskey Essos coveted. "He said I should decide once and for all which brother was better in bed."

"And did you?"

I laugh outright. "No, of course not. Once Essos and I were able to get past that initial..." I search for the right word "...hiccup, we were solid. I never regretted not going on that date with Galen, and I never looked twice at Xavier. Essos was my world." For a moment I get lost in the memory of that night.

I'm sitting at my vanity, face clean after a shower. I'm wearing a silk camisole and shorts while applying my lotion. Essos is already in bed, hair wet from his shower—well, our shower. I rise, crossing the room to my side of the bed where the covers are pulled back, waiting for me. I can feel the desire in Essos's eyes. All night, he's been looking at me, and it makes heat pool low in my belly.

"You won't believe what happened tonight," I say, climbing into bed, snorting at the thought.

Essos throws the covers over my legs as he moves closer to me so our bodies touch. "Tell me, my love, and let's see how far my belief in you goes."

I pull back so I can see Essos's face when I tell him. He presses a kiss to my bare shoulder.

"Your brother wants me to sleep with him so I can decide who is the better lover." Essos doesn't so much as pause as his hand traces the band of my shorts. He trails his nose from my shoulder up to my ear, dropping kisses as he goes.

"If he weren't my brother, I would offer to let you have us both at the same time." His teeth capture my earlobe, giving a gentle tug. "But crossing swords with my brother is a line I will not cross, even for you."

"Are you saying you need another lover in our bed?" I tease.

Essos trails his hand up to my breast. "I'm saying that if it would please you to try something new, perhaps someone new, then I would be sporting about it. A millennium is a long time with the same lover. But I would much rather not share."

I place a hand on his chest, stopping him. He goes still, his eyes meeting mine. I watch them, the warmth hidden beneath the ice-blue color of his eyes.

"Is that what you want, Essos? Someone else in your bed? Are you tired of having just me?" That old insecurity rears its ugly head.

He moves his hand out from under my shirt and sits up. Then he cups my face so he's looking at me straight on. There will be no mistaking his intent.

"I want you and only you. I don't think I could stomach having someone not you beside me in this bed without you. I mean only to offer; if you want to try something new, that we do it together. Should one of us want to share our bed with someone else, it would be us and them. I will never tire of worshipping everything about you, even your toes."

"My toes are terrible." I curl them where they are under the covers, trying to distract myself from how vulnerable I feel. It's stupid to let this thing that happened hundreds of years ago matter now. He's my

husband; I trust him implicitly, but there is always that nagging voice in my head that I wasn't enough for him once.

"Your toes are marvelous, even the baby one without a toenail. In fact, they have made me reconsider my stance on foot fetishes. Perhaps I should give it a try." His hand traces down my leg toward my foot, and I giggle. "I'm sorry, my love, that I ever caused you this pain. You don't deserve it. I told you then that I'll spend the rest of our immortal lives trying to make up for it, and I meant it. If you want to sleep with my brother, go right ahead. I might have to find a way to kill him after, but if it's what you want...."

"No, it's not something I want. You said it perfectly: I want only you beside me."

He kisses me, his mouth working over mine until the kiss deepens. I slip down, lying back so he can cover my body with his and worship me the way he promised.

Cat is snapping her fingers in my face. "Where did you go?" she asks, her voice concerned.

"A memory." My voice is little more than a whisper. There is no precedent to follow when it comes to being a goddess getting your memories back. No one knows how long it will take for me to have them all back, or if I ever will get them all back. I suppose that's the nature of life, even my unnaturally long one; I can't remember every second of it. I just have to hope I'm not missing anything big.

"I can cancel with Kai today if you want," Cat offers.

My whole body deflates. I hadn't realized that he would be able to meet with me so soon. "No, no. I need this, especially if I'm going on memoryless dates with Galen. What time am I supposed to meet Kai?"

"You have an hour."

I glance at the clock on the mantle and realize I've missed

lunch. I'm not sure if that's because of the memory or from getting so lost in what I'm doing. There actually is no rest for the weary.

"Then I guess I have to get ready." I let the moss on my walls wither and die, becoming ash before fading to nothing, leaving no trace of my duplicity behind.

8

H elene is waiting outside my room when I emerge, dressed for a workout. As far as anyone else knows, including Muffin and Emily, I'm going to be doing yoga with Helene so I can help work on healing my mind and spirit.

I know those aren't their names, but I don't care to get the names of Posey's spies right. That might seem callous and cruel, but if I have my way, they're not going to be with me long.

Helene doesn't say anything, wordlessly leading me down the stairs and toward the back of the house. I think I'm going to get away scot-free until I hear a little voice clear its throat. I spin and find my other sister-in-law looking at me.

"Fuck," Helene curses under her breath before turning and giving a big smile.

"We need to plan the wedding!" Posey proclaims without caring that I'm clearly on my way somewhere else. She's an octave short of stomping her foot as she shrieks at us. I haven't figured out what her angle is in all this, other than I must have made some slight to her that I don't remember.

"You can have Melinda and Eloise put some time on my calendar. I have an appointment to get to." I gesture at the shadows standing behind Posey. If they want to be effective spies, they should at least pretend they're not plants. The blonde has her gaze turned down, while the brunette is looking at me straight on.

Posey glances between me and the women before lifting her head high. "Miranda and Ellie," she corrects through gritted teeth. Just to see her ruffled is worth never committing their names to memory. "And when I checked your schedule this morning, you had free time now."

"Things change, Posey-popsicle," Helene says, flashing a fake smile. Her nails dig into my forearm as if I'm to blame for her appearance. I want to glare at Helene for manhandling me, but she might be the only way I get out of this planning session.

"Where are you going? Can I come?" Posey asks. She's like the annoying little sister we don't want around, if that annoying little sister was actively trying to ruin my life at every chance. There were times that perhaps Helene and I were cruel to her, choosing to sit in our own corner and gossip at a party while Posey ran around micromanaging everyone. But I do have memories of trying to reach out to Posey before we all became entrenched in our roles. I thought if anyone was going to understand how it felt to be an interloper in the royal family, it would be her, but she rebuffed me at every turn. Eventually, I stopped trying.

Helene and I exchange a look, and I turn to answer her.

"We're going to do some yoga to try to stimulate my memories and my womb." The last bit comes out with a hint of uncertainty, but Helene nods along in confirmation, like that is absolutely the answer.

Posey looks positively delighted by this turn of events. "Then perhaps I *should* come along."

Helene steps between us, putting me somewhat behind her. When push comes to shove, I know I can count on Helene to back me up. "You really shouldn't. It's best to have minimal people around. After all, I am the Goddess of Wives and Wombs, and I know what's best. Ta ta!" Helene shoves me hard out onto the back deck, leaving Posey seething.

"You're the Goddess of the Stars and Victory, not wives and mothers," I scoff.

"Yeah, I know, which is why we need to leave before that occurs to her."

We scurry away toward another part of the estate.

The land that Essos and I built our home on is extensive, and I'm glad that people like Finn and Sybil remember every unique thing about the house and land, because I certainly don't. I recognize where we're going because during the Calling, Essos and I were headed this way on horseback when I accidentally kicked Abbott, the horse I was on, and sent him off at a gallop. An open-air arena lies right alongside the water, farther past where Essos was able to catch us. It's hidden from view by some clever shrubs that I helped to erect for Essos so he could have privacy when he trained. He used to joke that he wanted the barrier there to stop people from seeing what an embarrassment he had become. He was—is—a peaceful king, but he liked to be prepared in case of anything. His brothers used to rib him for going soft as the King of Death, a bastardization of his two titles.

Kai is there waiting, stretching under the expansive sky. The arena is somehow smaller than I remember, but I seldom came out here. Occasionally, I would watch, and even more infrequently, I would train with Essos, but after several sessions that ended with me on my back and him between my legs, I was banned until I promised to be serious about it.

In hindsight, I wish I *had* been more serious.

Helene jumps into her husband's arms. His back is to her, but he spins and catches her just as she launches into the air. She wraps her legs around his wide torso and peppers his face with kisses. Kai's hands rest firmly on his wife's ass as he responds to her passion. I have no doubt that they'll rail each other right now with me standing here if I don't speak up.

"Some of us haven't seen our husbands in over a month, and you two are disgustingly cute with your affection. I love you both, but also, stop."

Kai has the decency to look sheepish, but Helene doesn't let go of him. Her ankles are locked around his back. It's not strictly true that I haven't seen Essos, but I'm not letting anyone in on that secret.

"Go get a vibrator or fuck my other brother. Just because you're not feeling the love doesn't mean I'm not," Helene snaps, sticking her tongue out at me. My anger gets the better of me and I pop my hand at her, coating her tongue with flowers. It's a risky move, but she deserves it.

When she tries to pull her tongue back into her mouth, she realizes what I've done and turns her angry eyes on me. "Fith ith," she manages, her words mangled by the flowers. She points at her tongue, glaring. Kai lets out a large laugh, and she turns her attention to him.

"You're rude," I point out, crossing my arms. I keep up this false bravado because I'm terrified of what Helene will do to me if I *can't* fix this.

"You earned that, starfish. She's right, you were being rude." Kai is still holding her, even if it is just by her ass. Always, he has her.

Helene turns her murderous look back to me. I take pity on her and tug on the thread of my magic that created the flowers, dissolving them. Glad doesn't even cover my feelings when my powers act the way they should. I can't tell if that worked because I used my powers out of an emotional reaction, or if they're finally settling.

"I am irritated by your existence," Helene says to me, finally climbing off her husband. Helene's powers were never specific to her the way flowers call to me or emotions call to Luminara. Instead, she has mastery over most of the gifts other gods have. Goddess of Victory, indeed.

"If you would like, you can go back to having only Posey as your sister-in-law."

"I'm still irritated but want you to stick around." She wanders back to where Kai has set out weapons and what look like cruel implements of torture but are probably just different tools for working out, like weights and bands. "Besides, if you don't wind up with Essos, I dread to think of him winding up with someone else. You were the best of his bad taste in women."

She's teasing me. I know she is because, once upon a time, we were closer than sisters. We shared everything without any of the childish drama of competing for a parent's affection, but my mind strays. It strays to the faceless woman my husband slept with before we were married.

Unhelpfully, I remember Xavier mentioning that Essos had affairs before my Calling. Of course, he did—I don't want him to have spent all that time alone. But now, my mind is trying to put faces to the women he was with after my death. Were there many of them?

I'm spiraling further and further into myself, and my self-confidence is breaking. Why would he want to go through all the trouble I bring with me? He could cut ties and run and be free now, knowing that I chose Galen over him.

Kai doesn't wait for a greeting; he just approaches me and envelops me in a crushing hug. "Good to have you back, kid." I think I might disappear completely in his embrace when he squeezes and lifts me. "What can I do you for?" He lets me go and starts back to Helene.

Kai has managed to break my fall before I hit rock bottom. I *know* Essos. I know that we are supposed to be together. I need to bury all these icky emotions that shitty memory dredged up. I need to focus on the millions of good memories I have with him, on the feel of his body wrapped around mine and what it's like when he drives me closer and closer to ecstasy.

Coming back to the problem at hand, I answer Kai. "I need to learn how to defend myself against Galen if he tries to kill me again."

Kai's steps stutter. His massive back is to me, but I see him lift his head toward Helene, a silent conversation passing between the couple.

"You really think he would try to hurt you again?" He turns to fully look at me.

I don't understand why everyone keeps asking this question. Of course, I think that. He's proven time and time again that if he doesn't get his way, he'll do whatever it takes to win. The God of War is a sore loser.

"I do. Once he has the throne, he won't need me any longer." I don't mention how he wants to use my body or how he threatened to share me with his friends.

"There's a big difference between him not needing you anymore and him hurting you," Kai points out.

"You're right—only one of those things is fun for him." I lift my chin defiantly.

Kai shares another look with Helene, concern rimming both their eyes. "Then we have no time to waste. Let's get started."

Kai is not slow or gentle with me. The first thing he wants to work on is getting me stronger. He can't work with me on my powers, but he can work on my physical strength. Galen won't expect me to strike back against him with my hands, because he thinks I'll rely on my powers the way I once did. I won't have that weakness again.

I know where Helene got the idea for working with giant tires and running and her endless stamina from. Kai pushes and is relentless for the two hours we work together. Making me strong is going to be slow going and something we have to work on every day, but it's more than I had before.

My muscles shake as I lift a kettlebell, then it slips from my grasp. I let my body follow it to the ground, unsure of how I'm going to explain my exhaustion later. This is exactly what I needed. I'm too tired to even think about my problems, let alone obsess over them.

"Did you have anything to eat today?" Kai asks. He's hovering over me, his hands braced on his knees while he looks down at me.

"Do whiskey and tea count?" I pause. "Oh, I had bacon and toast this morning."

From the look on his face, that isn't much better. A scowl twists his lips. It's not a mean one, but it's enough to get his point across. He expects better of me.

"I'll work with Estelle to increase your protein intake. You may be a goddess, but you still have to get your energy from somewhere."

I want to glare at Kai, but he's only trying to help, and he's right. Problem is, this body subsisted on tequila and Chinese food for the three years that I was in college. There's nowhere for the energy to come from. Estelle, our cook, has been doing what she can to keep me fed, but since I started getting my memories and powers back, my appetite is miserable. It's like fear of the unknown is keeping my hunger at bay.

When I think about the next few months, all I see is me having to walk down the aisle to Galen, and it makes me sick. Right now, all I want to do is roll over and puke, but that could just be the whiskey and the exertion.

"I can't thank you enough for this, Kai," I say, taking his offered hand to get up.

"I'm only sorry we failed you the first time." Kai sounds miserable at this statement.

Helene glances up from her phone.

"I wish everyone would stop acting like they did something wrong. Galen is the only one responsible for plunging a knife into my chest. Not you, not Essos, not Finn. No one would have thought such a thing was possible." I grab my water from the bench and start sucking it down. "You're giving me what I need now, which is a chance to survive if something goes wrong again."

I don't know how to tell people that I think he *will* do it again —he'll get what he wants from me and then kill me. He's proven he can kill a god. He's proven that he won't hesitate to do it. As much as remembering Essos's long-ago betrayal hurts, losing focus will get me killed. We can deal with my feelings of betrayal and hurt for the second time when Essos is home safe. Even if it breaks my heart every day until this is over, I need to do what I didn't do during the Calling—I need to *trust*. Trust that Essos and I are solid. Trust that we will get out of this.

I no longer know what Galen wants. Every day, it's something different—to get me pregnant, to let his friends use me, to rule together over the Afterlife. I'm not sure it matters much either way, because I'm not going to let it come to that. I will be reunited with my husband, and I will be free of Galen, no matter the cost.

As I start to head back to the house, a rustle of leaves catches my attention. My head snaps in the direction of the sound, but all I can see is a flash of blonde hair.

9

I'm sitting in my room alone the next day, watching the clock count down toward my date with Galen. It's better than looking at the papers on my bed, which allude to the poor financial status of the Underworld. The headlines attribute the closing of the Garden of Evil to mismanagement of funds rather than a direct ploy by Galen to ruin Essos's kingdom. What I can't figure out is Galen's endgame. Ruining the Underworld won't benefit him if he's going to take over, unless he has other plans in play.

I distract myself from all the dangerous thoughts going through my mind by getting Dave to select my shoes for the night.

"This?" I ask Dave, holding up a pair of flats with a treat behind them. He's all about picking heels for me to wear, but I can't get him to participate in our usual game of picking my clothes for this date. His gaze shifts to the shoe that has the treat behind it, but he refuses to engage. Even my dog knows this is a mistake.

There's a light knock on my door.

"Enter," I call, expecting it to be Zara or Cat. Instead, Ellie walks in with a tray in her hand. Dave doesn't lift his head, moving only his eyes to track her as she crosses the room to where I sit at my vanity. There is a light rumble in his throat, and I appreciate him knowing not to trust her.

"You look beautiful, Your Majesty," she says, not making eye contact. She has tea for me, something I didn't know I needed. I watch her pour it into a cup before taking it in my hands and sipping it. I'm dressed and ready for the date, but I'm stalling, not yet ready to go down to do the thing. I changed at least five times, not out of an effort to impress Galen, but because I didn't know what sort of message I wanted to send.

This is supposed to be a reconciliation. I'm supposed to want to make Galen and I work. Attending this date as a queen, one who is holding on to her title and the husband who gave it to her, isn't going to send the same message if I appear as the girl in the green sweater who noticed Galen before getting entangled with Essos. But I'm no longer that girl. I'm a woman who has lived and died; I'm a reincarnation.

I'm a college coed who is still trying to figure out who she is.

My mortal life feels like a whisper of my identity, but I can't forget what it was like to live in a world rife with pain and suffering that blended with love and kindness. Mortals live for such a short amount of time compared to us gods, but they never let that stop them from loving and feeling and hurting others. Some of what I experienced has made me question if there should be more nuance to all aspects of the Underworld. Essos and I were able to view the actions of humans secondhand, but living as one gave me another perspective entirely.

It burns me a little inside to think of the active shooter drills I had to do in school because of a lack of mental health care access combined with easily accessible weapons, and comforting a girl on my floor freshman year after she was assaulted on a date. Mortals are capable of such good and evil in the same stroke, but so are gods. We like to believe that, as celestial beings, we're above mortal problems, but our delusions of grandeur are just that—delusions. It's why Essos was able to hurt me by cheating on me, and Galen is able to so effectively wield sexual assault as a threat to keep me in line.

It's going to be a long time before I forget what it was like to be human, and I need to hold on to those memories if I want to make effective change.

Unfortunately, none of that is going to help me tonight as I go back to being the young woman at Solarem University, eager for a date with a prince.

I'm wearing a simple green dress, going back to my roots as a child of spring and flowers. It has a full skirt that ends just above my knees and a high neckline. The dress may be simple, but my jewels speak to the queen I am. I leave the moon and sun motifs that defined my marriage to Essos behind in my jewelry box. Instead, I have on heavy diamond chandelier earrings and a large statement necklace made from both canary and colorless diamonds.

Ellie glances around the room, surprised, I think, to find that Cat and Zara aren't with me.

"Looking for something to report to Posey?" I ask, scratching Waffles's back as he saunters over the vanity top and pushes my lip gloss over the edge. He watches with marked curiosity as it lands without a sound, earning an undignified huff from the feline.

"No, ma'am. I was just thinking that this isn't what I expected from a queen's room."

I give her a tight smile. "The queen's room is that which she shares with her king. It doesn't feel right to occupy that room when I have no king to share it with." As I say it, I hear how wistful my tone is. To cover up my vulnerability, I take a sip of tea. This room is not where I belong.

"You don't remember me, do you?"

Her forwardness surprises me. I study her to try and place where I might know her from. "I'm afraid I can't say that I do, I'm sorry. My memories are returning slowly, and I met a lot of people the night of the Calling Ball that I still haven't been able to connect the dots with." I try to give her an appeasing smile, but it comes out as more of a grimace. Sometimes not having all my memories feels like walking into a room where everyone shares an inside joke except me.

Ellie shakes her head. "That's all right. We spoke briefly the night of the ball. If you need anything from me, you can ring for me. I'll be around." She takes the tray and my now-empty teacup and backs out of the room just as Cat is entering.

"Ready?" Cat asks hesitantly.

I rise from my seat, lifting my shoulders. Cat closes the door behind Ellie and gives me a once-over. She's my ride or die, I know that, but I still can't help but try to protect her from my mess. I haven't broached the subject since the night of the Calling Ball, but I can always offer her the choice to go on to her afterlife.

Then again, if Galen isn't done messing around with the Underworld, I could be putting her at more risk.

Damned if I do, damned if I don't.

"Do I have a choice?"

"I guess, not really." Cat crosses to me and fusses with my brown curls, which are pulled away from my face in a clip. "Why can't you and Essos just run away together?"

"I wish it were that easy, Cat. But we can't abandon our people, the souls in the Afterlife. Essos has certain abilities that are his by right of being king. To give them up, he would have to abdicate, and he won't. To him, abdication is failure. At Essos's coronation, Titus—the God Supreme—bestowed powers on Essos that have to do with maintaining souls. If he wanted to, Essos could go to the mortal realm and mark souls for where they'll go once they arrive here, but he doesn't, because he believes in a person's capacity to grow and evolve throughout their life. He can change people's Afterlife designation if he so chooses. He adjudicates, as you saw. And he can unmake souls. To give up his crown would mean passing these abilities to Galen, who has proven that he would be a capricious god.

"Essos doesn't trust Galen with anything. Which means the only way that Galen can get those powers and Essos's scepter is by marrying me and engaging in a blood bond. My blood was coded to the crown after my coronation. Which means that, in lieu of Essos's abdication, Galen can gain some of those abilities from me during the marriage ceremony.

"The vote of no confidence wasn't enough to strip the powers from Essos. It just put his ability to rule in question." It's another long-winded answer that doesn't even begin to adequately explain what's going on.

"What happens if Galen is crowned king?"

"Theoretically, Xavier, as King of the Gods, could strip the powers from Essos without him being present, but I don't know, and I'm not interested in finding out. The final piece of the puzzle is the Scepter of Death. It's rumored that the scepter is the basis for Essos's power over the dead. It's not, but it does carry a lot of the same powers and would allow another god to perform some of the duties of the God of the Dead. It's why Essos has kept it hidden all this time. Someone could do a whole lot of damage with access to the scepter."

There is an impatient knock at the door. "There is fashionably late, Daphne, and then there is just rude," Galen's voice calls from the other side of the door.

I roll my eyes at Cat, who grabs my hand and squeezes it. I don't hesitate to pull her into a tight hug. I want to talk more with Cat, just to check in with her. There are bags under her eyes, and I want to know what I can do to help. I need to know if Galen is causing her additional strife, or if it's the situation we're in. Either will be understandable, but if it's Galen, I need to put a stop to it.

"You're my ride or die," I tell her, and hope that I'm not adding additional pressure to her.

"I know it. Knock him dead, and I do mean that literally," she whispers to me with a grim grin.

"Would if I could." I open the door to find Galen leaning casually against the opposite wall. It takes a moment for his golden eyes to sweep over me. The natural makeup and simple hairdo seem to catch him off guard. He drinks in the sight of me, his lips parting before he remembers himself and offers me his arm.

"Shall I escort you to dinner?" he asks.

I spare one last glance at Cat, who gives me a reassuring look, before I slip my arm into his.

Luminara is waiting for us at the foot of the stairs, Sybil close to her side. It feels so wrong that I'm doing this—that I *have* to do this—but I'm playing by their rules for now.

"You two look charming together," Luminara says serenely.

Sybil looks at their girlfriend like she has six heads.

"How does this work?" I ask as Luminara raises her hand to my forehead. I'm thankful when she pauses. All the nerves I've been suppressing are rising in me in the form of vomit. I'm going to lose it all over Galen's shoes. This is so wrong on so many levels that I don't understand why I have to go through with it. It's my "choice," but not really. Yet, if I don't go through with it, I'll be made to seem like the irrational one. The one who is "difficult" for not wanting to be re-traumatized by my abuser.

Day in and day out, I'm expected to play the good girl, but knowing who I'm dealing with—knowing what a rotten god Galen is at his core—has helped protect me. He might be faking it and he might be playing nice, but I know who he really is deep down. With that knowledge taken away, I'm open to being hurt by him again in a very different way. Information helps me guard my heart and my mental well-being, and Luminara wants to strip that from me.

"This is going to take you both back to your headspace after the meadow. I will wipe Essos from your mind, and the last few millennia won't have happened. It won't be Essos who broke your heart, just some other god whom Galen doesn't think highly of. I want to keep Essos far from your mind because your history together is too prominent. The focus tonight is on the moment you two had in the meadow and rebuilding and finding what it was that made you special together."

I don't point out that there was no "together." A handful of nights dancing does not make a relationship.

Luminara gives me a meaningful look, perhaps to convey that I need to take this chance to reconnect.

I'm about to voice a rebuttal and change my mind, fuck the consequences, when Luminara's fingers brush my temples, and searing pain shoots through my head. I cry out and screw my eyes shut, afraid that any light or sound will be too much.

10

I open my eyes.

Galen and I are seated at a table by the beach, just the two of us. I'm confused how we got here, and where *here* is. Galen glances around, and then his eyes find me. There is a haziness to his gaze before it sharpens, like he's clearing cobwebs from his mind. Maybe we both pre-gamed this date a little too hard.

"Have I mentioned how beautiful you look tonight?"

At his words, I blush and look away. When I try to remember the five minutes before this, it's fuzzy.

"I can't say that you have," I reply.

His gaze drifts to my lips and I know he's thinking about that kiss in the meadow. The kiss that held the promise of more, the promise that, if I had asked, he would have made love to me in that meadow until I was exhausted from the pleasure. I've heard tales of his prowess, and if the way he moves on the dance floor is any indication, I'm sure it would be a memorable night.

A shudder runs through me, and it's not from anticipation; it's low-level fear.

But I don't have anything to fear, and pinpointing a cause for that feeling is difficult. Galen's reputation as God of War and Suffering is just that, a reputation. I'm sure I have nothing to fear from him.

"Well, you do," he reassures me.

I flip my hair over my shoulder, not even looking at the menu before me. "What, no more cheesy pickup lines?"

"What is there to say? You leave me speechless."

I laugh and take a sip from my wine glass, which is suspiciously full. "Why didn't you ask me out? I mean, before, when we were dancing." I can't even bear to think the name of the asshole who broke my heart. Maybe it's for the best that he did step all over me if it meant finding my way to Galen.

That thought feels wrong somehow, but I can't put my finger on why.

No, it's not just that it feels wrong. I feel *dirty* at the idea of being with Galen.

"Honestly?" He takes a sip from his glass.

"That would be why I asked, yes."

"You're untouchable. I mean that in the most sincere way. You're dizzyingly gorgeous, you have a light to you that all the plants just want to bend toward. Which makes sense, since you're the Goddess of Spring, but you snort when you laugh and you don't care, and my gods, if I could wake up next to you every day for the rest of my life, that would be all I needed."

"Pretty words from a pretty man." The plates before us fill without our needing to order. Galen's words feel like just that—words meant to woo without any sincerity behind them. At face value, they're enough to make anyone's panties drop, but his words don't trigger a rush of pleasure through me.

"What do you want? Do you want me to take you right here and prove my interest to you? Should I bend you over the table as I make my hand your new necklace? Is that what the asshole that broke your heart did?"

The thought of him wrapping his hand around my throat makes my blood run cold. My lips twist into a scowl at his vulgarity. If he's hoping to shock a response from me with his words, he's going to be sorely disappointed. I push food around my plate before taking a small bite, my stomach churning the second it hits my tongue.

"I would like to be romanced a little. We danced for a week straight, your body pressed against mine. I mean, we were practically having sex on that dance floor, and you never even asked my name." I let my anger from having my heart broken fuel me. The truth is, I was mad—I *am* mad—that he never wanted to know my name and who I was, but the moment I was with someone else, *that* was when he started to express his regret.

"But I already knew your name. I knew exactly who you were and, yes, I admit it... I was a chicken. I didn't think you wanted me."

I guffaw into my wine glass. "I was dry humping you when we danced—how much clearer could my intentions have been, Galen? Your excuses only get you so far when I've *seen* you take girls into backrooms at clubs and fuck them like your dick was going to fall off tomorrow. You never wanted me until you couldn't have me."

We're quiet for a moment. I didn't realize we needed to have this conversation, this argument.

"I never did that on nights when we were dancing," he says defensively, as if that excuses his behavior. "But, you're right."

I look up at him, surprised.

"There is nothing quite like losing the one good thing in your life to make you realize what you had."

"You're so full of shit, you know that, Galen?" There is anger in my voice that goes deeper than Galen being a fuckboy and me getting my heart broken by someone who cheated on me.

"What will it take to prove my intentions to you?" Galen demands. He's shaking with barely contained rage.

I lift my fork to my mouth while I think it over.

"Time, Galen. You need to prove yourself to me over time."

"I will do whatever it takes. You want me to battle a Gorgon or slay some beast? I'll do it."

I try to hide my smirk, but I'm unsuccessful. "You can start by being honest with me. How does that sound?"

"Whatever I have to do, my lady. I may not be one of the princes set to inherit a crown, but I *am* a prince. There is no task too big or small for me to face."

At his reference to his brothers, my heart swoops, and I can't imagine why. We fall quiet, talking pleasantries, what I'm studying at the university, what my plans are as the Goddess of Spring. Galen conjures a bottle of champagne, and we take it with us as we walk down the beach, just talking.

"I have these impossible standards to live up to, you know? Like, Xavier is set to be King of the Gods, as if he wasn't insufferable enough, and then Essos is going to rule the Afterlife, which has its own bullshit, and there's nothing left for me. I should have been given the seas, but no, Helene didn't want Xavier, and of course my father had to have a god worthy of his favorite, so he summoned Kai and made him King of the Seas."

When he said Essos's name, my heart did that same swoop. I know an embarrassing amount about all three princes, including the fact that they all have their affairs.

I frown at yet another unexpected reaction. Essos is the quietest of the three brothers, but when I try to think of more details about him, my mind goes blank.

"God of War sounds pretty mighty," I offer to appease this mercurial god. I take a swig from the bottle we're passing between us, hoping that if I can reach that light buzzy feeling, maybe I'll start to truly enjoy myself.

"War *and* Suffering. It's like I'm diseased or something. No one wants to get too close; no one wants to be associated with the God of Suffering." He's actually pouting, his lower lip sticking out a little.

I reach out and take his hand, hoping to soothe him. "You get to decide how people see you. If you want people to fear you and see you as the God of Suffering, then commit to that. But being God of War is mighty, and that alone makes you fearsome. You can't let what your brothers have get under your skin. Be your own god."

Galen stops walking and looks down at me, like I've said something profound. He surprises me when he grabs my hand and pulls me against him. I let out a little yip, but I don't pull back, even though he's giving me the chance to. His lips find mine, and then he's kissing me, and something about it just feels so *wrong*. It's like biting into a cookie thinking it's chocolate chip, only to find it's oatmeal raisin.

I commit to this, though. I told him I would give it a chance, that I would try and see if we could make things work, so I do. I tell myself that it's my stupid broken heart making me think this is wrong. What's that age-old advice? The best way to get over someone is to get under someone else. Maybe that's what I should be doing.

I pull away from Galen, and he looks like I've just taken his favorite toy. The desire to avoid rocking the boat after kissing him rises in me, and I give in to impulse.

"Want to go skinny dipping?" I offer, turning my back so he can help with the zipper. He pulls my hair to the side and slides my zipper down. I don't look back at him, but I hear the sound of his pants being undone. I shuck off my dress, hoping that the moonlight doesn't show too much of me. The Goddess of the

Moon, Esmaray, blesses me, and the moon is shadowed by a cloud, blocking the light.

I race into the ocean ahead of him, the water shockingly cold. My system jolts and prickles, reminding me that this is reckless. I'm not the sort of girl who goes skinny dipping on a first date, let alone with a prince. There is a non-zero chance that I already regret this. Getting naked feels like too much of an invitation.

Galen runs into the water but seems to have sense enough not to get too close to me. Perhaps because I'm bare physically, I feel like I might as well bare myself emotionally before him. My heart has already decided that I'm not going on a second date with Galen, so I go for broke to see if something's wrong with me.

"Do you think I'm undeserving?"

His head jerks toward me and he raises a brow. "Undeserving of what?" he asks, floating a little closer toward me.

I'm careful to keep my whole body submerged as I swim a little farther out. I turn my back on him, finding it easier to reveal my insecurities to the wide expanse of the sea than to the face of this gorgeous man who, against all odds, is interested in me.

"I don't know. Love? The guy I was seeing...I thought he cared about me, but I caught him with another woman and, like, maybe if that had happened with only one guy, I wouldn't feel so insecure, but my boyfriend before that did the same thing, and this man *knew* it. He knew that betrayal would hit me the hardest." My first ex, Cassius, the God of Vanity, was a mistake. He'd told me exactly who he was, and I should have listened, but I fell into the trap of thinking I was the special one capable of changing the tiger's stripes.

Spoiler alert: I wasn't.

I began crossing paths with Galen a few weeks afterward, when I was trying to get myself out of my mental funk.

Galen swims behind me. I feel his hands on my arms, then his body presses against me and he reaches for my hips. I can feel his erection against my body as he pulls me close.

I immediately want the touching to stop. Warning bells are going off in my mind, and I know to listen to my instincts.

"Do you think this feels undeserving?" he asks, his voice husky in my ear.

I splash him over my shoulder, getting him right in the face. He lets me go, and I turn to face him, finding the sandbar firm beneath my feet. I put a fair amount of distance between us, eager for this date to be over.

"I didn't say I was unfuckable. I'm not looking for casual sex—if I wanted that, I would fuck Xavier. Lord knows he's asked enough. If anything, you proved my point—I'm not worth more than that." Tears prick my eyes, and I'm suddenly furious. Furious that I let myself get so vulnerable with him, furious that I got into this water where it's hard to angrily make a good getaway when the water seems to be fighting me. I send a silent plea to Kai, King of the fucking Seas, to let me get out of here with ease, and a wave sweeps me off my feet, cradling me and carrying me to shore. A water cone hovers protectively around my body as I get dressed.

Galen doesn't have a similarly easy time and is struggling to reach the shore while I pull on my clothes. When he finally does emerge, I suck down another gulp of the champagne and start walking back toward our table.

Galen runs to catch up to me. I feel his hand on my arm, and he spins me to face him. I throw out a hand toward him, flowers exploding from my palm. He barely dodges them—not that they would have done him any harm. He twists my arm and pins it behind my back.

"Daphne, I'm sorry." He doesn't let me go, though. If I thought the alarm bells were loud before, now they're shrieking. I need to get out of this position immediately. We're too close, chest to chest, and I'm afraid of what will happen if I have to physically fight the God of War. I've never been one to want a physical fight; I would rather cut someone with my words.

"If you're sorry, then let me go."

Galen does, instantly releasing me from his grip. "I'm sorry. That's not what I mean to do. I'm stupid. Of *course*, you're worthy of love. If you would let me, I want to love you. I would never hurt you."

I look at him as he says this. "You're not doing a great job of convincing me that it's *me* you want."

He tries to kiss me again, his mouth pressing against mine. I pull back and slap him, so annoyed at him and this bullshit he's pulling tonight. I feel like I'm on a date with Dr. Jekyll and Mr. Hyde. He flips between charming and controlling too fast for this behavior to be outside his norm. After what happened with Cassius, I'm going to believe Galen when he shows me who he is. If I wasn't already convinced that Galen wasn't getting a second date, this would have cemented it.

His hand touches his cheek, and he turns his eyes on me, fury burning in them. He grabs my upper arms tightly. He's bruising me, I can feel it, so I do the only thing I can think of to get out of his hold.

I kiss him...and fight the upchuck response.

He's surprised by the kiss but doesn't fight me. He lets me go to twist his hands in my hair and grab my hips, pulling me closer still. I feel sick all over, but I need his grip on me to loosen, so I deepen the kiss, opening my mouth to him, and his tongue slides against mine. Finally, his hold on me relaxes, and I pull back.

"Goodnight, Galen," I say, trying to keep my voice even, and then I walk away, back toward the building. I'm not sure how I know that this is where I'm supposed to go, but I do.

Inside, I come to a halt when I realize I'm not even sure where exactly I am. The Goddess of Harmony is sitting on a couch with an unfamiliar person in a black dress with a long braid. My gaze flits between them as unease skitters down my spine.

"How was your evening, Daphne?" Luminara asks, getting to her feet and approaching me. Something that looks like pity crosses the other person's face, but it's gone just as quickly as it appeared.

"It was just ducky. I'm not really sure—" Her fingers are on my temples, and my head hurts again the way it did when the date began. I clutch my forehead... and everything slides back into place. The date, the way that Galen and I are supposed to be trying to see if we can work together. Kissing him, liking kissing him the first time, the way that the cold knife felt as it slid into my chest while Galen laughed and Essos, oh—*oh.*

Essos.

Tears prick my eyes, and I stand up straight. My hair is soaking wet, dripping on the floor, I realize, and I'm embarrassed. The looks of the staff tell me they're embarrassed for me. They know that their queen is being made a fool.

"If that's all, Luminara, I'll retire to my room for the night. Thank you for your assistance." I hold my head as high as I can and walk back to my room. I'm grateful it's empty and Cat is not waiting for an update. I lock the door behind me and go swiftly to the bathroom, where I throw up the contents of dinner until I have nothing more to give.

Dave crawls into the room on his belly and licks at the salt-water on my leg, as comforting as he can be. Waffles takes a more direct approach and curls up on my lap, then promptly falls asleep as if just daring me to disturb him.

It's cool, Waffles, not like I'm kneeling in the most uncomfortable position possible. I'll just live here. I stroke his fur and, for a marvelous moment, it's exactly the distraction I need. But in the silence, my mind starts to turn again to what just happened. I can't keep playing this game, not at the expense of my well-being and, worse still, my people.

My emotions are tearing me in a thousand different directions, but I'm alert enough to hear the door to the bedroom open. I twist, wielding a vine knife and startling Waffles, who gives a pitiful yowl and digs in his claws to stay on my lap. I'm aware of what I must look like, waterlogged and feral, but when I see who opened the door, I let the tears begin anew. I should have known it was Cat, given the lack of reaction from Dave.

She crosses the room and sits beside me, then wraps her arms around me as I cry. Shadow is, well, Cat's shadow, and follows her to my side. She too tries to climb onto our laps, stepping on Waffles's tail and Dave's head so she can get her licks in. Waffles, annoyed with what should have been a peaceful cuddle, retreats to the top of the sink, where he sits and gives us all the evil eye.

"I feel so stupid," I sniffle, leaning into the comfort my friend supplies. I feel worse than that—I feel like a monster for how I've been trying to push Cat away, and how I'm now leaning on her for support to get me through tonight. It's not going to stop, this drive to isolate myself so there will be less fallout if I fail to get out of this. I know Cat; she won't let me push her away if she can help it, but I would sooner sacrifice myself than let something happen to her.

"Shhhh," she soothes, rocking me. She strokes my hair like I'm a small child. I grew from a flower, so I never really knew the love of a mother. Being born out of nothing is not an unusual occurrence among the gods. It wasn't until I lived as a mortal that I realized how many little moments I missed out on by not being cherished as a child when I was formed as a goddess.

"No, Cat. I can't. All I *do* is keep my mouth shut. I'm trying to be this docile woman, to play along with the head games, but tonight pushed me too far. Taking my memories? I *wanted* to kiss him. I wondered what it would be like to take him to bed. This man who tormented me for years, who everyone says was harm-less—they made me forget who he really was to me, what he did, and I actually considered what angry sex with him would be like."

"Everyone thought he was harmless? He's the God of War and Suffering. I don't see how."

"You met him when he first showed up at the Calling. He was charming and sweet when he wanted to be. Essos believed me that he was relentlessly pursuing me, but even he didn't take the threat as seriously as he could have. We slowly pulled ourselves away from Solarem and events to avoid him. There was a time, before Essos, where Galen and I were...we weren't anything, really. We would go dancing and grind together, but not once did he ask my name. *Never*. We danced nearly every night for almost two weeks, and then one day I was nearly creamed by a chariot, and Essos saved me from being maimed. He asked that I repay him with a date, and I said yes to the gorgeous prince who saved my life—or, well, saved me from grievous harm. Things *clicked* with Essos in a way they never did with Galen, and I didn't give the God of War another thought."

Cat seems to sense that I'm done monologuing, and it feels good to get all those thoughts out of my head. It's a world better than any session I've had with Luminara. "Did Galen ever talk to you about your nights dancing?" she asks.

I pause, searching my memories. The question gives me a chance to get up and brush my teeth. Unashamed of being naked in front of my friend, I peel myself out of the dress, willing it to be incinerated on the floor. I watch it burn away to ash, and it's like a burden lifts.

Cat gets up and grabs my pajamas from the bedroom, and I take them gratefully. Maybe I can end this night with some comfort.

"Once. He waited until I'd met the family three or four times before he cornered me about it in the bathroom. Galen asked if our dances had meant anything to me, and I told him no, and that I was with Essos now. I thought that was the end of it. And then Essos and I..."

Cat waits for me to go on, and when I appear reluctant to continue, she pushes. "You've deprived me of girl talk and gossip for too long. I've tried to keep my distance while you figure your life out, but...spill it."

I sit at my vanity and start to take off my makeup, needing something to do other than look Cat in the face as I tell her this. "Remember when I told you Essos and I broke up briefly, back when we first got together?"

She nods, waiting for me to get past the information she already knows.

"Essos cheated on me."

Cat's mouth drops open, but she's quick to close it before going *off* in the way only a best friend can. "You've got to be *fucking* with me. Seriously? And you got back together with him? You bet your ass I wouldn't have stood for that if I had been in your life then!"

"If you had been in my life then, so much would be different. But we did obviously get back together. We were so young compared to now, and I did break up with him. I swore off the whole of his family, and then Galen stumbled upon me and kissed me and asked me out. I was going to go *just* for revenge. It was petty, and it *never* happened. Helene Parent-Trapped Essos and me at their family cabin. We weren't allowed to leave until we worked things out."

"So, how did he justify his actions?" Cat's tone is cutting.

"He didn't. He owned his fuck-up. You would have to know his parents to understand what really happened. Unlike Xavier and Posey, they always presented as a united front, but they hated each other, and it was obvious. My father-in-law, Titus, loved to pit his children against each other, making the boys compete to prove who was the best of his sons. It was toxic, and I hope you never meet Titus or Octavia."

We both climb into my bed, where Dave and Waffles are waiting.

"So, he played the daddy-didn't-love-me card and got back into your good graces?" Cat says.

"Hardly. It took a *lot* of work." I pause, feeling like I'm betraying the trust of my husband, but I think, in this case, he would understand. "Essos didn't think he was good enough for me—for us—to work. He thought that eventually the other shoe would drop, so rather than wait for it, he forced it to happen. It was weird—it felt so out of character for him to be needlessly cruel like that. And then, Helene literally locked us in a cabin until we worked our shit out, and we set all-new ground rules for our relationship, about communication and what we each needed from the other. It took time before I was able to trust him fully again, and longer still for me to work out my insecurities." None of the specifics of how we did that have filtered into my memories yet, just the general feel of our relationship as we progressed from that point on. "It helped that he transferred the woman to Xavier's office so I never had to see or deal with her again." Not that I would remember her now if she walked up to me. I could try to remember who it was, but that feels like it would be picking at the scab. If I came face-to-face with her now, I would probably lash out with my powers.

"I still might slap the shit out of him for it," Cat grumbles, sliding closer to me. "Do you feel better?"

Diving into my history with her actually did help. It got my mind off the disastrous date and got me focused on what I'm fighting for. A future with Essos.

"You know Essos—he'll take it. Sometimes I think he's still trying to make it up to me."

"As he should."

There's a lull, and it's not an uncomfortable silence.

"How are *you* doing?" I eventually ask. It's like college again, as we lay in the darkened room, asking our questions, unsure if the person we share a room with has already fallen asleep.

"I'm doing just fine. Every day is an adjustment. I mean, it was one thing when we were pretty much isolated by the Calling, but to see creatures turned into water like it's nothing...it was my fault, a few weeks ago."

I sit up, alarmed. "What was?"

"Relax, nothing happened. I was restless, and I had a very realistic, very bad dream, sometime after Helene's trial. I went downstairs to walk outside. I just needed some fresh air. Galen and his merry band of goons were sitting in the living room, talking about..." She hesitates. I can imagine what they were talking about. "Anyway, there was a chick literally riding Galen as his goons were cutting off their own fingers to see whose would grow back faster. I think Galen saw me, because he looked toward where I was standing in the shadows, and I swear my heart stopped."

"He didn't do anything, did he?" I ask, my voice dropping so low, I'm surprised she can hear me.

"Oh, no. He was just staring in my direction, and I was terrified to move because, what if he *did* see me? And then I had to wait until he was finished, and he left in the opposite direction of where I was hiding, so there's that."

"Next time that happens, tell me. I'll make sure they can't grow their fingers back for a good long while."

"You can *do* that?" she asks.

"I've never had the cause to try, but why not? I control the growth of flowers—I can speed growth up or slow it down if I so choose, so, why couldn't I do the same for fingers? It would be a fun challenge." I figure, worst-case scenario, I accidentally maim them for a short time.

"Bloodthirsty. I love it."

"What was your dream about?" I ask, looking for something, anything, to keep us both talking.

Cat sits up and pulls her ponytail out to shake her hair. It feels a little bit like she's stalling as she reaches for the pillow to flip it over and fluff it before proceeding. "It was stupid, really. I dreamt I was being beheaded for having sex with my brother, but it wasn't, like, modern times. That's what I get for watching a documentary on the Tudors before bed." She doesn't sound entirely convincing, but her flippant tone tells me she's not interested in elaborating.

When Cat wants to, she can be locked up tight, refusing to divulge secrets. If she doesn't want me to know, I won't know. I just hope that eventually, she'll tell me what's bothering her.

I can't blame her for not turning to me. I've been inaccessible for too long. My fear of keeping her too close has done what I wanted all along—it's driven her away. I just hope that, when the time comes, I can bridge the divide and fix what I've broken.

11

I'm supposed to attend therapy the next day with Galen and Luminara to talk about my *feelings* and how things went during the date, but I'm so angry and upset that I refuse to go. It doesn't help that there's a photo of Galen and me on the front of the *Solarem Sun* as he unzips my dress. *Queen of Kings* is the title of the article, and it goes on to talk about how I exercise control over men with the only useful attribute women have—my body.

I don't disappear into work the way I should. I rise before Cat and put on yoga pants and a comfortable shirt. I even manage to beat Maleficent and Elsa downstairs so they can't report where I'm going. I slip out the door, only to be caught by Zara. We lock eyes, and I want to reach out to her, let her know why I'm pushing her away. I want to tell her it's to protect her in a way I can't protect Cat. I want to make sure she knows so many things, but I don't say a word.

Zara turns around and walks back down the hallway she came from, pretending she doesn't see me. As she disappears from sight, I say goodbye to another chance to tell her what's happening. Maybe the Fates are intervening and trying to tell me that I shouldn't tell Zara why I'm keeping her at arm's length. I know my friends would understand, but I'm afraid they'll say *fuck the danger* and put themselves at risk unnecessarily.

Everyone I pass seems to sense that I don't want to be seen, and they continue with their duties, not addressing me in any way. I make my way into my gardens. Anyone who wants to use their brain will know to find me here. They'll know this is where I find calmness.

No one comes looking for me, and the time of my appointment with Luminara comes and goes. I spend hours sorting through the flowers, experimenting with new colors and breeds. It feels good to get my hands dirty. When I dare, I try gardening with my powers, but otherwise I'm on my knees doing it the manual way.

The sun is high in the sky when I finally hear footsteps approach. I turn, the gardening sheers in my hand not meant to be a weapon, but if they need to be, they will.

Xavier stands in the alcove, watching me with his hands in his pockets. He's wearing his signature tan suit, his perfect hair combed back.

"You missed your appointment," he remarks casually.

"What are you? The therapy police?" I snap, turning my back to him.

"Catalina mentioned you've been missing all morning." He's trying to keep his tone light, but when it comes to her, there's always something lurking behind his words.

This time when I turn around, the sheers are raised in a threatening manner. "You need to leave her alone before your wife turns her into a crane or some other stupid animal. The least you can do with your interest in my friend is give her a protective charm."

"Worried?" He's trying to taunt me, but his voice betrays his own note of concern.

"Between your wife and my fiancé, of course, I'm concerned. The last thing I want is for something to happen to either of my friends." My whole body deflates.

"The date went that well?"

"I really..." I look away from him. "I really don't know what I'm supposed to do. Kissing Galen last night felt wrong. It didn't matter that I didn't remember my feelings toward Essos—all that mattered was that Galen wasn't him, and my body knew it. Marrying him will kill me, Xavier."

It's the naked truth, and possibly the most honest I've been with him, ever. I'm hoping to appeal to some shred of decency that might live in Xavier. There's no real reason for me to expect him to help me, but I have to try—last night convinced me of that. Hearing what Cat witnessed also caused a flurry of my own nightmares, imagining a day when Galen's goons try to see if her fingers will grow back.

I toss the sheers to the ground, utterly defeated. Anger keeps me upright most days, but today it isn't enough.

Xavier surprises me by kneeling down and wrapping his arms around my smaller frame, despite the mud and other dirt all over me. I hug him back, fighting tears from this simple show of affection. I needed a hug more than I could put into words.

"Your realm needs you. I need you to do this. Marrying Galen will at least bring some peace to the Underworld, and Solarem." His voice is thick with emotion, and I pull back to look him in the eye. "You don't see it, but in Solarem, there is discord. Those who believe that Essos is the rightful king, and those who support Galen. Your marriage will put an end to it, because the only thing everyone agrees on is that *you* are the queen."

"Of course, I don't know what's happening in Solarem! The news I receive is censored, unless it's trivial information or something meant to knock me down a peg. Galen closed the Garden of Evil, a decision that *I* should have been a part of. And yet, you let him do it without me. There are going to be repercussions. Never mind that our financial system is in ruins because our tithe requirement has changed. Who will do the work if Galen fails and I'm not there to pick up the pieces?"

The look he gives me confirms that I'm not even remotely wrong, but there's something else there. Dare I dream that he might be fond of me? Once, it would have delighted me to see that Xavier cared even a fraction for me instead of having the barest tolerance for my existence, but now, I want to shove his sympathy up his ass.

"My family is fractured, and I don't want that to be the case any longer. It's been this way since you showed up in our lives, so forgive me for wanting my family to be whole again."

Oh. Not fondness then.

I disagree with him. Sure, we were never the type to get all four siblings and their significant others together for a game night, but the blame for that isn't mine. Posey frequently had to best Helene and me, while Galen's wife, Callista, was often withdrawn and refused to engage.

"The three of you never got along—you can't put that on me. You used to make a sport of going after the same woman to see who got her first. I'm just surprised that you didn't try harder to get in my pants."

"It's not too late for that. I know Posey wants you pregnant before the wedding, and I have proven myself exceedingly fertile." His comment lacks humor, but I appreciate him trying to lighten the mood. I level him with a look anyway, putting to rest any delusions he might have.

"I would sooner fuck your wife," I deadpan.

He gives a hearty laugh and sits on a bench. "Why not make it a party?" He sighs. "You need to accept your fate. Better yet, if you can find Essos, get him to accept his. He needs to come in and abdicate. The neater this is, the easier it will be for his supporters to accept."

"And what's to stop Galen from shoving that dagger into Essos's heart? It's not going to end there. It's not enough that Galen has taken his crown and his wife. Killing Essos is the only thing that will please the God of War and Suffering."

"You have to trust I won't let that happen." Xavier is emphatic, clasping his hands together and pressing them between his knees.

"The way I trusted you the first time?"

Surprise flashes on Xavier's face. "I miscalculated then."

We haven't spoken about this. About how I went to Xavier after Essos didn't take Galen seriously. Even Helene was dismissive, because none of us believed a goddess could die. Yet here we are, over a thousand years since my death.

"What's to say now isn't a miscalculation? Essos didn't think Galen would hurt me now that I was in his grasp, and yet, I bore the bruises of his hands around my throat."

"You're the one who instigated that."

I get into Xavier's face, "*Breathing* is an instigator with him. He wants me to be his doll that he can dress up and fuck or beat when he wants."

I would swear that Xavier flinches. "Yes well, it's all in the name. God of War and all that." Xavier rubs his jaw, not making eye contact. "You don't have to do anything you don't want to."

"You're not funny. You know I won't have a choice." My stomach turns, and I want to be sick again.

Xavier gets to his feet, no longer content to be below me. "I like to think I'm funny. But Daphne, if you're looking for someone to blame, look no further. *You* did this. You couldn't stick to the man whose heart you were competing for. You were the one who was told to have patience, but you were more interested in boning

Galen than sitting tight." Xavier walks toward me, and I back up until I'm pressed against a hedge.

"Don't act like you're blameless in this. You were there while he was manipulating me. You watched him play his games and you did nothing. *Nothing*. So don't act like I'm the only one who fucked up." I'm shouting now.

"Nice and angry?" There is a glint in Xavier's eyes.

"No, I'm furious!" I shove him back from crowding me. His body gives under me, and he steps back.

"Good. That's better than the weepy mess you've been lately. You don't want to marry Galen? Then fight back. You want your husband back? *Fight*. I thought that you had a backbone. I thought that you were worthy of the effort that both of them are putting into you, but if you're going to mope around, maybe I was wrong about you."

"What would you have me do, Xav? As you so kindly pointed out, I hold my crown at your mercy. I *have* to play by your rules, which are designed to work against me. You want to help me, design a trial that he will lose. *That's* how you can help me."

"Says the woman who went around the rules to land us in this current predicament. You know I can't do that. I don't know why you asked."

Xavier's right. I do need to hold on to my anger. I can't let last night get to me, even though thinking about it makes my skin crawl. I considered sleeping with him right there. I let him kiss me and touch me. My hand rises to the unmarked skin on my chest. I don't bear the mark of the dagger on this body, but there is still a phantom pain there to remind me what I went through.

"I'm sure you have your own kingly things to do. Perhaps you should get on with it." I twist my wrist, and a grass carpet unfurls to lead him out.

Xavier takes his cue, leaving me to my gardening.

113

WHEN I WALK into the house, Galen grabs my arm, stopping me dead in my tracks. I try not to freeze, still not ready to face him. Galen's fingers dig into my skin, and I take a deep breath in through my nose, not trusting myself to not vomit if I breathe through my mouth. I turn my head toward him, just a little, enough to look at him from the corner of my eye.

"You missed therapy this morning." Galen keeps his voice soft, like the caress of a lover, but I hear the edge hidden beneath the softness.

"I wasn't feeling well." Galen lets me go but doesn't move away from me.

"I was worried. You stormed off last night. We didn't get to finish our conversation." He raises the hand that was just holding my arm to caress my cheek. My eyes flick up to his, and there's no anger on his face.

I bury a shudder. "It was just...overwhelming." It's not a lie.

"I think we got off course during our talk." His mouth leans closer to mine, and I try to relax my body so I'm not flinching away from him. Galen's lips brush mine, just barely. I kiss him back, leaning into this other self I've created that can tolerate his touches.

I pull back, trying to get a read on him. "We did, I suppose. We did more kissing than talking, though."

A smile tugs at his lips, and that bright personality that made me fall for his bullshit during the Calling shines through. "I'm sorry if it was too much. I told Luminara that I thought we made some progress. It was good for me to have one-on-one time with her. Been out in your garden?" He brushes dirt from my forehead.

He smiles as if we didn't scream at each other last night. As if I didn't figure out that it was the thrill of the chase, him wanting something he couldn't have. It was never about me; it was about undermining his brother.

"Yeah, it helps clear my head."

"I can come up with a better way to help clear your head that's just as dirty."

The suggestion behind his words turns my stomach. "I'm wondering if we should keep some surprises for when we're married."

His hand slides down my side, following my curves to my bottom. He squeezes my ass and pulls me against his body. "I'm willing to wait, even if Posey doesn't think we should."

My emotions war within me. On the one hand, he's touching me, and I hate that, but on the other hand, he's conceded a major concern. *Willing to wait* means that I have one less thing to worry about. I just have to hope he doesn't change his mind.

I reward him with a kiss. Maybe if I give him an inch, he won't take a mile. It's a chaste kiss, and he takes it for exactly what it is without going any further.

An annoying little throat clears behind us, forcing us apart. I'm thankful for it, but only for a second.

Posey smiles at us, looking delighted to see us embracing. Her blonde hair is styled in a low ponytail, and she wears minimal makeup and a simple pink sundress. It's the most dressed down I've seen her in days, or possibly ever.

"Glad to see the young lovers are making their way to reconciliation. It makes me so sad when you fight."

I want to tell her exactly where she can stick her sadness. "Is there something I can help you with?" My voice is weary. I got my morning of solitude, but apparently letting Xavier find me meant that it was open season to harass me. This family, sometimes, I *swear.*

"Yes. You have now skipped not one, not two, but *five* wedding planning meetings, and I want to make sure that the blushing bride is happy on her happiest day. You sent that girl Zara in your place, and she doesn't seem to know how to handle the responsibility, or you're not very clear in your instructions to her."

I have to keep my eyebrows from lifting in surprise. I never gave Zara any task related to the wedding, but I really shouldn't be surprised that she found her own way to help.

"You are *so* right, Posey. I kept changing my mind and, really, I needed some time to adjust and for Galen and me to get on the same level." I wrap my arms around Galen, and he doesn't hide his surprise. He looks at me before folding his arm around my shoulders. I focus on breathing through my nose, and how satisfying it would feel to rip his arm off.

"Well, perhaps you can join me now. I've been tinkering away with ideas, and, of course, I need your approval."

I can't decide which is the worse fate—fucking Galen or being stuck in a meeting with Posey. Perhaps Posey missed her calling to be warden of the Deep. She's already mastered torture.

"You know what, Posey? This wedding is more about the marriage for me, not the celebration. I'm sure whatever you decide will be fine. But perhaps if you're having trouble with Zara's communication skills, you should try to be clearer with your requests."

Posey's mask falters, and I see the anger simmering beneath. Her hand shoots out, and she grabs my arm, digging her perfectly-manicured nails into my skin. I don't break eye contact with her, even as I feel my blood start to coat her nails. It hurts like a bitch, but I won't show her that. Galen is frozen beside us—does he take the side of his betrothed or that of his biggest champion? Glad to know where I stand—not that I expected any better.

"You will come to a wedding planning meeting—that is an order from your queen." Her voice doesn't betray her anger. It's the same annoying tone she's always had. It takes a stupid amount of effort not to mimic her words back at her like a bratty little sister.

"You forget." I yank my arm back, not caring that she drags her nails down my skin as I do so, leaving deep gashes. "This is my domain, *my* realm, and I am the highest queen here. I bow to no one in my own home."

Below our feet, the ground trembles, and while I would love to pretend that it's from my bleeding, I worry it's a larger ripple caused by the closing of the Garden of Evil. Since I can't do anything about it right now, I focus on the issue at hand.

I can hear the droplets of my blood hitting the tile floor. I break eye contact first to look at the mess she's made of my arm, and *ouch*. It would have looked better if I had gone toe to toe with a shark. My God of War fiancé? He's useless beside me, still not wanting to take a side in the battle of queens. Coward.

"Oh!" Galen exclaims, finally jumping into action and wrapping his hands tightly around my wound. He's an expert at treating battle wounds and helping to staunch blood flow. Blood is where he thrives.

Someday, I'll deliver a blow he won't recover from.

"I will meet with you in one hour. I need to shower and attend to this. If you will excuse me." I back away from Posey with Galen still holding my arm. Gently, I extract it from his grip.

With my bloody hand, I grip his chin, making him look me in the eye. "If you want to be my consort, you can start by growing a pair of balls in front of people who deign to hurt me." I release him to cast a glare at Posey before walking back to my room, leaving a trail of blood in my wake.

12

T he house trembles again, making me grip my dresser. Dave whines from his spot on my bed. Even Waffles lifts his head to look at me.

"Find Sybil," I order Dave, who winks out of the room as I try hard to unclench my jaw. He's lucky I didn't scold him for being so lax. He should be out there patrolling the realm and not sleeping in my room with the cat. If something's going on, he should alert me, not the other way around.

I shouldn't take my frustrations out on the animals, but damn it, I need *something* to be going my way. Xavier wanted me angry? I'm *angry*.

When I lift my head, my heart stops at the sight of something on my vanity. Hanging over my mirror is the necklace that Essos was wearing during the Calling. It's one he says I gifted him, but that's not the whole truth of it. It was one of the first things he gave me when we were trying to decide what the emblem of the Underworld was going to be. He wanted me to be represented as much as possible in the design, and I didn't fight him on it, because I loved that this was an *us* thing.

At times, adjusting to ruling and establishing the Afterlife was difficult. On those days when he questioned if we were doing anything right, I would give him my necklace to bring a little light to his days. We were practically trading it back and forth as a sort of good luck token. The last time I saw it around his neck was when the Calling started. I press my lips to it now as if I could send him a kiss before slipping it on.

I shower, careful with my arm. I might have let it bleed a little more than necessary for show, but that doesn't mean I'm not in pain. When I emerge from the shower, I'm surprised to see Zara and not Cat in my room, waiting with a tray of gauze.

"I wasn't sure what eternal beings needed when they were injured." Her voice is raw, like she hasn't spoken in days. Now is my moment to tell her the truth, to open up and explain why I'm treating her the way I am. But I can't bring myself to say the words.

"We bleed just like the rest of you." I rub the corner of my eye, pinching my nose. "Thank you for not saying anything this morning."

"Well, that's not totally true. Xavier cornered me," I look sharply at Zara. My brother-in-law isn't the type to force himself on a woman, but I don't know who he's become in the time since I've been gone. "He just wanted to know if I had seen you this morning or if you had fled to be with Essos. I told him that you were still on the grounds, but that was all. I didn't think you were going to run away, so the grounds sounded like a good answer."

I sit at the vanity and hold my arm out to her so she can dress the wounds. It shouldn't take long for them to heal, but I like the idea of making Posey think twice about hurting me. She's made it clear that, for Galen to take the throne, we *have* to get married, so at least I know that I won't be killed again.

It's that risk to Cat and Zara that keeps me playing the good girl.

"Tell me if anyone is harassing you. You are a member of my retinue and should be treated with respect."

Zara doesn't respond. She only nods. Zara has always held herself tall, but I'm noticing how tired she looks, like her usual shine is gone. I hate myself a little for being part of the problem, if not the entirety of it.

"Can you heal yourself?"

"I could, but I also want my injuries to serve as reminders that I won't be cowed into doing something I don't want. If someone wants to hurt me, then they will need to look at that reminder."

Zara swallows audibly, and I chuckle.

"Can you send me home?"

Her question makes me pause. "Home?"

"I want to go home, to my parents, to my family. Tiffany went home." Zara's big, dark eyes well with tears, and I push strands of her hair out of her face. Her voice breaks on the name of her best friend, and my heart breaks for her.

"I can't," I whisper, sorry for all the pain I have caused. "It's not as simple as Es made it look. He has powers and abilities I don't. Coupled with Steve, a mortal, showing up here, in the Afterlife? The Fates had other plans for them. We are in no position to question them." I stand, tugging the towel tighter around me, even though she's not done wrapping my arm.

"Then send me to the Afterlife." Her voice is a whisper.

I release my hold on my powers, moss and trees and life growing on the walls around us so I'm certain it is just us. I'm more exhausted than I let on from using my powers today in the garden, even though that stupid carpet for Xavier and changing the colors of flowers were such small things. That's the real reason I'm not healing myself. Each use of my powers costs me, so I'm trying to conserve them as much as I can, but this conversation is worth the use.

"Is this because of me? Because I'm sorry if I've been too hard

on you. I'm sorry if I've made you feel unwanted or unnecessary."
I have to tell her. I have to tell her to protect her heart. "I'm not
mad." My voice comes out as a whisper too.

"I just, I don't think I serve a purpose."

"You do," I gush, sitting down beside her on the edge of my
bed. "I'm afraid for you. I'm afraid of Galen learning my true
heart, that he will use you and Cat to punish me. If I keep you at
arm's length, then he won't hurt you. If he thinks you're here
because *I'm* punishing you, he won't hurt you. If you truly want
this, if you want to go into your afterlife, I won't stop you. But I
don't want you to go because you think that you're not useful to
me. I don't want you to do it because you think you don't matter. I
know we didn't get along before. We were frenemies at best. But I
like to think that you're more friend than enemy these days."

Zara laughs through the tears that have started to fall. "You're
just saying that because you got the guy in the end."

I laugh with her at that, but it's a sad laugh—the guy I got
isn't the right one. "I know I've been a bitch," I continue. "I know
that I've been ruthless lately, but Cat gives me the reports you've
been giving her. I know you've been keeping an eye on Posey,
cozying up to her under the guise of planning the wedding. I
know it all." I smooth her dark hair over her shoulder. "Think
about it. If going to your afterlife is what you truly desire, then of
course, I won't hold you back. But don't do it out of some
misguided attempt to, I don't know, hide from me. This is, after
all, my realm.

"If I'm honest with you, Zara, I would rather you wait. Right
now, Galen has more control over the Afterlife than I'm comfortable with."

She opens her mouth, but Sybil appears in my room, looking
frazzled. Their hair is unbound, and their dress is torn in spots.

"What is *happening?*" I demand, rising to my feet and crossing
to where Sybil is braced against my dresser. Dave barks behind

them, getting more and more insistent. When they lift their hand to push the hair from their face, I notice a smear of blood on the surface of my dresser. It makes my stomach drop.

"Uprising," they gasp out between deep breaths. "In the Deep."

I tap into my well of magic, hoping that I'm not making a catastrophic mistake. I drop my towel and clothe myself in a blood-red dress that hugs the curves of my body, the straps crossing in over my chest and closing at the nape of my neck. Heavy garnet earrings appear to match the red and gold crown on my head.

I look at Dave. "I need Finn, *quickly*." Dave doesn't need any prodding and disappears. He's able to move at will throughout the Underworld and Solarem, but he can't transport others and I don't trust myself to get me there.

Dave and Finn appear seconds behind each other. I don't waste time explaining, I just grab Finn's arm. I look at Dave, who has been so good that I'm going to need to up the treats and belly rubs tonight. "Get Shadow and Spot and meet me in the Deep."

"The Deep?" Finn asks warily.

I don't blame him; I seldom go there myself. It's not exactly a highlight on the tour.

"Yes, Finn. We need to go now."

He must hear something in my voice, because he takes my arm and threads it into his before transporting me to our version of Hell.

13

ave, Spot, and Shadow are standing shoulder to shoulder, looking at the fighting. My stomach turns with nausea from the transportation. I never liked it before I died, and I like it even less now.

Before my eyes, my dogs gradually grow in size, pressing their bodies together until they tower over the chasm where the Deep is located. The name of this particular part of our world came not only from the idea of putting the souls in the deepest, darkest depths but from the actual location of it, a deep valley between two different parts of the Garden of Evil.

I can hear the sounds of battle below, but I don't take my eyes off Dave, Shadow, and Spot until they're done with their transformation into one dog. Shadow lifts her head and howls at the sky while Dave growls and Spot lowers his head, constantly on a swivel.

It's eerie seeing the Garden of Evil as empty as it is now. Even when we first set the boundary lines, there were still souls on this level but now, I can't sense anything but Finn and the dogs.

Until that changes, and my heart starts to slam in my chest. I can't see him, but I know he's here. Essos is close. I can't let myself get distracted, so I raise my head and approach the edge of the cliff. It's a visual illusion. To the souls, I appear close, like they could reach out and grab the hem of my dress. In actuality, I'm not close to them at all. They will never be able to scale the cliff to reach me. It's why I feel comfortable standing here now.

"Enough!" My voice carries over the crowd, and there is a slow stop as the souls turn and see me. Only it's not just souls—I can see the people and the beings who act as security trying to keep things calm. Some of them lie unmoving on the ground, and that hurts my heart.

"'O the *fuck*'re you?" one bold soul calls. Josiah James, died in 1842 after a tree fell on him. He earned a one-way ticket to the Garden of Evil after stealing from his wife's family to fund his gambling addiction.

"Your reckoning," I snarl. I don't know if I'll be able to do this, but I'll fucking try.

I pray to the Fates to give me the power I need as I dig my hands down toward the ground like I'm delving them toward the soil and then I raise them slowly, putting every ounce of my will forward.

A gentle hand presses to my bare back, and I don't know if Essos is giving me the energy I need or if just having him close is enough, but it works.

The souls slowly start to grow roots and harden into macabre trees. As they realize what's happening, some try to run, but as my reach expands, they start to realize there is no hope.

"Mercy! Please!" one calls as they run toward me, and it's enough to make me pause. I need time to gather my strength again anyway.

Essos never removes his hand from my back. His touch is both soothing and heartbreaking as I remember how he hurt me.

I *have* to keep my attention here and away from the conversation I want—no, *need*—to have with Essos.

Curt Remhalt murdered his college professor after being confronted with evidence of cheating. It takes a lot of pent-up rage to stab someone thirteen times. I would know. He died in 1967, in his forties, after falling asleep on the train tracks after a bender.

"Why should I exercise mercy when you have slaughtered those meant to guard you?"

"Your Majesty!" This speaker is a man who is covered in grime, so undistinguishable I'm reminded of a history class I took as a mortal about workers in the coal mines. But I don't need to see his face to know this man. Edmund Montgomery, killed in a duel in 1781 after being caught having sex with his best friend's daughter. This alone shouldn't have been enough to send him to the Garden of Evil, but her age—only fifteen when they started their affair—sealed the deal. Not an unexpected age to be wed at the time, but she wasn't the only girl half his age that he'd been carrying on with, just the one he was caught with. "Please, we need *help*." His tone is pleading, and I wait.

"I'm listening."

"You eliminated the Garden of Evil so that our workload could be reduced, but instead, we're working harder. I don't know if it's possible to work a soul to death, but it feels like you're trying."

It's not possible, and I don't like the feeling of not knowing what he's talking about. When dreaming up plans for the Underworld, Essos and I discussed the viability of putting souls to work in the gem-mining department. The souls would create precious gems for the mortal realm by mining our world for gems to be found by humans. It seemed inhumane to force souls into what would effectively be slave labor, so Essos and I found a way around it by working with other gods and creatures to develop a new way of creating gems that didn't involve the blood and sweat of souls.

I unfreeze some of the faces immediately before me. "Verify."

"Yes, ma'am," Josiah James confirms. "We 'aven't been given a rest. And I know we're souls, so we don't need it, but if I could go back to my torture, I would rather do that."

I steeple my fingers, pointing downward, as I think about what to do. If I only had more time. It would give me a chance to consider how to deal with the closing of the Garden of Evil and working the souls of the Afterlife.

There is really only one thing for me to do now.

"As punishment for your crimes today, you will be sentenced to live as trees for the foreseeable future. When I feel satisfied, I will lift the enchantment." There is visible relief on the faces of those still standing.

Essos's palm presses flat on my back as it slides up to the nape of my neck. The soothing warmth from being skin to skin with my husband relaxes the tenseness in my muscles, and I want to fall back into his arms.

Before I continue, I turn to Finn. "I will need your assistance with those killed today."

"Of course," he agrees solemnly.

I don't know if he knows that Essos is here, but I'm not going to question him further.

I blow out a slow breath as I ready myself. All day my powers have been working as I need them to; I can only hope they stay consistent. Closing my eyes, I search for the source of my powers inside myself, and I let it unravel, finishing what I started. I go a step further, changing the frozen forms into magnolia trees in full bloom instead of the horrifying people-trees of before.

I start to sway and grow lightheaded before my knees give out.

The last thing I hear is, "I've got her." I'm swept into strong arms and crushed to a familiar chest, the scent of vanilla and cinnamon and sandalwood wrapping me in a safe cocoon.

"I THOUGHT WE DISCUSSED THIS," Cat's voice says on a crack.

I'm just coming to, finding the ashen face of my best friend hovering over me. I force a weak laugh. "It's been a hot minute. I didn't want you to forget about me." Even saying that is too much, and I feel sleep drag me under.

"LET HER SLEEP, *PLEASE*," Cat's voice pleads.

"She needs to explain what happened in the Deep. You've seen the papers today. People are demanding answers, and she needs to provide them." It's Xavier.

My eyelids lift, barely, and I see Cat squeezing his hand between hers.

"And she will, but clearly, she exhausted herself."

"Turning millions of souls into trees. The scent of magnolias is reaching Solarem. People—*my* people—died. I need answers, Catalina. Don't overplay my fondness for you."

She scoffs. "Fondness? I'm one of a handful of people on Daphne's side! You can take your 'fondness' and go scratch. I'm asking you to give her a few more hours. I'll do anything. Please, Xavier. This is the most peaceful she's looked since the Calling."

"Anything?" he asks, his curiosity clearly piqued.

"Water?" I ask, rasping my voice more than necessary so they won't know I was eavesdropping.

"Daphne!" Cat exclaims, and as I open my eyes fully, I see her rush toward me.

Xavier raises an eyebrow, probably seeing right through me.

"How long has it been?" I push myself into a sitting position.

"Eighteen hours. I've heard nothing but crying from Posey about how you skipped another wedding planning session. Galen is furious that you've depleted his workforce, and the citizens of Solarem want to know why ten of their people are dead." Xavier tosses a newspaper onto my lap. This time, I'm the Queen of Vengeance.

"Can't this *wait?*" Cat hisses, looking over her shoulder at Xavier. He moves like he wants to touch her but changes his mind. Noticeably absent are my dogs, no doubt patrolling the Underworld for more unrest.

"No, it can't."

I sigh. "Did you know, Xavier?"

"Know what?" He puts his hands in his pockets.

"That he was using my souls for slave labor? Essos and I specifically did not use souls from the Deep because of this risk. Because it is *wrong.*"

"Don't get preachy on me. Ten dead. Tell me why." He grits out the last words like a demand.

"Ask your brother. For someone who wants to be King of the Underworld, he was noticeably absent when I was dealing with the problem."

"You could have sent for Galen. You sent for Finn instead. Galen issued a complaint to the Council and mentioned that there should be sanctions for your lack of consideration for his role as temporary ruler of the Underworld."

I think there might be actual steam coming out of my ears. I throw back the blankets to get out of bed, and that's when I realize that someone changed me into sleepwear. It's not the usual matching sleep shirt and shorts I would wear to bed during the Calling. No, it's an old shirt, one that was Essos's when he played sports in college, that I stole. It has the Solarem University Starball team logo on it, and I know his name is on the back. For bottoms, I'm wearing an old pair of sweatpants featuring dogs dancing in stars. It takes some of the burn out of my anger. Only one person would have chosen these clothes for me, and I soften as I think about him taking the time with me while I was unconscious and then not being able to stay and see for himself how I fared after reducing every soul in the Deep to a tree.

"Sanctions?" Cat asks.

"They can be anything from a slap on the wrist to a heavy fine or punishment," I explain, and leave the two of them so I can pee in peace.

"He just wants you reprimanded in the papers," Xavier calls through the closed door.

I wash my hands and start to brush my teeth, coming out to lean against the door jam. "Just a scolding for all of Solarem to see? You make it sound *so* easy."

"He also offered up the option to condense the Trials to occur once a week till they're completed, so he can make the Underworld more secure. Which would you prefer?" Xavier raises both of his stupid eyebrows.

I give him a rude gesture as I slip back into my bathroom to spit and rinse.

"Have you already contacted Celestina what's-her-name at the *Solarem Sun*?" I ask, taking the same position I was just in with my arms crossed.

He lets out a heavy sigh, "You should know your reprimand is going to run in tomorrow's paper, but it will probably be a below-the-fold article. It would seem that a slightly more significant god's mistress came forward and offered a tell-all, but only if it ran as headline news tomorrow."

My mouth drops open, and Cat's does the same. "Mistress?" she asks, voice weak.

His jaw tightens, and he can't meet her eye. "Lux decided she wants to speak about how she's the only woman able to give me what Posey can't."

Cat clears her throat and looks away from Xavier to me.

"Dion's mother," I confirm. Fear and anger co-mingle with oddly surprising gratitude. Lux is famously private; it was a surprise when she took up with Xavier to have Dion. After his birth, she and Dion effectively retreated from the public eye, but Xavier was always a part of Dion's life. There have been rumors about Xavier fathering other children, but Dion is the only one he's claimed publicly. If that's because of some agreement with Posey, no one can say for certain.

"How did you talk her into that?" I ask uncrossing my arms and stepping back into the room.

"I didn't. Finn and Dion did." But Xavier still won't meet my eye. "It doesn't change that you still have to explain what happened. Finn told me all he could, but I don't know if it's enough."

"Enough for what?" I ask, sitting on the edge of my bed.

"Enough for the families who lost someone. Enough for the citizens who have had their faith in you shaken. You want to walk around and demand to be treated like you're still the queen, then you need to act like it. That means taking the bad with the good."

"But not Galen?"

Xavier remains silent.

No, of course not. One of the royal children would never be expected to actually take *responsibility* for their actions. "Fine, whatever you want," I tell him, not for any reason other than my guilt over the lives lost. I should have done more, anticipated something like this happening after the shit Galen pulled.

"Will you tell me...?" Xavier waits.

"No. Finn told you all of it, and I don't want to relive it. Galen is working souls to death. They actually asked me for torture instead. So, please, let me give my condolences to the families." I look at Cat. "Can you get me the files on these employees?"

"No, they were Galen's hires, men from Solarem who support chaos and war. They weren't from the Underworld," Xavier tells me.

Cat sits beside me and takes my hand. "What does that mean?" she asks.

"That it makes sense now why they were killed. Underworld employees are trained to leave immediately if the souls get hostile in the Deep or the Garden of Evil. The souls can rip someone to pieces. It sounds like that's what they did."

"How do you usually handle it, then?" Cat asks, but Xavier beats me to the answer as he chuckles, resting against my dresser where Sybil's blood was smeared yesterday.

"She sends in her dogs."

"Dogs? Like Dave, Shadow, and Spot?"

"The very same," Xavier confirms. "I once saw them devour a soul that put hands on Daphne."

It takes a second for the memory to click. It was shortly after Essos and I established the boundaries. We were walking through the Garden of Evil, showing off what we'd done to his parents and siblings. Alaric Rogers, a serial groper who died in 1616, grabbed my ass and his cock as we walked by him. Essos had Dave, Shadow, and Spot each on a leash. They wasted no time merging into one and fighting over who got to eat Alaric.

"Can souls die?" Cat asks, appalled.

This only makes Xavier laugh harder. "Nope, but they get

digested the same way they eat regular food. I think Essos dropped that soul into the Deep after that."

"It's possible for a soul to die, to be un-made, but only Essos can do that. The souls of those who died are probably stuck somewhere in the Inbetween, like all the others," I confirm, still lost in thought. I look back at my brother-in-law. "So, what do you want from me?"

"Go to a godsdamned wedding planning meeting with Posey so I can hear the end of it, please?"

I smirk, "Did you just say the *P*-word?"

"And it will be the last time I ever say it. I'll send Zara to you with information about the next meeting. She's been keeping Miranda and Ellie busy with tasks on your behalf, such as bathing your beasts when they're one dog."

Xavier's gaze lingers on Cat a second too long before he leaves us alone.

"Is Sybil all right?" I ask.

"They're good. I believe Luminara has been taking care of them. How are *you*?"

"I'm fine, just tapped out. I did too much, too fast. I'm lucky I didn't turn *myself* into a tree." It's a weak attempt at a joke, but I have to make it; I need to keep the mood up.

"Can you do that?"

"I can't say I've tried. How are you? You look exhausted." And she does. Her hair looks limp, and she has dark circles under her eyes.

"I stayed up to watch over you. I didn't want you to wake up alone and be confused." She eyes me. "By the way, you're a badass. I've seen the photos of the trees you turned the souls into."

"I didn't know what else to do, but I figure it buys me time. You sure you're good?" I feel silly asking twice, but I hope Cat will tell me whatever it is that's bugging her.

"Really, it's just lack of sleep."

I grab her hands and force her to look at me. When she meets my gaze, it's quick before she looks away over my shoulder. "You'll tell me if there is really something bothering you?"

"Not likely. You have enough on your plate. But I'm fine, so everything is fine."

There's a knock on the door, and Zara pokes her head in. "You look like death," she says.

"Well, as Queen of the Dead, I should represent, no?" I'm glad she feels comfortable enough to joke.

"Xavier sent me to let you know that Posey will meet you in the drawing room in thirty minutes."

I clench my hands. It's clear, at least to me, that I cannot weather this storm alone. Trying to keep myself completely isolated isn't doing me any good. I'm too damn tired. Attempting to keep these women who have done nothing but support me and be there for me away is too draining.

"I have a drawing room? Don't answer that. She's probably talking about the ballroom." I pause, then barrel on. "I can't do this anymore. I can't be alone. I'm sorry I've been a colossal bitch. I made the executive decision that I should keep you both at arm's length so you won't be a target, but I can't do it. Not if you're going to be asking to go to your Afterlife because you think I don't care. I do. I care too much, and what happened yesterday, even as a queen, was really fucking scary. I shouldn't be this exhausted after using my powers, but I am, and I need to keep you both close to keep you safe."

"You do know you're transparent as a window, right?" Cat teases.

"What?" I demand.

"Duh, *I* knew that's what you were doing. It's your M.O., same as you copped to having the booze in our room freshman year when our R.A. tried to bust us for it. You have always and will always throw yourself on the sword for other people. And blah, blah, blah, it's nice, but I knew what you were doing," Cat shrugs before going into the closet to grab me a dress.

"I, for the record, did *not* think that. I *did* think you were being a bitch on a power trip." Zara holds her hands up as if to say, *What are you going to do about it?*

I drag Cat over and hug both of them. "I need you both so much."

"Duh. Your fashion sense is tragic," Zara mutters, giving in to the hug.

"It's not too late for me to turn you into a succulent," I remind her.

"Yeah, right. You made a few souls into trees, and you were on your ass for a day and a half. I'd like to see you try."

We separate from the hug, and I wiggle my fingers at her. "Let's get this done. The last thing I want is to hear Posey go off on me for another reason." I feel lighter, almost like I'm fresh from a killer yoga class. I'm standing a little taller. The weight that I've been carrying alone has lifted. I may not have unloaded my burdens on them, but just knowing that they're aware that I still count on them is enough.

For wedding planning, I put on a white dress, trying to make it seem like I am sold on this whole thing. Cat and Zara follow me downstairs.

Posey is waiting for me in the ballroom, which has been reverted to its normal use as a living room space. Three lush couches surround a low coffee table—at least, I think it's a coffee table, because it's covered in flowers and card stock and linens. Beside the piano in the corner is a dress rack with five garment bags that are bursting at the seams. I can't imagine what sort of frock Posey wants to put me in.

"Ah, you're only thirty minutes late." Posey is seated on the edge of a couch. She doesn't have her own ladies-in-waiting behind her, she has mine, but I suppose as her spies, they're both. Though, the jury is out on if Miranda is a good spy or not. I suspect she was the flash of blonde hair I saw when I first started training with Kai, but we haven't been in a room alone since then for me to confront her about it. There is a spark in her eyes when she looks at me that I can't decipher.

"Well, you can't rush beauty." I give her a wan smile and flip my hair over my shoulder before sitting on the couch. Cat and Zara step back like they're not even there.

"You need to help decide the guest list and what colors you want for your wedding. I figure we can start small, and then you can decide on a dress."

Ellie disappears to get refreshments. I ponder this, sifting through what is on the table before me. Essos and I didn't have an extravagant wedding; we didn't want to. Planning was done by my mother-in-law, who had big dreams about what she wanted her sons' weddings to look like. Essos and I sat in those planning sessions eye-fucking each other across the table while his mother had us try different treats that would be offered for cocktail hour and dessert. Our marriage was more important than the stupid wedding. I never cared what color the tablecloths were, or if Helene was wearing pink or blue or was naked for the ceremony. What mattered was me and Essos at the end of the aisle.

I banish Essos from my mind. I won't have memories of our wedding tarnished by this charade.

"I want black and red. We're going to rule the Afterlife, and he is the God of War," I announce, dropping a handful of embossed invitations on the table before leaning back and crossing my legs at the knee. Posey looks at my position, and I can practically see the thought on her face that it's not the *most* ladylike position I could take. She, of course, is seated with her ankles crossed.

"Yes, but you are the Goddess of *Spring*," Posey protests, repositioning herself so she can *show* me how to sit with my ankles crossed. I ignore her.

Ellie places a tray in front of me, and I take my cup of tea and sip it. "Which means I care more about the flower choices than the colors. Red roses will match nicely with black roses."

"Black roses don't exist." Posey sniffs at me.

I lean forward and rest my arm on my crossed legs to look her in the eye. "They exist if I say they exist," I say, my tone cold. Who is she to question the Goddess of Spring? The flowers before us turn from the beautiful blush and pastel colors to black. My vision swims for a second, but I don't blink first. *Too much, all too much.*

Posey huffs at me, conceding. "Black and red it is."

The color scheme of everything in the room changes to match what I said I want, and it's tit for fucking tat with Posey for the rest of the afternoon. I want a standard cardstock for the invitations, she wants a thick one. I want to host the wedding in Solarem, she thinks I should host it here. I want a mac and cheese bar; she thinks a mashed potato bar is more sensible. I don't understand why I need to be here if she's just going to plan the whole fucking thing anyway.

I start to seriously question where the dagger that killed me is so I can shove it in her heart. But that would be too easy. Maybe I should chain her in a coffin and drop her into the depths of the ocean. Kai would cover for me.

I'm so focused on all the ways I want to kill Posey that I miss her question.

"I'm sorry, what decision do you want me to make now just so you can ignore my opinion and pick what you want?"

Posey frowns at me. "It's time to pick your dress, silly."

She gestures at Miranda to bring the dresses over, and I hold up a hand to stop her. "I'm done here, Miffy. No need to bring the dresses. You're all dismissed." Miranda doesn't even flinch at being called the wrong name. While Ellie hesitates, Miranda just backs out of the room.

Posey rises when I do, her chin lifted. "You don't need to be rude."

"Posey, I told you that I don't care about what you want for the wedding. You insisted, nay, you *demanded* my input. Here it is. Perhaps if you didn't actually want it, you should have listened to me in the first place."

Hoping she didn't see the sweat beading on my brow, I stride from the room, Cat and Zara close behind.

14

I manage to put off therapy an extra week under the guise of needing to do some introspection of my actions after turning a million souls into trees. In reality, I'm so drained by having used so much power that even going to the bathroom is exhausting. I used my last burst of energy to go toe to toe with Posey. Despite my exhaustion, I'm not sleeping well. I reach for the other side of the bed, knowing it's empty, and tell myself that Essos made it through over a thousand years without me by his side—I can make it through these next few months with my head held high, even though all I want is to see him. To know where he is.

Missing him makes it harder to get out of bed in the morning. Harder to fall asleep. It all serves only to make me weaker.

My exhaustion means my training with Kai has also been delayed, and Helene won't talk to me because she thinks I'm blowing her off. I can't please anyone, so I choose to please no one but myself—and Sybil, but only because they keep sneaking me reports on the Underworld. Galen, it would seem, is trying to siphon souls into the Deep even if their tithe isn't high enough, because he wants them working in his mines.

The numbers make my head swim as I try to reconcile the number of souls arriving with the number of souls going to their afterlives. Something isn't adding up, but I don't know where the problem lies.

Luminara waits for my response as I cross my legs on the couch. I'm sitting more in the middle now, closer to Galen. He's trying not to crowd me, like he can prove that, by listening to me once, he's changed. But he has one arm thrown casually over the back of the sofa, his thumb occasionally stroking my shoulder, yet again pushing my boundaries.

Luminara's question—why did I skip therapy last week—is one I prepared for. "I was overwhelmed. Confused. The date was..." I turn my head toward Galen, just slightly "...a lot. It was all a lot. I needed time to order my thoughts. I'm still working through my hurt feelings that Galen would demand I be reprimanded for doing what I thought was necessary in the Deep."

It's been a week since the date, a week since I skipped therapy. A week rebuilding my strength after demolishing it in the Deep. Galen has been as sweet as he can be, pulling me into alcoves around the house, whispering apologies to me, along with giving me unwanted kisses. They're the same alcoves my husband and I used to make love in, as if the staff didn't know exactly what we were doing as they walked by, going about their business.

It's also been a week of being unable to keep my dinner down. The gauntness of my face is a constant reminder that I'm not handling this situation with grace. I don't have enough energy to fight Posey on the wedding, isolate myself from Cat and Zara, avoid Ellie and Miranda, train with Kai and Helene, figure out what's happening in the Underworld, attend therapy, and dodge Galen at *every* turn. Something has to give, and my body decided to be the thing that does.

"I wanted to ensure that the citizens of Solarem know there will be accountability when I become king."

My lips purse, and I have to make a conscious effort to keep a sour look off my face. Accountability—that's fucking rich, coming from the guy who was able to murder me without consequence.

"Let's put the events of the Deep on the back burner, since it's not crucial to your relationship as a god and goddess, but rather as future king and queen. How did it make you feel, the date?" Luminara leans toward us, resting her elbows on her knees.

The back burner, AKA where it will never come up again. I guess for now we're just going to ignore the fact that the Underworld is in crisis and pretend this farce of a relationship is the most important thing in my life. I shouldn't be surprised that I'm not allowed to fully express just how pissed off I am. That I have to take responsibility for every action that led me to turn souls into trees even though *he* tripped the first domino.

Galen expects me to have bent to his will already. He believes I should be the one initiating and pulling him into those alcoves. His promise to wait for sex until we're married is already a distant memory for him, his hands always straying.

Just because his memory has the lifespan of a fly doesn't mean mine does.

"It made me feel excited." Lie. "It made me realize what I was missing." Lie. "It made me wonder if I made the wrong choice." Truth, but not in the way they want to think. It's easier to lie than to keep fighting during these mandatory sessions.

Galen believes himself entitled to the Underworld and me, but I don't think he's actually prepared for what it takes to be king. The way he's handled things thus far worries me. I don't know who gave him the false ego boost, but they deserve to step on Legos barefoot for the rest of their lives.

"Galen didn't think the date went that well," Luminara points out.

He's been suspiciously quiet. He already debriefed her last week, and whatever she said to him seems to have been effective, because he's giving me space, but I don't trust him. He's inconsistent about when he listens to me about my needs.

"I think that's why I needed some time to think about it. Some time to really seek out my feelings. I was unnecessarily hard on Galen during the date—I think some of my residual anger was still there, even though you took my memories. I needed time to process that Galen isn't the enemy in all this."

Luminara's eyebrows shoot up, and I wonder if I went too far with that last one. Yeah, now that I think about it, I did lay it on a little thick.

"And what do you mean by that?"

I bite my lips, looking pensive. "The Fates did this to us. The Fates meddling is the only reason I can think of for why we weren't together in the first place. My murder was a...drastic...step to take, and I'm not sure I've fully forgiven him for that, but we need to work more cohesively."

"More like it was my sister Helene's meddling. She's always putting her nose in where it doesn't belong."

I try not to react to the venom in Galen's voice, but he is right to an extent. Helene is the one who locked Essos and me into the cabin to have it out after I caught him cheating. I had planned to cut him out of my life entirely.

Helene doing that was the best thing for me and Essos.

I focus on filling the emptiness Essos's absence has left inside me with my hatred for Galen.

"We're not here to talk about Helene—we're here to sort out our problems." I try to lead the conversation away from his sister. I'm supposed to meet with her and Kai after this for another grueling workout. I've seen them after he's done training me. They're one of those obnoxious fitness couples who make everyone feel lazy because he's doing push-ups while she does a handstand on his back.

"You have another trial coming up soon. Are you ready, Galen?" Luminara asks, redirecting us.

"Of course. I'm ready for any challenge they throw my way, if that's what it takes to prove to the world that I'm worthy of my girl and the crown." Galen brushes the hair from my shoulder to kiss my neck in the same spot where he left bruises weeks ago. I'm thankful my body doesn't give an involuntary shudder. I turn to him and kiss him on the lips softly, then pull away to gaze into his eyes.

If Luminara's half the goddess she thinks she is, she should see this for exactly what it is—an act.

"I wish I could call off the Trials. It was dumb and said in a place of anger." It's a hollow statement. I can't call them off, but my words have the desired effect on Galen. He seems to melt toward me. He's desperate for me to love him, and he will eat any lie I feed him, so I make sure to stuff him with them.

"You two seem to be in a much better place." Luminara's voice is placid, but the shrewd look in her eyes tells me she sees more than she's letting on.

I flash her a toothless smile. "I think the date helped us get to a place of mutual understanding."

"She's certainly more open to the inevitable now," Galen says, resting his hand on my shoulder. So much for not crowding me.

"And how has ruling jointly been going?"

It hasn't been, thanks to Galen's insistence that I do next to nothing. Sybil is more on top of what Galen is doing, more aware of each move he makes, and they try to counter him as much as they can. I moved the tithe amounts back to where they should be, and he raised them again.

I can only hope the damage he's doing is reversible. I don't think six months is enough time to financially ruin the realm, but now I have to bet on it.

"It's been going well. After the debacle in the Deep, Daphne agreed that I should be left to make the decisions, and she'll focus on wedding planning and women's work."

I smile serenely, even if I'm about to crack a tooth from clenching my teeth. That's not at all how my discussion with Xavier went, but if that's what it's going to take to get through this, then that's what it's going to take. Maybe with Galen lulled into a false sense of security, I can pick a different battle.

"I just want what's best for the Afterlife, and having two warring leaders is not what's best. If Galen had been with me in the Deep, maybe we wouldn't have had to stop all gem production."

Luminara's eyebrows rise at my emphatic tone. Definitely coming on too strong.

Galen tugs me into his side, my words hitting *his* mark. "She's learning that she can't carry the weight of the world on her shoulders and that she has to count on me to carry the extra burden."

Gag. I mean, he's not *wrong*, but he will never be the one I rely on. It takes a little too much to force my lips to comply with my attempt at a smile. It doesn't feel convincing, more like a grimace than anything, so I drop it.

"I'm glad you've both made so much progress in so little time."

We're dismissed, and I don't storm off the way I usually do. Galen slips his hand into mine, and when I try to turn toward my office and rooms, he tugs me outside and toward the beach instead. I have a moment of panic that he knows I've been training with Kai by the water, that he wants to punish me, but there's no flush of anger or deception on his face.

Then again, he didn't look like he was deceiving me during the Calling either.

I tell myself to relax, kicking my shoes off when we get to the sand. It's not out of a desire to sink my feet into the sand; it's because if I have to run, I can't do it in heels.

I'm just being practical.

"I feel like we went about this all wrong."

I glance at him, unsure what he means. "I need you to elaborate."

We walk to the water where, once upon a time, he started to plant seeds of doubt in my mind. The hems of my tailored pants get wet, but I don't mind.

"I mean, *I* went about this wrong, and Luminara has been helping me see that." We walk along the shore, our feet and ankles getting wet as we go.

"Are you trying to apologize to me, Galen?" I stop walking and look up at him.

"If you would stop being so obtuse, yes, I am. I went about this all wrong. This whole process has been very hard on me." He's not specific in his non-apology. Is he sorry for stabbing me a millennium ago? For terrorizing me? For letting his brother think he raped me? Or for deceiving me during the Calling? How about the latest infraction of demanding I be sanctioned by the Council for taking action in the Deep when he failed to address the repercussions of his actions? There are so many options, and I don't think he's sincere about any of it.

I open my mouth to accept with my fingers crossed behind my back, to put this behind us, and he silences me with a kiss. Any—and by any, I mean all—kisses I've initiated, I've kept light. A simple peck, a sign of affection. His kiss now is deep and yearning for me, for what he thinks we should have.

He cuts off the kiss, pulling back and getting on one knee. In his hand is a small velvet box. My blood starts to pound in my head and all through my body. This outfit is too restrictive. The air, too thick.

144

"I mean, it was me who got you released from the dagger. I was the only one pushing for it. Essos forgot about you, but I never did."

I somehow doubt that.

He runs a hand through his hair, seeming agitated. "Shit, I'm fucking this up. I should have started by telling you how much you mean to me. How much I love you. I should have told you how I can't wait to rule and be with you. There are great things for us to accomplish, and I can't wait to experience them. I can't wait for our life together to begin. We've been robbed by Essos and Helene and so many others. I never needed the crown, I just needed you. At this point, the crown is just a bonus. I promise our lives together are going to be better than anything Essos ever offered you." He opens the box.

I have to hand it to him, the pear-shaped ruby is large, exquisite, and looks like a drop of blood gifted to me by the God of War.

"Our lives—" he reaches forward and presses a hand to my womb "—our children's lives—will be blessed to have you in them. I'm glad you've finally come to see that we were meant to be. Nothing, not even the Fates, can separate us forever."

There's no question about it; he's fucking unhinged. All this is just pretty words and pretty sentiments that he'll never follow through on.

He slides the ring on my finger, and when he rises, I don't say anything. When his lips meet mine again, I kiss him with my eyes open, looking at the promise that this stone holds.

It is a promise of blood and pain, and he will be the one to pay it.

I'M WAITING in the arena on my own, trying to meditate, but my garish new engagement ring is staring me in the face. *Deep breath in, deep breath out.* My hand rises to clasp the necklace from Essos, as if it can protect me or provide me with strength from him, wherever he is.

Essos is the one who carried me to my room from the Deep, who ensured I was changed and safe, but I never got to talk to him to confirm whether I handled the incident the way I should have. I'm lacking confidence and conviction that I did the right thing, and the papers have started to call me the Recluse Queen. There's no shortage of the vitriol they'll spew.

I comfort myself by thinking they wouldn't need to assassinate my character if I wasn't well-liked. But that doesn't change how much it hurts.

"Nice bling," Helene calls, malice in her words.

My eyes fly open to find her sauntering over. "I needed something befitting my station."

She rolls her blue eyes but doesn't offer to help me up. "Kai can't make it today, so you're stuck with me."

"What crawled up your ass and died?" I ask, getting to my feet.

She picks at imaginary lint on her grey-blue sports bra. "I'm just a little frustrated that I have to watch you dick over my one brother while being dicked down by my other."

"You can't seriously mean that," I say with a laugh. I thought she was on my side, but her attitude says otherwise.

"I can, and I do. I've seen you and Galen being all lovey. I read your apology statement, bending to his will. You do know I have my own life, right? But no, I've been ordered by Xavier to stay here and babysit you and Galen to ensure you don't kill each other. Instead, you two have been fornicating in the halls."

"Holy gods, Helene! You know I wouldn't do that to Essos!" I want to get in her face, but I don't; it would only rile her up more, and I know she can kick my ass.

"Do I know that? For all I know, you're getting back at him for cheating on you, like, a million years ago."

Her words have the desired effect of hitting me where it hurts most, not least of all because there is some measure of truth in them. What's worse about her attack is that she has no idea that I remember him cheating, and that might sting more—that she's intentionally trying to hurt me.

"That's a shitty thing to say."

"Is it? Your soul gets released from the dagger, and you spend the Calling panting after Essos *and* Galen, and then you choose the wrong brother!"

This time I do shove her. "You have as much culpability for this situation as I do. Why was my soul trapped for so long to begin with? Why not set me free? I've heard that Posey and Galen spearheaded the charge to delay my release. Why did all of you go for it? I thought we were friends. I thought we were *sisters*."

She steps back toward me, getting in my space. "Let's get one thing straight. Essos absolutely advocated to have your soul released. He came before the Council, but it was agreed that your release should be delayed. Was it shitty that your soul was stored in that gem for the last few centuries? Yes. But if I'd known you were going to throw away your second chance like this, maybe I would have voted for you to stay in there longer." Helene blows an angry breath out through her nose like she's a bull ready to charge. "A *lot* happened after you died, and we could spend a month straight talking about it and not touch on everything. Yeah, I thought we were sisters too, but I know what I'm seeing and what I'm hearing. I've even heard *Posey* gushing over how compliant you've been. You tell me to my face that you hate her, but now you're being chummy. Even your lady's maids are talking about it. Pick a fucking side, Daphne."

"Fuck you, Helene." I straighten my spine. "When you're done listening to Posey's poison, you know where to find me."

I shoulder-check Helene on my way past her to the house. Her words cut deep, but she failed to answer my question.

What does Posey have over the Council that is letting her get away with what happened after my death?

15

I haven't seen Essos in weeks, and it's getting under my skin. I should be used to it, his absence. How long did he have to live without me, and I can't last a few measly weeks without getting all sorts of bothered?

I swing blindly, not caring that my form is wrong, or that I'm not twisting my hips to follow the movement. I'm angry, and I need to work out my frustration. Kai dodges me easily, grabbing my wrist and twisting it behind me. It doesn't help that Helene is glaring daggers at me from the bench.

"This is hardly fair," I pant as he holds me against his bare chest. He's sweaty, and the look Helene gives him tells me that she would jump him here and now if he asked, even with me between them. It's truly impressive how she's able to alternate between wanting to murder me and fuck Kai with one blink.

"This is very fair—you're the one who's not *focusing*," he scolds.

I tap his hands, and Kai lets me go. I spin and try to strike again, but he sweeps his leg out, catching my ankles and dropping

149

me on my back. From the bench, Finn and Dion let out a joint whimper in commiseration with my pain. The breath whooshes from my lungs and I lie there, not moving.

Kai offers me a hand up, and I swat it away. "It's *not* fair. You're an expert at this, of course, you're going to kick my ass at every turn," I snap when I finally do catch my breath.

"And what, you think the God of War isn't adept at hand-to-hand combat? I've seen him rip a man's spine out with his bare hands. How do you expect to hold your own against him if you can't hold your own against me? This isn't meant to make you better than him—it's meant to make you strong enough to survive. Take my hand, Daph."

I take Kai's hand and stand up. Dion tries to offer me a glass of wine, but Kai levels him with a look.

"Why are you doing this?" Dion asks, leaning into Finn. Finn gets it; Finn doesn't question it. Finn saw how I fell prey to Galen.

"Because I refuse to let Galen best me again." I take a sip of water, then start to guzzle it.

Kai grabs my wrist to slow me down. He's commented on the sharper edges of my face, noting I'm expending too much energy and not taking in enough food to balance it. He keeps telling me I'll be stronger if I eat better.

It's not that I don't want to. But the hand on my knee under the table when I eat dinner, the kisses pressed to my lips after lunch... every piece of my soul that I am bargaining away with every sign of affection keeps me too nauseated to swallow.

This is how Galen beats me. Not with brute strength, but by slowly wearing down who I am.

"Then eat."

I don't know where Kai gets it from, and I should really know better than to ask, but he hands me a plate topped with salmon, rice, and veggies.

"You want me to eat your scaled friends?" I deadpan.

Finn rises and pushes me down onto the bench. "Eat."

Kai doesn't answer me, so I do as I'm told, angrily chewing at him. Behind me, Helene snorts. I turn and glare at her, but cut off another sliver of fish.

"Odds are against Galen. They think he's going to lose again," Helene tells me, showing me her phone. It might be her version of a peace offering. For whatever reason, she refuses to believe my actions and is focusing on the words that are coming out of other people's mouths.

Kai glances between the two of us, as if he can figure out why we're fighting. Maybe if he does, he can let me in on the secret.

"It's not going to matter. He gets his prize no matter what." My words sound bitter to my own ears. My friends fall silent around me. Dion wraps an arm around my shoulder and tugs me against his side.

"We won't let him have you." Dion assures me.

I vanish my empty plate.

The ground beneath us trembles, but no one comments. It's easier to ignore the giant elephant in the room than address just why the Underworld is shaking. Ever since the Garden of Evil was closed and I took action in the Deep, my realm has been in a state of unrest. It's not affecting Solarem—yet—but whoever is feeding the *Solarem Sun* stories about me has also mentioned the small quakes. Tremor Queen is the nickname of the week.

Whenever I learn who's been feeding them information, I'm going to ensure they regret it.

I wish I knew what Essos is doing, wherever he is. I know he has to be coming up with a plan, but will it be enough? I can't assume he'll swoop in and save me. I have to save myself. Problem is, I don't know how to begin to do that.

"I don't think my marriage is something you have a say in." I look at the ring on my hand, a constant reminder of what I am fighting, of who I am fighting. I've tried to remove the gleaming stone, but it won't budge, likely kept in place by some sort of enchantment so I always know who I belong to.

We're quiet for too long, and when Finn holds his hand out to me, I take it, rising again on weary legs.

He throws a punch right at me, surprising me and everyone else. I block, responding in kind with a jab of my own. Kai joins the attack, and I falter, unsure where to put my focus, which lands me on my back.

"Again," Kai orders helping me up.

We do this for hours until I'm sporting bruises and aches in places I didn't know could feel.

As I'm packing up my bag, I try not to eavesdrop, but I can't help it. Kai, finally panting from his efforts, holds Helene against his sweaty body.

"When do you come home, my starfish?" he asks, his voice low. His hand is cupping Helene's face, my beautiful sister-in-law, who has been relegated to babysitter.

"Soon, I hope. Only four months of this left."

My heart lurches. I hate that my actions continue to have far-reaching impacts I never expected. It's a relatively short amount of time for us, but for me, every moment away from Essos feels like a lifetime.

I look away when they kiss, all passion and heat, their yearning for the other crowding the open space. Dion and Finn left earlier, tired of watching me get my ass handed to me. They're all risking everything with such open defiance of Galen, who very well could become King of the Underworld in a few months. Death is very possibly on the table for pushing back against him. The dagger is somewhere, still in play, and I can only hope that Essos is trying to find it to get rid of it.

The walk back to the house is slow, my feet dragging as we go. Helene tries to be patient, but she lets out an annoyed sigh.

"You don't have to come back with me," I say, stopping short.

Helene, now a few paces ahead of me, turns to look at me. She works her jaw. "Why would you say a stupid thing like that?"

"Because you don't have to play peacekeeper. Galen and I aren't at each other's throats any longer—you don't have to be here to stop us from killing each other."

"No, I just have to be here so you don't sleep with Galen. I'm starting to wonder if maybe you've decided to go for the brother you have and not the brother who's gone."

I flinch like she's hit me. She said as much earlier, but it still surprises me that she thinks me capable of this.

"I have it under control. I am not going to sleep with Galen. He promised he wouldn't push me." That last assurance I offer has no weight behind it; we both know that the God of War's word isn't worth much.

"Right, okay, sure. This is why I'm staying behind—to make sure you keep your eye on the prize." She starts walking again, and I have to move my sore legs much too fast to catch up.

"What is your problem?" I ask, grabbing her shoulder and spinning her around. She shoves me, sending me flying back. I do what I can to create a net of vines to catch me and stop me from skidding across the sand. It's barely enough, and they disintegrate after breaking my fall.

"My problem, Daph? My problem is you. You've ruined pretty much everything. I just want to get back to normal, back to my life with *my* husband."

"I was literally *just* telling you to do that. Why are you taking your anger out on me? I didn't do this."

"Fucking clueless, as always." Helene snaps, walking away from me again. We're at the house by now, and I can't even push the issue with her, because she disappears toward her room.

I'm rubbing a throbbing vein in my head when Zara runs to me. "You need to come quick. It's Cat." She's breathless as she says it.

A spike of adrenaline has me bounding up the stairs two at a time to Cat's room, across the hall from mine.

Cat is lying in bed, and my heart nearly stutters with how frail she looks. With the introduction of Marge and Effie, Cat's been getting pushed out at the insistence of Posey. I've let her go, thinking that I was protecting her even though it isolated me. I want them all to think they're winning so I can watch the disbelief in their eyes when I best them.

Cat's eyes open and try to focus on me. Beside her, Shadow has her head resting on Cat's hip. I'm sweaty and gross and mindful of this as I pull over the vanity chair to sit beside my friend.

"What's wrong?" I ask, taking her hand in mine.

Her whole body shivers. "I don't know. I just...I feel run down." Her voice is weak.

I place the back of my hand against her forehead, feeling for fever like this could be a mortal problem. The truth is, I don't know what the problem could be. I assumed that whatever allowed our souls to stay at the house during the Calling would continue instead of pushing us toward our afterlives. But I doubt that Essos and Sybil had a contingency for this situation.

I glance at Zara to see how she's faring, and she looks beyond perfect, her skin bright and healthy in comparison to Cat's. I have to keep my face neutral so Cat doesn't see my concern.

"At least you're not trying to tell me you're fine." I conjure a cool damp cloth and wipe her brow.

"She's been like this for a few days. She didn't get out of bed today," Zara pipes up from behind me, and I curse myself for not noticing, for being so swept up in my own selfish problems that I completely missed the pain my best friend was in. Today seems to be all about how many different ways I can fumble and fuck up.

"Traitor," Cat grumbles trying to swat my hand away.

I turn to Zara. "Why am I only finding out about this now?" My tone is cutting. It's not Zara's fault, logically I know this, but I need someone to blame.

I'm failing Cat.

"I told her not to tell you," Cat croaks, struggling to sit up.

I press her back into the bed. "Get Sybil. See if they can help. Maybe there's something wrong that we just don't know about." I'm grasping at straws, because I don't want my mind to go looking for darker explanations, but it goes there anyway, ready to offer up the worst-case scenarios.

That this is intentional.

That Galen knows I'm faking.

That this is a direct attack against Cat to get at me.

"Sybil has tried," Zara says, watching Cat's eyes drift closed.

My heart squeezes until I think it might explode. I want my husband, who would know how to fix her. I need to talk to Sybil to figure out what they've done and what this could be.

I brush sweaty hair from Cat's forehead, and I hate the next words out of my mouth. "Get Xavier." My voice is hard. "Then I need tea and cold, wet towels." I sit quietly with Cat while Zara runs out to do what I've asked.

"Why didn't you say something sooner?" I try to make her as comfortable as I can.

"Hot," is all she manages in response. I shoo Shadow off her and pull back her comforter. The sheet over her is transparent with sweat, and she is naked underneath it, but her modesty can matter later. Right now, I need to save her life.

For a goddess who can bring life where there was none before, I am useless with people and gods and curing ailments. Cat nods in thanks, her body going still under the cool air I'm drawing in through her cracked window.

The door behind me slams open and Xavier edges me out of the way. "What is wrong with her?" he asks, taking her wrist. Her eyes have drifted closed, and my womanizing brother-in-law hasn't once glanced beneath the sheets.

Zara is a few seconds behind him with the things I asked for.

I take the tray and set it aside for now, and Zara takes up her post at the door. "I don't know. I've only been here for a few minutes. She hasn't been feeling well for at least a few days. Knowing Cat, probably longer."

"Why didn't you do anything sooner?" Xavier snaps at me. I don't like the way he cradles her cheek and whispers her name, trying to coax her awake.

"I didn't know any sooner. You think I would have let this happen?"

He glances at me before returning to Cat. "I gave her the charm like you asked. It should have protected her from any sort of attack. Give me your hand." Xavier holds out his hand to me, like he's looking for a life jacket to buoy him as he drowns.

I take his hand as instructed without asking for further explanation. His power seizes hold of mine in a way I have never felt before, and it drives me to my knees. I can feel the tether between our powers grow until he starts to pull on mine and feed it into Cat.

His hand presses against Cat's chest, his dark eyes fluttering closed. I feel lightning crackle in the room around us as one, two, lightbulbs explode. Distantly, I hear Zara shriek, but I focus on feeding Xavier my energy, letting it funnel through him into Cat. Xavier roars from the overwhelming amount of power he is using to heal her, and I worry that maybe using my reserves was a bad idea.

Cat sits up abruptly, gasping for air. The blanket falls from her chest as she clutches Xavier's hand where it hovers over her heart. He doesn't let go, lets her grasp his hand as he pulls the blanket up to cover her body, intrinsically knowing that she would hate being exposed like this. Watching them, I wonder if this is what it was like to see Essos and me together.

I slump to the floor, my ankles crushed beneath me. I lean against Cat's nightstand, watching as Shadow crawls across the bed to her.

"What happened?" Cat's voice is raw.

I gesture at Zara to bring the tea and broth to Cat. She obeys without my having to say a word, carefully skirting Xavier, who looks like a worried lover. Perhaps I'm too late in stopping the cataclysm that's between them. Now, I can only hope they're discrete enough to not catch Posey's attention.

"We were hoping you could tell us." Xavier pulls his hand back, and Cat sips from the tea, holding it in both her hands.

"I don't know. I've been feeling a little under the weather, with headaches and the like. I figured a nap couldn't hurt, and then I had a stupid dream that I was caught in a volcanic explosion, and my whole body felt like it was on fire."

"When did it start?" I ask. My voice is equally raw, but I clear my throat, wanting the focus to stay on Cat.

She looks sheepish. "A few weeks ago, maybe a month. It was mostly nonsense. I figured feeling a little tired wasn't worth distracting you." She tries to turn her attention to where I'm still on the floor, leaning against her nightstand. "Are you—?"

"I'm fine. You cannot keep things like this to yourself. I need to know. What if someone has been poisoning you slowly?" I stop my scolding and recenter. I've never had cause to find out if a soul can be poisoned, and I'm not about to test that theory now. When I almost died *again* because I was attacked by a sea monster attack during the Calling, Essos admitted that my soul would have been lost forever. The thought of something like that happening to Cat... Ice runs through my veins. "How do you feel now?" I rise on shaky legs.

"Much better. Totally fine, actually." Her voice and eyes are both clear, and sweat no longer drips from her forehead.

"Good. Please utilize Zara for the next week to get you anything you need." I look at Zara, who nods. "I want you on bed rest. No leaving this room. I understand you may be feeling better now, but we need to monitor you for further symptoms. I'm getting you a food tester. It's something you should have had from the beginning. I might be invulnerable, but you are not."

My hands are trembling, but I'm too weak to form a fist to try to stop them. My head is swimming, and black spots are appearing in my vision. There is a dull thumping through my whole body that I recognize as my heartbeat.

Gods, did Xavier just transfer her ailment to me? I'm leaning heavily on the nightstand for support.

"I'm really fine," Cat insists.

"This is my order as your queen." Now I look at Xavier, then back to Cat. "I already spoke with you both. Stay away from each other. I mean it." I try to imbue my words with strength, but everyone in the room can see it's not there. I want to stay with Cat, but I'm worried I'm going to pass out. I turn to Zara. "Stay with her tonight, and coordinate with Estelle to get you whatever you need to take care of Cat. I don't care what Posey gets from that, but Xavier's involvement has to stay quiet." I turn and look in what I hope is Xavier's direction. My vision is blurring, but I will walk out with my head held high.

"You know their names," Cat teases with a smile. It's the best hint that she's still there, still okay.

"Goodnight. If you need anything from me, don't hesitate." I say, before slipping out of the room and into my own. I close my bedroom door behind me and lock it tight, my breathing labored.

I thought I did a decent job of sounding fine in Cat's room, but now that I'm alone, I can be just as not fine as I feel.

I stumble toward my bathroom, focusing on lifting one foot and then the other, but I can barely do that, and I crash into the doorframe. I hold on to it as my whole world spins out of focus and my vision narrows to a pinprick... and my body drops to the ground, unconsciousness taking me.

16

"Open your eyes, my love." The words are whispered, and I think they might be a dream, but my body jostles in an unexpected way, and my eyes flutter open. Essos is holding me to his chest, blue eyes darkened with concern. We're sitting on the floor of my bedroom, with Essos's back pressed to my bed.

"Es?" I barely manage the one syllable. My memory slowly pieces the previous day together. The training, Cat being sick, Xavier taking my power, collapsing while trying to get to my bathroom.

"I'm here, my love. I'm here." He brushes the hair from my face, and I wonder if this isn't some elaborate trick. His touch is so tender that part of me wants to close my eyes and just relish in his closeness. My eyes start to do just that when he drags his thumb across my lower lip, causing them to shoot open.

"How...? Why...?" I start to sit up, my strength returning to me. Essos doesn't try to hold me back; he helps me sit up so I can look at him. It feels like it's been forever and a year since I've been able to drink in the sight of my husband. He looks as tired as I feel. His black hair is a mess, longer than he usually likes to keep it, and it curls around his ears. He's got on a simple T-shirt and jeans, and I want to climb into his lap and never leave it. I want to hide from all ugliness that's hounding us and just bask in his presence like a cat in a sunbeam.

"I came to check on you, and I'm glad I did." He doesn't question why I'm lying on the floor between my bedroom and bathroom; he doesn't push for answers. He trusts that if I want to tell him, I will. And I do, I do want to tell him, and open my heart up to him, but he has enough burdens without having to hear from me about how I keep letting his brother kiss me, about how I keep kissing his brother. Without me bringing up my newest memory. It's been only a few weeks since the first trial, and so much has happened that we need to talk about, but he won't want to rehash our fight over me catching him cheating any more than I do. We have to do it, even if it's only for my sanity, but it doesn't need to be today.

"Cat was sick. Xavier healed her but needed some of my power to do so, and I'm just exhausted."

Essos's face darkens. "I'm going to fucking kill him," he growls.

I move closer to him, wanting contact of any kind. "Don't. I'm glad he saved her life."

"Even if it came at the expense of your own?" He sighs, knowing the answer is yes. Essos pulls me farther onto his lap. "How is Cat?" His knuckle drags along my cheekbone, his gaze flicking to my lips, before he meets my eyes. He may want me, but he won't act on it when I'm so fragile.

For once, I wish he wouldn't treat me like I'm fine china.

"She's okay. Much better. I would do it again in a heartbeat."

"I know you would, my queen. I know you would." I don't wait for him to kiss me; I lean up, pressing my lips against his, needing to feel something real. Essos reciprocates immediately, as if he needs the affirmation just as badly.

I wonder if he's heard the details about his traitorous queen who abandoned her husband for his brother. I wonder if he's heard how I kiss Galen and now wear his ring. The ring that feels like it's tightening around my finger in Essos's presence like a noose around a hanged man.

I twist so I'm facing Essos more straight on, and I deepen the kiss, opening my mouth to him, coaxing him to open his lips. He does, and I feel his tongue flick against mine. I light up like a pinball machine at his touch. My belly swoops as my desire for him only grows, my need to have him inside me becoming an insatiable beast and my core clenching at the very *idea* of our joining. He must feel it too, because the kiss changes again, and it's feral. We're all lips and teeth and tongue, and I'm reaching for his shirt, pulling it up and over his head. We break apart for just one second to cast it aside before he pulls me onto his lap, my legs straddling him.

His hands move deftly to unhook my bra, the one I wore while working out with Kai and Helene and Finn, and then I'm skin to skin with my husband. I want more of him. Essos's hand comes up to the back of my neck and cradles it as he lowers me to the floor with ease. His sinful mouth moves away from mine, nipping and sucking and kissing as he moves down the column of my throat. One hand palms my breast before he captures the other with his mouth. Everywhere we touch, I burn with awareness of him.

My hips jerk at the hot, wet sensation of his mouth closing over my nipple, and I feel him grin. I must be coated in salt from the workout, and he just doesn't care. Part of me registers that maybe *I* should care, but if things keep going the way they're headed, I'm going to be a boneless, sweaty mess anyway. I watch him, biting my lip as he tugs on the nipple with his teeth, eliciting a jolt through my body like I've touched a live wire. He pulls off my workout pants slowly, teasing me as he peals them away and casts them aside then beholds me, spread before him. I open my legs wider, inviting him to me.

The grin Essos gives me makes me tremble. He watches me, taking a finger and sliding it through my slick folds, feeling how badly I want him. I gasp as Essos touches the most sensitive nerves in my body. I don't want to wait for him any longer. I sit up, crunching toward him, but he puts a hand on my chest, pushing me back down.

"You never were very patient, my love." His voice is husky, thick with desire and the same need I have. The same dark, lustful need for the other. Essos would make cities tremble to have me back. To torture me, he's slow about taking off his pants. He starts with his belt, undoing the buckle, then sliding it slowly out of the loops. I wet my lips then slide my hand down my stomach and between my legs, rubbing my clit.

Essos hisses, watching as I circle my seam before pumping fingers in and out of myself. My lips part as my breathing gets heavier. Two can play this game.

I've driven him to the brink of his control as his eyes flit from my face to between my legs and he finishes disrobing, tossing his pants aside. He covers his body with mine, slowly and gently. Essos nudges my hands aside as he positions himself at my entrance. We hold eye contact, even as I want to close them as he slides into me. My back arches, pressing my body against his, the feeling of us being one again warming me everywhere, and for just a second, we hold ourselves this way.

Essos is braced on his forearms, and I give in to sensation, my eyes sliding shut as he slowly pulls back before sliding into me again at the same speed he withdrew. This is everything I've been wanting and wishing for during the past two months. I simultaneously want him to move faster and slow down.

"Eyes on me, my love," he orders, and I obey.

My hands hold his sides as our bodies find that familiar rhythm that we had for centuries. I savor the sensations, the delicious way he stretches my body to accommodate him as he pistons inside me, as his movements get more frantic, more full of need. My nails dig into his sides and his back. Essos must feel the change in me, the rising tide of my orgasm, because his hand clamps over my mouth, silencing me. He's barely in time, because it crashes over me, and he muffles my cries then moves his hand and threads it into my hair as his orgasm takes over. I bite down on his shoulder, whimpering as our releases subside. Essos gives one last shudder before burying his face in the crook of my neck while bracing himself on one forearm.

We lie there, bodies entwined and hearts beating rapidly in our chests as aftershocks of pleasure work through us. Essos kisses my lips, then my forehead, before rising.

"I'm in need of a good shower, but I worry I might slip," I say. I'm not totally lying, but I want him to stay as long as he can. I've been pushing myself too hard, and this release, while everything I needed, cost me more energy than I have. Essos smiles indulgently, offering me a hand up. I sway for a second, and he pulls me against him, worry creasing his brow.

We step into the shower, and it's almost like no time has passed since we last did this. I really do just need a shower, but Essos lifts me in his arms and presses me against the cold wall. I barely notice the chill, focusing on his mouth and his kisses. I wait for him to line himself up at my entrance before he slowly sheaths himself inside me.

We make love torturously slowly this time, each snap of his hips is driving me closer and closer toward ecstasy. I want us to take our time together, relearning each and every sound, every inch of each other's bodies, but we don't have that luxury, so I let myself tumble and fall into the oblivion that he has started.

By the time we're done, the steam of the shower has enveloped us.

Essos squirts my shampoo into his hand and lathers my hair while I wash my body. It's decadent having someone wash my hair for me, and I never realized how much I missed my husband's hands digging into my scalp. I condition my hair and then do the same for him, washing his hair even if there is a lot less of it. He faces me, keeping a tight hold on my waist, as if he knows my legs are weak.

"I was worried about you," he admits as I'm scraping my nails into his scalp the way he likes.

"I know," I admit, apologetic.

"I keep wanting to pop back in here, make sure you're alive and okay and that you're real. I'm always afraid it's been a cruel trick and I'm going to come back and find you lying in bed with a dagger in your heart again. Seeing you unconscious, I think my soul might have left my body for a minute, knowing that I would follow you into whatever our kind has as an afterlife."

My hands slow, and I drag them down his chest, needing to feel the beat of his heart. I look him in the eye, stepping as close to him as I can. My heart breaks all over again for the pain I've caused us both. "I'm right here. I'm still fighting," I swear.

Essos reaches for my left hand to look at the red stone adorning my fourth finger. "My brother always did have a flair for the dramatic." There's a bitter edge to his voice, a reminder that we're both suffering.

I sigh. "I don't know what you've heard."

Essos drops my hand and steps under the water to rinse the shampoo from his hair. I don't continue my statement, waiting to look him in the eye. When he emerges from under the water, he steps back toward me, crowding my space. His hand slides along my side, dipping at my waist before settling on my hips.

"I don't know what you may have heard," I begin again, "but I'm not. I'm not giving up on us."

"I think you just made that abundantly clear." He smirks, reaching for the spigot and turning it off.

I swat at him, annoyed. "What I mean is—"

"I know what you're trying to say, Daphne, and I love you for it. I'm aware that this game we're playing requires deception. You're doing what you need to, and I trust you. I don't care what anyone else says or thinks about what you and Galen are doing."

"I'm not sleeping with him."

Essos freezes at these words. "It will wreck me if you feel like you have to, but I can live with it if it means you surviving to fight another day. It won't ever change how I feel about you. I will love you until every star falls from the sky, and even that can't stop my feelings for you," he whispers, unable to meet my eye. He reaches for a towel and wraps it around me.

I do something I haven't done in centuries. I slap him across the face. It startles him just as much as it startles me, but I can't take it back, so I ground myself, clenching my teeth.

"*I* couldn't live with it."

Essos eyes me, a smirk tugging up his lips as he rubs the towel on my sides.

"I just meant that...I understand how deep this deception may have to go. Fuck, Daphne." I startle at him cursing. "I don't want you to sleep with my brother. I don't want you to be in a position where you have to decide between fucking him to save your life or betraying me. I just want you to know that I under-stand. Nothing that happens during these months will be held against you by me, and if it's held against you by someone else, fuck them."

All I want is to fuck *him* again. I want to climb on this vicious, dirty side of my husband that he seldom lets out, and I want him to fuck my brains out for the next year. But we can't, so I settle for the next best thing. "You know I love you, right? Nothing is going to change that."

"Not even Chad from your meteorology class?" Essos kisses my neck, and I remember the one time I mentioned having a casual relationship with Chad in college.

"Not even Chad from meteorology." I pass my towel to him and grab my silk bathrobe from behind the door, letting my wet hair hang around my face and drip onto the delicate fabric.

"As long as you know you have every defense avenue open to you, I'll leave it alone."

I tie the robe around me tightly before running my hands down his hardened chest. He's been working out all this time on the run with nothing to do but plot and do sit-ups.

"Saying that is not leaving it alone. That's the second time in like five minutes that you've insulted my commitment to you. I'm not fucking around, Essos. Stop saying that. Stop telling me it would be okay. Stop acting like you would be okay with it. It's pissing me off."

"What am I supposed to say, Daphne? I want you to live through this. I'm looking for the dagger, but I don't know what happened to it after your soul was released, and the idea that it could still be in his possession causes me to lose sleep every night. Losing you almost killed me once. I won't live through it a second time."

Heat sizzles through our gazes as I look at him, understanding passing between us, but I won't let it come to that.

Essos shifts the conversation. "I can see that working out with Kai has had its benefits, but what's with all these sharp edges, my love?" His fingers trace my prominent collarbone before gently grasping my elbows and tugging me closer to him. I stumble as he tugs me. Part of me wants to push back from him, scream at him for being so willing to let me barter away a chunk of my soul I would never get back. But on a baser level, I understand. There might come a time when I won't have a choice, but thinking about it isn't something I can allow.

"It's hard to keep dinner down when I have to keep kissing my murderer. Everyone expects me to bury that. They act like I should forget it, that I should have already forgiven and forgotten, but I haven't. I think about it every single day. You giving me permission to sleep with him to save my life is nice in theory, but it fucking *hurts*."

Essos cups my face when my voice wavers. His lips are a caress against mine, and my eyes flutter closed the same way they opened. It's over just as quickly.

He's already been here too long, and I don't know how long he sat there with me unconscious on his lap.

Essos pulls my robe open, and I want to question just how badly he needs to see my boobs, when he kisses the spot on my chest where the knife sank in with the killing blow. Galen stabbed me six times in the chest, but it's that one spot that got me, that broke me into nothing more than a wisp of soul. I try to hide the tremor trying to work through my body, but Essos knows.

He closes his arms around me, pressing me tightly to him so we're skin to skin. "I'm sorry. I never intended to hurt you. I won't say it again." Essos leans forward, kissing my cheek. "Talk to Estelle. Tell her that you're having a hard time keeping food down. She can help." He brushes a strand of wet hair behind my ear.

"I miss you," I whisper, because I don't know what else to say. So much still hangs between us. We spent this precious time not talking as we should have about the Deep, or the past, but reconnecting in a way that soothed a broken part in both of us.

"This will all be over soon. I miss you constantly. I will *not* let Galen have you. So long as you still want me, I won't let him take you from me again."

I kiss him urgently, knowing that he's leaving now. Even

though I'm greedy for every minute I can have him with me, I know he needs to go.

"When will I see you again?" His visits have been sporadic, with no pattern to them, likely intentional. I follow him into the bedroom so he can pull his clothes back on, hating how the feel of his skin on mine is already just a memory.

"Soon, I promise."

I kiss him fervently, one last time. Essos grabs his Yankees hat, slips it on… and disappears before my eyes.

17

Early the next morning, I rise before anyone else. My hair is still in damp clumps from where I slept on it. I'm shaky, but I'm going to rectify how poorly I've been taking care of myself. Seeing Essos last night put an extra pep in my step. He's reminded me that I'm not facing this alone, even when it feels like I am. He is out there too, fighting for us.

I step into the kitchen and pause, relishing in the flurry of activity. Even without the pomp and circumstance of the Calling, the staff is running around, readying themselves for the next big event. In this case, it's the next trial, which is less than a week away. I don't know whose trial it is, but I'm anxious for the Trials to be over. I wanted time to find a way out of this travesty of an arrangement, but the grimmer my situation looks, the more eager I am for it to just be finished.

"Where are the test dishes for the trial? It's an entirely seafood-based menu, and you were all told to have your ideas plated by this morning. How is it going to look to Her Majesty when the menu doesn't match?"

"I imagine it will look like you're busy running a kitchen," I say, clasping my hands behind my back.

One of the younger staff sees me and drops what he's holding to bend to one knee. It's the highest form of deference, one that Posey prefers but rarely gets.

"Now you've done it!" Estelle shouts, walking to me. I bend to help pick up the plate, and she swats at my hand. "I allowed you to clean up that one time when the king was here, but not now. *Now* is about appearances, and you need to be the queen we all know you are." Estelle winks at me, and I want to hug her. "Ma'am," she adds as an afterthought.

The poor boy is still on bended knee, and I tap his shoulder gently, only to realize most of the kitchen has done the same.

A flush burns up my skin, but I take Estelle's advice and raise my chin. "Please rise." And they do, immediately jumping back to what they were doing. "Might I have a word, alone?" I ask Estelle.

She glances around her kitchen, lips pursed and eyes narrowed.

"It will only take a second," I assure her. I know having Posey around isn't good for anyone's nerves, much less people she believes are beneath her. "I also need a plate for Cat for breakfast, if someone could put something together."

"Of course, of course, Your Majesty. You heard the queen! Lady Catalina is taking breakfast in her room, and prepare an extra plate for Shadow!" Estelle turns to me, lowering her voice. "Right this way."

She leads me to her office, a room off the kitchen. It's full of recipe books and hard-to-find ingredients.

"What can I do, ma'am?"

"I find I've been having difficulty keeping my meals down," I confess. "I wanted to see if you could help. I know Kai spoke with you about increasing my protein, but that doesn't matter if I never have a chance to digest it."

She reaches out and squeezes my hand. "You always had a devil of a time keeping food down when you were pregnant, but of course, this is probably just nerves. I know just the cure, and I'll be sure to include it when putting together your meals."

My heart stops at the comment about my past pregnancies. I didn't expect the reference, and I almost sway, grabbing onto the side table I'm standing near. We tried, of course we tried, and we'd started off joking about how it took time and we would enjoy the journey, but my body was never the perfect host. I never got a chance to find out if the last attempt was successful. I had forgotten. Forgotten how the nausea made it impossible to get out of bed at first. It happened only twice in hundreds of years. I thought maybe I was cursed.

I touch the corner of my eye as if tired, but it's just to wipe the tear that was threatening to fall. Galen did more than just extinguish my life. He extinguished the hope that was just taking root in my abdomen, nothing more than a cluster of cells.

"Wonderful. I appreciate it." My voice sounds breathy.

"I have it in pill form now. You can take it so you can keep breakfast down, but I'll make sure it's mixed into your food so no one is the wiser that you can't keep your food down around him. I know I wouldn't be able to." She pulls something from her desk and hands me a pill.

I've known Estelle for years, and Essos trusts her, so I take the pill, swallowing it dry with no questions asked. She gives me a terse smile.

"Thank you."

We walk back out, where there is a full breakfast tray waiting for my best friend and me.

My hands are full with the food, so I unspool a vine bracelet and make it wrap itself around Cat's door handle and pull to let myself in. It's a new little experiment I'm trying, so I always have something ready to use on me.

Cat is sitting up in bed. I place the tray on her lap, then drop onto the bed beside her.

"Well, this is a spread fit for a queen. Are you sure this isn't meant for you?" Cat takes a piece of bacon, too crispy for my taste, and pops it in her mouth.

"Three queens in, fact." I take Shadow's food bowl and place it on the floor, where she greedily gobbles it up.

"Well, if I'm to be treated as a queen..." Cat digs in, her appetite returning.

"Don't get mad..." I hedge. Cat's sharp green eyes look at me, and she raises one perfect eyebrow, waiting for the hammer to drop. "Are you sleeping with Xavier?"

Cat laughs. "No, but he wishes. He even gave me this a few weeks back." She reaches under her shirt—which she didn't have on last night—and shows me a necklace I didn't notice before. It's lapis lazuli, with lightning bolts of gold shot through it. His lake house estate has these very stones littered along the coast where it's built, but none this striking. For Xavier, it's understated, but it's also completely him. I touch it gently and can feel a hum of energy. Was creating this charm why Xavier needed my power? I can't even imagine the shitstorm we would be in if the King of the Gods was out of power.

"Did he tell you anything about it?" I should tell her that I did this, that I wanted her protected. But I want to see what Xavier said more.

"Just that it was a symbol of luck in Solarem."

I snort but let it go. "It's a protective charm. It helps to ward you from harm. The nymph that got turned to water during the last trial? It would protect you from something like that."

"But not the flu?"

"No, not the flu. It's meant to ward you against malicious magic." I savor a bite of her waffles.

"But you're benching me anyway?" Cat infers. I did put her on strict bedrest last night, so she's not wrong. She's mad about it but won't say so directly. I gave her an order as her queen. She might be new to the power dynamic of the gods, but she's able to read a situation.

"Just until after the next trial. I can't afford to have my focus split." As soon as the words leave my mouth, I grimace. I've made a dangerous misstep, insinuating that she's a distraction. Which she is, if I'm being perfectly honest, but it doesn't change that I need her, as selfish as that might be.

"So, now I'm a liability." Cat pushes her tray away, anger simmering in her words.

I want to be a better friend, but I can't. For now, I need to keep her locked in her room and out of the mess that is my life. "Yes, you are. I'm worried that someone targeted you to pave the way for someone else to get close to me."

She ponders this, taking a sip from the juice. "Someone like Miranda and Ellie?"

"Someone like Miranda and Ellie," I confirm.

"That's devious and fucking rude. But how?"

"I don't know," I confess softly. I want to tell her about Essos and seeing him and how good and right it felt, but like everything in my life right now, I have to play it close to the chest.

"Right, so I'll just sit tight and hope that whoever tried to hurt me won't try again?"

"That's the idea," I say in a dry tone, but it's a genuine concern. "Do *not* let Posey see that necklace. Don't ever take it off. She's the jealous type."

"Noted. How are you feeling? You looked like you were going to collapse last night."

"I did, in my bathroom." I probably shouldn't have told her. The burden should be mine to bear alone, but gods, I don't want to be alone anymore.

"Oh gods, Daph! Why didn't you lead with that?"

"Because I'm totally fine. I was just...spent. I'm going to tell Kai that I need a break. Even though I really need to keep training, my body is rebelling, and I can't fight it."

"I'm sorry if I'm causing problems," Cat says, deflating.

"Oh, shut up, will you? You're the only thing keeping me from crashing and burning around here. I would probably level the place if I didn't have you, and Essos and I took too long to build this house to do that."

Cat's breath hitches as this catches her attention. "You and Essos built this house?"

"We did. We lived in Solarem right after we got married because it was closer to his family and Xavier, but we ruled the Underworld. We needed to be closer to the Afterlife, and this house acts as an entrance to it. We have a separate home in Solarem, but we wanted something in between. Something that wasn't in Solarem surrounded by sycophants, and something that wasn't in the Afterlife, so we chose here. This space exists in the mortal realm, but also in Solarem—just not in the city."

It hurts to think of every decision we made—what type of wood and flooring, how many kitchens, how many guest rooms. Would Kai and Helene have their own apartments within the house? Did that mean we had to extend an offer to all my husband's siblings, or worse, my mother-in-law?

The reminder fuels my longing for Essos, even though I had him last night. We were supposed to spend our eternity here, ruling our kingdom and making babies. We were meant to have a bright and joyous future...until Galen stole it.

No. Our dream is not totally lost. There may have been a hiccup, but that future is still attainable. It's what we're fighting for.

"I'm sorry for everything that's happened," Cat says.

I lift my coffee to my lips and take a long sip. "Appreciate that, but it's not necessary. I've been dealing with these people for so long I don't think twice about it. I want you to tell me if you're feeling unwell again. It's my job to protect you, friend or not. You belong to the realm of the dead. An attack against you is an attack against me."

Cat nods.

"I know..." I pause. "I know I've been a shitty friend since the ball." I hold up my hand to silence any objections. "I'm being pulled in a thousand directions, and that's not an excuse, after all you've done for me, but I'm sorry. I'm sorry for being a bad friend, and I will make it up to you."

"You can start by giving me something to do. I'm so bored, and if Xavier comes calling, I may not be able to resist his charms." She singsongs this last bit, trying to bait me, and damned if it doesn't work.

I was starting to get out of bed when she said it, and I stop, leveling her with a look. "Do not even *think* about it. And I know, telling you not to is just as good as begging you to do it, but my sister-in-law is the jealous type. If you get turned into a heifer, it's not my fault." I pause beside my friend's sickbed, scared that I might lose her.

"Ick, cow is so not my type. Do you think she takes requests?"

Cat grins when I glare. "I'm kidding! I'll do as you say, just as long as you give me something to do."

"Can't I just have Zara keep you company? Maybe have you win Miranda to my side?" There's something about Ellie that's more off-putting, and I can't put my finger on it.

"I'll take both of those, but I need something more mentally stimulating."

I can't blame her for wanting to do more, even though I want the opposite. "Fine. I'll have Sybil give you a stack of files that need to be adjudicated. Sort them into the blatantly guilty and those you think deserve a second look."

Cat grins, sagging with relief at having something to keep her busy. It feels more like a punishment to give her my work, but I've been neglecting it the same way Essos did during the Calling. Our people deserve better.

When Cat starts to doze, I slip out of the room and find Zara there.

"I was just waiting for you to finish with her," she confesses.

I grasp her forearm, giving it an affirming squeeze. "You could have come in at any time."

"I appreciate that, but I wanted to give you two some time on your own. I would have wanted that, if it was Tiffy."

"Thank you." The reminder of her friend is another reminder of my failure. I intended to check in and see how Tiffany was doing after being returned to the mortal realm, to see if any memories of the Calling slipped through.

"I've sent Miranda and Ellie on a task, and I hope that's all right. I told Ellie that you wanted to sample bath salts as wedding favors, and I told Miranda that you possibly wanted another feline friend for Waffles, so she needed to visit the shelters in Solarem to provide a comprehensive list of available cats. I don't know if you have animal shelters, but she didn't argue about it so I guess there are, and I figured it could be good busywork."

A smirk tugs at my lips. "And do you happen to know where I can find Xavier?"

"I believe I saw him at the stables."

I thank her before striding toward my stables to confront Xavier.

He's right where she said he would be, brushing down his brown and white spotted horse. I hear him murmuring to her, but it's not clear what he's whispering. He's dressed for riding in tan riding breeches and a white shirt.

"You owe me an explanation," I demand, approaching him from behind.

"Take a ride with me, Daphne." He doesn't turn to face me.

"You've propositioned me before, and I've declined. I hardly think bedding the King of the Gods will help my approval rating."

"Stop being a brat and get on a horse, Daphne."

"I'm not dressed for it," I point out, gesturing at the sweater dress I chose for the day.

Xavier looks over his shoulder at me and, damn him, he changes my outfit into butter-soft jeans, a grey sweater, and riding boots.

"Who do you want to ride? There's always Abbott and Costello, or you can ride one of these babies. This is Espinhos, and his mate is Rosas. I would suggest the more mild-mannered Rosas for a chickenshit like you."

Just for that, I get Espinhos ready, and really, his name is fitting, since it translates to *thorns* in English. It takes some work for me to tack him up, and while I'm doing that, Xavier prepares Rosas.

We ease into a slow jog to warm up, and then we race through the vineyard to a wide-open field where the horses can graze. We're far from the house and the ocean, having climbed in altitude, and the vista offers sweeping views of the coast.

"What do you want?" Xavier asks, staring at all the land Essos and I have.

I take a deep breath. "Why did you need my powers last night?"

"Because Posey can feel when I use mine." His answer is swift as if he knew what I was coming to ask. "I drew primarily from yours and bolstered them with mine. Your well is deep, and the amount of mine I used wasn't enough that she'd know."

I look up, surprised that he's giving me the information I'm requesting so freely. "Really?"

"You weren't able to feel it when Essos used a huge amount of his powers?"

"No, but I was usually with him when he did. We also never shared our powers like that."

"Hmm. I would have thought that the blood bond from your marriage ceremony would have done that."

"But you didn't do a blood bond," I point out, easing Espinhos closer to Rosas.

I try to remember what I can from their wedding. It happened after Essos and I got back together, and the *Solarem Sun* was insistent that the only reason Essos had bothered to rekindle our flame was because I was carrying his love child. The truth of our breakup was never leaked, so Essos's extra attentiveness to me leading up to the ceremony—which was all groveling—was attributed to him being a doting father-to-be. Posey was, of course, livid that she had to share an above-the-fold story with my bump watch.

Now that I think about it, it was unusual for them to have not done a blood bond.

"She didn't want to," Xavier muses, drumming his fingers on his thigh.

"So how would she know..." I ask, trying to lead him back to the conversation.

The blood bond is meant to share powers between couples. As far as I know, blood-bonded couples don't sense each other using their abilities, they just...boost them. The only other blood-bonded couple I know of is Kai and Helene, and she and I aren't on the best of terms at this point for me to ask how it works for them. Galen and Callista also opted out of the ritual.

"How does who know what? Stop talking in riddles, Daphne. Why did you want to talk?" His tone is sharp, his gaze more so when he turns to look at me.

I open my mouth, then close it, not sure what riddles he means. "Do you not know what we were just talking about?" I press, reaching my hand out to touch him.

"You were asking asinine questions about powers. I didn't want Posey to know that I was using my powers and potentially trace the power surge back to Catalina. It took time for me to make the necklace with a powerful enough charm. It was more efficient if I just drew from you to heal her."

"I didn't think you knew much about healing."

He raises his cold blue eyes to mine. "The things you don't know about me could fill a book, Daphne."

"Then maybe I should double down here. Stay away from Cat. The last thing she needs is to attract Posey's attention."

"Maybe the fault doesn't lie with my affections but rather your lack of them. Try cleaning up your own house before you cast blame on mine."

Xavier turns Rosas away from me and doesn't look back as he rides away.

As I start my own ride back to the house, I'm left with more questions than answers.

18

Now that I can keep food down, I expect to feel stronger, but I don't. Even trying to call my powers is becoming troublesome, and I start to limit my attempts. Every morning, it's harder and harder to get out of bed as the realization that I'm fighting a losing battle grips me. Why should I get up? I'm thankful to Kai and Finn, because they're the ones who insist that I need to keep training.

Today, I'm seated in an arena by the sea at my estate, surrounded again by the bloodthirsty citizens of Solarem. Posey decided that, due to the nature of this event, she fancied setting it up like the Roman Colosseum, as if this were a gladiator battle feeding right into the wants of her people for the first time ever. Hopefully, today will satiate them.

I am alone on my dais, with Zara and Ellie standing a good distance behind me against the back wall of my enclosed suite. Miranda is oddly absent, but I take it as a good thing that Posey hasn't confronted me about training with Kai.

I'm thankful that the Council is located one level below me so

I can't see Helene's face during this trial. I'm going to be worried enough without adding Helene's worries to mine.

Today, Kai and Galen will fight in hand-to-hand combat until one yields to the other, and I'm not convinced we won't be here for days. Both of them are incredibly stubborn, and both have a vested interest in their side. Kai is trying to protect me; Galen is trying to own me.

I walk with Posey from the dais down into the fighting pit to mark the beginning of the trial. Galen watches me descend, tracking my every move. My skirt has several panels of red gauzy fabric that part as I walk, exposing my freshly-toned legs. The bodice is metal, the sun glinting off the gold scales. Metal-winged dragons rise over my shoulders, wings open. The armor is for show, the sweetheart neckline dipping low, leaving the tops of my breasts and my heart exposed. I look like the embodiment of what the God of War wants in a wife.

"Finally dressing for your new role?" Posey asks as we walk side by side, our skirts gathered in our hands.

"I beg your pardon?" I clench my skirts just a little tighter to keep myself from stopping and slapping her for speaking like I don't deserve to be queen. Or maybe I'm assuming that based on her tone and how much I hate her.

"The armor. You look much better suited to being the wife of the God of War instead of the God of Death."

God of *the* Dead. Why is that so hard to keep straight?

Essos doesn't want people to see him as a grim reaper, although he's so often cast in that role. The God of the Dead is a shepherd, a king who keeps the souls of those who have passed safe. He is not the specter that haunts people's dreams, seeking to rob their loved ones of their lives too soon.

"I thought it suited the event." My words sound stilted to my own ears, and I need to remember that I'm playing the part of a besotted woman.

Posey tuts. "I wish you would give more thought to using the time before the wedding to get pregnant."

This time I do stumble, and Posey is there with a soft hand to "catch" me, though I don't know how much help she's really giving, with her grip barely holding me. It's enough for the flash of a camera to capture.

"Motherhood isn't everything."

"Well, you wouldn't know, would you?" She dares to meet my eye when she says it, and I'm sure that no one would hold me responsible if I hit her for saying that. Essos and I stuck to the line that we were happy, just the two of us. That when you have eternity, children are no rush. I still jealously eyed Helene's bump when she grew pregnant and cried at home in my husband's arms on the days that it felt like everyone everywhere was pregnant and I wasn't.

"Because motherhood with all your children has worked out so well?" I ask. It's bitchy and low, and I don't know what she's dealt with or what her struggles are, but she hit me in the ovaries first, so I think I'm justified in hitting back.

She gives me a serene smile. "Daphne." She says it like she's talking to a small child. In my mind, I break her nose. "You know that I am too busy being mother to all of Solarem to deal with something like having Xavier's offspring." She gestures behind me. "Your betrothed awaits. Think about what I've said. Perhaps after this trial."

Galen's chest is bare and glistening with sweat under the sun. There are no clouds to shield the fighters on this perfect day. He wears shorts that hang indecently low on his hips, letting everyone admire the perfect cut of his abdomen, the alluring vee of his Adonis belt, and the broad set of his shoulders. The God of War is in his element. He is virile and young and vicious, and I worry that this challenge will not defeat him but only empower him.

Kai stands across from him, looking unworried. The corners of his lips lift as if he has a secret. There are no weapons in this battle; it will just be brutal man versus brutal man. Kai has a size advantage over Galen, but that may not be all it's cracked up to be if it means Galen is faster and able to dodge more easily.

I don't know if they've ever sparred together. I don't know if they've ever fought for real. Kai mentioned seeing Galen fight, but I don't remember a time that they would have been adversaries. Kai's chest is covered in tattoos, a story of the man he is and who he became. Over his heart is a starfish tattoo, and I know it's for Helene. His pants are snug on his hips, showing just how different these fighters are.

Galen approaches me first. He will not bend to his knees before me; I know this. Instead, he grips my upper arms before kissing me roughly. It's a bruising kiss, intended to show his power over me, over everything around us, and it drives his point across clearly. The crowd around us erupts, even as he opens my mouth with his and his tongue plunges in, another fight for dominance over me.

We have an audience, and I give them want they want. I keep my eyes tightly closed, envisioning that it's Essos's hair I'm threading my fingers into, the stubble on his cheeks that I feel on my palms, my husband's body that I press against. It's the only way I can get through this moment, even as tears spring to my eyes. Galen releases my arms, and one hand moves to the outside of my thigh. His fingers press into the taut muscles, and he lifts my leg to curl around his hip. I let him; I let him manhandle me, pressing me against him so I feel his arousal at my body on his, at the impending bloodshed.

I hope that Kai finds a way to do irreparable damage to this part of him.

"Enough already. We don't want to watch you copulate. We want to watch a fight!" Xavier shouts, his voice ringing over the crowd. There is some booing at this. They would love to watch us fuck and *then* watch the fight—entertainment is entertainment, after all.

Galen releases me, a fire in his eyes that wasn't there before. I hope he's overconfident in having me now, and that it will make him slip up.

Kai, King of the Oceans, kneels before me. I'm shocked to see the act of deference, his one knee on the ground, the other bracing his arm as he lowers his head. He is a king who doesn't even bow to Xavier or Essos. As far as I know, the only person he kneels for is Helene. I want to glance at her, but I keep my eyes on Kai, standing up straighter.

"You may rise." I keep my voice level and loud as I shout it. Kai gets to his feet, waiting for further instruction, not that he needs it—this is his challenge. "The objective today is to defeat Kai, King of the Oceans and Seas, in hand-to-hand combat. Weapons are forbidden. You will battle until the floor is yielded. These are the only rules." I pause, swallowing hard. I look from Galen to Kai, raising my hands into the air. The metal dragon wings bite into my skin as I wait, and wait and *wait*, before lowering my hands. "YOU MAY BEGIN!" I shout, stepping back.

They both wait until I'm clear of the pit before they start to circle each other. Each sizes the other up, waiting to see who will make the first move. It seems my betrothed is waiting for me to turn my full attention to him before striking.

Once I'm seated again, Galen makes the first move. He tries to fake out Kai by feigning right, but he twists left instead. Kai expects this and locks Galen in a chokehold. I nearly rise from my seat, expecting this to be over quickly, but Galen plays dirty, going for a nut shot, prompting Kai to release him.

They're back to circling, and Kai moves lighting-fast, driving his fist into Galen's face. Galen's head snaps back, and the crowd cheers. Zara learned at the last trial not to react, and I'm proud when she doesn't this time, her sharp intake of breath behind me barely audible. Blood drips down Galen's face in thick rivulets, and the psychopath grins. It reminds me too much of when we fought. Of when he killed me.

I look away, gesturing to Ellie for tea. I need something to settle my stomach, because I just might throw up.

I look back to see that Galen has now landed punches of his own. Kai has a cut near his eye, and his mouth is bleeding. I grip the arms of my chair, terrified about how this is going to go. Ellie presents me with a teacup, and I'm slow to sip it.

Kai flips Galen over his back like he's a rag doll and not a grown man. I can't even look at Helene to see how she is handling this. It's unbearable to watch, but watch I must.

The fight wages on for hours, and they're both wearing down with impatience. Each of them thought this was going to be a quick, easy victory, and it's not. They're getting sloppy in their attacks. Both of them have been kicked and punched countless times. They're bleeding from their legs, faces, and knuckles, skin tearing with each hit.

Galen glances up at me and finds his resolve. He strikes fast, kicking out one of Kai's feet, driving him back to the knee he bent to me hours earlier. When he staggers, Galen takes advantage, planting one foot to the inside of Kai's opposite thigh. His hands grip the back of Kai's head, and he rams his knee into his face.

It's the beginning of the end, and I know it. One of them has to come out the victor, and Galen has decided it's him. Still, Kai tries to fight on, but he doesn't have the incentive, doesn't have the same drive that Galen does. The horse Kai has in this fight doesn't mean nearly as much as Galen's horse means to him. I don't blame Kai—he's only trying to help clean up my mess.

"Do you yield?" Galen shouts as he kicks Kai in the chest. The whole earth seems to shake as the man hits the ground, his body prone. He still has some fight in him and tries to get up, but Galen is on him, raining punches onto his face, brutal and efficient. I hear my friend—my sister—cry out as her husband is beaten badly by her brother. I want Kai to surrender, to give in to Galen.

"Yield," I whisper, hoping the wind carries my words to Kai. His head turns just a little, and I think I've been successful, that he has heard me.

"I yield," Kai confirms, his voice gravely and low. The amplifiers in the stadium were planted there to catch this moment of defeat.

Galen rises and shows he can be a good sport by offering his hand to Kai. They clasp hands, and Galen helps his brother-in-law to his feet.

The Trials are now tied, one-to-one.

I'm expected to go to him now, my victorious betrothed, and congratulate him. I find I don't want to, but my feet carry me there all the same. Kai begins to drop to his knee before me again, and I rush forward, stopping him. Helene is right on my heels, pushing me out of the way and giving me a scathing glare.

"This is your fault," she hisses, and I rear back as if she hit me. I have no idea what she means, but I'm not going to pick a fight in front of onlookers. She's just trying to get to her husband; I can understand that.

"You defended my honor well. Thank you," I whisper, my voice weak in the face of Helene's vitriol. I want to hug Kai, covered in blood, sweaty and dirty though he may be, but Galen doesn't let me get close enough to even think about it.

Again, Galen pulls me against him in a searing kiss that I feel down to my soul, like he's branding me as his. I can taste the blood that stains his teeth as he does it. From what I know of Galen, he relishes in a good fuck after battle, but it won't be me he takes to bed.

I think, despite his promises, he expects to do so.

His hand moves to my ass, hauling me even closer against him with no escape. I let him lift me. I let my legs wrap around his waist as he kisses me deeply. I let my soul be chipped away with each stroke of my tongue against his. I do a better job keeping my tears at bay this time, numb to what this win for him may mean.

Kai's booming voice is what breaks us apart. "Galen has passed this trial."

I hear how it hurts him to say this. I disentangle myself from Galen, glad to have a reason to step away. I lift Galen's hand in the air, and the crowd around us erupts in cheers.

19

Kai and Galen both need to change and be healed before the party that Posey insisted on having. As they depart for their rooms, I mingle with the crowd on the beach, refusing to look Posey in the eye because I know her stupid face will just be gloating over Galen's win. I don't delude myself into thinking this is anything but her victory.

What I *can* keep from her clutches is my womb. My lady bits are *closed* for business.

The look Helene gives me as she brushes by could peel the skin off a mortal. I want to wither and die under her glare.

The pool has been covered with a clear pane, allowing people to walk over it, and there are so many in attendance that the party spills from the deck onto the sand. The last trial was so short that people lost interest by the end, but now, there is a suffocating crush all around. Noticeably, there are fewer white lilies on the lapels of the guests.

"Well, if it isn't the woman of every man's desire. If I didn't know how good-looking I was, I would be worried you came back as the Goddess of Vanity."

Slowly, so slowly, I turn to face Cassius, the actual God of Vanity. We dated so many moons ago that I don't even bother to call him an ex.

"I thought events of blood and gore were beneath you, Cassius."

He's always been in-your-face charming with a sliminess just under the surface. His brown hair is perfectly styled up and away, and if we weren't gods with magic, I would wonder just how much hair product he needs to keep it that way. His blue eyes lack warmth, only cunning interest shining from within.

But Cassius has never been cunning. Even with a giant dick, he's the reason that women know size isn't everything, it's how you use it. And he just uses it like a jackhammer. As if that's ever gotten a woman off.

"Well, I figured the Trials were a special event, and I wanted to see how my girl was doing." He slides an arm around my shoulder, and I knock it off.

"What do you want, Cassius?"

He leers at me, but I get the impression it's just for the sake of leering, not because of any actual interest. No. Cassius was always happiest watching himself jerk off in a mirror while telling himself what a great lover he is.

"Call it fondness. Call it guilt for what happened between us. I wanted to warn you."

I perk up. He tried to "warn" me once before, after we broke up and I started dating Essos. He was quite effusive in warning me that I would never enjoy the kinks that Essos did before extolling all the ways that Essos was a brutal Dom who enjoyed blood play and pain. I have to stifle a snort at the memory.

"Warn me?"

"Yes. I was at an orgy with some nymphs. They were talking about how the Council never intended to reinstate you as proper queen." His voice drops as explains.

"I *am* a proper queen."

Cassius rolls his eyes. "Sure, and I'm the God of Bad Sex. You may be given the respect of a queen—"

I do snort at this, casting my gaze about for a tray of drinks. No one around us seems to be paying attention to our conversation, but there is a photographer. Awesome.

"But without a new coronation, you're not fully a queen, not in the ways that matter. There's also talk of you not making it out of your marital bed with the God of War. I just..." Now he glances around. "You aren't a bad person. You made a great queen, and having bagged a queen was pretty great on my resume." His smirk fades. "But really, watch your back. I may not be wearing one of those stupid flowers, but that's because I'm still hoping to get in Posey's pants. It's all about that pussy bucket list."

"Ew, you still have that?" His revelations aren't all that shocking. I suspected I wouldn't survive long if I married Galen. This confirms what I already knew.

"Still need to find that Goddess Supreme. It's gotta be a supreme pussy." The slimy smile is back for half a second before he nails me with a serious look. Well... I assume it's serious, because I've never seen him without a stupid smile on his face before this moment. "One last thing—someone isn't what they seem. Don't ask for more, because I was half-stoned when I heard that, but someone right under your nose isn't who they claim to be."

This feels like more evidence that Miranda and Ellie were planted to gather information. I do want to ask him about it, even though he said not to, but Posey walks over to us. She doesn't look twice at Cassius.

"It is not appropriate for you to be talking to an ex after your betrothed just bled for you," Posey scolds, dragging me away. I try to look back at him, but he's already melted into the crowd.

"Have you seen anyone with a beverage tray?" The words are

out of my mouth before I can stop them, but it drags Posey's attention off me for just a moment. She looks around, trying to find someone circling with drinks, but there is no one to be found.

Posey releases me to find someone else to harass.

Xavier sidles up to me while his wife yells at someone about the need for passed beverages. "How is—"

"Don't ask. Not now, not ever. I appreciate your help, and she's fine, but she only stays fine if your wife doesn't know you care." Because he does care, and I think that scares me more than anything. We haven't spoken since going for that ride, but the way that he seemed unable to talk about Posey weighs on me.

"Fine."

I start to walk away but then turn quickly, looking him over. I decide to try again. "Why did you need my power to heal Cat?"

Xavier frowns. "You have a stronger affinity for healing. Lightning only brings destruction."

"And your concern about your use of power being felt? How does Posey know when you use your powers?"

Xavier's gaze clouds—this time I'm sure I see it. "Two wells of power are better than one. If you'll excuse me, I have more important people to talk to."

I let the words hang in the air for a moment, then I turn and walk away, shoulders stiff in annoyance. More important people, my ass.

I promised Cat I would let her know once the trial was over, but I'm afraid to go in the house and be cornered by Galen and find out that his promise not to push me physically was for nothing when I won't go further with him. There are some lines you can't cross and keep your soul intact.

While healers see to Kai and Galen, knitting together skin and broken bones, I have to turn on the shine for my guests, including those who tell me they're jealous that I share a bed with Galen. They're mostly minor deities who've been part of his unofficial fan club for ages and think he's some prodigious lover. From an outsider's perspective, it must look like that, with the way he lifted me up so I could practically mount him in the arena.

Other guests whisper under their breaths that I'm a traitorous whore, their allegiance to Essos still strong. I mark those faces so I know who is actually an ally, even if they think I'm not.

Galen finally joins the party, telling anyone who'll listen that his brother-in-law is still licking his wounds, as if this makes him the better man.

"Quite an accomplishment today." I offer a sweet smile as Galen sweeps me into his arms. I will not congratulate him or tell him I am proud; I will offer only quaint platitudes until I am out of his arms.

But Galen is empowered by the win. He holds me to him as we sway, not a bruise to be seen or a hair out of place.

"It's easy when I'm fighting for you. I will always fight for you." The way he says it, placing a line of kisses up my neck, makes me sick. But years of adjudicating the trials of remorseless criminals prepared me for this. It just took a month for my old mask to slide back into place. I have to look like I'm enjoying our dance, so I let my eyes drift closed as I pretend that his kisses are that of a reverent lover.

"Are you fully healed?" If he kept some bruise to show off, I can press on it and cause him a fraction of the pain he's causing me.

Galen never gets a chance to answer, because the roar of a motorcycle rips through the pathway around the side of my house.

Gods and goddesses and nymphs alike are jumping out of the way of the machine as it barrels into the party. Galen, to his credit, pushes me behind him in an effort to protect me. I want to shove him away. The person I need protection from is him.

The rider—a man, by the look of his body type—lifts his helmet, and my heart sinks.

"Well, excuse the godsdamned shit out of me. Where was my invitation to this little soiree?" My father-in-law flashes a toothy grin and looks around. I'm frozen in place, torn by the fear of having him here and the hope that maybe he'll be on my side. Galen was always very clearly the least favorite of his children.

Helene emerges from the house with Kai by her side. When she sees her father, her eyes light up. "Daddy!" she cries, running toward him. He dismounts his bike and catches Helene around the waist. She clings to him, her arms around his neck.

Once Xavier and Essos ascended to their thrones, my in-laws made themselves scarce. I haven't seen Titus since shortly after my wedding. Back when Galen started to get more aggressive toward me the first time, I tried to reach out to them to see if they could curb him. Titus admitted then that Galen was a problem— he was probably the only person who took my concerns to heart —but rather than do anything about it, he told me that the baby birds were free of the nest and I was on my own. My mother-in-law, Octavia, was equally unhelpful, refusing to admit there was anything problematic about Galen. Classic golden-child syndrome, if I learned anything from my psychology classes in college.

Galen is tense beside me, his hand curved around my hip, holding me tight. Xavier steps out of the crowd, his wife at his side for once.

"Children." My father-in-law's voice is smooth, like aged whiskey. He holds his hands open to his sons, waiting for them to embrace him. Xavier steps forward first into his father's arms. Galen hesitates, then goes to him so that his father is holding all three of his attending offspring at once.

Posey steps up beside me, and Kai flanks me on the other side, observing. My father-in-law looks incredible for his age. His dark hair is combed out of his face, which perfectly shows off his salt-and-pepper beard—more salt than pepper. This, of course, is his own doing—like the rest of us, he doesn't age. Even his leather jacket looks well-worn and scuffed, like they've seen some things together.

The siblings step apart, and Helene seems to be the only one truly excited to see him. The rest of the party shuffles around, unsure what to do.

My father-in-law steps toward me, eyes flicking from Kai to Posey. "Daphne. You look spectacular for a dead woman." His swagger is undeniable as he reaches for me. He's gentle as his calloused hands grip my arms. His rough beard scratches my cheeks as he kisses first the left then the right.

"Titus, always generous with the compliments," I greet, surprised by the genuine hint of a smile on my face. He flashes me that million-dollar grin before turning to Kai and giving him a firm handshake, and he slights Posey by approaching her last. She has no leg to stand on to make demands of him for how to address her.

Titus created the universe and us all, and she will never be as important as him.

I gesture to the musicians, and they begin to play again. Titus's discerning dark eyes study me as I set the party back in motion, and his bike moves to the front of the house by some unseen force.

"Does someone want to tell me what's going on before I call your mother? Where is Essos?" His voice is casual, but I can feel its sharp edge.

"That's what we'd all like to know," Xavier says, giving me a look. Really, whose side is he on?

Dion saves me from having to answer, walking over with the same swagger as his grandfather. His appearance brings a smile to Titus's face.

"Granddaddy!" Dion exclaims, hugging him tightly. I feel more than see Posey's eyes roll; after all, Dion is the result of one of Xavier's many affairs.

A warm hand settles on the small of my back, and I turn to see Finn, lending me strength to deal with this whole situation.

"I appreciate the affection, but I would like some answers." Titus holds my gaze, and the earth trembles beneath my feet.

"I don't know where Essos is." I spread my hands in front of me. It's not a lie that rolls off my tongue, but it just as easily could have been.

Galen steps close to me, slinging an arm around my shoulders, and Finn removes his hand to avoid detection. "Daphne and I are righting a cosmic wrong. At the end of the Trials in four months, we are to be married." To punctuate his point, Galen kisses me on the mouth. I can feel Titus watching me, waiting for more answers.

"The penchant for forgiveness knows no bounds." Titus's whiskey voice is mocking. He would know all the dirty little details about my death.

I lean against Galen, my eyes moony and only for him. "It was easy once I was able to see the wrong that the Fates did us." I cling to Galen like he is my only hope in the face of his father. I can use that Galen and Titus have never gotten along. I can use that Galen hates that Titus didn't trust him with his own kingdom, choosing instead to summon Kai from the depths of the ocean to take that crown.

"The Fates." Titus's tone is disbelieving, almost mocking. "The witches the people of Solarem put all their faith in?"

"The very same," I confirm.

"Can't forget Helene was a party that did us wrong too. She meddled in things that were none of her business," Galen snaps.

A growl escapes Kai. He might have been beaten earlier, but invoking Helene's name like that will bring a hurt that Galen couldn't imagine. Kai might not have been properly motivated to fight for me, but he will tear Galen limb from limb if he so much as thinks about hurting Helene.

"I'll repeat my earlier question. Was my invitation lost in the mail?" Titus looks from me to Finn, of course, the Messenger of the Gods. Finn tries to shrink from the look, but Dion won't let him, holding his hand tightly.

"Posey was in charge of the invitations," Dion says, not sounding apologetic at all. Posey's blue eyes flash red as she looks at Dion, who outed her without hesitation. They've never gotten along, Posey referring to Dion as *that bastard* when she thinks no one's listening, particularly Xavier, who ripped her a new asshole the first and only time he heard it.

I can't say I blame Posey for not inviting Titus and Octavia. The God and Goddess Supreme have made themselves difficult to find in their retirement. But she has no choice but to cop to it.

"I believed such affairs were beneath you. Your retirement was meant to be enjoyed, not troubled by such middling trifles as this." Posey's voice is hard. She's angry that she has to defend herself. Good. For once she needs to be on the defense.

"My son is to get married! Again! To my other son's wife. Of course, I would want a front-row seat. Essos had years of training with me to ensure he was capable of taking over the Underworld. It's only fitting that I step in again."

That training was part of what drove a wedge between me and Essos. I was a minor goddess faced with the great power that his family held. It was a culmination of meals questioning what *right* I had to date a future king, while none of those questions were lobbed at Posey. Who never, not *once*, spoke up in my defense.

I can't remember the entirety of my and Essos's time locked in the cabin, but I remember snatches of conversations between us, trying to get to the root of what went so wrong that he chose to do something so unforgivable.

I do remember that part of it was fear. After seeing the way his parents showed love, he chose to push me away.

Helene understood that and helped him to face it. She knew what her brother was doing as soon as he did it. Each of the royal children has been guilty of self-sabotage at one point or another. Their parents royally fucked them over, drilling into their heads that they could never truly be happy. Happiness was a farce; it was why Xavier was perpetually unfaithful, why Galen always wanted that which he could not have, why Helene was brutal and harsh to everyone she met, and why Essos kept almost everyone at arm's length. If they weren't close enough to hurt him, they would never be close enough for him to hurt.

I was the exception, and look what good it did him. Not only did he have to live through losing me, but he had to watch me pick Galen over him.

"That's not necessary, *Dad*." Galen snaps.

I've seen firsthand how Titus pitted his children against each other. There were little remarks at dinner about what one child did better than the other, bringing their competitive streaks to the surface. Helene could get away with murder, Galen could do no wrong, and Xavier always took the easy way out. It worked, until Essos chose not to engage any longer. But watching Titus interact with his children now, I realize something. Essos was wrong when he thought he was the odd child out and that Galen was the golden boy. Galen might have been the apple of his mother's eye, but he wasn't the apple of his father's.

"That's not up to you, son." Titus closes his hand over Galen's shoulder and squeezes. His thumb digs into the hollow of Galen's clavicle, exerting an unnamed amount of pressure. Galen refuses to blink until his father withdraws his hand.

"I can have your rooms here readied. Had I known you were

left off the guest list, I would have remedied the situation," I say, gesturing for a server.

"Don't be such a brownnoser, Daphne, it's unattractive. Enough of this crowding me. Let me have a dance with my daughter-in-law and soon to be daughter-in-law again." Titus holds out a hand for me to take, and I do. Out of the frying pan, right into the fire.

Our movements are part of choreographed dance, one we have done for centuries that Titus never seems to tire of.

When I'm close in his grip, Titus looks down at me. "You seem different."

I look up at his face. "Murder tends to have that effect on someone."

Titus laughs at my tone. "There's that fire I knew you had. Interesting, is it not? Murder of a god? Who thought a thing would be possible."

"I imagine, as the creator of all things, *you* would."

He doesn't like my tone or insinuation but can't do much about it besides crush my hand in his.

"It's not something I would have deigned to do. My scheming wife...perhaps she did. Galen was always her favorite." Titus studies my face, watching how his blow lands.

A chill skitters down my spine, but I can't show the effect his words have on me. I had considered the possibility. Was Galen clever enough to have found or forged a weapon capable of killing gods? What of the stone that captured my soul?

I keep my mask in place. "And here I thought she just hated me like a normal mother-in-law. I didn't think she wanted me dead."

"That was your first mistake—underestimating my wife and her desire to see her golden boy happy. You haven't seen her in a long time. Would you even recognize my old lady if you saw her today?"

I stare, mouth open, at Titus, who laughs in delight at breaking my mask. I think about it. Octavia's cold eyes are similar to Essos's blue, but when you make it past the ice in his, there is warmth and love. Beneath the icy shade of her eyes are mischief and anger and hate. Last time I saw her hair, it was long and a warm reddish brown, but changing hair color is easy enough to do. He's right, she could be here right now, and I might not have realized it. Fates, I do not need this whole new level of paranoia.

"Enough with the games. Titus, do you know something about the dagger that killed me?" Seconds pass as I wait for an answer, as I wait for him to decide if I deserve to know more about my death.

He seems content to let me suffer in silence, and I wonder if he'll even answer. But then...

"If someone wanted to learn something, maybe the best place to start would be the library."

The song ends, leaving Titus and I to bow to each other. I dip into a low curtsey, as I should have done when he arrived, but like me, he likes to dispense with formality. Unless, of course, he's throwing his weight around as God Supreme and all that.

Galen swoops in, pulling me away from Titus, who is only amused and offers his hand to his daughter for the next dance. Helene looks uncertainly between her husband and father, but Kai slaps her ass gently, urging her forward.

"Are you okay? Did he hurt you or say anything?"

I turn my attention to Galen, who is trying to sweep me back onto the dance floor. Rich, coming from him, but I say nothing. The arrogant prick still hasn't apologized for murdering me.

I pull back a little, grabbing a raw oyster on the half shell and a glass of champagne. "I'm fine, Galen. He just wanted to check in and see how I was adjusting." Not a total lie. I'm sure in the morning, Titus will have feedback about how I've been handling the Afterlife. Cat has done what she can from her post in bed, reviewing reports I should be looking at. She could really be up and about, but I want to keep her out of the public eye.

What a sorry queen I make.

"Did he say how long he plans on staying?" Galen sounds almost worried. Maybe having his father around will keep him on a tighter leash. He's on edge, glancing at Titus, who has his head thrown back in laughter at something Helene has said.

"I imagine until our wedding."

Galen turns his eyes on me, a fire burning in them that makes me uncomfortable. "We should see what we can do about getting him out."

Galen is shaken by his father's appearance, and I am here for it.

I reach out, putting my hand on his forearm, feigning a comforting touch. "Galen, he's not going anywhere. Get used to him being around. Otherwise, it's going to be a long four months."

I tug Galen onto the dance floor, depositing my empty cup on a waiter's tray along the way.

This might be the kindest I've been to him, the least I have fought him, since before the Calling Ball, when I was pliant and easy to mold to his wishes.

Galen lingers by my side all night, a hand around my waist, a kiss on the neck, a turn about the dancefloor. Finn keeps trying to get me alone, but every time I try to step away, Galen is right there. By the end of the night, I realize I'll have to talk to Finn at training the next day.

When I excuse myself for the night, Galen's gaze travels my body. We've been sitting around a firepit, talking to his friends, the same chumps who patrol my home at night, waiting for my husband to appear. As if Essos would do something as ridiculous as walk up to the front door. No, I think they're meant to serve as a reminder to me that, while we might be in my home, Galen and his men are the ones occupying it.

My whole being is heavy as I get ready for bed, drowning my teeth and tongue in mouthwash to rid myself of Galen's kiss. I never got a chance to talk to Kai, to thank him again for what he did. Besides Galen not letting me out of his sight, Helene wouldn't let me near Kai either.

My nightgown is smooth against my skin, and as I wipe off my makeup, I wish I could see Essos. I wish I could just lie with him, his arms wrapped around me, and hear him telling me that it will all be okay. I miss his touch, the taste of him, the feel of him on me and in me. I crack open my bedroom window, feeling stifled by the expectations around me, especially now that Titus is staying. I know that Posey's trial is next, and she already told me that she wants to plan the party immediately and have it mirror some elements of the trial.

What she really means is she wants me to plan it to keep me in her clutches as much as possible.

I plop on my bed, lying on top of the covers and missing more than just my husband. With the arrival of Titus, I have Dave and Spot patrolling the house to better keep an eye on things. They can't speak, but they have acted as our guards and our spies long enough for them to get the point across when something is amiss. I don't trust Titus. There is no way that he missed that the Trials were beginning, so I'm not sure why he decided to show up *now*. But he does love those dogs, so I'm fine having Dave watch him.

I tug the wind through my window as best I can. Doing this shouldn't be difficult, but it is. I wish I knew why my powers were on the backslide. I was doing so well the day I had to go into the Deep, but since then—really since Xavier siphoned from me—I can't even make a leaf quiver.

At least in my dreams, I have Essos.

I'm in a meeting with Posey, Helene, and a few other goddesses.

We're discussing the impact of war on marriage and childbirth when Essos pokes his head in.

"Apologies, ladies, but I need my wife." We've been married half a century, but hearing him say wife with a lift of his lips still makes my heart beat faster. I push back from my chair so fast it almost topples over, and Helene gives me a knowing look, but she doesn't say anything. Posey seethes in her seat but doesn't challenge Essos as he takes my hand.

"Is everything all right?" I ask as the door closes for the benefit of the members of my meeting. Essos leads me toward his office. Until our house is built, we're using office space at his brother's new headquarters. It makes it easier for us all to have meetings, but Essos and I still want a place of our own that doesn't leave us beholden to Xavier.

The door to his office is barely closed behind me when he pins me to it, kissing me like he's a dying man and my lips are his cure. He keeps me pulled tight against him as he navigates backward toward his desk. He breaks away from me only long enough to sweep everything from the desktop, papers fluttering to the ground. His hands grip my waist, and he lifts me, settling me onto the hardwood.

"What's gotten into you?" I laugh as he kisses down my neck. His fingers fumble with my top button, but he soon grows impatient and rips my shirt open. This is a side of Essos that he keeps caged. Whatever meeting he just had did something to his mood, and I haven't decided that I don't like it. This rough side of Essos is different, and it sends a thrill through me. My legs are spread just as much as my tight skirt allows.

"The question should be how I'm getting into you. I missed you. I shouldn't need a reason to ravish my wife."

"Do your worst, husband."

Essos drops to his knees before me, his hands reaching up to grab my underwear, which he tugs down my legs. It isn't lost on me that he's still in his full three-piece suit. He tucks my underwear in his pocket with a sneaky grin on his face.

"Perhaps, if you behave, you'll earn those back." He eases my skirt up my thighs, his hands feeling me as he goes. He doesn't kiss me, just watches my face as he does it. He likes seeing me get worked up, that my need for him is just as bad as his for me.

His breath is hot on my neck, his weight on my whole body. But that isn't right. We're on his desk. He never gets on top of me—

I blink away sleep, as lips brush my neck and a body presses between my legs. Panic flares in me, and I freeze. I need to get myself together, bring myself under control, because this person doesn't smell of cinnamon and vanilla and sandalwood. He smells like blood and pine and violence.

"Galen," I whisper, aware not only of him between my legs but also the fact that I'm wearing only a nightgown. "Stop."

"I need you," he says, his words lightly slurred. He's the God of War; it takes a tremendous amount of alcohol to get him tipsy, let alone drunk.

"Not like this," I say, still whispering. I'm afraid of getting louder, and I'm afraid of him forcing it anyway. My insides tremble as his weight settles over me.

His mouth finds mine, and I can feel him press against my middle as he deepens the kiss.

"I am battling for you. I won today. I deserve a reward." One hand moves to the hem of my nightgown and starts to hike it up. If I struggle, he'll like that. He enjoys it when I fight back. It's a game to him, but I can't just give up and lie here, because he will take what he thinks he is owed. He will take what I do not freely give.

"Galen, you promised me you would wait." It takes tremendous effort to keep the tremor from my voice. I reach for his hand to still it. He rears back, looking at me, and his hand closes around my throat instead. I grab for it to try to stop him, to put my fingers between his and my throat to keep some breathing space, but he's too fast.

"What? No cute tricks tonight?" His slur is gone, and in the moonlight I see that his eyes are clear. He knows exactly what he's doing; he thought if he pretended to be drunk, he could get away with it.

I reach for my powers, but there is no answer to my need. I couldn't even wilt a flower right now. Panic claws at my throat, at the very real chance that he will take something from me that I'm not willing to give.

I could lie here and let him get it over with, but the thought of that brings tears to my eyes. It is no more palatable now than it was when Essos told me I could do it. Fear and panic will not serve me now. They will serve only the God of War and Suffering. I need to get my head on straight and out of this position.

"Galen." My voice rasps around his hand. I'm no longer reaching for the hand around my throat but instead for my night-stand. My fingers close on the engraved metal of my letter opener, and I'm thankful I left it there after opening some correspondence yesterday. I maneuver it between us and my legs, the point just shy of his manhood.

"I need to make sure you're not defective. The only way to do that is to ensure you're carrying my child when you walk down the aisle."

Fuck that. I welcome the rage that pours through me. Adrenaline floods my veins, and I embrace this feeling of physical strength. Kai has been training me for this moment.

I press the tip of the letter opener against him, a little surprised at the way his skin gives under the weapon. I don't think he even realizes it, the prick too small to register.

"If you move another muscle, you won't be siring any more children."

He must feel it now, because even in the light of the moon I see him blanch. He releases my throat and sits up, holding up his hands in surrender. It's all for show, because then his closed fist strikes my mouth. As warmth seeps over my teeth, I don't have a chance to think, I just thrust the letter opener into his abdomen, missing his dick by an inch.

I guess they're right; every inch does matter.

"You stabbed me," he says in disbelief.

"You stabbed me first," I spit out, not removing the opener. Instead, I wrench it to the side, hoping I can eviscerate him.

I sit up and scramble out of bed as he bleeds all over my sheets, keeping the weapon in my hand between us. I'm shaking, and we can both see it, but he doesn't advance on me. Instead, he holds his gut.

"Get out." My voice waivers, but my resolve doesn't. Slowly, I inch toward the door. I open it, trying to keep my emotions from overwhelming me. My heart has crawled into my throat—or maybe that's just dinner.

Either way, I need to get a hold of myself, because if I speak right now, my words will sound strangled. I keep the blade pointed in his direction. I'll need to talk to Kai about weapons work.

"We're to be married. You are to be my wife." His hand presses the wound. It felt sizable when I was pulling against his skin, but it's smaller than his palm. The letter opener was a gift from the Goddess of the Hunt, Bria, who said it was always good to have something sharp around in case you had to put something out of its misery. I doubt she envisioned me castrating the God of War when she gifted it.

"And until that time, you can fuck anyone else you want, but *not* me. You're able to make quite the fist—try your own hand the next time the urge to rape me crosses your mind. Now, *get out* before I scream and we find out what your father thinks about you trying to force yourself on me."

Galen rises from the bed, his eyes red with fury. I can see his gaze slip to my mouth. I'm not sure if I'm bleeding from when he hit me or if he's considering kissing me again. I grip the letter opener tight, moving it just enough to draw his attention, and he seems to think better of it. It might not kill him, but it will hurt like a motherfucker; I will make sure of that. He huffs out of the room, and I watch him retreat toward his own space or to wherever it is that he plans on going.

Once he's out of sight, I close my door quietly and jam the lock. I don't think he'll come back, but I need to think.

I bring my hand toward my mouth only to see the letter opener, and I drop it with a heavy thump. I choke on a sob, refusing to let fear surface and take hold of me. I need a clear head, even if tears are falling down my face. My hands are shaking, and I want to bury my face in them but they're coated in Galen's blood.

That fact warms me. I survived his attack, and I will survive the aftermath of this too.

I want to be alone, but the urge to be free of the blood matters more, so I do something I never do—I press the bell for my ladies-in-waiting. It's going to ring to all but Cat, whom I fought to get off the summoning list while she recovered, but I have to live with that.

I sit beside the door, blocking it with my body weight until there is a knock.

I lean forward, opening the door just enough for Ellie, Miranda, and Zara to walk in. They see the bed first, the blood, and I can only imagine the thoughts running through their minds. I shut the door behind them, and all three of them jump, turning to look at me. They've all hastily dressed, hair pulled back into ponytails, robes tied around them.

I grip the doorknob and use it to rise. "Change the sheets." I leave nothing up for discussion in my tone. Zara looks at me, bewildered, before springing into action. Miranda's blue eyes find mine, void of any emotion, and she turns and immediately helps Zara strip the bed, looking at Ellie.

"Get clean sheets for Her Majesty," Miranda orders. Ellie jumps, clearly eager to be away from the blood. She pulls the door open, and before she can leave, I shove it shut, not caring that the door slams.

"If you so much as *think* about this outside the room, I will end you. That goes for all of you. Posey is not to hear about this." My voice packs the punch I want it to, because Ellie meets my eye and nods. Posey is the last person I want in my business. I release the door, and she scurries out. I look to Miranda, who has already balled the sheets and is holding them in her hands, looking unsure of what to do with them.

"Burn them," I order.

Zara picks up the letter opener, and I take it from her and wipe off the blood with my nightgown. She takes it back from me and sets it on my vanity. I realize my hands are still shaking.

"Are you okay?" Zara asks, putting a hand on my shoulder.

I flinch away from her and step back toward my bathroom.

"I expect my room to be clean of any traces of blood when I get out of the shower." I take off my nightgown and leave it on the outside door handle, then I close them out, trying hard to stop shaking. It's spread from just my hands to my whole body like I've been left in the cold with nothing on. I can't look at my hands and the blood starting to dry around my nails. I can't look at where it had stuck my nightgown to my skin. Not anymore, because that initial flood of success has left me and now I'm left with thoughts of what could have been.

For a second, I wonder if this is where Essos's mind went when he found me on the bed with my skirts hiked up and a dagger in my chest. I can't stop the keening noise as it claws out of my throat.

All I want is Essos. I want him there to soothe me and reinforce that I am okay, that I am *safe*. But this is the way of life, wanting the thing you cannot have.

I turn on the shower and sit in it, watching the water turn lighter and lighter shades of pink until it runs clear. I don't wash my hair, or move. I just sit until I feel that the ground is sturdy below me. I scrub every place Galen touched me. I scrub my thighs and my hands and my belly where the blood was; I scrub my neck and my mouth, not caring that as I scrub harder, I am beginning to bleed. I stop scrubbing only when I heard the door to the bathroom open.

Fear grips me again, and I curse myself for being so stupid as to not lock the door.

"Daph?" Zara's voice is as uncertain as I feel.

I realize the water has started to go cold, and it makes me laugh. The house is magic but still manages to empty the water heater. What were Essos and I thinking when we designed the house with such a mortal flaw? I can't stop laughing, even as Zara walks in, looking at me like I've lost my mind, which I'm fairly certain I have.

Cat is behind her, looking like Zara just roused her from sleep. She probably did, now that I think about it, and my laughter turns into tears. My two friends climb into the shower with me and hold me as I fight to recenter my world around what happened.

Neither of them speaks as they turn off the shower and help me dry and dress in clean pajamas. When we come out, Miranda and Ellie are gone, and Shadow and Spot are sitting in my bedroom, watching with their soulful eyes as my friends try to hold me together. Our next steps go unspoken as we cross the hall into Cat's room, but I can't sleep.

My mind is whirling with all I need to do.

I have to go to the Solarem library. I have to find out more about the dagger that killed me, where it is or how to forge my own. I have to do it, because I *will* kill Galen. Tonight was a step too far.

I can pretend. I can pretend in front of people that murdering me was forgivable; it happened ages ago, after all. I can pretend like the fledgling life inside me that he also killed was nothing more than a bundle of cells at that point, not even the dream of a tiny god. I can pretend I have rediscovered my feelings for him.

But I cannot pretend my way past this transgression. I cannot pretend that, if he had pushed it, if he had gotten what he wanted, I would have been able to get out of bed again. I wouldn't have been able to do it. But I don't have to, because I'm prepared.

I will not be caught defenseless again. I need to figure out what is happening with my powers, and I need to step up my training with Kai. Everyone else can be damned. I don't care if they know what I'm doing. I don't care if they can see what I'm up to. I don't care if I'm transparent as a window.

Galen has to die.

20

Titus gazes at me from across the table. We're eating breakfast outside, as a family, something that he requested. Even Xavier and Posey have graced us with their presence. Titus said it's something he wants, that he's missed his children and wants to see them all in one place, even if it's sans Essos.

I think he's a sadist. We'd all sooner stab each other than hug. Helene and I still aren't talking, and I've been ignoring Galen all morning. When I have looked at him, there's been no sign of shame on his face.

Galen tries to catch my eye, but I've taken a seat as far from him as possible, sitting at the end of the table, away from most of the family. I would have sat by Helene, but her glare when I looked at that seat made me second-guess myself.

I've chosen to read the paper instead.

Which was my mistake. I expected a brutal photo of Kai and Galen trading blows. But no. Instead, there's a gallery of images showing my kiss with Galen, including one of Kai giving us a dirty look. The caption below that one muses on the thought that Kai is perhaps jealous of the attention I've been giving other men and that he chose this fight to make a case for my hand.

Well, that explains why Helene looks like she wants to knock my teeth in. Of course, there is also a great shot of me and Cassius gazing into each other's eyes. Queen of War. Queen of the Rebound. What clever name will they think of next?

The picture of my kiss with Galen chokes my insides. I look like I'm enjoying it, and I know that was the message I meant to send, but did I do too good of a job? Why else would Galen have felt brave enough to come to my room?

My fists close around the paper, tearing it.

No. I didn't ask for Galen to come to my room last night. No amount of kissing equals consent. What is going to keep me upright today is the reminder that I got away. It doesn't make it better, it doesn't minimize what happened, but for me, for now, I need to hold on to that message, because I cannot afford to let this break me. I cannot afford to let my mind be derailed by Galen's actions. If I keep looking ahead, I can keep going.

Kai slams his fits on the table, dragging our attention to him. "These are the best damn waffles I have ever had," he says through a full mouth.

I appreciate the attempt to diffuse the situation. I still have a bruise on my face from where Galen struck me, and Titus's eyes are drawn to it as he idly rubs his beard. I couldn't heal it even if I wanted to, with my powers so useless. And I don't want to heal it. I want Galen to have to explain what happened last night.

I should have known better. No one asks me about it.

"I will give your compliments to Estelle. I'm sure she'll appreciate the praise," I manage to choke out, my eyes flicking to Kai then back to my plate. I push the scrambled eggs around.

"Estelle is still here?" Titus asks, his eyebrows raised. "I was curious to see who she went with after we closed the main house." As each child went to their own marital home, Titus and

Octavia stopped trying to maintain the illusion that they had a functioning marriage and moved into separate spaces.

"Yes, well, Essos managed to charm her to come here, and then he tucked and ran," Xavier snaps, sending a scowl my way.

Estelle came here because I was always nice to her when I visited their family. I asked her to teach me to bake cookies.

"He isn't here because someone was usurping his throne and all you did was stand in the corner, sipping your drink and letting it happen." I keep my tone even. Titus clearly hasn't been brought up to speed about what his children have been up to in his absence.

"Someone else already set the charges on that particular explosion. All I did was watch," Xavier hisses at me.

"Well, I'm looking forward to my trial! It may not be the most exciting visually, but I think it will be fascinating," Posey says to no one in particular. Although Estelle made her requested breakfast of egg whites with diced peppers, she hasn't touched it.

"No one cares," Xavier, Helene, and I all snap at her. I have no patience today.

Titus leans his elbows on the table. "What did my son do? You were all lovey-dovey last night, and today, I'm afraid you're going to peel his face off with a spoon." Titus stares at me.

"That's not a bad idea," I mutter under my breath. It's mostly to myself, but the grin on Titus's face tells me he heard me. This is my moment to deflect blame back on Galen, but before I have a chance to answer, Helene jumps in.

"Daddy, how long are you staying?" she asks, flashing me a blank glance. I don't know if she meant to draw attention away from me, but it leaves me feeling conflicted. I want Galen to answer for trying to take liberties, but I'm afraid of what I'll hear if I speak up.

You were asking for it. You're a tease. You should stop being so much trouble.

I stay silent and pick pomegranate seeds from the fruit.

"Oh, my little Goddess of Stars, I'm staying until the wedding. Maybe *this* wife will do your brother some good."

My nostrils flare. Callista was too good for Galen—too good for all of us. She was the Goddess of Healers, and she and Galen were wed shortly after Essos and me. But I can't think of any other details about her, and it frustrates me.

I don't have the patience for games today. I push back my seat to stand. Kai, Xavier, and Titus all jump up in a gentlemanly way, but Galen watches me, seething. *Good.* Fucking stew for all I care.

"If you'll excuse me, I have work to do." I had said that I would leave ruling the Underworld to Galen, but I won't anymore. I can't. I'll do anything I can to save it, even if that means only reading reports and planning how to fix what is broken by the God of War.

"We have therapy in an hour," Galen says smugly.

I can barely stand to look at him.

"Some things not even therapy can help." I leave without another word.

When I open the door to the office, Waffles yowls and sprints for the stairs. There are deep gouges on the inside of the door, and I realize where my cat was last night. It makes me want to cry, but I focus on feeling numb instead.

I have five blessed minutes alone before Titus shows up. He never knocks, just opens the door and closes it behind him. I ignore him, hoping that if I pretend he's not there, he'll tire of this and leave.

"Avoiding everyone today?" Titus drops into the chair across from me.

I look up from the report in front of me, one that Cat provided, summing up information that Sybil has been able to sneak us. Fewer and fewer souls are passing into their afterlives. The tithe requirements have been set higher and higher. The only upside is, with souls stuck in the Inbetween, there are fewer cases to adjudicate. Not that I can do anything about that anyway. The stack of adjudication requests sits on the corner of my desk, mocking me.

"Something like that."

"You know, for someone who wants to rule, you're doing a terrible job of it. I've seen reports from the Underworld. You're failing in spectacular fashion."

My head snaps up to him. "*You're* seeing reports?"

"Not all of them. I used to get a monthly status, but I haven't since the Calling ended."

Essos and I *never* provided reports to anyone, so I have to ask. "Who's been giving you the information?"

"Sybil, of course. I'm the one who sent them to Essos after your unfortunate accident."

I can't help but feel a stab of betrayal. I'm sure Sybil didn't see how it could be a problem. Maybe Essos knew they were sending the reports, but it feels like something else I've been kept in the dark about.

I look away from Titus to what is in front of me now. Cat has been providing me with a summary of our finances, the cases that need adjudicating, and the rate of attrition for our workers. With souls not passing on, my employees have less work to do. The barriers between the levels are further eroding. I can only hope that something like what happened in the Deep doesn't happen again. The tremors have nearly stopped, but every so often, I notice a ripple in my beverage.

I rub my temples and read the report of a skirmish around a diamond mine in the mortal realm. Over five hundred dead after a rogue gang decided to take over the operation. They massacred the town around the mine and all the workers, only for the government to sweep in and eradicate them. The loss of human life is staggering, and my heart hurts not just for my people, but the mortals.

"I have an actual realm to run. While your son might think that taking over for Essos means not having anything to do, he's wrong. Essos was damn good at his job."

"I know. I *am* the one who trained him." Titus isn't smug, but matter-of-fact.

I reshuffle the papers on my desk. "Is there something I can actually help you with?" I ask, glancing at him before looking for a pen on my desk. I should be able to conjure one, but I'm still tapped out. This is all sorts of cause for concern, but at this point, I feel like the dead horse everyone is beating.

Titus conjures a pen himself and offers it to me before taking a file from my desk and thumbing through it. "Where are the financial statements from the banking system? Has Xavier reviewed them?"

I reach across my desk and snatch the file back from him. "When you retired and relinquished power to your sons, you gave up the right to have input on how business in the realm is conducted." I drop the file into a drawer. I don't know what that particular file was about, but I don't want him to have it. I could see if he'll help me, but I'm wary. I feel like a dog who's been kicked too many times. It's easier to make him an outlet for my frustration. My bad mood hasn't driven him from the room yet, so maybe there's a chance for me to get my head on straight when it comes to Titus.

"I relinquished power to my son, not his wife, the Goddess of Spring." His smooth voice doesn't reflect the amused look on his face.

"Haven't you heard? The Goddess of Spring is dead. Long live the Queen of the Dead."

Titus doesn't have anything to say about that, but I can see his respect for me tick up, just a little. Whatever good that does me.

"How has Galen's involvement been in management?"

In answer, I rise from my chair and pour us both a stiff drink. I hand one to Titus and take a sip of my own, despite it being before noon. "I'm sure you can imagine. There's a reason you didn't give him his own kingdom, is there not?"

Titus laughs, taking a sip. "Among other reasons, yes. Gods, Essos did always have good taste, in drink and in women."

"I'm going to pretend you're not talking about my husband's involvement with other women."

"Why couldn't I be talking about you, Daphne?" There's a mischievous glint in his eyes when he says it, and I can't help but snort into my drink.

"Because I don't need a Daddy. I need my husband. Why are you really here, Titus? It's not because of the Trials, and it's not because of the wedding. So, level with me. I always was your favorite child-in-law." I sit on my desk right in front of him.

"So, you're going to pretend that you weren't all over your husband's brother yesterday? You can have your dalliances, but he can't have his? That's awfully sexist. And you're wrong—I brought Kai into the world all on my own, dragging him from the depths of the ocean, which makes *him* my favorite. It's perfect that he married my favorite child as well." When I remain silent, making it clear to him that I'm not going to play ball, he huffs. "I'm here because a change in power worries me."

"You can undo this. You can put Galen back into whatever terrible little hole he crawled out of. He closed the Garden of Evil. He tried to use the souls as slave labor. Essos and I had meeting after meeting with you to establish the boundaries for the Underworld. You were there when we spilled our blood to draw the lines between where each part of the Afterlife started and ended. You can fix this." I feel stupid hope rising in my chest. It takes a herculean effort to not grab him by his lapels and shake him.

"I could, but I won't. Maybe I underestimated Galen. Maybe he does have the chops to rule this cute little empire you have set up."

217

"Cute little empire?" I take in a deep breath through my nose, letting my eyes close.

"I said what I said, sweetheart."

"I have honestly *had* it with all of you. The condescension, the barbed comments. I'm a member of this family and have been for centuries. Why is everyone acting like I *just* got here? Essos and I built this *together* from what you left in shambles. We made it so there wasn't just vast emptiness for mortals to deal with when they came to the Afterlife. We established the Deep and the Garden of Evil and real places for souls to go after they died. We built *your fucking economy* with the tithes of my people, and you want to act like, what? Like it's all disposable? You want to know what's happening?" I lean back on my desk, shuffling folders and pages until I find what I'm looking for—the report on the funds set to keep our kingdom running, which clearly shows that the surplus we've had for eons is slowly but surely dwindling away right there in black, white, and red ink. The little red arrow highlights the not-so-steady decline.

Titus takes the report and looks at it, his mouth stuck in a grim line as he studies the numbers. Occasionally, he lifts his finger to track the columns on the page in front of him.

"These are not the numbers I've been seeing," he tells me stiffly.

"No, because there's been a total lockout. I'm not able to do anything with this information. I'm barely allowed to know. Whoever said knowledge is power was wrong. Having this knowledge does nothing for me or the Underworld."

"I'm not sure what you're extrapolating from this data, but to me, it looks like ring-around-the-Posey has too many rings."

I throw my hands up. "That *would* be your takeaway. That Xavier has a spending problem, not that Galen is choking the financial system to death."

"And how, sweetheart, is he doing that?"

The pet name chafes.

"If you need me to explain it to you, then maybe you're not the all-powerful God you pretend to be."

He stands, moving faster than any natural being, faster than Finn, if I were to guess, and I'm slammed against the wall behind the fireplace. My head hits hard enough that I see stars, but I refuse to break eye contact with him.

Being in Titus's grip doesn't send me down the same panic spiral I would have expected after last night. Maybe on some level, I know I don't have anything to fear from Titus. He holds me by the throat, but it's not the same crushing grip his son had last night. It's a reminder that he *is* the all-powerful being in the room, and I am nothing but a minor goddess in his presence who should be honored that he would deign to talk to her. I'm tired of being manhandled, but right now, I'm outclassed.

"Do you need a lesson in who I am?" Titus's voice is low and gruff, rough edges all around.

"No, Supreme One, I do not." My voice drips with sarcasm and condescension, but still, Titus lets me go. I try not to sag with relief. His fingers come to my jaw, where the bruise from Galen darkens my skin.

"I trust you didn't let this stand?" Of course, his father knows what a monster his son is. He raised him. By pitting his sons against each other, he created the toxic environment that made each of them the way they are. Xavier and his inability to stay faithful, Galen with his brutal determination to take what isn't his, and Essos...my sweet Essos and his inability to see that he is worthy of so much.

"I couldn't afford to." If I let Galen get away unscathed last night, what else would he dare to try?

Titus walks back to the decanter and pours himself another drink. "I'll have a conversation with my son."

"I don't need you to fight my battles for me, Titus." Galen will see it as weakness, and I'm sure whatever punishment Galen would choose to dole out for me telling tales would be all the worse for involving Titus. I don't think there's a being Galen hates more than his father.

My father-in-law took pity on me once. I was a being born of the ground, the Goddess of Spring, taking root and sprouting on the petals of a flower.

I was born fully formed, the way all gods and goddesses were, and I came to Solarem to learn what it meant to be a goddess, what my life meant. As the God Supreme, Titus liked to claim all the minor gods and goddesses as his children, but only Essos, Xavier, Helene, and Galen were literally born from him and his wife.

I stay where I am beside the fireplace, watching Titus's movements, recognizing Essos in the way he rubs his jaw, deep in thought, and how he grips his drink. It awakens this ache in me that I didn't realize I had. I miss the idiosyncrasies of my husband.

"I should leave you to it, ruling your realm. I do mean that sincerely. I'll be having a conversation with Xavier about interference. Your sister-in-law was looking for you before I came by, something about having to plan the party after her trial." That means Posey, and I would rather hide in my lit fireplace than seek her out.

"Thank you for the warning," I say.

"I would also stop drinking that tea—it could be the reason you can't even make a leaf quiver right now." He motions to the tray on my desk, where my half-drunk tea has gone cold.

I impale him with my stare. "What?" I snap, my voice sharp enough to cut a man in half. I almost want it to, but now I need answers.

"Your powers. Someone is trying to bind them." Now he's smug, knowing something I don't.

"How could you know that?" I look at the teacup as if it might attack me.

"I'm the God Supreme. I can feel power radiate off every being. It's why I allowed Posey to marry into the family—she has a lot of untapped power. I know what your power should feel like, and it doesn't feel right. That could be because you've been killed and brought back, but you recently turned the entirety of the Deep into a grove of magnolia trees, and now you feel weak. Somehow, I don't think the depth of your powers is the problem."

"Why tell me this now?"

"Because it suits my interests. Simply stopping the tea should reverse the limitations."

I think of my desperation last night, reaching for my powers and finding only the absence of them. The world shifts below me, and I collapse into the chair Titus had been sitting in.

Titus opts not to elaborate on how I could serve his interests, instead exiting my office and leaving me alone.

I want to scream and rage. I get up and grab the tray to lift it and hurl it across the room, but I pause, looking into the drink. I swirl the liquid around the dainty teacup as if I can divine something from it.

Another deception...or is this an attempt on my life? Why can't I catch a fucking break?

I shouldn't be surprised, but I've never heard of something with the ability to bind powers. Then again, before Galen murdered me, I'd also never heard of a weapon that could kill a god, and here I am, back from the dead. There seems to be a first for everything.

I set the teacup down gingerly on the tray before carrying the tray to the kitchens. I'm glad I don't encounter any of my meddling in-laws as I go. I don't say anything as I step into the kitchens, trying to remain as unseen as I can.

Estelle doesn't miss anything in her kitchen, and she follows me when I go straight to her office. She shuts the door behind her.

"How can I help you, Your Majesty?"

"I need you to find out what's in the tea I'm being served." I'm careful when I place the cup on her desk, trying not to spill the remaining liquid.

"It's your standard tea, the one you've always been served. Vanilla, cinnamon, and butterscotch with rose petals."

Realization makes my knees weak—the tea always makes me feel so warm inside because it has hints of Essos in its scent. But I have to focus on the issue at hand.

"Someone has been putting something in my tea. I have my suspicions as to who. Now I need to know what. Whatever's in it is binding my powers."

Estelle stiffens. "Someone is trying to bind your powers? Why would they do that? How would they do that?"

"I think *why* is easy enough. I want to know how, and I want that way eliminated. I know I don't have to stress the need for discretion. You are, however, to allow the tea to continue to be served. When it is, discreetly have another tea sent to me within the hour. You are only, *only,* allowed to send the clean tea with Sybil, Zara, or Cat."

Estelle nods, studying the cup as if it's going to attack her. "Of course, ma'am."

"Thank you."

Estelle looks like she wants to say something more, but she hesitates. I wait one more moment for her to speak and, when she doesn't seize the opportunity, I leave.

21

Cat is in bed reading the same issue of *Solarem Times* that I read this morning. The article she's reading is all about the fight between Kai and Galen. When I realize that was only yesterday, I want to sleep for a week. I don't understand *how* it was only yesterday, but time is funny like that.

She lowers the paper to look at me, her gaze flicking to my bruise then back to my eyes. Her blond hair is pulled into a ponytail at the top of her head, a mug in her hand. Since I put her on bed rest, she seems to have gotten better. I think. Despite what she says, she wouldn't tell me otherwise anyway. Cat is reading about Galen's victory; she won't want to worry me.

I flop facedown onto the pillows beside her. This morning when I woke up, she let me slip out of the room to get ready on my own. I wasn't ready to talk about what happened last night, and I'm still not. I appreciate the space she's giving me. I need it more than I thought.

"How was the victory party?" she asks.

"Can we talk about literally anything else except Galen and the stupid Trials?"

"Are you okay?" she asks, placing a hand on my shoulder. "Never mind, that was a stupid question. Of course, you aren't okay."

I ignore all that. "Like, Chad from meteorology. Do you think he's achieved his dreams? Do you think that he's working for the Weather Channel yet? What about that girl Missy from our floor freshman year, who would always self-sabotage her dates? Do you think she's okay?"

"Wow, you really do want to talk about anything else."

Shadow scootches closer and licks my face.

"Yes." I pop up. "Let's go for a walk. I need to beat the shit out of something. I've kept you cooped up long enough."

This is enough to distract Cat, who nearly leaps to her feet as she buzzes with excitement. "Meet in the hall in a few minutes? I'm still in my sleepwear chic." She gestures at her pajamas.

I appreciate the gesture; it allows me to go change as well.

I try to be all smiles and provide happy chatter as we head outside to the beach and then to the training arena. Titus is outside, tanning himself in one of the lounge chairs by the pool. Where everyone else is I don't much care. Titus was right. If I have to see Galen again, I will peel his face off with a spoon or the nearest blunt instrument I can find.

I frown when I see that the training grounds are not empty as I hoped. Kai is there, working on the wooden Wing Chun dummy. His hands fly through the air artfully, not missing a beat as he flows gracefully through the movements. That is, until he hits one of the dummy's arms so hard it flies off and lands at our feet. One hard kick from Kai, and the entire piece shatters from his frustration.

"So, you're not the only one working out your anger today," Cat mutters to me.

Kai looks up. "Daphne, Catalina. I'm—"

"Stop. If you're about to apologize, I don't want to hear it." I squeeze his arm in sympathy. I hate that Galen has left Kai feeling inadequate and like he needs to apologize to us. We're all learning that we've underestimated Galen for too long.

"Think you can teach me how to do that?" Cat asks without giving Kai and me a chance to address the proverbial elephant in the arena. The trial Kai had been so confident in couldn't have gone worse. He lost, and it left Galen emboldened enough to enter my rooms in the middle of the night.

"Of course, I can." Kai waves her forward, and seawater creeps unnaturally onto the floor before him. Slowly, it takes the shape of the dummy that was there before, the water rippling until it settles into the form and solidifies. It makes me miss my powers even more. Sure, they were unruly, and I struggled to have a firm grasp on their capabilities, but they were a part of me that made me who I am. Not having them, even briefly, feels like I'm missing a limb.

"Holy shit," Cat says, awe in her voice. She's still adjusting to this world of powers and total magic. During the Calling, Essos was conservative with his powers and what he showed us he could do. We saw the magic closets and the tricks he pulled out for us from time to time, but he kept most of his skills hidden.

Unlike his brothers. Xavier never hesitates to flaunt his abilities, and Galen is a showoff in equal measure.

"Did you come here to beat the shit out of something too?" Kai asks me as Cat pokes at the dummy.

"I did."

Kai grips my chin, and it reminds me of the way Essos did the same, months ago when we were playing a stupid flag football game. He studies the bruise on my cheek, his eyes darkening.

"Did he do this?" Kai's voice is on the edge of losing control.

"I handled it." I turn my head so my chin is no longer in his grasp. I should open up to him, to my friends. Not just about the pressure I feel to protect the Underworld, but about what happened last night. But it feels too daunting.

"Did you? He was walking just fine this morning."

"The blood on my sheets tells a different story."

Kai gives me an approving nod. I grit my teeth, and Kai seems to take the hint.

Nothing happened. Nothing happened. Nothing.

"Let's work out our anger in a productive way." Kai starts by setting me up with some exercises I can do on my own while he gives Cat pointers in self-defense.

Taking control back, even if it's just by being active, feels good today. Since talking to Estelle about my nausea, it's gotten better. I've been able to eat more, and my energy is finally making a comeback. I still have bouts of nausea as the day starts, as if my body is re-remembering the situation we're in and is sick all over again, but they soon pass.

Cat doesn't last long with the exercises. She tires quickly, and I think it's more than just being a mortal soul; I think she's still not feeling well but won't tell me. It's barely been a half hour, and she's sitting off to the side, drinking water under the guise of not wanting to impede my anger management.

I ask Kai to teach me what to do if I'm pinned to the ground. I can feel a change in the air when I ask, anger flooding his veins that I even need to ask this question. I should feel safe in my own home, but the truth is, I don't. And I'm not. I've already resolved to sleeping in different rooms for the time being, until my powers are back or I can ask someone to put additional locks on my door. The ones there now are magical, to prevent someone from tampering with them. Never in my life did I think that would be a necessity. But the number and type of locks I have won't help me if I forget to lock them.

I won't make that mistake again.

I get angry all over again. My powers should be able to protect me. I shouldn't need to ask for help. The emotions rise in me, and I close my eyes to squash my tears. *It could have been worse* becomes my mantra.

Kai gestures for me to get on the ground. "Are you sure?" he asks, as I lower myself to lie on my back.

"This is what self-defense is about, right? I need to be able to get myself out of any type of bind." I'm trying to keep my breathing steady, but it's already erratic.

"If at any point it's too much, I'll stop. We'll go at your speed."

I nod, knowing that I have to focus on this being Kai. Nothing happened, but the fear of what could have happened still makes my heart slam in my chest. My mantra keeps me going for now. Surviving day by day is the name of the game at this point.

Kai sets himself between my legs with space between us so I can ease into the feeling. He's instructing me how to move my arms and shift my weight. If I don't think about the weight of him on top of me, I'm able to push past the claustrophobia, the feeling of being trapped. This is Kai, and Kai isn't going to hurt me. My chest feels tight, as an invisible force closes itself around me. I want to draw my knees up to my chest to escape the mounting pressure, but I can't. *I can do this.* A slow breath out through my nose.

I am okay.

I am not okay.

I am not okay, but I can't let the world see me break. I have to keep my gaze on Kai's kind brown eyes, even as his brow dips with worry.

I focus on doing what I'm told, and then Kai has me go through the whole thing. We go through it once, and then I have him start again. By the time we reset, so has my mind, and I need him to coach me through it.

"What, two of my brothers isn't enough? Now you want my

227

husband too? You think you can get him hurt and fuck it better?" Helene's voice calls as she approaches. Kai gets up, offering me his hand, which I take.

"Starfish," Kai chides, walking to embrace her. He wraps his broad arms around her, but she glares at me over his shoulder.

Helene doesn't know what happened. At least this is an easy enough issue to explain away. Maybe it can start to clear the air between us.

"I thought if you two were training, I was the cover story. Or did you just use me for no good reason, Daphne, the way you seem to use everyone in your life?" She sniffs.

"We ran into each other out here, Hel. I wanted to blow off some steam with Cat." I sigh. I'm tired of fighting with her when I don't know what I did wrong.

"You don't need to be a bitch," Cat snaps, walking over and sliding an arm around my waist. Her thin frame leans against me, and I can feel just how much weight she's lost since getting sick. I need to be better about checking in with her more.

What a mess I have made of my court.

"Talk back to me one more time, and I'll turn you into a beetle and squash you." Helene takes a threatening step toward Cat, with no intention of doing anything, but I still reach for my powers. For the thing within me that isn't there. The others see it too, the way I raise my arm to defend, but nothing happens. Even nature seems to take notice, the waves no longer crashing and the birds silent where they sit.

"You will do no such thing. Lest you forget, this is my home, Cat is a member of my court, and any action against her is an action against me."

Helene is still focused on my raised hand, and she lashes out, blasting me with a gale of wind. The last time she pulled this move, I was able to react, catch myself. But this time, I hit the ground hard and roll backward onto my stomach. The wind is thoroughly knocked out of me, and I struggle to suck in even a little bit of air.

I lie there, aching all over. Too tired of it all to even move. It was a targeted blast, leaving Cat standing.

I glare at Helene. "I'm not dealing with one of your temper tantrums, Helene. Go cry to someone who cares." I push up from the ground and limp past her, an uncomfortable ache in my knee from when I rolled.

"Why didn't you use your powers to block me?" Helene asks. She sounds more curious than anything.

"If you want to pick a fight, find someone else. I'm not in the mood. Not with your father lurking around, not with Posey trying to get me to plan another stupid fucking party. I have enough on my plate." I push past her, not looking to see if Cat is following. I can hear her steps, so I know she is. "If you're not going to stand behind me, get the fuck out of my way."

Kai stays silent. I don't blame him.

"I *saw* him. I saw him go to your room last night. If you aren't fighting for Essos anymore, just tell us so we don't waste our breath keeping you in the know."

I turn slowly at what she said. "You saw Galen...walking into my room last night...and you didn't *stop* him?" My voice is dead. Helene was supposed to be my friend; she was supposed to be like a sister to me. This doesn't make sense.

"I figured you invited him, with the way you acted after he beat my husband half to death. You didn't even ask how Kai was after he bled to defend you. I thought you were doing what you always do, taking the easy way out."

There is so much to unpack in her statement that I don't even know where to start. "Has it not occurred to you that I *want* him to think that? Has it never dawned on you that if I pretend to be interested in him, he might let his guard down? Do you not realize that I'm bartering away my soul to my murderer to *save my husband*?

"Because that's what I'm doing. And what do you mean, I always take the easy way out? I'm *here*. I'm fighting *every day* to maintain the scraps of control I do have. My life isn't my own. If I step too far out of line, Galen will kill Cat and Zara. He could still have the fucking dagger, and he could just kill me *again*." Tears are burning my eyes. "Feel free to tell your brother to fuck off from my rooms if you ever see him near them again. While you're at it, you can fuck off out of my life."

There is a stunned silence as my words sink in.

"Daphne, you don't mean that." Kai's words might be true eventually, but right now, in this moment, with my anger welled up with nowhere to go, I *do* mean it.

"You were ready to give up on Essos once before in favor of Galen. You picked him during the Calling. You've been sucking his face at every turn. What was I supposed to think?"

"You were supposed to be my sister, Helene. You were supposed to trust me. Trust *me*. Galen almost raped me last night." I choke out the words. They're not ones I was ready to say out loud, but it's too late to claw them back. Immediately, I try to minimize what happened, because it *didn't*, and in the grand scheme of things, isn't that what matters? "He didn't. It didn't get that far. But last night could have gone so much worse, and it would have been all your fault. I can't look at you." It's unfair of me to lay that on her, but I need to put these feelings somewhere, because I can't carry them alone anymore.

I limp off, faster than I expected. Cat catches up to me and slips her arm into mine.

"What am I supposed to think, Daphne?" I can hear the anguish in Helene's voice as she calls after me, but I can't look at her, not right now. I know what I'll see in her eyes—pity—and I won't accept that. "You won't talk to me. You won't talk to *anyone*. Even Cat says you hardly come see her, and Zara perpetually looks like she's one bad mood away from being voted off the island. Don't get me started on Finn. You want to take this all on yourself, fine, but don't cry to the rest of us when we don't know what's going on in your head! You come here, you train, and that's it. Stop pushing us away. This isn't your burden to bear alone."

Helene sounds almost desperate, and when I do stop and look back at her, safe in her husband's arms, I get mad all over again. Despite what she says, I'm not pushing everyone away. I'm just trying to handle things the best I can, and that means protecting everyone as best I can. The less everyone knows, the better. If they don't know anything, Galen can't hold it against them.

I huff off, not giving Helene an answer. It's a slow huff, my knee aching with every step I take.

"Do you want to talk about last night?" Cat asks quietly. I stop and look at her, then glance back at where Kai and Helene are now arguing.

I shut my eyes tight to stop the tears. I need to look at this like it happened to someone else in another life. "Nothing actually happened. He...he came to my room expecting to collect the spoils of war, and I was not willing to reward him. I stabbed him with that letter opener you like so much.

"But what scares me more than Galen is the fact that I can't access my powers. I'm completely powerless right now." The last part comes out as a whisper. I'm afraid to say it too loudly, in case someone hears me and uses it against me.

Cat hugs me tightly. "Just because he didn't get what he wanted doesn't mean that something traumatic didn't happen. I get that you're a goddess and a queen, but it sounds like last night was really rough. You don't have to downplay it to me, and if you ever want to talk more about it, I'm always here."

I start crying harder, holding on to Cat. She's my life preserver when I didn't realize how badly I was drowning. I thought I was treading water, but I haven't been for a long time. "I don't know why you are. I've been a terrible friend to you. You nearly died. My actions last night could get you killed," I say, squeezing her. "I've been neglectful and trying to shield you from all of this. Last night with Galen's win, and with Galen himself, and now my powers, I just... I feel like I'm failing on every front, and I don't know how to fix it." I pull away and wipe my eyes.

Cat reaches out to catch a few errant tears as well. "Can I be honest with you? Like without offending you, your grace majesty highness or whatever I'm supposed to call you?"

I snort and nod. "Now's your time. Chances of being smote are pretty low while I'm powerless." My joke falls embarrassingly flat.

She grips my upper arms, looking me in the eyes.

"You're trying to do too much. I get it, you're a queen and you're supposed to, but you've been back for like fifteen minutes! You're trying to run your realm, get your husband back, keep your brother-in-law at bay, train, work on your powers, attend therapy, and plan a monthly party. Let's not forget that you're also trying to keep me and Zara safe and plan a wedding. It's a lot, and I'm sure there's still more you're not telling us, about your memories coming back and your powers and everything. You need to give yourself a break. Like, a real break. If Galen wants to run the realm, let him see what it takes. If Posey wants to plan the party, let her. I think you should be seeing Luminara separately from your little couples therapy, and if not Luminara, then another professional, but you need a *break*. A break from the house, a break from everyone."

"Those aren't smitable words."

"You never know. I mean, Posey turned someone into water."

"Yes, well, she tends to overreact. I just—if I leave Galen in charge, I'm failing. I'm letting my people down. He's already destroyed the Garden of Evil—those little tremors you've prob-ably been feeling are from the Underworld—but I don't dare try to return without him after what happened when I went to the Deep. He has his people working security, and they'll report back to him. He's wreaking havoc, both on my world and on the mortal world. I hate to see what he's going to continue to do."

"Right, but you can't fix it at all if he wins. You need to let your body and mind heal. Is there somewhere you could say you're going for a spa trip?"

I think about my conversation with Titus, about needing to look into the type of weapon that could kill a god. He was cryptic about what I could find, annoyingly so, but it got me thinking. I need to do some research, and the best place to do that is the library in Solarem.

"There's a spa in Solarem, but I don't know if we can get there before Posey's challenge. With Titus here, I'm not sure I can convince them to let me go."

"Then you just have to spend the next month the way everyone else around here does—do nothing and cry about how busy you are. I mean, Xavier talks about how important he is as King of the Gods, but I never see him *doing* anything other than leveling people who dare question him with a glare. I swear, he spends more time gelling his hair than he does even reading the paper."

I don't slow my steps. "You're still talking then?"

Cat winces. "I hoped you hadn't noticed that. I mean, he pops in to check on me every so often, and you've been so busy. I can't resist."

It's another reminder of what a shitty friend I've been. "He is pretty hard to resist. I get it, I just...you really can do what you want, but he's *married*."

"And that means I hate it even more when he comes to see me

and makes me laugh. I would never *do* anything with him. I just like having someone to talk to."

Add that to the list of my failures lately. "How have you been feeling—and please be honest. None of this 'I'm fine' bullshit you've been peddling." We're in sight of the house now, so I stop us while we're still on the beach, dropping into the sand unceremoniously. She follows me down, kicking off her shoes.

"I'm exhausted. I think if I lie down right now, I'll pass out. I don't know what to do about it either. Nothing seems to be working. The charm was a good idea, but I'm not sure it's doing the trick."

I reach toward the necklace but lower my hand before touching it. "Keep it on anyway. I don't want to risk it, if it is doing some good. It took considerable power for him to make it."

"How did Xavier and Posey end up together anyway?" I hear the interest in her voice, and I've already warned her off all I can.

"You'll have to get the full story from him, but she sort of just appeared one day. It was before Essos and I were married. If my memory serves—and it's like Swiss cheese, so take this with a grain of salt—I think she and Xavier met just before Essos and I did. Xavier and Posey supposedly had a love-at-first-sight thing, and they got married just after Essos and I got back together. It's always been the two of them plus whoever else Xavier is sleeping with at the time. I mean, Dion isn't Posey's son, but he is Xavier's firstborn. That's why he has a seat on the council."

"Did I hear my name?"

I jerk my head up.

Dion stands over us, looking down. At some point after my death, Essos took down the wards limiting where people could teleport around the house. With them down, anyone can drop by whenever they want, much to my annoyance. It means Galen can have a steady stream of visitors.

"You did." Today he's in an emerald green suit that matches his eyes. The suit makes a vibrant statement against his dark skin.

"I would join you, but I don't want to get sand in my suit."

"Don't stand up for him if he's being a baby," Finn calls, approaching us as well. His boyfriend might be dressed in a suit, but Finn is ready for the beach, wearing only his swim trunks.

"Phineas." I smile sweetly at him.

He stops and stares at me. "Whatever you're about to ask, no. It's never good when you use that voice and smile like that."

"It's really, really simple actually." I try to play coy.

"I somehow doubt it, but do go on, you have my attention." Finn drops onto the sand beside me. Dion does as well, his outfit changing from a full suit to a swimsuit in the same color as he moves toward the ground.

"After Posey's trial, I need you to take Zara, Cat, and me to my apartment in Solarem. Possibly Miranda and Ellie, too, but not if I can help it." The trial's still a few weeks away, but I know Posey. She's going to want to monopolize my time with planning the most ridiculous party for her trial. If I leave before then, she's just going to whine and probably invite herself along in the name of party planning. No fucking way.

"Seriously? I'm not a taxi." He flips his blonde hair out of his face.

"You're the Messenger God. You deliver things," I point out stubbornly.

"*Messages.* People are not messages. Why can't you do it?"

I twist so I'm facing him. "My powers are unreliable right now. The last thing I want to do is accidentally kill Cat or Zara mid-transit."

"But Ellie and Miranda are fair game? Bloodthirsty. I guess you heard," Finn says with a laugh, still not giving an answer.

"Of course, I don't want to hurt them either. What is it you think I heard?" I ask, suddenly confused.

Finn and Dion both still, exchanging a glance. Cat's head tilts curiously. Finn opens his mouth, looking for something to say.

"That they're Posey's spies," Dion answers, covering for whatever that was. His answer is both too slow and quick at the same time.

I narrow my eyes but let it go. "Of course, they are. That's been obvious since they got here. So, will you take us to Solarem?"

"Absolutely, I will gladly play chauffeur. We can sort out details once we know the timing of her challenge." Finn's voice has a forced sincerity behind it.

"I have to go plan that with her. I've sort of been ignoring what I'm supposed to be doing all day." I groan at the thought of being locked in a room with her to plan the party and my wedding.

My *wedding*.

Thinking about it makes me want to fall into the same deep crack in the ocean that Kai emerged from. It's right up there with going to the dentist or eating brussels sprouts when there's cake in the same room.

"It's about time. You rulers of death like to work yourself to death," Finn quips. I can hear actual crickets trying to fill the void left by his words.

"We are the Gods of *the* Dead. It's not the same thing at all. That's someone else's job. And someone in this whole empire actually needs to work—we can't all be drinking wine all day or carrying on with our affairs."

"Sounds like you're thinking of some very specific people when you say that. Does this happen to be someone I call 'dad'?" Dion asks with a smirk.

I get up. If these two clowns found me, it's only a matter of time before Posey does.

Cat reaches up to me for a hand up.

"Only get up if you want to," I tell her. "You've been cooped up. I trust these two to take care of you. I'm going to go and tackle wedding planning or whatever absurd thing Posey wants from me now." I hope my words convince Cat to stay. I've been unfair, asking her to stay in the house all the time.

She nods, reaching for the bottle of wine that Dion is offering her and taking a swig. I wink. "Enjoy. Ask Finn about his favorite spots in Solarem—maybe we can go out while we're there." With that, I leave the fun behind.

Titus is where I left him a few hours ago, only he's a few shades darker, his tan coming in nicely.

"Do you know where the Goddess Supreme is these days?" I don't expect him to have an answer for me, but I have to ask.

"Nope. The only one who probably does know is Galen, but I'm not sure he's in a particularly sharing mood with you." He's wearing sunglasses, but I can tell his eyes are on me. I can feel them burning through me.

"Thanks for your assistance, I guess."

I steel myself to deal with Posey, who is sitting just inside with Miranda and Ellie. I pull open the French doors and sweep into the room with as much ethereal grace as I can muster while limping. Whatever happened to my knee when Helene blasted me hurts more and more with each step.

On the table is a teapot with two cups waiting to be filled. I have to assume that this tea is safe, given that Posey will be drinking it, but I plan on letting her drink first.

"There you are. Shirking your responsibilities again? And skipping therapy? It's almost like you don't want this wedding to happen." There's a challenge in Posey's voice.

"What are we deciding today?" I ask, my tone neutral.

"You know, it's not like Essos was some celibate monk while you were dead. I don't know why you're trying to hold a torch for a man who couldn't wait until you were cold to start a dalliance with some other woman. I mean, for all we know, it was happening while you were still alive."

Ellie and Miranda go completely still, like deer afraid to draw attention to themselves. Posey's words are meant to create doubt and mistrust, and they strike the intended target. I have to fight not to recoil or flinch. I keep my face impassive, the mask of a woman who has moved on from her husband to his brother. But inside, I'm crumbling. Xavier alluded to this during the Calling, and there've been other mentions here and there. That's the only reason I believe Posey about it now.

This is something I would have wanted Essos to tell me, not something to hear from someone else, especially not Posey. I know my husband was faithful when I was in this realm, but I never thought about him seeking comfort in the arms of another while I was dead. But of course, he would. There was no guarantee I would ever return. He needed to find a new consort; in fact, it's why the farce that was the Calling was held.

Such bullshit he sold us about the Calling being something he had to do. Was it something he invented as a way to get me back? He never *had* to have a co-ruler before. Titus would have been just fine if Essos had been the one leading the dead alone. Sometimes I think it's what Titus would have preferred. When we established the Underworld, Essos wanted to make it clear that I belonged, so we set up our own system of checks and balances intended to keep the work from wearing one of us down too much.

"Are your words supposed to shock me? Am I supposed to start crying and spill my heart out to you about what a traitor Essos is? I was *dead*, Posey. I never would have expected him to remain celibate for the rest of eternity." Because I'm feeling particularly cruel, I push on. "Men have needs that they can't always get from their wives, but you would know that better than most." I reach forward and pour tea into each of our cups. I don't believe that sentiment at all, but I know it will get under Posey's skin, and that's what I want.

Posey looks like I just took a shit in her lap. She never could take it the way she dished it. I wish I *had* taken a shit in her lap. Maybe then she would never speak to me again. But I pass her the cup of tea and wait to see if she'll drink from it. When she does, I take a sip from my cup.

"You and Galen seemed to be having a fight this morning. I wanted to make sure there weren't any residual feelings."

I try not to roll my eyes, but inside, my heart is ready to burst from all the pressure. I don't want to hear about last night ever again. "We were having a lovers' spat. I'll forgive him when he comes groveling back. What are we planning today, the wedding or the party after your trial?"

I get her talking about her plans while Ellie and Miranda take notes and show off samples of her ideas. I let her make decision after decision, having learned my lesson that she's just going to do what she wants. I pretend to have differing opinions now and then, just so she thinks I'm interested. If I roll over too quickly, she'll be suspicious.

"Since I have your attention for once, I'm thinking maybe we can look at wedding dresses. We'll need to have them tailored, after all."

"We're gods, Posey. Is there a reason I can't just make it fit me once I pick one?"

Posey looks at me, her lips pursed. "I suppose not. We should still pick one—that way we can make sure to accessorize it just right."

I stand up, prompting Ellie and Miranda to do the same. "I'll pick a dress after your trial. I need time to envision the look I want for the day. If you'll excuse me."

"We're not done here!" Posey calls after me, but I don't stop. Thankfully, I've done a good enough job reiterating that this is my *home,* and she doesn't try to force the issue. I walk out, hoping to find solitude in my room.

Only Waffles is there, grooming himself on my bed.

Even though my muscles are aching, I push my dresser in front of the door. I regret not asking Finn or Dion to add more locks. The only other person who could help who knows I'm lacking in powers right now is Titus, and I'm already in debt to him for that tip. I don't think Galen will try anything again so soon, but I don't want to tempt fate.

Fool me once and all that.

I fill the tub, uselessly trying to pull at my powers to do something, and I want to scream at the futility. There's nothing there for me to find. I can feel the hole they've left, now that Titus pointed it out, and I can't do anything about it. I wish I'd done yoga with Helene, even though I am mad at her. Maybe I could draw on that meditative state to center myself and find a way through the next month without killing Posey or Galen or Titus.

I slip into the hot water, the burn of it sending a *zing* of pain all up my body. I welcome the sensation, the reminder that I'm not dead, the reminder that I still have fight left in me. With my eyes closed, I envision Essos in the tub behind me, holding me the way he would after a long day. We wouldn't need to talk, just bask in the comfort of each other. I try to imagine what he would tell me, how he would make me feel better after today.

He would kiss each and every tear as it fell from my face, and he would remind me that what happened wasn't my fault. It wasn't Helene's fault either, and while she might have been out of line, I owe her an apology for trying to throw the blame at her feet. Essos would remind me that I'm stronger than I think. I've gotten back up every time someone has tried to keep me down, and this time shouldn't be any different.

He would make love to me and remind me that I'm worthy.

He wouldn't let me stew in my feelings; he would make me talk through them when I was ready.

I sink lower in the tub, as if the water can soothe the ache of missing him. This was the pep talk I needed to remind me what I'm fighting for, and for just a second, I feel like he's there with me and I'm not alone in this.

22

G alen has the good sense to avoid me for a week before coming to grovel. He finds me in the barn, brushing one of my four horses. It makes sense now, why Essos brought me to Abbott and Costello for a horseback ride during the Calling. We used to ride up and down the beach, finding new spots in the dunes to make love or to stargaze, and I adore the horses.

Abbott and Costello are the more mild-mannered of our horses. Bonnie and Clyde are our other two black Friesians, and they're more temperamental, living up to their names. Bonnie whinnies as I brush her.

"Daphne," Galen calls out to me. One of the stable boys is picking Bonnie's hooves as he approaches. There's defiance in the boy's gaze as he looks up, ready to stand between Galen and me, but I won't let him. He's not a god, and I won't have his blood on my hands. I give a simple nod, dismissing him. I close Bonnie in her stall, not interested in getting kicked during this conversation.

I step out to face Galen, crossing my arms. I will not make this easy for him.

"Daphne," he begins again, clearing his throat. He looks repentant and holds something in his hands, his golden eyes downturned along with the edges of his lips. He's still trying to emulate Essos by wearing a suit, but he looks rumpled. His shirt is half tucked in, and he's lacking a tie. Since his father showed up, he's been putting in an effort to show that he does have what it takes to rule. I've heard the screaming matches between them running late into the night.

"Daphne, I'm sorry." It's the first time he's ever actually said those words to me with something that sounds an awful lot like sincerity.

I glance down at the ruby on my finger. I tried to smash it off my hand, but it's been reinforced by some sort of magic that keeps it from so much as being damaged.

I look past him and behind me, confusing Galen.

"Are you looking for someone?" he asks, taking another step toward me.

"I'm looking for who the fuck you think I am. A week later I get an apology? A *week* after you hit me? A week..." I pause, unable to finish the thought.

My powers stirred this morning. I'm not sure I would have noticed it, but at some point last night, the rose I gave Essos during the Calling turned up on the pillow beside me. When I reached for it, it bloomed further. All it took was my fingers grazing flowers on my nightstand to make them stand a little taller, their petals a little wider. I wish I could have talked to Essos, but just the reminder that he's still here was enough to strengthen me.

For the first time in a week, I'm not worried that I won't get my powers back. I'm not flexing that muscle, not till it feels a little stronger and a lack of response won't break me, but I'm not as freaked out.

"I said I'm *sorry*." He repeats it with more emphasis.

I raise my hands in the air and start to walk past him. He grabs my arm. I stare at where he is touching me, wondering if I could burn him or grow thorns to make him let me go, but I decided to let whoever was dosing me think that I'm still bound.

They don't know that I'm not a thing that can be bound. I will fight and claw my way back from the grave if it so suits me, and I will not be made a pawn.

"For what, Galen? Surely your mother explained that a proper apology includes admitting how you wronged a person."

I know now that Ellie is the one giving me the dosed tea. She brings it to me with a smile on her face. Whether she's getting it pre-dosed from the kitchen or she's dosing it herself, I haven't figured out. I'm also not *positive* which puppet master is pulling her strings. Posey is the most likely culprit, but I can't count out Galen, or anyone else who might be holding a grudge for a slight I don't even remember. As far as I can tell, neither Ellie nor Miranda mentioned the bloody sheets to Posey. That's something she would hold over my head to keep me in line, and she hasn't brought it up.

"I'm sorry for not being a better man to you. That I keep failing you when I'm trying so hard not to. I misread the situation. I thought that things were changing between us, and that meant you would welcome a nighttime visit. When you rejected me, I lashed out. I'm trying to learn to be a better man *for* you, and sometimes that means that I forget myself and I'm not a better man *to* you. Please, forgive me." He pulls out a long box. I scowl at him as he pops it open.

The necklace is beautiful, but I don't want to say so. It's a cluster of small diamonds connected by platinum bars seemingly at random. I want to reach out and touch it, but I hold back.

As far as apologies go, it was a decent one, but I don't believe he's sincere. The apology was also cheapened by the gift. He can't buy my love and affection, and he needs to learn that.

I don't have a chance to say anything before he takes out the necklace and loops it around my neck.

I go still as he steps behind me. "It's the constellation Lyra. You used to love to play the instrument." My fingers come up to the necklace, which now rests around my throat like a noose.

I turn to look at him.

I had to take an instrument as part of my university courses, but I hated every moment of playing the lyre. Titus and Octavia enjoyed making us play our instruments at dinners, saying we were more cultured for it. Helene played the viola with excellence, Xavier was passable with the aulos, and Galen was a brute with the drums. Kai, meanwhile, would accompany Helene on the cello, while Posey was commended for her lovely use of the larger version of my instrument, the harp. Callista played the flute whenever she showed up, but would often just stop mid-performance as if tired of being a performing monkey.

Essos was gifted on the piano. The first night we moved into this house, he laid me out on the one in the ballroom, hooking my legs over his shoulders and making me his personal feast as he played until he was too distracted by me, which wasn't very long.

"You can't buy my love or forgiveness, Galen. You crossed a huge boundary, and it's going to take time for me to trust you again. I made it clear that I was not going to sleep with you before we got married, and it doesn't matter what messages you thought I was sending. I was explicit. I don't know how things worked with you and Callista, but I will not let you bully me. You're used to being given everything on a golden spoon, and you're not used to hearing the word *no*, but hear me now, Galen. No. No to *everything* right now."

He flushes red, and I worry that I've gone too far. "I don't want to talk about Callie. I don't want to talk about all the things that went wrong, I want to focus on the things that will go right for us." He reaches for my face, cupping it in his hands, and I have to fight the urge to flinch and pull away. I'm supposed to make him think that I want this to work, but sometimes it's hard to sell it.

"I think maybe you should see Luminara without me. You clearly have some problems to work out that have to do with your ex. This would be a good way to start to get into my good graces again. Until you commit to seeing her without me, I'm going to ask that you not even kiss me. We can't be intimate in any way until we trust each other, and right now, I can't trust you."

"So, I said I'm sorry and you're still punishing me?" he snaps, but he lets me go.

I try a different tactic and let him see how I'm trembling. If he thinks that I'm some mewling woman who's afraid of him, maybe he won't push it. He knows I'll fight back if I'm backed into a corner. This kitten has claws, and I'm not afraid to use them.

"I'm not punishing you, Galen. I'm trying to make our relationship stronger. We can't work effectively as a unit if we don't trust each other. That's why I want you to take over handling the kingdom with your father. It's a small token of trust that I can give you. Show me that you're worthy of my trust."

Titus may want to put everything back on my shoulders, but I won't allow it. If he doesn't want to exercise his right to fix this, then he gets to show Galen how to rule.

"So, I'm not forgiven, you're making demands of me to go to therapy, *and* you're abandoning your responsibilities." His voice is dry, bordering on annoyed.

"What responsibilities do I have to abandon? You've made it clear you don't *want* my help. You've restricted my access to the point where Sybil won't even make eye contact with me for me to even *ask* about what is happening in my realm. I see snippets of information some days, when you're feeling magnanimous about letting me do my job. You can't have it both ways, Galen. You can't insist on leaving me out of decisions like closing the Garden of Evil and then get angry with me for how I chose to deal with it."

I've gotten far off the point, but all those words needed an outlet. The horses stomp their feet around us and I move us out into the yard away from the animals. "I'm putting in the work too," I say, my voice calmer.

"How?"

"I'm going to take some time to recenter myself by going to Solarem. I haven't been there in so long. I'll take Cat and Zara to see it, and we'll spend a week at the spa, but I'm going to spend the month between Posey's trial and Xavier's away from this house. I'll see if I can track down Rafferty so we don't have the issue of my scattered memories hanging over our heads. Our wedding is fast approaching, only three months till the big day, and as much as I realize that you have some things to work through around whatever happened with Callista, I have to work on myself too. It's a team effort." I touch his arm gently.

"What the hell have you been doing at yoga with Helene every day if you're not centering yourself or whatever?"

"We're doing that too, but it's been a bit more about gossiping. I missed so much, and I feel so inadequate at these balls following the Trials, where everyone is talking about things I missed. I had no idea that Finn and Dion were dating the Goddess of the Hunt, and that Xavier had another child, or that Helene did too. I missed a lot. You can't blame me for wanting to catch up." I place a hand on his chest, then move it to his cheek.

Galen makes a disgruntled groan. "I guess I don't have a choice, do I?"

"As a reward for trusting and respecting my wishes, and as proof of my commitment to trying to make this work, you can kiss me, but only this time until I say otherwise."

Galen's eyes meet mine, questioning. I lean up and close my eyes, pretending he's Chad from meteorology or literally any other person alive. Our lips meet, and it must be everything he wanted, because I can hear his sigh of pleasure. For me, it feels like the world is crumbling, like it's on fire and there's nothing I can do about it.

I pull back first, and he looks disappointed.

"Can I walk you back to the house?" He offers his arm to me, and I slide mine into his.

"You may." A fresh wave of sickness rises in me as we walk. I miss my husband. I haven't seen him since well before the last trial, and I want to take comfort in his arms, in the reminder that I love a good and honest man.

A good and honest man who will help me put Galen in the ground.

"Again," Finn orders as I try to summon my powers faster. My whole body is trembling as I reach for that which remains elusive.

I came clean to Finn when he caught me trying to make a flower bloom in the gardens and proved myself incapable of doing so. I've *actually* been meditating with him and Dion the way I said I was with Helene from the start. Finding that quiet space in my mind and feeling out my well-being has been beneficial, to say the least. My powers aren't what they once were, but getting faster at what I can do makes all the difference, even if I tire quickly.

"Where is Essos?" I ask, looking at Finn, not summoning my vine dagger as demanded.

"You know I can't tell you that. Even I don't know," Finn tells me with a shake of his head as he advances on me.

Kai comes up behind me, pinning my arms to my sides. I form a vine dagger in my hand and drive it into his thigh as I stomp on his instep and whip my head back, twisting until he lets me go.

I'm breathing heavily as I turn from Finn to see Kai rip the dagger from his leg. It's coated in his blood, and he tosses it to the side with the others I've made. My focus today has been on making weapons and not unmaking them.

"You're getting too good at that," Kai whines as seawater travels up to his leg and soothes it with a seaweed bandage. He'll heal himself completely later, after I've poked a few more holes in his skin. Kai wants to make sure I know how to exploit injuries next.

"I've had a good teacher," I tell him with a pleased smile.

Helene scoffs from where she sits, perusing social media on her phone. She's been full of snarky comments for the past two weeks since our fight. We're both stubborn pains in the ass and refuse to take the first step toward fixing what is broken. We should have resolved this immediately after our argument, because the more time that passes, the more uncomfortable it becomes to address, and now we're avoiding addressing each other. Instead, we pretend the other isn't even there.

"I've had enough, starfish." Kai snaps. He crosses to her in three long steps. Kai has no qualms about manhandling his wife and, I think on a good day, she would enjoy it, but as he tosses her over his shoulder in a fireman's carry, she flushes red with anger. He slaps her ass for good measure before dropping her in front of me.

"If you know what's good for you..." Helene's threat hangs in the air. She turns to throttle him, but I can see a faint light enveloping us. I reach toward Finn and encounter a physical barrier.

"Make nice, the two of you, please, for all that is good in the realms," Finn pleads.

I cross my arms. "Not until she apologizes to me." I turn to Helene, knowing she won't; she's the stupid type of stubborn who would starve to death rather than eat something offered by someone she didn't like.

"I can't apologize." Helene spins to face me.

"You blasted me, *twice*. You doubted me and my commitment to Essos. You owe me an apology."

"No. You said heinous shit to me about..." She casts her gaze toward Finn and Dion, asking without words how much they know. Even that little consideration touches me. "About what happened, and I could have understood your side, but blaming me was uncalled for, and I deserve an apology first. Even if you're just pretending, as you claim, Essos wouldn't stand for it. He wouldn't want you to be kissing Galen."

I screw my eyes shut, debating. I could refute her words, but I shouldn't. They're my allies; they won't use it against me or Essos, not intentionally. Helene has a way of getting under my skin, so I don't hold my tongue.

"He knows," I say softly.

"And another thing, if you want—wait, I'm sorry, did you just say he knows?"

Both Kai and Finn uncross their arms, watching me curiously. Even Dion glances up from where he's stretching by the bench. I wave a hand, dissolving the barrier that held Helene and me in. I could have dissolved it the moment it came up; I could sense that when my hands touched it, but I want to clear the air with Helene. She's right. I have been pushing everyone away. Finn's brow furrows, but he offers a grin.

"Yes, Essos knows. I've seen him a handful of times since the Calling ended. He knows everything." At least, he knows everything up to the last time I saw him. I don't know what else Finn has told him, or what other spies he has in the house. He'd been showing up when I need him most, except for the most recent incident. It's been two weeks since Kai lost to Galen and a little over a month since I last saw Essos, after Cat was sick.

"And you're just now telling me? How is he? Is he okay? What did he say? What is he planning?" Helene clings to me, desperate for answers I can't give her.

"He's okay. We talked about the Trials. He's looking for a way out of this, but we keep details nonspecific. He came by once before your trial, Helene, to collect some things from his office that he needs to protect." I don't tell her more. The secrets of being rulers of the dead are things that we don't share with anyone.

Titus has been in Essos's office teaching Galen some of these things, but not all of them, not yet. Galen will face Posey's trial next, though I have no doubt that he'll come out victorious. She's sure to give him something easy to handle, if she hasn't outright told him what it is.

I'm grateful to Titus for stepping in and guiding Galen in running the realm. It's keeping Galen from harassing me, giving me time to focus on my powers and my mental well-being. From the screaming I can hear from my office sometimes, it doesn't sound like it's going well, and my debt to Titus gets larger every day.

"Why didn't you say anything before? He's my brother, and I miss him too. You used to trust me, and now you're keeping secrets, trying to face this all alone. You're *not* alone, and what happened wasn't your f-fault." Helene's voice breaks on the last word.

For all I've been going through, I've forgotten that she's lost her brother in this whole mess. "Because none of what was shared was relevant, and the last—the *last*—thing I want Galen to know is that Essos can come and go from the property without his thugs being aware of it."

Helene still looks utterly betrayed by my words. "You had no right to keep that from me."

"I had *every* right, Hel. This is my *home*. He is my *husband*. I love you for supporting him while I was gone, but my priorities are him and the realm, not you and your feelings. I'm sorry if that sucks, but it's the truth. I also don't know where the dagger that killed me is. What if Galen has it? What if he catches Essos when he's leaving here one night? What if he kills him? I cannot let that happen. I won't. I have to be kept in the dark about what his master plan is and what he's going to do to get us out of this mess." I pause and meet Helene's gaze so there's no mistaking my words. "I'm sorry. What I said after Kai's trial wasn't fair. I shouldn't have put that on your shoulders."

Helene makes a strangled noise deep in her throat. "That's the whole fucking point, Daphne. You *can* put that on my shoulders. I'm not just here for Essos or because Xavier told me I had to stay. I am here for *you*. I'm here because we were sisters once, and you need me, even if you fucking refuse to admit it. Give me some of that pain and let me carry it for you so you don't carry it alone."

She looks like she wants to step toward me, but she doesn't, choosing instead to move into Kai's arms and avoid another possible rejection from me.

"I get it," Finn reassures me, snaking an arm around my shoulders for a genuine hug.

I close my arms around his middle, my fingers fisting in his shirt. "I know you do. But you've seen him—the rest of his family hasn't," I tell him.

Finn rests his chin on the top of my head. "They've all had an extra thousand years that you didn't. Helene can grow up."

"Do you have something you would like to say, starfish?" Kai asks Helene softly.

"I'm sorry. I'm sorry you felt like you couldn't tell me anything and that you chose to bear this burden alone." As far as apologies go, it's not the worst I've received, but it leaves room for improvement. There's still tension in the set of her shoulders, and I realize there's only one way we can really put this whole thing to bed.

"Helene!" Finn scolds.

"I'm sorry you feel so powerless right now that you have to attack me." My voice is saccharine sweet. Helene starts toward me, but Finn places himself between us before we can start to fight.

"Enough, ladies. Essos wouldn't want you fighting like this. What happened to being on the same team? We all want the same thing. We need to stop fighting each other and focus on the real problem," Finn begs.

"I'm going to Solarem after Posey's trial. Come with me." My olive branch to Helene is metaphorical and literal. I hold out my hand to her, hoping that she'll take it.

Helene frowns but slips her hand into mine. "No. If you're not going to be around, I'm going to my own home. But...we can put this behind us." Her voice is saccharine sweet as she begrudgingly squeezes my hand, but then she tugs me forward and brings her fist toward my face. I don't have a chance to block or dodge, and I feel the burn as my lip splits. She follows up with a kick, which I successfully block with both forearms. I don't hesitate to strike back, feigning a punch but instead spinning and kicking her in the face.

We trade blows without using our powers, focusing on blocking and defending. She's not the same size as Galen, but she's craftier than Kai. Helene is more willing to take cheap shots, like wrapping a fist around my ponytail and slamming her other fist into my stomach again and again. I drive my elbow into her face, and she lets me go.

We're both bleeding and bruised by the time we're done, lying on our backs side by side. Finn and Kai wisely stayed out of it, choosing to spar on their own. My breathing is labored and I'm pretty sure I broke a rib, but I don't move.

"I'm sorry," I start, wincing as I say it. "I'm sorry that I didn't tell you about Essos. I thought I was doing the right thing. And I'm sorry I've been pushing you away. You were right when you said it two weeks ago, and you're still right now. I can admit when I'm wrong, and I was wrong here, but you also totally overstepped."

Helene turns on her side to face me. I try to make the same effort, but wince and settle onto my back and turn my head.

"I've been a bitch, I get it, but you upended my whole life, and you're not even a little sorry about it. I can't be home with *my* husband. I worked hard to help you and Essos get back together, so to see you and Galen making out all the time...it hurts. When you died, my heart broke too, and it's like you don't even care. You're too busy getting your rocks off with my brother to even realize the harm you're doing."

I wince. She's right about getting my jollies with one of her brothers, although it's the wrong one.

"I'm *not* sleeping with Galen," I vehemently deny. I turn to face her again, not caring when I feel the stabbing sensation in my side.

"You're doing a good job of making it seem like you are."

"Good! I want it to be believable to him, to you, to Titus, to anyone who sees us together. I want him to believe I could love him, right up until the moment that I take everything from him the way he took *everything from me*." My voice is thick with emotion when I say it, exhaustion and anger lowering my shields, leaving me vulnerable. Tears are in my eyes, and I wipe them away hastily.

"I just don't want you falling for your own deception. I wish this could be over tomorrow. This yo-yo-ing is awful. I'm tired of Galen thinking he's superior and I'm tired of being away from Kai."

"Kai has been staying here every night. At least you know where your husband is and that he's safe. I don't know where Essos has been sleeping or who he's seeing. I don't know what he's doing or if it's dangerous. We can sit here all day and bitch about who has it worse, but I'm trying to do what I can to survive this, the same as you are. You need to trust me. You need to know that I'm not willingly betraying Essos. Everything I'm doing is for Essos, for my realm. Please don't ever think that's not what I'm doing. Have more faith in me than that."

Helene stands and offers me her hand. I take it, clutching my side as I get up, the pulling sensation uncomfortable.

"Let me heal that." Helene touches a hand to my side, and my rib warms and pulses back together where it was cracked. A weird look crosses her face, but she draws her hand back once most of my other injuries healed.

"Thank you." I touch the spot where my lip had been cut earlier and find the wound still there.

"I still want you to bear a reminder of what it means to cross me."

I nudge her with my elbow. "You and your stupid power plays."

Helene scowls at me. "We know I'm not the power player in the house you have to worry about."

I let out a derisive snort. "Her trial is in two more weeks. I can survive that. I think."

I would rather go head-to-head in a fight with Helene than spend a second with Posey. At least when Helene is pissed, she has the decency to punch me in the face.

"Speaking of, I think you have some party planning to get back to." There's a sick level of delight in Helene's voice, and it makes me wonder if she enjoys knowing I'm being slowly tortured.

"Wouldn't you rather kick my ass again?" I offer. I twist the ruby ring on my finger, a new nervous tick I've developed. If I keep it up, I'm going to rub my finger raw.

"Name the time and place, asshole. I'm always ready to kick

your ass for some reason or other." Her tone is teasing as she hugs me to her side.

When we get back to the house, for once, Sybil isn't trying to duck me. I approach them, waiving Helene on, and cross my arms.

"I didn't know Titus hired you." It's been weighing on me, this feeling of betrayal.

"Technically, Essos hired me. Titus introduced us. Does it matter?"

"Not much, but I don't appreciate that you've been passing reports to Titus."

"Would you like me to give you an actual update, or would you rather pick apart decisions that were made after your death?"

I scowl but gesture for them to go on. "By all means, provide your update."

"The tremors." Now they have my attention. "They're being caused by the shifting boundaries."

"I wasn't aware that the different Afterlife boundaries were sentient."

"They're not, but you and Essos coded them to automatically grow to ensure there was plentiful space for the souls. With the absence of the Garden of Evil, the Deep is trying to compensate."

I remember the decision being made. Titus tried to reason that the souls would never need that much accommodation, but Essos and I insisted. The souls might be doomed for all eternity, but that didn't mean they needed to be forced into little boxes.

"Can anything be done to stop the tremors?"

"No. And there's one more thing."

"For fuck's sake, now what?"

"Titus has asked that, while he tries to work with Galen on becoming a ruler, you take no part in ruling. That means I'm not allowed to give you any more reports or information."

I purse my lips. "And yet, here you stand, giving me information."

"I never said I wouldn't. I'm just not supposed to."

"That is an awfully murky way of looking at it," I point out.

They grace me with a grin. "You're not wrong, but just because Daddy says heel doesn't mean I will. My loyalty is to the Underworld, and to an extent, you and Essos. I will not stand by and let some dolt with a superiority complex ruin everything you've built. I know you've been avoiding her, but it's not what Luminara wants either."

"I thought therapy was supposed to be confidential. Having a little pillow talk?" It might be unkind, but I'm not thrilled with the way Luminara has been handling this situation. Really, I just can't get past that she thought it was okay to take my memories and let me step into a situation with the lion.

"Daphne, you of all people should know that not everything is as it seems."

23

I'm sitting in my office, yearning to be in Essos's space, when I hear something shatter in the room beside mine. True to my word, I'm not doing any work for the Underworld, just answering the endless correspondence of people glad for my return. I go to open a letter when another glass shatters. My hands pause. I rise and open the door that divides the offices to see what is going on.

Essos's crystal decanter set is in pieces, and the table it sat on is splintered as well. Titus is glaring at his youngest son, while Galen breathes heavily. We all know that he's going to win the next trial, but any stress relief he might have had from that is counterbalanced by the stress of having to be with Titus all the time.

Secretly, I love it, but I can't let Galen know that.

"What in all of Solarem is happening?" I ask. When Galen rears his arm back to hurtle a shard of glass at Titus, I reach for my powers but tamp down that reflex immediately. I'm supposed to be powerless. If Galen is the one poisoning me, it won't do to have him know it's not working.

The glass seems to pass through a barrier and turns into a fine powder that coats the desk.

I regret pushing for the Trials to be six months long. I needed to buy Essos time to save us both from my mistakes, but the sooner this is over, the better.

"Just as I suspected, Galen doesn't have the temperament to handle being regent of this realm," Titus declares, sounding glad of this.

I start to gather chunks of glass, again avoiding the use of my powers. I see a flash of red in Galen's eyes and know that he's going to do something that will get him evaporated. I should let him do it, I should let Titus wipe the floor with him, but it won't stop Galen's supporters from coming for me, so I drag the thick edge of a piece of glass along my palm.

"You're not being—oh!" I fumble with the glass I had gathered, dropping the pieces to the floor.

It's not enough to stop Galen, though, because his muscles tense as he charges for his father. Titus stops his son easily. He grabs Galen by the lapels of his shirt and tosses him clean through the bookcase and into my office. That's going to be a *bitch* to clean.

"Think twice the next time you consider raising a hand at me. There is no power greater than mine. I created you, son. Don't forget that I can unmake you too."

Galen gets up, the scent of blood thick in the air, and he chooses to tend to me instead of attacking his father again. His hand covers mine, healing the cut before I can bleed onto the carpet.

He doesn't ask why I don't heal myself, doesn't question why I was picking up the glass shards with my hands. Another indictment of his likely involvement in trying to bind my powers. Titus rolls his eyes at my theatrics.

"Why are you fighting?" I ask again, trying to tidy some of the mess they made in Essos's office. He's so organized and clean;

Essos would weep to see his room like this. Books left open on tables and straddling the armrest of the couch, cups sitting on the mantle, and at least two of the throw pillows from the couch torn to pieces. The room looks less like an office and more like a battle-ground. Galen is still red with anger, but Titus looks unbothered. Neither one of them makes an effort to do anything with the broken bookcase and wall.

"Leave it," Galen orders, pulling me to his side. "He doesn't think I can do it." Galen's voice reveals the deep level of betrayal he feels. He's still that same boy I met on the dance floor who fought for his father's approval.

"Because you can't," Titus says matter-of-factly.

"Hush." I throw a look over my shoulder at Titus.

Titus straightens up, raising an eyebrow at me. "Did you just—"

"Are you planning to prove him right by throwing a temper tantrum, or are you planning to prove him wrong?" I rest my hands on Galen's forearms and give them a gentle squeeze.

"There's nothing he can do to prove me wrong. His actions already—" Titus rises and throws a folder onto the desk "—proved me right. He's misappropriating funds, causing needless wars in the mortal world, and generally—what's the term the kids use today?—fucking shit up. And you're complicit, with your desire to take a vacation and abandon all it is that you swore to protect. You're no queen."

Now I'm the one who's seeing red, but I don't do anything about it. I don't let so much as a flower petal fall in that room. I try to remember that breathing is a two-step process, that air has to enter my lungs and then it has to leave. I push the air out and drag it back in before I speak again.

"I feel confident enough to take a step back because I have complete faith in Galen. He will make an excellent king. I'm sorry you don't see him the way I do." My voice is docile and sweet. I give Galen my best starry-eyed look. He tentatively reaches out and rubs my back in thanks for that support before closing a possessive hand over my shoulder.

Titus's eyes narrow on me for just a second before he lifts his gaze to his son. There isn't a snowball's chance in hell that he believes the shit I'm slinging, but he doesn't say as much.

"Without the scepter, I don't think you'll be much of a king."

I have to fight every instinct in my body not to freeze when Titus says this. The absence of natural movement from me would give away that I have something to hide.

And boy, do I have something to hide. The scepter is a tool Essos seldom needed to use. He didn't use it in front of us at the Calling, but I know he called on it somehow—it's the only way that Tiffany and Steve were able to make it back to the human realm. I didn't see him wield it, but with my memories returning, I know he did.

It's an ugly, garish thing. The top is a skull cast in pure gold with two rubies for eyes that seem to track you as you move. The length of it was once rather short, but Essos had it extended to cane-size. Eventually, we tucked it out of sight in a chest, and there was an invisible tether between Essos and the scepter so that if he ever needed it, he could call it to him. But anyone could use it...if they knew what it was.

If Galen ever gets his hands on it, the results could be catastrophic. It holds the power to vanquish souls or return them to the mortal realm. We could use it for reincarnation or to close the Underworld to new souls if we wanted—not that we ever would. The scepter was presented to Essos during his coronation, and again to me during mine. I'm not sure that anyone other than Titus remembered it existed, let alone what it looked like. It was shown off for only those two events and, if I recall, Galen didn't attend either. He could be staring right at it and never know. But it hasn't been in the house since the night of the

Calling Ball—the night I rejected my husband. Sybil and Essos ensured that.

If I find Rafferty, I can erase the memory of the scepter from people's minds.

Just the thought of the God of Memory reminds me that I wanted to track him down, and yet every time I think about Rafferty, as soon as I've moved on to the next thought, I fail to remember wanting to engage with him.

Curious.

"Do you know where it is?" Galen demands after Titus leaves the room. His fingers are digging into my skin, greedily seeking this source of power.

"I don't. I haven't seen it since before my death." I want to see him flinch at the thought of my murder, even though a docile fiancée wouldn't push him like that.

"I *need* it. Where did he keep it? You have to know." He's desperate to prove himself to Titus, gain the approval of his father.

Essos was off-base thinking he wasn't the favorite child. He was the one they had to worry about the least, the one they trusted—there's a reason he was put in charge of the banks, the real seat of power. All the influence Xavier has is a charade. Essos was the one in charge.

"I can check a few places, but not until after Posey's trial. She wants me here to plan." I pull out of his grip, but he reaches for me again.

"Just tell me, and I'll send my people to look for it."

I pull away again, able to do it easily thanks to all the training from Kai and Finn. "I can't just tell you. They're protected locations, meant to be accessed only by Essos or myself. One of your men could be looking right at it and not see it. It has to be me."

"What if he set a trap? I can't imagine what I would do if you were hurt." He caresses my cheek.

I almost snort. Maybe, terrorize me in my own home? Stab me to death? Choke me out? Or how about punch me in the face for not giving him what he wants?

"I don't think he would. Honestly? He used it so rarely, I don't know that he would have thought about it." I hope I'm convincing, but I can't rely on his attention span to make him forget, so I kiss him.

It's clear I've surprised him. His lips move against mine cautiously, as if he doesn't want to risk upsetting me. Which means I have him right where I want him. Keeping him wary means he won't come on to me, I hope.

I pull back. "I'll take some time after Posey's trial to search. I know Dion's trial comes next, but hopefully, Posey won't need as much input from me for his party." I give Galen a wan smile. "We'll find the scepter, and all will be right."

Galen nods, letting me go. "I trust you." He says it with conviction, but his eyes tell a different story. He doesn't know if he can truly trust me, but he wants to, and that's what I need to prey on. The guise of looking for the scepter gives me the perfect coverage to go to the Solarem library and search for the answers to all my questions.

I smile and let him believe the lie.

24

osey's trial was an utter farce, and I'm still stewing in
my anger about it. I knew it would be, but I can't help
how it rankles that he's now up in victories two to one.
"Lost Diadem" my ass. The ugly tiara that Posey allegedly lost
should have stayed lost. The trial lacked the pomp and circumstance that everyone wanted. There was no watch party, and no
spectators the way Posey wanted all the other trials to have.
Instead, my backyard has been turned into a press junket, with
Galen answering questions as to how he sleuthed out the
crown.

Galen had a week to find a tiara that Posey lost centuries ago,
allegedly to time, but she forgets that I've been remembering
everything. It may have been long ago to others, but I still
remember the clear night when she hurled the five-inch-tall tacky
collection of gems and metal into the lake at her second home in
Solarem after someone complimented me on my crown before
they complimented hers. She knew exactly where it was.

My only satisfaction is that she's wearing it tonight. Posey
tried to jam every type of precious gem known to mankind onto it,

264

and it looks like a five-year-old's attempt to make their own crown.

I want to laugh with Zara and Cat about it, but I had Finn take them to my home in Solarem proper ahead of the trial. Cat tried to put on a brave face, pretend she was fine, but she never leaves her room anymore and gets winded walking to the bathroom. Whatever healing Xavier and I did was temporary. No one can seem to pinpoint why she's still declining, and I'm starting to worry that I have no way to help her. Going to the Afterlife isn't a good option because of the tithes, and I worry it would put her more at risk than being here.

"You seem displeased that your betrothed won."

I turn to look at Titus. He's wearing an impeccable suit, finally dressed up from the jeans and ratty shirts he's been wearing around my house.

Galen is by the pool, talking to the crowd of reporters while I stand on the sand as far from him as I can get. I thought I was going to have a moment alone, but alas, the God Supreme demands my attention.

"That tiara is offensive to me. It hurts to look at." I turn from the party before me toward a buffet table and grab a tiny piece of toast in the shape of a tiara with avocado dumped on top. I feel bad for whoever had to make them.

"I have to agree with you on that. I hear you're taking a bit of a vacation." Titus reaches around me for his own little avocado toast. He says this like he didn't call me out for it last week while simultaneously dressing down his son.

"I'm not going on a vacation. I'm taking time to clear my head and to see if the fresh air of Solarem will help Cat." I don't tell him that I'm going to the library at his suggestion. I don't tell him that I'm pretending to look for the scepter for Galen, or that I'm going to try to push the boundaries of my magic while I'm there, away from everyone else.

265

Titus sees more than he lets on and, for now, our interests align.

"What's so great about these little avocado toasts that is driving an entire generation into debt?" Titus asks, ignoring me as he shoves a sixth one into his mouth.

"Okay, boomer," I say, swatting at his hand. "If you can't appreciate the avocado toast, then stop devouring them and leave them to the rest of us."

He scowls at me. "No respect. Not from you, not from my son. I don't know what's wrong with kids these days." Titus grabs another toast.

Out of the corner of my eye, I see Galen coming toward us. "Dance with me," I order, dragging the God Supreme onto the dance floor. He doesn't question, just swoops in, arm around my back with the same agile grace that Essos had—has, that Essos *has*.

"Figure out who wants to leave you powerless?" His grip on me is relaxed.

"I would have to think it's someone who wants me beholden to your son for everything. That leaves your son and someone who has the power to create a god-killing weapon, which would be you or your wife. I have to guess that it's not you, since you were kind enough to point this out to me."

Titus doesn't meet my eyes, glancing out at the crowd. "I can't tell you if it's my wife—well, ex-wife—or not. Is it truly possible to divorce yourself from the Goddess Supreme?"

His question feels rhetorical, but I jump on the chance for a little supreme-being gossip. "You tell me. You both always seemed so..." I trail off. They seemed miserable together, but in the way that only someone who truly understands you can drive you up a wall.

"I don't think that's any of your business." His eyes are rock-solid glaciers as they bore into mine, but I don't blink.

"If she's trying to usurp my crown with your son, I would think that makes it my business."

"What need does the Goddess Supreme have of your crown? Everything you can do is within her abilities, as it is within mine."

I intentionally step on his foot. "Maybe it's less about the Goddess Supreme and more about her favorite son?"

"What kind of Greek tragedy do you think we're living? Octavia and I never played favorites." Titus is affronted by the suggestion and stumbles because of my words.

"Never played favorites? My husband spent *years* wondering why he got the least love from you. Helene was easily your favorite, and you groomed Xavier from the start to be a king. Galen was always Octavia's favorite. That left Essos to be the child who did as he was told, waiting for you to see his worth. He was the smartest, cleverest of your children, and you disregarded him."

"Did it occur to you that we worried about him the least because we knew he was the most capable? That he was going to do just fine?"

"That's bullshit, Titus. Did it occur to *you* that capability doesn't change his need for love? Despite you, he never lost the capacity for love." I don't like how still Titus gets as I say this. Thankfully, the song ends, and we step away from each other.

"May I cut in, Father? I want to dance with my lovely bride-to-be." Galen extends his hand to me, and I beam at him, taking it.

"It would be my pleasure. I haven't had a chance to congratulate you on such a miraculous job." I tell him, as if he wasn't basically handed the tiara. Galen sweeps me into his arms, his golden eyes flickering.

Today's celebration is a brunch. It's part of Posey's attempt to separate herself from the rest of the parties. I don't mind; it's nice to be outside with the sun on my face during the day when we would otherwise have been cooped up inside.

"It was a breeze. I think it was nice to have a lay-up. I know that Xavier is probably planning something humiliating, and fighting Kai was not easy, though I'm sure it looked it." Galen flexes his muscles under his tuxedo.

"I'm glad this was easier for you." I keep my voice placid.

"I'm going to miss you while you're gone." I can feel his hot breath on my neck.

"I'll miss you too. I appreciate your willingness to let me take this time for myself."

"Of course, my dear. I hope you're successful in all your endeavors." He winks at me. His golden eyes sparkle in delight, no doubt at the hope that I will come back with the scepter.

I feign comfort in his arms as we sway on the dance floor. Posey preens while everyone compliments her on such a clever challenge. But she doesn't get a single compliment on her tiara. It gives me a petty flush of glee.

When I'm able to break free of Galen's grip, I make sure to be one of those people approaching her. Subtly, I adjust the crown on my head. "Posey, I just want to compliment you on such a well-thought-out trial. It was truly one of the best challenges so far. It's such a good thing to get your...*unique* diadem back."

Posey turns to look at me with a blindingly fake smile. Once no one is close enough to us, she frowns. My own tiara has a low profile today. I swapped it out as soon as I knew what she was wearing. Standing beside her with the cycles of the moon resting comfortably on my head while her crown is as large as her face lets people see exactly the types of rulers we are.

"Why must you be so patronizing, Daphne? It's very unbecoming."

"That crown is what's unbecoming. Stop moving your head; it's actually blinding me. Really, Posey, don't be so jealous. Green isn't your color." I shield my eyes as the sun glints off one of the gargantuan diamonds right into my eyes. I remember when she commissioned it. It angered her to no end that she had to ask us for the materials, since her requests were for gems larger than any of the usual stones the jewelers carried.

Posey goes for the jugular this time. "Why are you being such a bitch?"

I look at Posey, really look at her, when she asks this. She's this tiny ball of anger that's ready to erupt at any moment. I bite back the sigh that I want to release; that would open a whole other issue with her.

"Maybe it's because you rejected every idea I had for this garden party, and it's a smashing success. It's hard not to be intimidated by your party planning prowess." Maybe I laid it on a little thick, but I try to inject sincerity into my words.

They earn me an eyeroll, but she stands up just a little taller, and her mouth starts to turn up. This game between us with surface-level niceties and aggressive subtext is getting old, and I'll be glad to have a month-long break from her.

"What are we talking about?" Helene asks, approaching with her own drink.

"How well Posey did planning the party. I think she should plan Xavier's trial party without my input. I didn't make any difference either way."

Posey looks stricken at the suggestion. All her plans to keep me in her thrall are slipping away. Posey has been trying for months to bring me to heel, and I keep denying her. She's been a one-woman party-planning machine anyway.

"Why? This whole operation was your idea. I shouldn't bear the responsibility for planning more parties in addition to my Council responsibilities." Posey's hands curl into fists. As if the Council is doing anything right now. Each member has their own trial to designate, and I know for a fact they're more focused on what's going to happen with the Underworld than anything else. There *are* no other responsibilities.

"I'm going to take some much-needed time away to get my head straight. Between the memories, and..." I pause here for dramatic effect "...if I'm being totally honest? My powers don't want to cooperate with me. I can't *bear* to let it continue. I need to focus on that."

"But you promised we would pick your dress." Posey's expression gives nothing away, and I know that Helene is watching her face just as closely as I am. Posey would be more worried about the stupid wedding than me possibly losing my powers. She seems to actually read the look on my face. "Don't get me wrong, that *is* awful, but I think you're focused on something trivial. Everything will fall into place after the wedding, when you're where you're meant to be. By Galen's side."

"It's still concerning. Finn is taking me away tonight."

"You still haven't taken my suggestion of consummation before the wedding if you're not spending the night with your betrothed after his second victory."

I try not to see red at her words. I can feel Helene close her hand over my wrist to hold me back.

"We decided it was for the best to wait." Galen's voice is cold when he approaches us. "You need to stay out of matters that don't concern you, Posey."

"These matters do concern me." Her voice has taken on a hard edge.

I glance between the two of them. Much as I would like to see them come to blows, I don't want to overcomplicate things.

I place my hand gently on Galen's forearm and signal for drinks. "We should be celebrating, not fighting. Another victory for Galen means we're one step closer to the Trials being over." I inject false cheer into my voice.

"I was thinking over the timing. Perhaps it's in the best interests of everyone that we start to move forward."

I take a sip from my drink to buy time. Helene looks ready to object, but I speak first. "What is it you propose, Posey?"

"That we shorten the window between trials so you have time to focus on and plan the wedding. There are three months before the end of the Trials *and* when you're supposed to be wed. Since you're so enamored of your beau, I'm *sure* having more time for wedding planning would be your preference."

I open my mouth, but no words come out. This is quite possibly the worst of all proposals, and I've been proposed to by Galen. The glint in Posey's eyes tells me she knows that she has me. I've done *such* a good job of selling my feelings that I have no choice but to accept this.

"Posey, don't be so pushy. Let Daphne enjoy the wedding-planning process. You've crawled so far up her ass about it that I don't think she's had an original thought about what she wants."

"She wanted black and red, so we're doing black and red. She said she doesn't want traditional invitations, so we're not doing traditional invitations."

I fight a smirk. That was one of my more devious decisions. I told her we should do hand-folded origami roses for a personal touch. Miranda and Ellie have been the ones doing all the folding. It's kept them out of my hair.

"Talk it over with the Council. I still intend to take a month for my own rest and rejuvenation. If we move to the two-week window, I will return for the next trial and party only."

Across the yard, Xavier is talking to a pretty redhead. I watch him brush her hair over her shoulder.

As if he senses me watching him, he glances at me and tilts his head. His interest in her seems superficial, his eyes not on her, but on the party around us.

The festivities continue, oblivious to the matters of life and death that hang in the balance. Posey seems delighted by my willingness to compromise and takes the win.

271

Once she's disappeared into the crowd, Helene tugging her along, I stick out my tongue at her back.

"Well, that wasn't very queenly," Celestina points out as she walks over to me. She's been turning her attention more to me than to Galen, and now she has the balls to approach me again.

I pick at lint on one of the pleats on my green dress before dusting it off. "I don't suppose that could be kept from your column tomorrow?"

"Depends on if you have anything better for me to work with."

I take a drink off a passing waiter's tray and sip the mimosa. "I'm not at liberty to discuss anything with the press."

"But if you were to remain an unnamed source?"

I face her fully, trying to decide what I can or cannot say to her. She looks earnest but shrewd.

"But nothing. Galen has been doing a great job managing the tremors that resulted from the closing of the Garden of Evil, and I have total faith in the training Titus is putting him through, even if it comes at the expense of my office being trashed. I know they haven't had the easiest of relationships, but that makes their time together all the more meaningful. After all, Essos spent his whole life leading up to his coronation being groomed to rule the Under-world. I'm fortunate I can trust Galen to run the realm while I take time to reacclimate. I was thrust into ruling too quickly." The news that the Garden of Evil was closed is no surprise, but her eyebrows lift with these two tasty nuggets I've given her.

"Then I wish you the best," Celestina says as she backs away, an eager gleam in her eyes to chase down the rest of the story.

I dance with Dion and Finn and Kai and Xavier. Dion reassures me that Galen will never win his trial and that he has my back. Xavier asks after Cat, but I pointedly ignore his question. Finn finally offers to help me make a quick exit. Anyone I want to contact me will know how.

I step into the foyer, where Spot, Shadow, and Dave are

pacing in front of the front door, tails wagging. I lift a hand, palm up, the command obvious to them. The three dogs drop onto their haunches, waiting for directions. A quick glance around tells me I only have Finn and Dion with me. I summon three treats and set them on each of their noses. They wait, watching, until I give the command that they can eat them. I nod my head, and they devour the treats. It was the easiest way that Essos and I could figure out to give them treats without a fight when both of us weren't there.

"Be good. Watch the house. Be the fearsome creatures I know you are." I drop to my knees, and all three dogs crowd me. I scratch behind their ears, letting them lick my face. Dave nearly topples me over trying to get close to me the same way he did the first time he saw me after over a millennium away.

Finn holds a hand out to me, and I take it. Dion steps up on his other side, his hand resting on his lover's shoulder. Finn pulls me close.

"You sure you're ready? It's been a while since you did this," Finn teases.

I scowl. "I'm sure."

I am not sure. The ability to teleport is something we all have, but the way we move through time and space always left me feeling like a jumbled mess. My weak stomach could barely tolerate it, and I would be laid up for hours with a headache, eating crackers and drinking ginger fizzy drinks. Maybe the extra champagne today was a bad idea.

"If you vomit on me..." His eyes narrow, and he waits for me to tell him I'm ready to go.

"How did Cat and Zara handle it?" I ask, mad at my thoughtlessness for not asking sooner.

"Cat passed out. Zara only managed to hold it together because Cat passed out. I stayed till she woke up. She was okay when I left—she actually seemed to be breathing easier."

More desperate to get to my friends now, I screw my eyes shut and squeeze Finn's middle. "I'm ready."

Finn doesn't hesitate. There is a weightlessness to our bodies, like we're floating in space with no gravity. If I opened my eyes, I would see the world moving quickly as we bypass it all until we get to our destination.

We stop, and my arms refuse to let go of Finn as I ground myself, first with my eyes still closed. My head is still swooping dangerously and the avocado toast and champagne are fighting their way back up. I take a second to look around. We're outside my old apartment building in Solarem. It's my first time back, and seeing the neighborhood nearly drives me to my knees.

Nothing and everything has changed all at the same time. The cobblestone street is a thruway for people to access the larger avenues on either side of the block. Short brownstones are welcoming, with yearlong lights strung along the railings leading up to the front doors. On the corner is the flower shop I would always frequent, offering exclusive blooms when business was down to drive people to them.

My favorite market is beside the florist, the awning a brighter shade of yellow than I remember, like it's been painted or updated. The bistro where Essos and I would have wine with the owners still sets their tables outside. Each store has a white lily attached to the doorway, and that touches me in more ways than I can put into words.

In the distance, the bright lights of Solarem City burn. They look taller, sleeker than the last time I was here, but I wonder how much of that is actual change versus me misremembering. The scent of magnolia is so strong, it's no wonder the papers have been writing about it for weeks. You can't escape it.

Essos and I picked this neighborhood because the street was quiet. We wanted to have privacy but still be close to Essos's family. It's early in the evening, so people are still milling about, heading to shops and restaurants. There are families and couples and singles everywhere, and I'm overwhelmed by the way the world kept turning after I died. It was different seeing everyone in a bubble at my house. People came to me, but they felt like props —they weren't really there. Here, there is no denying that life moved on.

I grip Finn's arm as I reach out to touch the brick façade. Behind us is the large lake that Solarem grew around. It's the same lake that Essos and I would sneak into in the middle of the night when we wanted to feel the cold water on our skin and each other.

Long ago, after Finn dropped in unannounced once, we made it so no one could transport directly into our apartment. Essos had me bent over the kitchen table when Finn showed up. It was a lesson we learned early, and after that, people had to check in with the front desk.

Finn grips my chin, tilting my head up. I can feel tears pricking the backs of my eyes.

"Head up, my queen. You don't want your first time back to be as a blubbery mess."

I close my eyes, blinking away my tears. Finn is right, I would hate that.

I reach for my powers and pull the doors open, then I stride through with my head held high. The workers at the front desk and even other residents turn their heads at my entrance. I'm flanked by Finn and Dion as I walk in.

People drop to one knee, foreheads pressed to their forearms. It's not a slow realization; it's immediate once they're over the shock.

"Please, you know I hate that formality." The people rise to their feet, starting to whisper amongst themselves.

"Might I be the first to welcome you home, Your Majesty?" One of the doormen approaches me, his hand outstretched.

I smile, taking it and giving it a shake. "Thank you, Luca."

He beams when I remember his name. "If there is anything you need, Your Majesty, please let us know. Will you be with us long?"

"I'll let you know. I have two friends staying with me, and I would appreciate if you could tend to them as well as you tend to me. They're new to Solarem."

"Of course, of course!" Luca is still pumping my hand, not ready to let me go.

"I should see to them."

Luca releases my hand and I give him a genuine smile.

"It's good to be back."

"His Majesty...he missed you. If you don't mind my saying," Luca says as Finn, Dion, and I step into the lift to my penthouse apartment.

My smile falters. I wonder if Essos brought other women here, to our apartment. The doors close, and I let the smile fall.

"I thought you would be happier to be home." Finn gives me a worried look, and I hit the stop button and turn on the two of them.

"I would be happier if a friend had told me that my husband had other lovers while I was gone."

Dion's dark skin drains of color. He casts a furtive glance at Finn, who looks guilty as sin. I could have confronted them back at the house, but I wanted the privacy to get an explanation.

Essos's earlier betrayal rears its ugly head. Self-doubt whispers in my ear that he's cheated on me before. Why not again, here?

No. Those feelings, that memory being fresh, doesn't give me a good enough reason to doubt Essos. He is my constant. He is my anchor. He is all that is good in my life.

"How did you find out?" Not a denial.

"Posey." I spit out her name, finally feeling like I can release these feelings. I had to pretend not to be bothered by it. Bury the revelation in my mind, even when it tried to creep up on me while I was falling asleep. "I got a hint of it from Xavier during the Calling, but I didn't think twice about it—not until his wife decided to rub it in my face."

"She had no right." Dion's voice has an anger that usually isn't there.

"No, but at least she told me, which is more than I can say for my *friends*." I start the lift again, turning my back to them.

I know this isn't an argument for me to have with them; it's for me to talk to Essos about... if I ever see him again. But I wish someone I trusted had told me, or someone who was at least friendly toward me, who wouldn't have used the information as a weapon.

We're silent as we get to my front door. I lay my palm against the wood, expecting to see...what? Feel what? Memories of when we got this place? Feelings of love? I trace the embellishments carved into the wood, our symbol. I can't question the decisions I have made that brought me to this moment. I grip the cold metal of the handle, which is coded to open at my touch, twisting it and pushing the door open.

The apartment is exactly as I left it, with the exception of Zara and Cat, who are snuggled under a blanket, watching TV. The walls are the same rich purple I struggled over picking. The jewel-toned walls complement the teal velvet couch. Essos suggested making the space look like my jewelry box, bright and opulent. I want to weep at the sight of the sun setting over the lake that I can see from the window to our balcony.

Zara throws off the blanket and runs to me. I can smell the wine on her as she squeezes me in a hug. Cat rises to her feet, and Waffles crawls out from under the blanket Zara tossed aside, a scowl on his little face as he prances right onto her warmed spot.

"I see you found my wine collection," I tease lightly, welcoming Cat into the group hug.

"Finn made sure to show us where it was." Cat's cheeks are rosy, but I don't think it's from drink; I think she's finally starting to look like herself.

"That was generous of him," I say with a look over my shoulder.

He's unapologetic as he and Dion close the door. "I figure a thousand years is more than enough time to let them age."

"So, what's the grand plan?" Dion asks, dropping himself on the couch. With a simple gesture, he covers the glass coffee table with wine glasses and an elaborate charcuterie board with perfectly cut meats and cheeses. Waffles meows loudly at the couch being jostled before he moves and makes himself comfortable on Dion's lap.

"Grand plan?" I ask, seating myself on an ottoman so my friends can sit again on the couch.

"I thought this was some sort of strategy meeting." Dion gestures again, and our glasses are filled with varying shades of liquid, likely to our personal preferences. My affection for this man never ceases, especially since his wedding gifts to Essos and me were bottomless wine glasses that filled with a simple thought of whatever we were craving. We could have done it ourselves, but his magic always made the wine sweeter and more savory.

"Well, my strategy is to figure out who is trying to bind my powers, how the dagger that killed me was created, and how Galen got it in the first place. From there, I don't know. I just want my husband back." I glance at the hallway that leads to our bedroom. I can practically see him leaning against the doorway, hands in his pockets, as if saying, *Here I am baby, I never left.* But the doorway is empty, and I am left to deal with this in my own way.

"That sounds like a lot of boring research," Finn says, making a face.

"I can help with research." Cat offers, but I shake my head.

"I appreciate that, but I need you to focus on healing. If you're not fully on the rebound by the end of this week, I'm having specialized healers come to see you. You look better already, but when we healed you the first time, we used enough power to light a city block. There's no reason for you to have declined again."

Cat scowls at me and I stick out my tongue at her.

"So, you're going to the library?" Finn asks.

"Does the Goddess of Wisdom still prefer double-fudge brownies?" My eyes flick to my kitchen, where I'm going to need to work hard on perfecting them.

"She has recently developed a taste for caramel drizzled in them," Dion points out helpfully.

"When are you going to the library?" Zara asks, slathering a piece of meat with cheese spread and honey. She shoves the whole thing in her mouth, waiting for a response.

"Day after next. Tomorrow, I want to get you settled in, and I need to bake. I'm a little rusty. Finn, I need you to check with Estelle, see if she found out what could be binding my powers." He nods. "And if there's time, I want to track down Rafferty, the God of Memory, to see if he can restore my memories completely. I need them all back. I can't still have things floating out there that I *should* know but don't." That's something else I dread, having to bring someone else into this whole situation. Though it occurs to me that Rafferty must be the one who bound my memories in the first place, so maybe I won't need to tell him about everything.

If we can find him. As rulers of the dead, Essos and I worked with Rafferty to craft a potion for souls who were suffering from trauma, to give them the option of forgetting the horrors of their life or death. But the god was difficult to get a hold of regularly and was well-known for being a hermit. Even Finn, who has God GPS, struggles with locating the elusive god.

"And tonight?" Cat asks.

"Tonight, we relax." I reach up and pull the pin from my hair, letting my curls loose. I feel more at ease here than I have since I got my memories back. I shake my empty glass at Dion for a refill, and he obliges with a laugh.

We spend the night drinking and laughing and dancing. I keep an eye on Cat, who puts on a brave face, but I see her exhaustion. Also on the itinerary is an actual visit to the wellness spa at the center of the lake. Posey's proposal to change to two-week intervals between trials is inconvenient, but I will make it work.

Somehow, I always do.

25

"So, why are we doing this?" Cat asks as I layer brownie batter into a pan. She's ready to drizzle the caramel with perfect accuracy. It's our third batch of the day, and I've tried something a little different with each round. I forgot how the oven worked, the best spot in the oven that didn't burn the brownies, and how best to fold in the caramel. I needed time to adjust.

"Because Gisella is the librarian, and she holds the key to all the knowledge. She has books that center around the creation of time and the birth of Titus and his wife Octavia. If there's any knowledge about the dagger that killed me or about how we can reverse the vote of no confidence, then she has it." I pop the latest tray into the oven and set the timer. "The library is vast, storing not just knowledge of the gods but also the mortal realms. She could send me on a wild goose chase or trap me in the labyrinth that is the library."

"Literal labyrinth?" Cat asks, grabbing a crumb from an earlier batch.

"Literal labyrinth," I confirm. "At Solarem University, at least once a semester, we would have to go into the library for something or other, and every time, she would send someone in the wrong direction and they'd be trapped for days. She never let it go further for fear of someone damaging the books, but no one ever made the same mistake twice."

"Why doesn't Titus just reverse what Galen has done, if he's this supreme being, and why don't you use the dagger to kill Galen?" Zara asks, picking at a discarded brownie.

I pause in my licking of the spoon and contemplate the right way to explain. "Killing Galen wouldn't solve the underlying problem. *Someone* had to give him the dagger that killed me, and we need to find out who, because killing Galen doesn't guarantee that I'm safe or that Essos is safe. Titus? Well, he doesn't *want* to help. Joke's on him. He's stuck at the house trying to train Galen to be a ruler." I set the bowl in the sink to soak it before I wash it.

Nausea rises and burns the back of my throat, but I swallow the urge to throw up. Maybe five pounds of brownie batter wasn't the best breakfast.

"And you think your house will still be standing in a month?" Cat asks with a laugh. I'm pleased she managed to finish the eggs and toast I made her for breakfast. I don't think I'll be able to stomach asking Cat to come back to the house with me. She's flourishing here in a way she hasn't in my home since after the first trial.

"I left Galen specific instructions to not burn the house down. He thinks I'm busy looking for the scepter."

"Do you know where it is?" Cat grabs another brownie crumb and pops it into her mouth.

"Of course. Essos has it. It would be hell on Earth if Galen ever got the scepter. I can't imagine what terrors the God of War would use it for. It's what Essos used to allow Tiffany back into the moral realm."

Zara deflates at the mention of her best friend, whom I'm sure she's missing. Cat reaches out and rubs her back.

"Tiffany." The word is a whisper on Zara's lips.

"Do you want to see her?"

Zara and Cat both look at me. Zara nods. I gesture at the TV. It turns on, and Tiffany's voice filters through the air.

She's standing at a podium on a platform in the quad at school in a somber black dress. Behind her is a red curtain. Steve is on one side, giving her an encouraging smile.

"I should be preparing for fall semester finals. I should be talking to my sisters about job offers or grad school plans. I should be looking forward to spring semester of our senior year and gushing with them over the future. I should be busy planning for my future, but a part of me is stuck in the past.

"Six months ago, I missed my alarm. I overslept and never got on a bus with my friends headed to Santa Monica. It should have been an amazing weekend of hitting the beach, watching my boyfriend play beach volleyball, and building memories. Instead, it was spent in mourning over the twenty lives lost after the bus that was carrying them plunged over a cliff." Tiffany sounds pained as she reads on.

"None of them deserved to have their lives cut short. They all deserved to live the lives they wanted, as an accountant, a lawyer, a president. They deserved to live out their lives as wives and daughters and girlfriends and mothers, but I'm left behind to live out their dreams.

"The sisters of Epsilon Lambda Delta have decided to build a lily garden in honor of the sisters we lost, and a scholarship has been created in honor of Daphne Hale, who was not a sister but a beloved friend. The scholarship is being provided by her parents, Congressman Phil Hale and his wife, Melinda."

Tiffany pulls a tassel, dropping the curtain. Behind it is a lovely garden with varying colors of lilies and benches arranged throughout. It's a lovely gesture, but I know it's just going to be used by freshmen to hide their puke after they've had too much to drink. A small rock at the entrance holds a plaque engraved with the names of all the sisters who perished.

"This garden will serve as a reminder that life is short and to love everyone in your life. I miss my friends dearly, but I'm comforted by the knowledge that they're in a better place." Tiffany steps off the stage and into Steve's arms.

She did a great job of holding it together, but she falls apart in his embrace. Beside him, my adoptive parents stand with somber expressions, answering questions for a reporter about the scholarship and how much they miss me. I catch a question about a possible run for a senate seat, and I hope Phil makes the jump.

But this isn't about me, it's about Tiffany, so we follow her as she and Steve step into the garden. They sit on a bench, and I see my name on a plaque on the back, since it isn't on the rock with all the sisters.

"You did so great." Steve's arm is slung over Tiffany's shoulders. His fingers trace circles on her arm.

"I wish I didn't have to do it at all. Why did Zara leave without me?" The way she says it sounds like she's asked this question plenty of times in the last six months.

A choked sound escapes from Zara.

"You can ask yourself that a thousand times and never have an answer. I will never not be thankful that she didn't wake you up, because if she had, I would have been standing where you stood. I love you, and I'm sorry that you're in pain, but you will heal from this eventually." Steve kisses her forehead.

"Still sure you're okay naming our first daughter Zara?"

Steve laughs gently. "She has a strong namesake to live up to. I would be proud to name our future daughter Zara. You promised to marry me; that's all I need."

Tiffany holds out her hand, showing off a dainty solitaire

diamond ring. She nestles closer into his side, and I turn off the TV.

"She seems mostly happy." Zara's voice is choked, probably from realizing they're going to name their first daughter after her. She leans against Cat.

"She is. I check in on her from time to time to see if she has any memory of her involvement in the Calling. Today is just a hard day for her for obvious reasons." The timer goes off, and I step back into my kitchen to take care of the brownies.

"Can you look in on anyone in the world?" Zara asks. Cat already knows the answer—Essos let her look in on her parents during the Calling—but this is new to Zara.

"I can look in on both the living and the dead. Well, at least, I could. It's in my wheelhouse. Essos was a little stingy with this power, but having been to the mortal realm myself, I have the desire to look in on it now and then." I set aside the pan and start measuring ingredients while this batch cools.

"Did you always want to be a queen?" Zara wasn't privy to the late-night conversations Cat and I had as my memories started to come back.

I plan on having enough brownies to suffocate Gisella. I don't know how many days I'll need to be in the library, but it's important that she lets me in and doesn't ask too many questions. She also can't let anyone know I've been sniffing around.

"Nope. I was in school learning what it meant to be a goddess and what my responsibilities were to the mortal realm. I was content being the Goddess of Spring, growing flowers for the mortals and helping to fertilize their crops. Even after I met Essos, I still wasn't sure I wanted to be queen, or if I was good enough to hold the crown. We had a lot of conversations about it. I was never the strongest physically, and with my powers, I could grow flowers and kill them as well, but there are many powers the gods share, like teleportation and matter creation, that I struggled with. I also didn't have as much power to draw on. It's part of why what happened with Galen—well, why I wasn't able to hold him off. He was a much better fighter, and more adept with his abilities, all of them. I don't plan on making that mistake again."

As part of my self-guided workout, I use my powers to make the next batch. I watch the batter mix before pouring it into another pan and drizzling the caramel. The oven door swings open, and I pop them inside before closing it again, the timer set.

I collapse onto the couch with my friends, huddling under a shared blanket. Since we're settling down, Waffles makes his way over and climbs on us.

"How can you do it? Make nice with Galen. I would cut his balls off at the first chance." Most of Zara's questions are ones that Cat and I spoke of before, when I was trying to play mad at Zara to protect her.

"With a lot of antacids and anti-nausea medication. It's hard to make nice with your murderer, but I have to. I don't know where the dagger is now, and I don't trust that Galen won't use it on Essos. He wanted me, and he still killed me. He has no love for Essos. I'm not willing to risk the murder of my husband."

"Hopefully, this will all be over soon," Cat says, wrapping one of my curls around her fingers.

"I mean, I don't know how this can end—that's why I'm here for a month. I need time to find a way out. Essos is looking too, but I don't know what he plans to do."

"If we can help, let us know," Cat pleads.

I scratch Waffles's head, triggering a purr. "You can help me by staying safe and away from Galen. You feeling better helps me. Eating the leftover brownies helps me. Now, I have like a thousand years to catch up on some of my shows. What do you say you watch with me?"

GISELLA HASN'T CHANGED. She's sitting behind her desk at the Library of Solarem, her long dark braids pulled back into a ponytail and her glasses on the bridge of her nose. Like all the librarians under her authority, she's wearing a navy blue tunic that covers most of her. Her lips are colored royal purple, and I hope the lipstick is smudge-proof when I place down the six containers of brownies. The Goddess of Wisdom lifts her eyes to the containers then to me, a small smile ghosting her lips.

"Your Majesty." She tips her head to me but doesn't rise from her chair. If she's surprised to see me, she doesn't show it.

"Gisella, it's lovely to see you as always." I keep my voice low to avoid disturbing the scholars within.

Behind her are some of the oldest tomes to ever exist. The honeycomb building extends above and below ground, the lower levels requiring special permission to access, and she seldom provides it. The building itself is in walking distance from my apartment, on the border between my neighborhood and Solarem City, and on the opposite side of the city from Solarem University. Really, all of the city is walkable, with some homes, like Xavier's, located just outside the city limits.

"Is there something you want?"

I smooth down my red skirt. Today's outfit is modest and sophisticated. The pencil skirt extends past my knees, a dark blue belt separating it from the powder blue top. My hair is pulled into a side ponytail, with curls in soft ringlets falling down my front.

"I would appreciate access to the archives related to weaponry."

Her eyebrows shoot into her hairline. Finally, a reaction. "That seems outside your usual department."

I push one of the containers closer to her. "Yes, but I did make brownies. I heard you developed a taste for caramel."

Her nostrils flare as she sniffs. "Are these all made with caramel?"

I rest my elbows on the counter and my chin in my hands. "Varying levels of gooeyness."

With a simple glare at where my elbows rest, she has me pulling my arms off the counter.

Gisella pulls a container of brownies onto her lower desk and drops an access bracelet in its place. "Good luck with your research."

As a pair of bookshelves behind her separate, opening to a lift that will let me down into the bowels of the honeycomb, I hear the sound of her opening the container.

Once I get down there, I'm overwhelmed. The stacks feel endless, and I don't know where to start. The lights turn on as I go, letting me know that I am alone down here. It's eerie, the only sounds that of my flats hitting the ground as I go farther down the hall.

I stop periodically to check the content of the stacks I'm passing, and I start grabbing leather tomes. I drop them onto a cart and settle down at a table and begin reading. Of course, none of these books have a table of contents or an index to help me figure out where to look.

My vision starts to blur as I set aside my third book, unsure how much time has passed. Daylight doesn't reach down here, and I understand how easy it would be to get lost in the books or yourself.

I've made some headway with the section I just started pulling books from, so I return, hoping to find something more. Gisella would kill me if she knew I was doing it, but I stand on the bottom shelf and stretch for a book on the top that is *just* out of reach.

"I hope you plan on putting those books back." The male voice startles me, and I stumble back right into the source. Strong hands catch me around the waist and pull me against a hard chest. A gentle kiss is pressed to my exposed neck, and I relax. I turn to face Essos.

He's clean-shaven but wearing glasses. I run the back of my knuckles along his cheek, loving the feel of his smooth skin. I have so much I want to talk to him about, but I kiss him instead.

He meets me with equal fervor, his hands tightening around my hips. Essos tugs me against him, his arms locking around me. I let my hands slide up into his hair, my fingers tightening in his dark locks. I rise on my toes, trying to get as close to him as I can. He turns me gently, walking me back to the wall.

I let him, let him move his lips from my mouth down my neck.

He inhales deeply. "You smell like brownies." He's breathless, his teeth scraping against my skin.

I stifle the sound in the back of my throat. I forgot what an exhibitionist my husband is. "I had to bribe Gisella. You and I have to have a serious conversation later." I'm breathless because he's kissing me again. His hands are in my hair, pulling my hair tie out.

"I love your hair," he whispers, shaking out the curls. "I've missed how soft it is."

His hands move to my skirt and start pulling it up. I hear the fabric tear, but I ignore it. I'm focused on undoing his jeans button and zipper. His hands are greedy, hiking my skirt up to my waist and pulling my underwear down. I finish the job, dropping them to my ankles and casting them aside with a kick. I grab his face and yank him back down to me. He lifts me, and I'm able to wrap my legs around his hips. I can feel him pressing against my core, and I bite down on his lip, fighting another moan.

"I've missed *you*," I whisper, reaching between us, removing his cock from his boxers and positioning him at my entrance. His movement to enter me is quick and precise, and I don't fight the sound I make when he's in me. Each thrust is powerful, and I worry for a moment he might fuck me through the wall. I want to cry out, but if Gisella doesn't know what we're doing in her library, she certainly will if I do.

His hand cups my breast as we find an even rhythm. He drives into me, and I meet his thrusts, rocking my hips. I don't want this moment to end, but I can already feel my release coming. Essos increases his tempo, wringing pleasure from my body with ease. I hold my moan in but can't stop a small whimper that seems to set Essos over the edge. I feel his muscles tense, and I clench around him as my orgasm recedes and his begins. It adds an interesting symmetry to our story, as my everything begins and ends with him.

He slows down, his hips pressing to mine, until he's spent. We stay there for a moment, our bodies crushed together, sharing kisses until he withdraws and sets me gently on the ground. I pull down my skirt as he fixes himself, but I reach up again and bring his face to mine for one last long kiss before we talk business.

"I love you," I say when I lean back.

He kisses the tip of my nose, then my forehead and each cheek. "Love is such an insufficient word for what I feel for you. I spend my days longing for you, unable to think straight. But until I create a word for how you make me feel, *love* will just have to cover it." His words have me melting into a puddle of adoration; when he says things like this, it's so hard to muster the frustration I feel.

He holds up my underwear, and I shrug. "Keep them. Makes it easier if we want a repeat later on a table." He smirks, shoving them deep into his pocket. I don't admit to him that I love the filthy feeling of having his mess dripping down the insides of my thighs.

"My exhibitionist little minx."

I shove him gently before looking at the tear up the side seam on my skirt. "You started it," I point out with a grin. He can't take his eyes off me and looks like he wants to fuck me again until I scream loud enough to shake the building.

"And I'll gladly start it again. What book were you reaching for?"

I point to the one I want, and he grabs it with ease. We go back to my table.

Having time with Essos is all I've been pleading with the Fates for. This is everything I want it to be, and yet in this post-sex haze, the first thing on my mind is not the dagger I should be hunting for. It's that he slept with someone else while I was dead. It's bad enough that I never cleared the air with him after the memory of him cheating on me resurfaced. No amount of lying to or cajoling myself can hide the fact that it still *hurt*. It *still* hurts my heart to think about him with someone else, and these two issues are getting conflated in my head and heart, and it will taint our time together if I don't clear the air with him.

"I'm trying to find out more about the dagger that killed me. Your father suggested it, and maybe once we're done with that, you can tell me about who you slept with while I was dead?"

Essos stops short where he is and turns to look at me. There is shame written all over his face, in the dip of his brow to the frown on his lips.

"You already know." His tone is flat. Blue eyes struggle to meet mine, but they do, and remorse fills them. "Who told you?"

"Does it matter? *You* didn't." I stab a finger into his chest.

He reaches out to cup my cheek. "When, my love, would you have liked me to bring it up? When you chose my brother over me after I watched you two kissing like it was the only way you would

291

survive?" His use of the term of endearment doesn't soften the anger in his words. I hurt him, deeply, at the Calling Ball.

Things between us are getting so complicated, so tangled, when he is supposed to be the sure thing in my life.

I swat his hand away. "It *is* the only way for me to survive there, Essos."

His eyes soften, and his posture deflates just a little. "I'm sorry. I know that, and I didn't mean it." Essos grabs a book and drops into a chair in front of me.

I remain standing. "I don't want Galen. I never did. I hate this as much as you do."

Essos reaches for my hand and tugs me onto his lap. I sit, cognizant that my lower lip is sticking out in a pout.

He reaches up, his thumb pulling on my lip before he steals another quick kiss. "What do you want to know? I'm an open book."

I know it too. I know he wouldn't keep secrets from me, not intentionally, and the few times we've gotten to see each other since the Calling have been too brief. Too brief to drop a bomb like that into the middle of our newly revived marriage.

"I shouldn't have said anything. We have more important things to worry about, like Titus and Galen and the scepter and the dagger."

Essos pushes my hair over my shoulder. "It is clearly bothering you, and the whole world can be damned. Ask what you want, and I will tell you my side. It sort of just happened and I know that's stupid to say, but it's the truth. She was, well, she is a nymph. I'm obviously not doing anything with her any longer. I just got lonely. She was always more interested in me than I was in her. It's tacky to say, but it was just sex, and it was brief. It left me feeling emptier than before." Essos rubs his thumb along my bare leg, where his hand rests. His blue eyes don't break contact with mine, letting me see how sincere he is. "You are my soulmate, and without you in my life, I was half a man. I barely got out of bed. I barely functioned. Sybil helped make sure the realm was running, but you and I had done such a good job making ourselves redundant that I barely had to do anything."

"What was her name?" I hate the insecure note in my voice.

"Eliana. I ran into her again at some party that Xavier and Posey were throwing. I accidentally spilled my drink on her dress, and I was a little drunk, and it just happened. It was nothing like before."

Before, when he cheated on me with some random woman in his office. Maybe when I track down Rafferty, I'll ask him to erase that particular memory.

"How long?" I ask not even registering his last sentence.

"It was only in the last quarter century. I—"

I cut him off with a kiss. "I believe you. I don't need to know any more." It hits me then, Finn's comments, and even Cassius's warning. My blood runs cold as a thought catches and sticks. I lean back, trying to keep my breathing even. "Can you describe her?"

"She doesn't hold a candle to your beauty."

I roll my eyes but don't fight the smile on my face. Essos strokes my cheek, gazing at me like he could stare at me all day and never get bored.

"I love you, I really do, but be serious," I scold. "Is she short? Long black hair? Brown eyes? Always looks a little like she smelled something rancid?"

Confusion flickers in Essos's eyes. "That's her to a tee."

I get off his lap, pacing back to the stacks before looking at him. "She's one of my ladies-in-waiting, I'm pretty sure she's been binding my powers."

Essos leaps out of his seat as if shocked. "Binding your powers? What are you talking about?" There is a lethal edge to his voice.

I cover my face with my hands and scream into them as quietly as I can. All of the annoyed glances I got from Ellie start to make sense. She was *sleeping with my husband.* I was the person who stood between them, even from the grave. I was the reason she would never have Essos. Our love triangle just grew into a love quadrilateral.

Essos waits for me to come back to him.

As calmly as I can, I start from the beginning. "Titus kindly alerted me to it. Someone was using my tea to bind my powers. It was being delivered to me by Ellie—Eliana. Once I found out, I stopped drinking it, and my powers are rebounding, but I'm still a little sluggish, on top of trying to relearn how my powers work."

"He never gives without taking something in return. But your powers *are* returning?" Essos rubs his jaw, looking past me, concern etched into his features. We don't age, but I could swear my husband is starting to go grey.

"I know. And they are coming back," I assure him, conjuring a blue lily for him.

Essos takes it with a half-smile. "Where are you staying while you're in Solarem? I assume you're here for at least a few days? This type of research is going to take a while."

"I'm staying at the penthouse. With any luck, I'll be there until the next trial. But full disclosure, I have Cat and Zara with me, and Posey is trying to shorten the window between trials." I watch Essos's Adam's apple bob as he swallows. "How did you even know I was here?" I ask, but I know the answer.

"Finn told me. Can I stay with you?"

My face softens and I reach for him, knowing that he needs reassurance the same way I do. I hurt him, even if unintentionally, by choosing Galen at the ball, and I hurt Essos all the time by kissing his brother to sell the lie.

"Of course. There is no one—*no one*—I want beside me but you."

Essos's hand slides into mine. In one swift jerk of his hand, he tugs me against his hard body. "Good. I'm tired of sharing you. You are my *wife*, and I'm tired of hearing about other people with their hands on you."

I tilt my head up to him. "I am your wife, not your property," I remind him.

His knuckles follow the line of my jaw before lifting my chin. "You are your own woman and I love you, but don't mistake my intent. I am *burning* with jealousy over how possessive Galen has been over you. I keep wanting someone to tell me that you've socked him in front of everyone."

I capture his lips with mine. The kiss sizzles as I press his lips open and his tongue dances with mine. "I did stab him in the gut and nearly castrate him, if that makes you feel better."

I realize my mistake once the words are out of my mouth.

Essos goes perfectly still, a hunter who realizes that his prey has been alerted to his presence. "Why did you do that, and why didn't I hear about it? I imagine you stabbing him in front of everyone would have made the papers."

Not wanting to get into it right now, I shake my head. "It's a long story."

Essos's brow furrows, but he doesn't push further. I will tell him everything, just not now, when I finally have him back for the foreseeable future. Not when we need to get this whole situation figured out. If I tell Essos what happened, I have no doubt that he will go back to our house and start a war with Galen.

"Clearly, we have much to discuss. We can deal with Galen later. First, let's finish researching the dagger and what could possibly be able to bind your power."

Things start to go much faster with Essos across the table from me. It reminds me of when I was in university here. Essos would be working on homework provided by his father, devising plans on how to manage the Afterlife, while I read up on the history of Solarem and learned simple tricks for managing my abilities.

We swap books and share details and information that we're finding. I'm tracking the information in a notebook, but I know I'm going to have to burn it or find a way to leave it with Essos if I can. Things would go poorly if Galen ever found out—it would be evidence enough to prove I'm working against him.

I rest my feet on Essos's lap, and he rubs them absently while reading. He stops and turns his book toward me. I look up and rub my tired eyes. Without natural light, I have no idea what time it even is.

"This mentions an alloy imbibed with the blood of the God and Goddess Supreme. It doesn't say what happened to it, just that it was created. The next page talks about a gem forged from pieces of each of their hearts, joined and hardened."

My fingers trace the words. "You think maybe it's the gem that held my soul?"

"It has to be, right? I mean, I'm sure this alloy is what made the dagger. It discusses the properties of it here." He flips the page and points to another passage. "The ability to do lasting damage to gods, and the stone has retention properties. It looks like these stones were originally created to be part of the Afterlife, to retain souls as a power source. The metal was supposed to hold the stones but was instead fashioned into a weapon. It looks like two daggers were made."

"Do you think the daggers were supposed to go in the scepter?" I ask, starting to make connections.

"Maybe. Maybe the scepter is made of the same alloy? This talks about a lot more metal being created. They had to use it somewhere, why not the scepter? Maybe the eyes were meant to hold the stones. They are rubies." Essos is thinking out loud. He sucks in his lower lip and bites it. We're almost entirely in darkness now; since we settled at our table, the lights around us have turned off.

A light behind Essos winks on, and he turns toward it, pulling on his hat. I watch my husband fade to darkness. Quietly, he slips out of the seat, and the only reason I know that is because he places my feet on the seat he vacated.

"Your Majesty," Gisella says as she approaches.

"Gisella. I promise I've followed the library rules and I haven't had any food."

She glances at the books littering the table. "I'm less concerned about that. You haven't left the library since you arrived when we opened. It is now well past closing. If you would like to come back tomorrow, I can set your books aside."

"Closing?" I stand up and close the books. I shove my notebook into my bag and try not to glance at where I think Essos is standing.

"Yes, I do like to go home. This place isn't my whole life."

"Of course. I'm sorry. I simply lost track of time. I'll be right up."

Gisella raises her eyebrow but walks ahead to the lift. I start to follow and feel a hand on the small of my back. I can't see Essos, but I can smell him.

Gisella waits an extra beat once I'm inside the lift before sending it back to the main floor.

"Is there anything I can do to help you with your research?" Her voice is knowing when she offers.

"I think this is something I have to do on my own, but if you happen to know anything about weapons that can make gods vulnerable or anything like that, I would appreciate your guidance." I take a chance on Gisella, hoping that as the Goddess of Wisdom, she will side with us.

"I'll leave any books I know of at your station. So long as there are more brownies coming my way."

We reach the main floor, and I step out. "I'll work on a fresh batch tonight."

She hesitates a beat, as if waiting for someone else to get off, then she nods and grabs a container of brownies from behind her desk. "See that you do."

26

I want to walk out holding Essos's hand, but I know we can't. I have to trust that he stays close to me.

I'm startled to find that it's dusk, the sun nearly completely set over the lake. Most of the shops I pass, I remember. The market where I would get fresh strawberries, the bookshop that carried new releases. I see a salesperson in the clothing store where I loved to shop. All of these places made this neighborhood home.

The walk from the library to the apartment isn't long. When we arrive, I'm careful about how long I leave the door open as I enter the building, and I scoot over slightly when I get in the lift. I can feel Essos with me as we ride up.

"You should have gotten something to eat at that little bistro we loved." His breath tickles my neck.

"I was wondering if you could make me your famous carbonara. I've been craving it for what feels like weeks."

He's still invisible, but I can feel him beaming as I twist the knob to our apartment. The wards around it should protect him.

He waits until the door behind us is closed to reveal himself to

Cat and Zara, who are on my couch, watching some of the shows I got them hooked on while we were baking brownies. They're slow to look up, likely thinking that it's just me.

"You were gone forever. Where was this dedication during finals?" Cat teases, finally raising her eyes to me. She catches sight of Essos and screams, startling Zara, who also screams when she sees him.

They both jump up and seem unsure what to do. They start to bow, but Essos holds up a hand to stop them. Waffles is left disgruntled again, hissing at the disruption before moving to the cat bed in front of the window, seemingly tired of the humans.

"Don't start with that now," Essos says. "I never made you bow before, and this isn't any different. I'm glad you both look well."

It's awkward for a moment as Zara shies back now that she's face-to-face with Essos. She carried a major torch for him during the Calling, and I was thankful that she dropped it in front of me immediately once the truth came out. But this is the first time the three of us have been together. Cat and Essos were never serious during the Calling; she stayed purely for my benefit, much like she is now.

Essos embraces Cat, grinning at her. Zara doesn't approach him, and a possessive part of me is glad. I know that he's faithful to me and only to me now, but the image of them kissing is forever seared into my brain. I can't imagine how he's dealing with Galen and me kissing. I need to remember this and give them both some grace.

"Did you guys eat already?" I ask, setting my bag down on the kitchen island.

"No. Did the books fight back? What happened to your skirt?" Zara asks.

Essos's hand rests on the small of my back, a blush creeping up his cheeks.

"Yes, these books are full of ancient and monstrous magic," I say, but I can't stop grinning. I glance at Essos, and he leans into me. We can't get enough of being near each other.

"He totally ripped your skirt fucking you on a table, didn't he?" Cat deadpans. A smile tugs at her lips, and I can only laugh. It is so good to see her back.

"It was against a wall, but yes." I realize the clarification is making Zara doubly uncomfortable, so I nudge Essos. His blue eyes spring to me, then where I am motioning, and he clears his throat.

"Right, well, since you haven't eaten, I'm going to whip up my famous carbonara, so you ladies sit back and enjoy." Essos kisses my forehead, his hands not leaving my body until he has to use them to cook.

"Can I just say, I'm, like, super sorry about throwing myself at you?" Zara says, sliding onto one of the stools at the island.

Essos glances at me, before turning to her. "You have nothing to be sorry about. I'm irresistible, I get it." Essos gives me a wink before being serious. "But honestly, you have nothing to be sorry about. I'm the one who should be apologizing. I never meant to toy with your affections. It was unfair of me to lead you on like that and make you a pawn. I thought what I was doing was for the best, but I was very clearly misguided. I do want to thank you for continuing to support Daphne. This was not how I wanted this all to play out."

I drop into a chair across from Essos and watch him pull out ingredients and, when there are none, magic them onto the table.

"Well, Daphne always did have a flair for making things complicated," Cat says, bumping shoulders with me.

"I feel I am being unfairly vilified here and am going to change." I slip off the chair and huff toward my bedroom.

Last night I fell asleep on the couch with Zara and Cat. Waffles was settled between us all, the sounds of the TV lulling us to sleep. I showered in the shared bathroom and summoned an outfit, convincing myself that it was all for the sake of flexing my abilities.

But it was because I was afraid. Afraid of what was behind that door. Would it be just like I left it the last time I was at the apartment? A half-finished paperback on my side table, an ancient tube of Chapstick sitting in my drawer? Has my make-up dried out at my vanity? Did Essos take Ellie here and make love to her the way he did to me? Will it be her makeup littered on the counters? Will I find her clothes in my drawers? So many questions I don't want answered lay behind that door, and now I'm going to open it.

Open Pandora's box, so to speak. Two hands settle on my hips.

"I haven't been here in I don't even know how long," Essos says, bringing his arms around to fold them across my chest.

I lean against him, staring at the door. "Where did you go?"

"I got a different place. I couldn't handle being surrounded by memories of you. I thought I was going crazy, that I could hear you laughing on the other side of the door and that this was all just one big joke. When I opened the door and it was dark inside, the curtains still drawn, and you weren't there, I just closed the door and left." His arms tighten around me. I take a steadying breath and push the door open, stepping out of his arms. My body relaxes at the idea that he didn't bring Ellie here, but then the thought that maybe they were screwing in our bed in our *home* hits me, and I'm tense all over again.

The king-size bed is still unmade, the sheets rumpled from the last time we were here. A pile of my shoes lies on the floor near my side of the bed; a dress is haphazardly discarded over a chair.

The last time we were in Solarem was for Posey's birthday party. She threw this huge bash and made everyone spend twenty-four hours celebrating with her. I was exhausted before even going. Essos promised that he would be the ruse to get us out that night, and he did a spectacular job. He got plastered within the first four hours and started to turn Posey's staff into animals. It was endlessly amusing for us to watch as one of the waiters-turned-monkey dropped down from the chandelier in his full livery with a tray of drinks for Posey to pick from. She turned shades of red that were unnatural. Essos had pre-planned with the staff and compensated anyone affected. We laughed on the entire walk home, my shoes in his hands, his arm wrapped around my shoulders. We made love slowly as the sun rose, peeking through our blinds.

I'm pretty sure that was the night we conceived. I never told him I was pregnant. It was still too new, I was too afraid, and if it didn't work out again, I wanted it to be my burden to bear alone. Even now, I haven't told him that two lives were lost the day that his brother stabbed a knife through my heart. I don't know if he ever found out, but I won't bring it up. He's already dealt with so much.

Two months after that night, I was dead.

"Here," Essos calls, tossing me my underwear. I catch it with a laugh and throw it toward the hamper, which I'm surprised has been emptied.

"I love you," I blurt out as he moves back toward the door.

He smiles. "Say it again," he demands in a harsh whisper, moving back to where I stand at the foot of the bed.

"I love you." It's a whisper now, my fingers fisted in his shirt, and I don't know if I want to scream or cry or throw myself at him until we're both too exhausted to move.

"I'll never get tired of hearing you say that. You could read a dictionary to me, and I would never get tired of the sound of your voice." He brushes a strand of hair out of my face.

"I'm pretty sure that's not true. I would be bored to tears trying. But I'll endeavor to speak as much at you as possible."

"As long as you're naked eighty percent of the time, you'll hear no complaints from me."

"Suddenly, there are stipulations as to how much you want to hear my voice? I'm appalled at your roguish behavior."

The smile Essos gives me brightens his eyes, and I can see the flames of desire dancing in them. "Keep talking like that, and everyone in the apartment will go hungry. Change. I'll get working on dinner. I love you." He closes the door gently behind him. My husband sometimes has the self-control of a saint.

I emerge a few minutes later in my royal blue Solarem University Alumni shirt and matching pair of shorts with the letters *SU* on the ass. Essos is folding in the beaten eggs and cheese when I walk in.

"So, Daphne walks up to this girl—mind you, Daphne and I had been on all of one date at this point—and I swear, she looks her in the eye, and says, 'You're in my seat.' And dear Daph doesn't bat an eye, staring down a literal warrior until she gets off my lap. Then Daph slides herself onto my knee, flipping her curls over her shoulder, and she looks back at her and goes, 'I'll need a margarita to wash away the memory of you.' The Amazon was of course so confused, and Daphne, in her regal voice, says, 'Make that sugar on the rim. Sometime today.'"

Essos is laughing as he tells one of the more embarrassing stories of our youth, but I suppose I deserve it. There are moments I'm not proud of, just as Essos has a few that, if he could go back and do them over, he would.

"Telling tall tales?" I ask, clearing the small table we have for dining. We never used this space for entertaining, so we never needed the extravagant furniture we have at the main house. This table is just big enough for the four of us.

"Only the best ones. I knew at that moment that I was a goner and she was going to be my queen." Essos winks at me as he pours the pasta into a large bowl for us each to pull from. Behind him, the oven beeps.

I'm setting the table when the memory slides to the forefront of my mind. It's from not long after his story.

ESSOS IS SWAMPED at work and can't meet me for lunch like he promised. It's not the first time that's happened as the pressure from his father mounts. He needs to present three options for how to handle the Underworld for the mortal realm. Essos doesn't know I overheard his father one night in his study, asking if Essos is up to the challenge or if he's too distracted by me to do it right. So, I've been helping him brainstorm and keeping him focused and well-fed with snacks when he's busy.

Today is no different. I know him, even though our relationship is so new compared to our lifespan. Essos will work through lunch and dinner and will realize three days later that he still hasn't had anything to eat.

I get us both sandwiches from the vendor across from his office, and I'm nearly bouncing on my toes to get to him. Maybe if he relaxes a little, he'll be able to focus better on the task ahead. A blow job wouldn't be the most insane idea I've had, and I wouldn't be opposed to a quickie.

I've got my long hair pulled back into a ponytail to show off the ruby drop earrings that Essos gave me last week. The look is ostentatious for the office, but they match the red bra and underwear I have on.

As I walk toward his office, I notice no one's meeting my eye, and I wonder if something has happened. He's never been the type to yell; he's more fond of attracting bees with honey and is a firm believer that if your staff is too scared of you to come to you with a mistake, then you're doing something wrong.

Once I get to his office, I notice his assistant isn't at her desk. I decide to slip in quietly, in case he's on a call or in a meeting.

As my hand closes on the door handle, I hear it.

The sounds of grunts and moans and flesh meeting flesh. The panting, the thump of a body being slammed against his desk. I open the door, my brain trying to reason with me that that isn't what I'm hearing, but I make eye contact with him, and I know. He has a woman with black hair bent over his desk, and his pants are around his ankles.

The hurt on his face matches the pain in my chest, but there's a grim determination there. His blue eyes don't look away from me; he wanted me to see this, wanted me to catch him in the act.

I barely looked at the woman. Only when she lifts her head to see the interruption does my gaze flick to her. Her long dark hair had veiled her face, but it slides off, showing the perfectly round shape and the contour of her dark eyes.

"Do you mind?" she snaps before lifting her hips for him. My gaze meets Essos's again, and this time, regret burns in his eyes. I drop his food on the ground, letting the door close as I fight tears. I can't break down in front of anyone. I barely notice the desk plants wilting as I pass.

"Daphne, wait!" Essos calls, finally emerging from his office. It sounds like he's stumbling after me.

I don't look at him. I don't want to give him the satisfaction of seeing my tears. I become unmovable, like a redwood tree, firm and sturdy. I get into the lift before he can reach me, and when I get outside, I walk deep into the park across the street, where we liked to have lunch together sometimes. I scream, not caring anymore who's around, not caring who sees me or if they know who I am. I scream, and the grass and flowers and trees around me are reduced to ash.

THE PLATES in my hand shatter when they hit the floor as the final pieces lock into place. Things I missed, that I had forgotten, all make sense, and I look at Essos.

He looks worried, immediately placing the tray with the garlic bread down to move toward me, and I hate myself for doing it, but I flinch away from him. He stops short, giving me my space.

"It was Ellie." My words are a whisper.

"What?" he asks, looking at me, his brow creased.

I can barely meet his eyes, so I study that little wrinkle, following it around the muscle in his jaw that jumps. I finally do look into his blue, blue eyes that I would love to get lost in.

"It was Ellie all those years ago, and you went back to her again."

27

I'm not crying, though I feel like I should be. I'm just, disappointed.

Essos pulls his shoulders back, standing taller, ready to receive the punishment for his crimes. "Yes, but it wasn't like that. I didn't seek her out. I was true to you, true to my word back then. I'm still true to you now." He takes a step toward me to see if I'll let him, and I do.

"We're going to go look at the city lights," Cat says, ushering Zara to the balcony.

I don't even acknowledge them, but Essos nods. I'm beyond words right now.

"After what happened before we got married, you asked for me to have her transferred, and I did. I never saw her or spoke to her again until that party. I thought you knew who she was. I'm sorry. I'm so sorry, Daphne."

"But what? You thought, 'Well, fuck it. My wife's dead, I might as well stick my prick in the last living being she would ever want me to sleep with?'" I drop into the chair at the table and look up at him. I rub my chest, not over the stab wound, but just below, over my heart.

"What do you want me to say? I wasn't thinking straight. I was in a near-permanent state of drunk. I couldn't get through my days. Sybil was running the Afterlife—I was barely involved in the day-to-day. At least Ellie helped me get sober." Essos drops to the chair in front of me. He scrubs his hand over his face before he turns his pleading blue eyes on me.

"Is that supposed to make it better? That she was the *one* person who was able to draw you out of your depression?"

He reaches out a shaking hand and brushes the hair out of my face. The evidence of my broken heart is written all over his face in the deep set of the crease in his brow and how his lips tug down at the sides.

"Literally any other person in Solarem would have been better. Hell, you could have had an entire *harem* of women. I was dead—it's not like I would have expected you to stay celibate." I wipe away my tears angrily.

"No, that's not supposed to make it better. And she wasn't the one person. But when I was with her, I could close my eyes and pretend. I don't care how much of a monster it makes me. I could think of you, and I could think that this miserable life was still worth living because there was hope that I could find you again. If I had gotten my hands on the dagger, I can't promise you that I wouldn't have sunk it into my own heart. Life was unbearable without you.

"This isn't how I wanted to tell you, and before you ask, of course, I would have told you. You might have died, but you were never dead for me. There was a dagger out there with your soul in it. I felt it happen, felt your soul leave your body and stay in that stone. I had to watch as the gem filled with the essence of you. I'd say the Council, but it was Posey who tucked your dagger away for 'safe-keeping' until she thought it was best to release your soul. Xavier, thank the Fates, took pity on me, and assured me that it—that you—were safe. I always knew there was a chance I could get you back, but as my requests to the Council were denied, over and over again, I lost hope.

"I never should have. I should have known that as soon as I lost that hope, *that* was when you would come back to me." He cups my face. "I have a lot to atone for from the last millennium. But I would do it all again if it meant that I would get you back.

"I'm sorry you found out like this. I'm sorry I didn't tell you about Ellie to begin with. I'm sorry that I slept with her the first time, and I'm sorry I was stupid enough to do it again."

There are so many things I *still* don't know about what happened after my death, but this fills in a small amount. Essos has laid out the truth, however unfortunate it may be for me to digest, and that's what I have to do. I have to take time to absorb what happened.

"It's just a lot. The memories coming back make it feel fresh, and, I missed so, *so* much, I feel like I'm on unsteady ground. Every time I turn around, another hit comes my way, and I can't get up before something else comes for me."

"I asked you once to trust me, and I know that didn't work out great, but I still trust you, and you never have to worry about me." Essos holds my gaze, unflinching. "I will be your sturdy ground. I will be your constant. I will do whatever it takes to prove myself to you. I'm not bound by arbitrary rules. I'm an open book. Whatever you want to know I'll tell you."

"I..just...Ellie? *Really?*" I slide my fingers into his, my acceptance of his apologies. The warmth of our touch is as much for me as it is for him. It's a reminder that he's at least here for us to work through these issues.

"I'm a dumb fuck. I was lost without you. I can't explain it."

We sit in silence as I try to digest all of this. Of all the memories to come back, it had to be the one thing I want to forget. It's the truth when I say we worked past those problems, past his self-sabotaging. He sought help for it, because he truly wanted to be a better man. I forgave him with the understanding that, if it happened again, I was done. When we made up, it was for good, and he didn't lie. He was faithful to me from then on.

"It just feels like such a betrayal to know you went back to her. And I know, I *know* I don't have a leg to stand on. But Essos..."

"I don't know what I can say to make this better, other than I will do everything in my power to make it up to you. Can we start with a home-cooked meal? Your poor friends didn't bring their coats outside, and it was a bit nippy on our walk back."

"You're going to have to do more than feed me to make it up to me. Ellie is trying to poison me, and I'm not entirely sure it's not so she can be queen." I press my lips to his quickly. There is nothing to forgive him for, except choosing Ellie. It could have been anyone else, and I could have recovered with a slight misstep, but her?

She's the one I'll take my revenge on.

Getting involved with Essos when we were together was misguided on her part, but he was the one in a relationship. That was on him.

Trying to poison me? That's on her.

"No other woman will *ever* be my queen. No one on Earth or in Solarem is as kind, generous, and powerful as you. Go rescue Zara and Cat. I'll clean this up." He rolls up his sleeves to pick up the broken glass. It would be easier to use his powers to do it, but I guess this is his way of showing me he wants to put in the work.

There is still so much left unresolved between us, but like all our problems, we can't solve it overnight. I'm not even sure we can resolve this in the next year. I open the sliding glass door where Zara and Cat have made themselves cozy on the bench swing.

"Dinner time," I announce.

Cat beckons me over, so I close the door behind me. "Is everything all right?"

I drop into an egg-shaped chair across from them. "It will be. There's just a lot to process." I look at Zara to fill her in. "A long time ago, Essos slept with someone else, and that's old news, and we moved past it, but he slept with her again—regularly—after I died, and also it's Ellie." Zara's eyes keep getting wider. "So, I have a lot of feelings about it, but we can deal with it later. After we defeat Galen, there will be plenty of time." I get up and pull Zara and Cat with me.

"No, wait, I'm sorry—that sniveling little brat who likes to talk back to me when I tell her to do things because she thinks she's above me because I'm a mortal and she's not? Nope. No, ma'am. I am going to roast her like the little nothing she is. I'm going to make her regret the day she thought she could sink my OTP. Oh, I know *exactly* who will be scooping Waffles's litter box. She fancies herself a queen? More like queen of the grunt work."

Cat and I can only blink as Zara goes off with even more tasks she's going to dream up to put Ellie in her place. My heart grows three sizes at her words, and I melt a little. It makes me extra glad that I have Zara as a friend and not an enemy.

"How are you doing with this?" Cat asks, once Zara is done.

"It is not the worst thing to ever happen to me. But it hurts nonetheless." I take a deep breath. "Essos and I will figure it out. After we repaired our relationship the first time, we made a promise to each other that we wouldn't have secrets. And I can't hold him not telling me against him, because when would he have had a chance to? But...*her*?" I hate that my voice breaks.

Cat and Zara wrap their arms around me tightly. "I can kick him in the balls," Cat offers.

"No, don't. I can't blame him. If I was dead for real, I wouldn't have wanted him to be alone for the rest of eternity. It just feels like the Fates are playing a cruel joke on me, to keep putting the three of us in each other's paths. Then again, it's a lot easier for me to hate her for having been with Essos once before. Could you imagine if I actually liked the person he moved on to?"

"But he never really moved on, did he?" Zara asks. "The Calling was for you. He only had eyes for you that whole time. It's why I threw myself at him so aggressively, if we're all being honest. I had no chance with him—no one did."

Cat shivers, reminding me why I came out here in the first place.

"Let's go inside. I promise his carbonara is to die for."

"Been there, done that. I have no interest in repeating *that* experience again," Cat teases, opening the sliding glass door. The first thing my best friend does is level the King of the Dead with a blood-chilling glare before making the universal signal for *I'm watching you.*

Essos nods in acceptance before gesturing for us to sit.

He finished setting the table, the dishes I dropped put back together. Our meals have been plated, and candles burn at the table. Essos looks repentant waiting for us. I forgot how much I missed his carbonara. He tried to teach me how to cook it, but I would always lose focus and have him make it instead.

I sit beside Essos and put a hand on his knee. He takes my hand in his, giving it a squeeze. I can almost pretend this is normal, a nice domestic night with my husband and friends. We talk all around the problems we're having, avoiding mentioning Ellie and Titus and Galen most of all.

"We need to give Sybil a raise," I say, swirling my wine.

Essos is relaxed, his legs spread out in front of him as he leans back. It's possibly the most relaxed I've seen him look, even during the Calling.

"I don't disagree, but any particular reason?" He reaches out an absent hand and plays with my hair.

Cat stands abruptly. "I think it's time for bed. All this lying around is exhausting. Let's go." She holds her hand out to Zara.

"I'm glad to see you're feeling better. Reports told me that you were nearly on your deathbed." Essos's words stop my heart when he says it.

"It wasn't nearly that dramatic. Being in Solarem has been nice though." Cat's downplaying it.

"Are you feeling well now?" he presses.

"As well a dead woman can." She reaches up to toy with her necklace, the lightning bolt charm from Xavier.

"Can I ask about your necklace?" He leans forward, almost reaching for it but seems to think better of it.

"Xavier gave it to me. It's a protection charm."

"Nothing to protect you from here. You should give it some time to rest. I'll recharge it myself and add a little extra to it."

"Does it need that?" She reaches up, unclasping it and dropping it into Essos's outstretched hand. She stands a little taller, like the magic within the charm had been weighing her down.

"Not necessarily, but it doesn't hurt. I promise, you're safe here. If Xavier gave it to you, I imagine it's Posey you're worried about. She can't get you here—we specifically spelled this place against her. I'll take care of it. Have a good night."

Zara and Cat go to their separate rooms, leaving Essos and me to clean up. Essos waves a hand, clearing the table and all the dishes and pots.

Wordlessly, we go to our room and go through the same nighttime routine we used to follow. It's a small slice of normalcy that I've been craving without even knowing it. My heart starts to beat a little faster, even as shame floods my system. I ruined this. *I* am the reason we can't have this consistency every night.

That dangerous line of thinking is halted when Essos takes off his shirt and then strips off his pants and leaves them on a chair. His boxers rest low on his hips, revealing every fine muscle on his body. Heat pools low in my belly. A bemused smile is on Essos's lips as he watches me check him out. How easily distracted I am when his clothes come off.

Clearing my throat, I try to keep my desire at bay and focus on the things we still haven't talked about. "Where have you been staying?" I ask, popping out a fresh toothbrush for each of us.

"Here and there. The mortal realm for the most part, and various safe houses in Solarem."

We brush our teeth in silence, and then I start to brush my hair. Gently, Essos plucks the brush from my hand and guides me toward my vanity. I sit obediently and close my eyes. Essos runs the brush through my curls. Just enough to be soothing.

"What have you been doing?"

We move into the bedroom, hesitating on either side of our bed. Together, we pull back our comforter and climb into the cold sheets, then settle awkwardly in bed. You would think this was our first time in such proximity, that we hadn't spent thousands of years sleeping side by side, curled into each other.

"I've been looking for answers of my own, allies, mostly the dagger."

My blood runs cold as I turn to face him. I can't help but feel responsible for the discomfort between us. "Have you had any luck?"

Essos lies on his side, one arm curled under his head as he studies me. There is wanton desire in his blue eyes; clearly, memories of us being together are never far from his mind. I wonder if I measure up to who I used to be. I feel like a shell of the woman I was, no longer the eternal Goddess of Spring and no longer the college girl either. With each memory I gain, I try to thread these two lives together as best I can.

Maybe I'm imagining this distance between us.

"I wish I could say yes. I've had a few leads that didn't pan out. After your soul was released, I didn't even think about it, I was so focused on how I would get you back in our realm. Xavier confessed to not even knowing that your soul had been released when it was. Which...shouldn't surprise me?" He says it like a question. "There was a lot of interference by the Council to keep you from me in those early days. I could never get a straight answer why—there were always vague reasons provided about it not being the right timing and how the realm needed more stability first. No one would meet my eye and tell me *why*. And that hurt." He rolls over so he's on his back, staring at the ceiling. His hand rests on his stomach. "I never thought Helene and Kai would vote for that, but they did. Mum even interjected with her own two cents that this never would have happened if Galen had been allowed to court you properly first. As if we broke some rule by going out before he grew a pair and even asked your name. All I could come up with was that Mum was the one who encouraged Helene and Kai to vote like that."

"I thought no one had seen Octavia in years." I scoot closer to him, earning a small smile.

He wastes no time reaching out and placing his hand on my hip, then sliding his fingers under the hem of my shirt.

"A goddess died, people mourned, my parents had to make an appearance, though they didn't talk to each other. My mother comforted Galen, who was more of a wreck than me, as if he wasn't the cause of everything. I don't think I can ever look at her the same after that." A shadow settles in his eyes, and he won't look at me. I can see it even in the dim light of the bedroom.

"I'm sorry I caused all these issues," I whisper. I wish I could go back and change something, but at this point, I don't even know what I could change. I did nothing to encourage Galen's behavior.

Essos's gaze snaps to me, and he moves with a feline grace as he flips me onto my back so he can settle over me. "You did *nothing* wrong. You were murdered. Someone hurt you. You don't have to apologize." His words are fierce, his gaze boring into mine.

"I kissed Galen," I confess, not looking away from my husband.

"I know you have, and I get why."

"No, Essos. I kissed Galen when we broke up, after Ellie."

His face softens. I don't expect the kiss he plants on my lips, but I should have.

"I know. You think he didn't gloat about it? You think he didn't describe to me in detail what he wanted to do to you on your date? Helene helped me see how wrong my life would be without you. Daph, we both made mistakes, mine bigger than others, but the past is just that—the past."

I kiss him. "You're just saying that because the Ellie stuff has come up, again," I tease, and he returns my smile.

"I'm really not. You didn't deserve to have Galen hound you the way he did, the same way I didn't deserve to have my wife and child killed."

My heart lurches. "Do I have no secrets from you?" I whisper, tears welling in my eyes.

Essos rests his weight on one elbow so he can catch my tears with reverent swipes of his thumb. "My love, you are many things, but subtle is not one of them. When you realized you were pregnant again, you cried into a pint of ice cream for three hours, and when I asked you why, you threw the carton at me and told me to —and I'm quoting you here—'Mind your fucking business.'"

I laugh at the memory, the tears still falling. I had been so overwhelmed, arguing with myself over telling him or not. It was the day I found out I was pregnant again, something we had been desperately hoping and wishing for, but I was cautious after our previous heartbreaks not to get too excited.

I latch on to the one thing that can possibly stop my tears in their tracks. "Posey wants me to get pregnant with Galen's child before the end of the Trials." I should tell Essos now about Galen coming to my room, but I'm spoiling this moment enough without that confession.

Essos snorts, but it's forced. He tugs me even closer to him, if that's possible. "Right, because being pregnant at a time of turmoil like this is where your priorities should be. What is she even thinking?"

"Something about proving that I'm capable of being a broodmare."

Essos's hand smooths the flat of my lower belly. "When the time is right, when our world has settled, we will try again, because the trying was the best part. We will try in the living room and in the kitchen, and in the shower and in the lake." He trails off, kissing my neck. "I will enjoy taking my time with you until you swell with our child. There is no rush, not for me, and I don't think for you. We need to reacquaint ourselves."

He gives me a roguish grin, but I can see the little lines around his eyes. Not even immortality can keep the stress of losing your other half at bay.

It makes my tears resurface stronger than before.

"How did you survive?" I know that losing him would have ruined me. I would say my mood swings would have been out of control, but that would imply having an emotion other than depression. I wouldn't have been able to get out of bed. Even the thought of it sends me spiraling hard enough that I have to close my eyes to stop more tears.

"Hey, hey. I'm right here. I'm not going anywhere. It's going to take a lot more than an empty ice cream carton to scare me away. I survived because I had hope for this moment. I had hope that we would share a bed again, that I could hold you close, although I will admit, my idea of how we would spend time together was less than pure." He presses his hips forward so I can feel his arousal.

"Is that a request?" I tease, resting my hands on his hips. I run my fingers along the edge of his boxers.

"No. I just want you to know the constant effect you have on me. Then, now, and always. I would be content just to lie next to you and sleep. You never stopped being my whole world, the Calling be damned. I'm not a fool. I know how my brother tricked you. I know that I was left with no choice but to let you play into his hands. You've had a long day and need rest." He rolls off me, and I think I might be disappointed. I can't deny it though. He settles back into the same position he was in earlier. His arm is tucked under the pillows, and he faces me, watching the war within my heart and mind.

I relent, flicking off the lights and lying beside my husband. I face him for only a moment, pressing a soft, tender kiss to his lips, then I roll over and tuck my bottom into his lap. The arm under the pillows snakes out and folds across my chest, and the other snakes around my waist, pulling me against him completely.

I don't expect to fall asleep quickly, but my body seems to know it's home and it's safe, and I get the best night's sleep I've had since the Calling began.

28

I'm in a deep sleep when I'm startled by pressure on my body. Slowly, it tugs me from my dream, where I'm being chased by brownie-eating books. My eyes open, and I can just see a mess of dark hair resting on my chest.

"Essos?" I croak. He lifts his head and looks at me, eyes watery.

"Did I wake you? I'm so sorry." He shifts back toward his side of the bed.

I'm still trying to wake up, but I reach a hand toward him and find his cheek. His stubble has started to grow back in, and the prickliness helps wake me up a touch more. I can feel dampness there and I rouse myself further.

"It's fine. Is everything okay?" My voice is still sleepy. He cups my face and kisses me hard. If I wasn't awake before, I certainly am now. His lips press against mine, pulling me to him.

"I just...you were so still, I couldn't even see your chest rising, and I..." He looks broken. "I had to hear your heart beating. I felt it —when you died, I felt it when your heart stopped, like a part of my soul had been cleaved clean off, and in my dream..." His words choke off with a sob.

I clutch him to my chest, unable to fathom what he was dreaming about, what the past three months have been like having those dreams, unable to verify for himself that I was just fine. I wonder if he constantly woke up in a sweat, wondering if I was still alive. Would there be anything left of him if I died again?

"Hush, hush. I'm okay. We're okay." I hold him to me, and he clutches me, his tears wetting the fabric of my shirt. I soothe him as best as I can, rubbing his back.

"I have this recurring dream where, during the Calling Ball, Galen makes you pick him. He makes you kiss me, and just as our lips meet, he stabs you again through the back, and I have to hold you as you bleed out again." He withdraws from me so he can see me with his own eyes.

"I can't imagine." Words are insufficient for what he went through. He hugs me to his chest so my cheek is pressed to his bare skin. I listen to the thumping of his heart, my own reminder that he's alive and well.

"Just try to go back to sleep, I'm sorry for waking you." His tone is quiet now, little more than a whisper.

"It's really okay. I'm happy to bring you peace." I slip my knee between his, twining our legs together.

"I know it's a shared sentiment, but I just want this to be over. Not having to hide, being able to sleep beside my wife every night —*that* will bring me peace."

"I'm here until the next trial in a month. You should stay at least that long."

He kisses the top of my head. "I will. Do you know what the trial is?" His fingers tangle in my hair. Neither of us is going back to sleep anytime soon.

"No, but I told Posey I need to focus on my wellness. I told Galen I was going to look for the scepter."

Essos's hands still for just a moment before resuming the mindless twirling. "The scepter? How does he know about it?" I don't miss the edge to his words.

"Titus told Galen he would never be king without it. I don't understand why Titus won't do something about this. He has the power to set things right, and he won't. I've asked him to point blank."

"For now, it suits his plans for me to be out of the picture and Galen to do whatever it is he's doing. But Galen won't find the scepter—it's out of his reach."

"Good. Keep it that way. You won't even believe what he's doing to our realm. Solarem is practically bankrupt. Any and all reserves we had are depleted, he's upped the tithes, and he refuses to adjudicate. I tried to do it on my own, but the Council shut me down. I was supposed to do everything *with* him, but he seems to have no actual interest in learning how to rule. The only reason he's having lessons now is that Titus insists on it." That doesn't even begin to touch on what happened in the Garden of Evil and the Deep.

"And, of course, Dad mentioned the scepter." Essos heaves a sigh. "If he'll leave you out of it, I'll gladly give Galen my kingdom. It's worthless without you. He needs only to ask."

I push away from Essos to look him in the eye. "You don't mean that," I tell him, sitting up a little. I can't believe he could mean it. The Afterlife is the pride of Essos's long life.

"And why wouldn't I? I know what it is to have you in my life. I know what it is to lose you. If you think that *anything* is worth not having you in my life, you're delusional." His arms tighten around me.

I push back and roll over so I'm straddling him. He reaches out to rest his hands on my thighs, but I catch them and pin his arms down.

"Our people need you. They're suffering under Galen, and it's only going to get worse."

Essos watches me, his eyes thoughtful before he flips me onto my back in an easy movement. Now his hands pin mine.

"I'm not giving up. I'm just saying that it's not worth losing you to him. I know his vicious streak better than most. I know what he is capable of, and you do too. I won't leave you to that life. If it's just the crown he is after, he can have it. This matters so much more." Essos rolls his hips against me.

I bite my lip, feeling my core turn molten against him. I let out a harsh breath, annoyed at how my body betrays me. Now is not the time to think about how it feels when he's inside me.

"We're having a serious conversation, Es," I protest, and he rolls his hips again, the corner of his mouth quirking up. I feel his erection press against me.

"I'm sorry, but this is a very serious situation too. I have a hard-on for my wife, whom I haven't seen in over a thousand years."

I don't protest when he kisses my neck, his mouth working over the sensitive spot that sends my body arching up into his.

"Essos, you've been with me since yesterday."

He kisses all around my mouth before finally meeting my lips.

"Yes, but we have a thousand years of orgasms to make up for, and I am eager to get started."

I don't object, my hands running along the bare skin of his sides. My fingers tease the band of his boxers, and then my hand dips down between us and I stroke the length of him.

Essos grunts, thrusting in my hand. "We seem to have an unfair distribution of clothing," he purrs, nipping my earlobe. One of his hands strays to my hip and tugs my shirt up. I try to sit up to make it easier, and we wind up knocking heads. You would think that we hadn't done this thousands of times before. Essos laughs, pulling away to sit on his knees. His hands grip my head, and he presses a kiss to the spot where we collided.

Gently, he pulls my shirt off and away, then carelessly throws it behind him. He takes in my chest before I drop back onto the mattress.

"I'll never get tired of the sight of you bare before me." He lowers himself to me again, tugging my shorts off this time.

"You're just saying that because my breasts won't get old and saggy and hang down to my knees."

He tosses my shorts aside, leaving me exposed. "I would love them even then. I don't believe there was any fine print in my vow to you with regard to your breasts or any other part of you." He silences me with his mouth and cups one breast, circling my nipple with his finger, swirling sensation around the alert skin. I can't think straight as his other hand slides between us and grabs my wrist and then sets it aside. His whole body slides down mine, kisses peppering all the way from my mouth, down my neck, along my collarbone, to the other breast he hasn't toyed with, and along the plane of my stomach.

I know where this is headed, and I don't stop him, don't dare breathe too hard. His mouth kisses the crease of my hip. He nudges my legs farther apart before settling between them, his breath hot against my sex.

Essos pauses, waiting for any sort of objection I might voice, before he presses his mouth against me. I can feel my magic unspooling, moss covering the walls to silence the room. I whimper and writhe as his tongue slips between my folds. He slides one finger and then another inside me, pulling me closer and closer to the edge. My hips roll against him, and I work my fingers into his hair as I start to cry out. My throat is raw as the sound rips from me.

My body squirms, eager to find release in every way. Essos

doesn't remove his mouth or fingers until he's sure I'm spent. I open my eyes and see him watching me with fascination.

"That was new." Essos murmurs.

When my eyes refocus, I see what he means. The room erupted in more than just moss to silence us—there's a full garden. Wisteria hangs from my ceiling, and along the walls, roses peek out in full bloom, blocking the window that had shown the light of daybreak.

"Wow," is all I can manage.

Essos stretches his body up over mine and covers my lips with his. I can taste myself on him, and it's intoxicating. I reach for him again, feeling him pressing against my center. When I try to set him against my entrance so he can slide into me with one smooth movement, he removes my hand.

"It's about you today." He nudges my nose with his so he can kiss me again.

"And what I want is you inside of me."

His eyes burn with desire, and he won't deny me. I didn't need to position him because, with one easy thrust, he is inside of me, and I gasp, lifting my hips to meet him in equal measure. We're slow and tender together in a way we haven't been able to be. He draws out each moan, each whine that is unlocked from within me. Our joinings before this were frantic, never knowing if we would be caught or if he would have to abruptly leave, but now we can take the time for lovemaking. Our hips move against each other, our bodies able to settle into the movements that have been rusty. Our hands entwine as our sweat-slicked bodies remember the feel of the other.

When we're done, and it's just the two of us panting, our bodies still connected, my head rests on his chest, and I listen to his heartbeat. The sound breathes life into me. My eyes glance around the room, the thicket having grown more during the last hour. I was able to relax here in a way that I haven't been able to back at the house.

"So much for your powers being bound," Essos quips, dragging his fingers lazily down my spine.

"I guess they're back."

"Can I speak freely without fear of reprisal?"

I rest my chin on his chest and look up at Essos. "Always."

"You always held yourself back a little before. Like you were afraid of the depth of your abilities. You avoided teleporting yourself because of how it made you feel, and you never went deeper than the superficial with your power. I never understood why, but I think that this——" he lets me go only long enough to gesture at the garden around us "——is proof of how much power you have. You didn't even try, and we're in a garden."

"What do you mean?" My tone is defensive, mostly because there's an element of truth to what Essos is saying. I was content being a low-level goddess; I never needed to see if I had more powers or really pushed myself to explore them. I saw the power plays of stronger gods, and I had no desire to be involved. Did people look a little closer at me because I was married to Essos? Sure, but it was never more than a passing glance, because I was just that flower girl who sat beside the real power.

"I'm trying to say that maybe getting in touch with your abilities isn't the worst thing in the world. Talk to Gisella. She's a fountain of knowledge."

"Hardy har har," I snap, but he's right. I also know that the sun is rising, but I can't help the heavy feeling in my eyes.

"Sleep, my love," Essos whispers, resuming his mindless caresses.

I settle down beside my husband and let sleep carry me off again.

I'M ALONE when I wake up, and there's a moment of panic that last night was a dream, that Essos isn't here and that I haven't even gone to the library yet. But the room smells heavily of flowers, and when I look around, I see the evidence of our lovemaking in full bloom.

I find a small notecard on Essos's pillow, the words written in his elegant script.

Making breakfast and brownies.
-E

I run my fingers over his handwriting then move to get ready for the day. I quickly shower, leaving my dark tresses damp when I emerge from our room. Immediately, I see that the expanse of my power was pretty wide. The apartment looks like a wall that Pictogram influencers use to take photos against. The walls are lush and green, peppered with tiny trumpet flowers in varying colors. Waffles meows loudly in annoyance at all this greenery; all the corners he would rub himself against are covered in plant life.

"My love." Essos greets me with a smile as he plates pancakes for Cat and Zara.

"How long have you all been up?" I ask, taking the plate Essos holds out to me. He hands it over with a kiss.

"I couldn't fall back asleep, so I went to work on some brownies for our favorite librarian. Zara and Cat were both awake."

"Yeah, someone decided to wake us up by growing a garden in

our rooms," Cat teases. She's not wearing the charmed necklace; I can see where it rests in a box. I wonder if Essos has already infused it with his powers.

"The morning glories were perhaps a touch too on the nose, my love," Essos says, tapping me on the tip of my nose. He nods at the small trumpet-like flowers I noticed while walking down the hall.

I blush furiously and roll all of the flowers out of existence. "Whose fault is that, really?" I snap, trying to deflect.

"Entirely mine, and I'm not sorry about it." Essos slaps my ass when I lean against the counter. I roll my eyes at him, but I'm delighted at the attention.

"So, I have a theory," Cat announces.

"It could be bunnies?" I quip with a laugh, thinking of the summer when all we did was listen to the *Buffy* musical episode soundtrack.

Essos perks up. "I understood that reference." He breaks off a chewier part of a piece of bacon and drops it onto my plate while he eats the burnt end.

"You two are so cheesy, and it's disgusting, and I love you both, but focus. Please. I feel like I'm able to think clearly for the first time in weeks." Cat barrels on, "I think your mother-in-law might be behind this entire situation."

I furrow my brow. "Octavia?" I glance at Essos to see how he reacts. I've thought it myself, but outright saying it feels wrong. No matter our differences, I don't know that I'm capable of accusing Essos's mother to his face.

Essos glances at me and, from the guilty look in his eyes, I know that he's considered it too.

"Yes," Cat says. "Hear me out. You mentioned the dagger and gems were made with the blood of the God and Goddess Supreme, hereafter referred to as Titus and Octavia. It sounds to me like Titus was not a big fan of Galen's, which is why Galen got the shaft on kingdoms, right? Titus *literally* dragged Kai from the depths of the oceans and gave him power over water rather than make his last son, the golden boy, a king. Are you following?" This is the Cat I knew in college, clever and quick, talking like a lawyer, laying out the facts. I can only nod.

"Where did you get all this information?" Zara asks, sipping from her tea.

"Okay, well, I actually listened during our lessons in the Calling, and also, I've been on bedrest with nothing to do but read the histories of these people. We probably could have figured out who Daphne was just by picking up a single book in the library."

A faint smile ghosts over Essos's lips. "Where were you when I was stuck needing loopholes?" he asks, sliding an easy arm around my waist. I lean into him, gesturing her on.

"I was too busy being an accessory to a coup. But I digress.

"Titus has made it very clear that he does not support Galen becoming king. He never wanted him to be king of anything, let alone the entire financial system. I've been looking over the reports, and I won't lie, it gave me a massive headache, but he's been looting the Afterlife, and not just by increasing tithes and halting gem production. He's added increased fees to every account, he's been making deposits into his own accounts as payment for being interim king, and, lest we forget, he closed the Garden of Evil, forcing all those souls into the Deep."

Essos already knew this, but it doesn't mean it's not hard to hear. His whole body tenses, but he waits for Cat to continue. I love him, but I know that he will *never* be content with giving the Underworld to his brother.

"Right, so we know that they were involved in making the dagger. Essos—the weapon was unknown, right? So, in theory, one of them had to give it to Galen, right?"

The timer for the brownies goes off, and Essos leaves my side to retrieve them. "Theoretically, but we don't know who else might have known it was forged." He places the brownies on the counter to cool.

"Okay, but if it walks like a duck and looks like a duck, it's probably a duck. I think, based only on what you've said, it's pretty likely that Galen is her favorite, no offense. Someone needed to like him enough to introduce a weapon that could kill you all, someone willing to risk having the knowledge out in the world that there is a weapon that you are vulnerable to. If people know about it, no one feels safe, and now petty grudges that were once easily dismissed can bring death if the wrong person gets their hands on it.

"How did you explain Daphne's death?"

"That she wanted to give up her immortality for a year to better understand mortals, and that something went wrong when she did that. We didn't want anyone to know about the dagger," Essos confirms. "People were bereft. They loved Daphne. She was kind and compassionate to more than just our people."

"She's still kind and compassionate, but for someone to want to kill her, they either have to hate her or love someone else. Titus seems generally indifferent. All signs point to your mother."

"That is cold. For your mother to help murder your wife," Zara says. "On second thought, I'm glad you didn't pick me. Your family sounds like a bunch of megalomaniac sociopaths."

"Xavier's not all bad." Cat's eyes stray to the box with her necklace.

"Stay away from him," Essos and I say in tandem. We share a look, somewhere between glad we're still on the same page and annoyed with Xavier for having to say it.

"I know, I know, you tell me constantly. I'm not getting involved with him, I'm just saying that he's not all bad. Helene and Kai are also pretty chill." Cat's deflecting, and I'm letting her.

I look at Essos. "Joining me for another study session?" I ask.

He nods, handing me my bag from yesterday with my notebook. "I'll make inquiries about my mother. I haven't seen her since the funeral, so...maybe. I just...I can't believe she would do this to me, to us." Essos's hand grips the back of my neck gently. I can't blame him. I wouldn't want to think the worst of my parents either. It's part of why I love him so much—despite his parents showing him time and time again who they are, he still hopes for better from them.

"Gives a whole new meaning to monster-in-law," I joke with a tight smile.

Essos plants a kiss on my temple.

I turn to my friends. "I want to give you a tour of Solarem and really welcome you here, but..."

"No, this is more important," Cat says.

A knock at the door has Essos sliding on his cap. Zara isn't prepared for Essos to vanish, and she lets out a gasp.

"Daphne, Cat, Zara, it's me open up!" Finn calls from the hall. I smile, anticipating him. I wave the door open, and it indeed reveals Finn on the other side. He steps in with a box in his hands.

"Finn," I greet, covering Essos's hand with mine. Once the door is closed, Essos removes his hat.

"Today, I'll be playing your tour guide, boat captain, therapist, and if you don't laugh at my jokes, your swim instructor." Finn slides the box across the counter to me. If he's surprised by Essos's presence, he doesn't show it. Instead, he throws his arms around Zara's and Cat's shoulders.

"Is there a reason we would need swim instructors?" Zara asks, leaning into his side.

"I thought we could go out on the lake, after we do some shopping. On Daph and Essos, of course."

"Of course," Essos mutters before turning to me. "We should get going, since you slept in today. Gisella will be disappointed."

I take a look at the clock and realize that Essos is right, I did sleep in, and the library has already been open for a few hours.

331

Somehow, I still feel exhausted.

"That thing you wanted me to research..." Finn starts.

"You can say it. I have no secrets from Essos. He knows someone was trying to bind my powers. And *I* now know that it was his mistress." My tone is biting, and both Finn and Essos look shamed.

"Right. Estelle said it's something called red tide algae? It's apparently only available in the mortal realm, so maybe research that too."

I nod and look at the box he brought with him. It contains brownies from Estelle and a supply of my usual tea. I'm hesitant to take the risk, so I toss the tea and grab a cup of coffee to drink on the walk.

When we arrive at the library, Gisella is sitting behind her desk, a stack of books at her side.

"More brownies," I offer, setting them before her. She pushes a stack of books with an access badge on top of it toward me.

"I request that you not have sex in the stacks, if it can be avoided."

A hot flush creeps up my neck and cheeks. "Of course, Gisella."

She smirks. "Hello, Essos," she says to the vacant air beside me.

"Lovely to see you, Gisella," he murmurs as we pass her.

We look for data on everything from the red tide algae to his mother to the dagger and stones. I feel like I'm reading in circles. Books that should have the information are missing those pages, and I want to tear my hair out over it.

We spend two days like this, occasionally asking for help from Gisella.

We do try to be good, but each time I get frustrated to the point of tears, Essos finds some clever new way to draw an orgasm from me while making me stay as silent as possible.

On day three, I'm lying on the table with my eyes closed and my chest heaving. Essos is on the chair between my legs, rubbing my knees. I learned after the first day to wear clothes with easy access, so I smooth down my skater skirt and sit up.

Essos wipes my desire from his mouth before pressing a kiss to the inside of my knee.

"Let me take you away for a day," he says as I rub my eyes.

I tilt my head, considering. I shouldn't let myself get distracted. Well, much more distracted than we have been. I need to find a way to balance my sanity along with defeating Galen.

"What did you have in mind?" I run a finger along the edge of a torn page. It was one of the final straws before I started to scream. Essos acted quickly, turning the scream from one of frustration to pleasure, but I'm starting to worry that we've reached the end of the information available in the library.

I slide off the table, already down with this plan. I close the book and heft it into the pile of damaged books.

"Anything. We can go to the mortal realm. We can visit some gardens. We can go to the cabin and..."

"And fool around?" I ask, my eyebrows shooting up.

Essos laughs, leaning back and sliding his hand up my skirt to grab my ass. "Insatiable minx. I was going to say, 'and test your powers.'"

"You're the one who put the idea of a thousand orgasms out in the universe. I thought you were looking for some solitude so we won't disturb Cat and Zara anymore." I pout just a little. I'm enjoying this mock honeymoon phase with Essos.

"I wouldn't want to keep you too long in case Galen decides to visit you."

I pace away from him, my anger swift and sudden. I should control myself better, but I don't. Instead, I slam my fist into the frame of a shelf.

Essos rises and crosses to me. "Easy, killer. We can do whatever you want. We don't have to go away." Essos's hands grip my upper arms before rubbing them gently.

"I just want this to be *over*. I'm exhausted. I'm exhausted playing pretend every day, pretending that I care. I don't care about the Trials, or the wedding, or schmoozing with people. I only care about making sure Cat feels better and that I get you and our life back."

"These missions go hand in hand, my love."

I brush him off, and hurt flashes across his face. He covers it with a mask of indifference just as quickly, and I feel bad.

"I know that. I *know*, but I'm losing myself. I'm failing Cat and our people, and I am so, so tired."

Essos surprises me by grabbing me around the hips and setting me on the table. I let out a squeak but spread my legs so he can settle between them.

"I wish there was something I could do, my love. I wish I could take some of this burden from you." He sounds as exhausted as I feel, and guilt settles low in my gut. I shouldn't be saddling him with my concerns; he shares them and more.

I drape my arms over his shoulders. "You're already doing so much. I abandoned you, and you're trying to clean up my mess."

"Isn't that what love is? Cleaning up each other's messes?" he asks lightly.

"I like to think that we're more than just a collection of mistakes."

"You're being obtuse, Daphne. Whatever it is that's going to make your stay better, I'm happy to oblige, with my mouth or my cock or any other part of me." He kisses my neck.

I heave a huge sigh, leaning into him totally. Moments like these have made the last few months bearable. I feel less alone knowing I have him in my corner.

"I think we've hit the limits of what the library knows, and we have more questions than answers." I can't help but sound defeated.

"We do, but I also have things to focus my research on after you return to the house."

"After I return to Galen, you mean?" I challenge. It's bitter and unfair, but a cruel part of me doesn't want to be the only one suffering, even if I know that Essos is in the same boat.

Essos squeezes my thighs, his blue eyes sad. "I would rather not think about you having to return to his grasp. I'm terrified every day that he's going to hurt you, and I can't do anything about it." I see that Essos needs the break just as badly as I do. How hard has he been working on getting us out of this mess I've made?

"Let's go. Somewhere, anywhere. The cabin, a park, anywhere you want," I offer.

"I know just the spot," Essos says.

We gather our books and set them back where they belong, with the exception of the damaged ones. Essos slips his baseball cap on, vanishing, and my heart stutters with him out of sight. He stays close to me as I take the lift back up to Gisella's desk.

When she sees the books in my hand, she frowns. "You could have put them back yourself." She accepts the pile and sets them on her desk.

"I could have, but then you wouldn't know that someone tore pages out of your books."

Gisella's face shows every emotion. She moves from shock to anger to livid in a span of seconds. "I'm not sure I understand you," she says in disbelief.

I grab the book on the top and flip it open to a missing page. I can feel her anguish as she touches the frayed edge. The details contained were supposed to reveal how the dagger was forged and, specifically, who forged it.

"I think this is pretty clear. Thank you for your help, Gisella. Enjoy the brownies."

"Whatever crusade you're on, I hope you're happy that it cost us valuable information. Clearly whatever you're looking for was important enough for someone to steal it to ensure you don't find it." Her words are cutting and unfair, but I *try* to understand her frustration. The books never leave her library—someone did this under her nose.

"Gisella, I didn't rip out those pages. I don't know who did. But I would be interested to know if the Goddess Supreme has been to the library since my death."

The flush on Gisella's face tells me that I'm not far from the truth. I just don't know how close after my death it was.

I don't say anything further, just walk out with Essos at my back. Once we're clear of the building, Essos grabs my upper arms...and whisks us away.

29

We land in a clearing, the city in the distance. Behind Essos rests the old cabin he used to share with his brothers when they were younger. A pang shoots through my whole body at the sight of the building that was the setting for our reconciliation. It's like there's a crack in my soul that anyone can see.

It looks dark and overgrown, like no one has been here in centuries. The bushes that used to line the deck have overtaken it, and the once-meticulous flower beds are flooded with weeds. A tree branch rests on the roof, and I imagine if not for protective charms, the house would be in ruins. I can't remember the last time we were here ourselves. A solstice celebration, perhaps.

It feels wrong for a place that has such emotional significance to look so forgotten.

"It looks like no one has been here forever," I muse aloud.

Essos comes up behind me and pulls me to his chest. I melt into his embrace. "They haven't. I think Finn, Dion, and Bria came here during the first quarter century of their relationship. They hosted epic orgies."

Bria, the Goddess of the Hunt, a woman to whom I owed a great deal. If I saw her again, I would have to thank her.

"What happened between them all? Helene said one day Bria was part of them, and the next, she wasn't."

Essos shrugs then pulls away. "I can't say. I wasn't exactly up to speed on gossip."

I smirk and tilt my head at him. "But up to date enough to know that there were orgies at the cabin? If I pushed a little, would I find out you attended those orgies?"

I'm teasing him, but all humor drops from his face. "No. Never. There was a period, around that time, when Finn reached out to me every day, but he would come over and just talk nonsense. Some days I listened better than others."

It seems I have more still to be thankful for. "I'm sorry. I was only teasing."

This pulls a smile from Essos's lips. "Well, it was a logical leap." He gives me a quick kiss. "Try clearing it out," Essos prods once I'm settled.

"I'm sorry, what?"

"You heard me perfectly. Clear out the debris, and let's see how far we can push your powers."

I get what he's trying to do, but outside of the accidental surges when we're having sex, I haven't used my powers in such a big way since the battle in the Deep.

It takes a moment to focus on how the yard would look with the bushes trimmed and the branches cleared. I concentrate less on turning them to ashes and more on unmaking them, turning back the clock on the growth. It requires more energy, and I do it around the property, shrinking away weeds and grass.

I'm hit by a powerful force on my shoulder, and it sends me spiraling. I panic while I'm airborne. That Galen has found me, that he knows that I've been with Essos, that maybe Galen still has the dagger and will kill us both. I hit the ground with enough force to knock the wind out of me, but when I look up, Essos has his gaze trained on me. I jump to my feet, swirling my hands around each other to form a small, dense wooden ball, and I hurl it right back at him. He catches it barehanded, burning it to ash.

"You're an asshole." I snap, furious with him.

When he sees I'm genuinely angry, his smile fades. "I'm sorry," he says, immediately apologetic when he realizes how pissed I am. "I was trying to get you to shift your focus and be able to do two things at once. I went about it the wrong way."

I scowl at him and go back to focusing on what I'm doing. I shouldn't be surprised when he does it again, but I am. When this blow hits me, it's right at my center, sending me ass over teakettle backward. I stop only when I hit a tree. Everything hurts, trying to move my arm most of all.

"What the actual *fuck*?" I demand. I pull back on the roots from the tree behind me, hauling it out of the earth and right at him. Essos has to pull his hands out of his pockets to block the oncoming tree, blasting it into splinters and then turning those splinters into butterflies. He looks proud as he walks over to me, hand extended. I swat at it and climb to my feet without his help. The pain in my arm is blinding for a second, and I gasp. Essos moves toward me, but I shift my arm away from him.

"What are you trying to do here?" I demand, giving him a little shove with my good arm. I probably just tweaked my shoulder, but holy shit.

"I'm trying to show you how capable you are. You're stronger than you think, but you're afraid to see how deep your powers actually go because you don't want to hurt my delicate ego," Essos taunts.

I laugh in his face. "Right, your *ego* is what I'm protecting. Maybe you need to reevaluate that ego, because you're really pissing me off."

"Good. Use your anger. Delve into it, and focus it."

I glare at Essos. "You want me to fight back? You want to see what I am capable of?" The house behind Essos crumbles, and I reach deep into the land for all the saplings and seedlings of trees and make them rise, I make them *grow* until they tower over us, and then I shape them like my little vine dagger, only now they're wooden swords, dense and hard and unyielding. I launch another tree at Essos, who waves a hand, petals raining on the ground.

Whatever happened between us when we made love unlocked something deep within me. It opened up a box of my abilities that have sat untapped, unused for I don't even know how long. Essos throws a smaller blast at me, nothing like before when he sent me spiraling, but enough to make me stumble. My hands shoot forward, curling into fists before I pull them back toward me like I'm tugging a blanket up at bedtime. The grass below Essos's feet lifts and moves toward me at the same speed, knocking him on his ass.

"I yield!" he shouts as I hover the wooden swords and knives over him. I snap, and they all turn into tiny acorns that rain down on him, burying him. He sits up, the mound falling to the side.

"You're a jackass." I walk over to him and offer him a hand, helping him up.

"Well, you blew up the house, so I suppose we're even." He pauses. "Are you all right?"

My gut reaction is to tell him that I'm fine, but my shoulder throbs something fierce.

"No. My arm hurts," I admit.

Essos gestures for me to give him my arm. I comply gladly and welcome the healing warmth of his touch. I could do it myself, but having him take care of me is what I need.

"I'm sorry, love," he says, releasing my arm.

"I appreciate what you're trying to do, but it was also the wrong thing." I dust off my shirt and Essos's, then flick an acorn cap from his hair.

"I'm not excusing myself, but I'm terrified. I'm terrified of what happens if you don't have every weapon in your arsenal at your disposal. I'm worried about what happens when I lose. I can't fail you, not again."

My brow furrows as I catch on one word. *When.* Not if he fails, when.

"You're not going to fail," I say softly. "*We're* not going to fail. It's not an option. Just like when Helene locked us in this cabin for a week."

Essos looks at me, and I know he's remembering what led to us needing to be locked in the cabin. I can practically taste the salt from my tears when I showed up. It's enough to drag me into the memory of it.

"You two will talk *about this and resolve your little bullshit problem.*" *Helene's voice is hard. Behind me, I can hear the sounds of food being shuffled around in the cabinets, filling them to the brim.*

"*This is not a little bullshit problem—he cheated on me.*" *I grit my teeth. I told myself I wouldn't cry in front of him. I refuse. I try to leave but find that I can't—it feels like gravity is weighing me down, or maybe that's just the crushing burden of my broken heart. Defiance flashes in Helene's eyes, like she knows what I attempted.*

"*She can't even bear to be in the same room as me,*" *Essos says. He looks sick, like he hasn't showered in weeks, or eaten. His face is gaunt, eyes sunken with dark smudges under them. I want to reach out to him, but I won't. I might love him, but I have to move on. He doesn't respect me or our relationship.*

"*This* is a little bullshit communication problem. Just *talk to each other, really and truly. You two are on a whole other level of meant to be, and you owe it to each other. You—*" *Helene rounds on Essos, pointing an accusing finger at him* "*—told me you love her, so what*

341

happened? And you—" she turns to me "—need to give him a chance to apologize and explain. Galen is not your future. Essos is."

She's gone before I can say another word. I actually do try to leave then, feeling the weightlessness of my body, but when I reach the boundary that Helene has set, I drop out of the air, and Essos catches me. Concern flashes in his eyes. My body tenses against his, and he lets me go, stepping away. He checks the doors, confirming that Helene meant it. We're not leaving until we sort this out, for better or worse.

Essos is the first to break, moving into the kitchen to start poking around to find whatever it is that Helene left us with.

"There is this moment, right before you wake up every day, where I know you're starting to stir."

I stay quiet with my lips pursed as my gaze tracks him.

He pulls out the ingredients for his carbonara. "I always wondered what you were dreaming about, because you'd start smiling, and sigh this happy, contented sigh, like you were right where you were meant to be. It took so much effort for me to not wake you, to not kiss you, because part of me wanted you to live in that happy moment forever, but the other half of me wanted to see you open your eyes and hear you say my name."

Knowing that he watched me like that hurts even more, because how can you pay that much attention to someone and then betray them? How can you act like you have this pure form of love and then tarnish it?

"What is your point, Essos?" I demand.

His back is to me, and I see his shoulders turn in just a little more, like defeat and resignation have their claws in him. "My point..." He exhales. "I guess I really don't have a point. My point is that I'm not going to waste your time with excuses, because there aren't any. There will never be a reason good enough to have hurt you like that. I can tell you it was a one-time thing, I can promise you that she meant nothing to me, but that would almost make it worse, I think."

He finally turns to face me, the silence stretching out between us. I thought I loved him—no, I know I still do, because if I didn't, it wouldn't feel like my heart is being carved from my chest anew every time I look at him.

"I don't know if we can fix this," I tell him. I thought all the pieces of my heart were already broken, but admitting to him that I do want to fix it might shatter me completely. It was easy to want to pull away from the gravity that is Essos when I wasn't near him, but standing here now, all I want is to go to him.

He inhales and I notice garlic crushed in his fist. "I realized a few months ago that I was more than besotted with you. I was in love with you, for better or worse. And that was it for me. I knew you were too good for me, that I was never going to deserve you and so, rather than strive to make myself better every day, I did the opposite. I'm not going to make that mistake again."

He moves around the counter so he's closer to me. "I am not above begging you to give me a second chance. Let me learn from my mistake, because I know exactly what it was. I let my inner demons convince me that I wasn't good enough for you. Give me the chance to defeat them and show you that I can be a man, a god, a king worthy of you. I have no excuse. I fucked up tremendously, and there will be no making up for it. But I want to try, for as long as you're willing to let me try. If you decide I'm not meant for you after that, then I will bow out gracefully." Essos falls to his knees. "But you have a prince on his knees for you, one who is willing to do whatever it takes to win back your heart. However long it takes, I will prove it."

With each word, each declaration, my heart begins to knit itself back together. I know tears are tracking down my face again, because I can taste the salt on my lips.

"Maybe we can talk over dinner."

It's not a yes, but it's a start.

. . .

HIS MOUTH PRESSES into a thin line. "I feel like all I do is fail you. I should have protected you, and I didn't. I should have taken Galen seriously. But never in my wildest dreams did I think he was capable of murdering the woman I love. I won't make that mistake again."

I wrap my arms around his center, closing my eyes, breathing in the scent of him, which is now mixed with the earthy scents around us. I visualize the house returning to its original form, rebuilding itself the way Essos and I rebuilt after coming here. My affinity for plants and flowers means that this is harder, but I do it. I clutch Essos, my knees going weak from the exertion, and he holds me tighter.

We've made our mistakes—what eternal being hasn't fucked things up along the way once or twice? But when it mattered, we fixed things. Essos is right. He is my soulmate. I let my mind get muddied by Galen, but my pull to Essos was always there during the Calling.

"You haven't failed me, Essos, not since we fixed things. I don't think that you could." It's obvious that Essos needs reassurance too, that he needs to know it's not too late for us. My heart is nearly pounding out of my chest, and I don't think it's only from how he makes me feel.

"We can debate that later—you feel a little warm. Are you all right?" His lips press to my forehead, and his brow furrows.

"Probably just overexerted myself. I had no idea I could do things like unmake a house, let alone rebuild one." I glance at the house. It's not exactly the same. The colors are brighter, and I've made it bigger so that, when things settle, I can bring my friends here. I didn't want it to be the same—I wanted a reminder that sometimes rebuilding can be better.

"The ability to make and unmake things is something all gods have. It's why we're able to summon things. You just never tried to do something so large—you always hesitated to push the boundaries of your powers, which was fine. You did what came naturally to you, and destruction was never your forte. It makes sense that you're exhausted from the effort."

I lean into him, accepting the support, which he provides no matter when, no matter why. "Can we just go home, eat more carbonara and garlic bread, drink wine, and maybe take a long bath?" I plead. My head feels heavy, and I want desperately to lie down.

Essos chuckles. "Anything for you, my love." His arms tighten around me, and I don't feel that usual dropped-stomach feeling as we move through time and space.

But when our feet touch the carpet in our bedroom, I break away from Essos and sprint to the bathroom, hurling straight into the toilet. Essos is a beat behind me, pulling my hair back and rubbing my back with his other hand.

"I never understood why that upset you so much."

I throw up again. "Now is really not the time for criticism," I whine, and I slump to the floor.

"What can I get you?" When he touches my skin, he frowns.

"A ginger fizzy? Why the face?"

He rises, brushing his hands on his jeans before crossing to the tub and starting to fill it. This is the Essos I knew best, casual and caring. He always looks amazing in his three-piece suits, but nothing beats the way jeans hang low on his slim hips.

"You're sweating, and I'm worried I pushed you too far."

"You worry too much. Ginger fizzy," I repeat, more urgently this time. I need something to settle my stomach.

"Yes, my love." Essos slips out. I take stock of how my whole body aches. He did a number on me with those few blasts he shot out. They weren't overly powerful, nothing like what Kai or Finn or Helene have shot at me, but he caught me off guard. I slip my shirt over my head and try not to whimper at the pain shooting through my side. His healing was targeted before; maybe I should ask for the full body treatment.

I'm unbuttoning my pants when Essos strolls in with a ginger fizzy. He holds it out to me, a straw sticking out of the long glass bottle.

"This is my favorite part. How dare you rob me?" He smiles when I take the drink from him.

I let him tend to me, knowing that unnecessary guilt is gnawing away at him. When he sees the mottled bruise on my side, he doesn't hesitate to touch me, his hands so featherlight on my skin I can barely feel them. His warmth suffuses my body, and I melt as each little ache and pain in my bones subsides. The nausea, however, seems here to stay.

"Lift your hips," Essos orders, and he pulls down my jeans. It's an order I would expect to lead to him taking me right there on the floor of the bathroom, but there's nothing sexual behind it, even if the feel of his hands on my thighs makes my heart beat wildly.

I suck on the ginger fizzy slowly, hoping it will magically settle my stomach. I know it won't—my body feels off in ways that even the drink can't cure.

Once I'm bare, Essos scoops me up. He doesn't bother removing his clothes; instead, he magics them away so we're skin to skin as he carefully steps into the tub. The hot water sends a shock of pain through my body all the way up the back of my throat. Feeling me tense, Essos cools the water and raises the level so once we sink into it, we're submerged to our chins.

"I feel like our reunion has gone all wrong," he confesses while I hold my drink and nestle in his lap. When we renovated the space, I said I wanted a tub large enough to hold five, which only got me questions about who else would be joining us. Really, I just wanted space for the two of us to spread out, whether for something relaxing or erotic. Moments like this, where I'm curled into his lap, are what I had in mind.

"Why do you think that?" I rest my hand on his cheek. If anything, it's my fault.

"I wanted us to disappear for at least five years and spend more time with our clothes off than on." He nuzzles my neck. "How are you feeling?"

"Better now, though sore everywhere. I think you owe me a nice deep-tissue massage." I can feel him harden against my bottom.

"I can get as deep as you want," he murmurs, kissing my neck.

I can't help but laugh. "First you kick my ass, now you want to go to pound town. I don't think so. Besides, I'm not feeling that well."

Essos lazily drags his fingers along my arm. "What can I do?"

"Holding me is good."

His arms tighten around me. "Rest, sweet girl. I've got you." I let my eyes drift closed in the warmth of the tub, knowing that Essos will always have me.

I'M TUCKED against Essos's bare chest, our bodies twined together, when someone grabs my shoulder and gives me a hard shake.

"Daph! Daphne!" The voice is urgent, and I roll toward them. I blink my eyes open to find Cat kneeling beside my bed. Essos's hand curls in the sheet and tugs it up to cover him.

"What is it?" I ask, aware that all I have on is Essos's shirt. I slumbered in his arms in the tub until I woke as he carried me out.

I got the massage he promised, his hands gingerly rubbing my body, healing every ache as he went. A little soreness didn't stop me from spreading my legs and welcoming him to me, eager to feel his skin on me in a different way.

"Galen is here."

30

My whole body freezes. I turn toward Essos, who is already looking around the room for his things. I bite my lower lip.

"Is he already in the apartment?" I whisper, fear getting the better of me. Cat shakes her head. No, of course, he wouldn't be; we warded it to protect against anyone coming in uninvited. I say to Essos, "He'll know I was with you." I can taste my fear, tangy and bitter against the back of my throat, or maybe that's just vomit at the thought of seeing Galen. I thought I had more time away from him. It hasn't even been a week.

"He won't. There is no way he can."

"He *can*. He knew during the Calling Ball that we had been together. He...he...he told me I was used up and that he would hold me down so his friends could use me." I cover my mouth as bile tries to force its way back up my throat. I can't see straight. I can't think. *Oh my gods.* He could just decide I'm not worth the trouble and kill me, kill us all.

Essos grips my shoulders and squeezes hard enough to cause pain and jolt me out of my downward spiral. "We will discuss *that* revelation later. Right now, I need you to take a breath. Cat, tell him that Daphne will be right out. It's the middle of the night. What is he thinking?" Essos stays where he is on the bed, hands still on me as I try to pull myself together. Cat sweeps out and, once the door closes, Essos moves quickly, grabbing his clothes off the floor.

I pull my hair back into a bun, then shower quickly, scrubbing my body and between my legs roughly. I have to scrub everywhere Essos touched me or kissed me.

It's irrational, this need to clean myself. Essos is right; there is no way Galen can smell Essos on me, but why take the risk? I emerge from the shower and dry my body quickly with magic. Essos is leaning against the bathroom counter, dressed, hat in hand, watching me.

"I'll stay right here," he swears.

I shake my head vehemently, pulling on a pair of shorts and a clean shirt.

"I love you for wanting to stay, but you *have* to go. Please. I can handle him."

Essos crosses to me, wanting to reach for me, but thinks better of it. "I'll be close by." Essos slides on his hat on, and I don't see him leave, but I can feel the absence of him. I let my hair down, shaking it so I can hide any accidental hickeys Essos was careless about giving me. I heal what I can see, just in case.

I take in a deep, steadying breath and then open the door and step into the main apartment.

Galen is pacing, waiting for me. "There you are! These two wouldn't let me past to see you." He rushes toward me and grabs for me, but I pull back a step.

"When I opened the door to tell him that you would be right out, he pushed his way in," Cat tells me, explaining how he got inside.

"What are you doing here? It's the middle of the night." I stifle a fake yawn and pull my robe tighter around me.

"I had a revelation, and I had to share it with you." His golden eyes are bloodshot, and I smell booze on his breath.

"So, you had to come in the middle of the night?" I repeat. Cat and Zara both look unsure. "Go back to bed," I tell them, facing Galen.

Cat and Zara shuffle past me into one of the guest rooms. I catch Cat leaving the door open a crack and I frown. I can feel a presence behind me, and I curse Essos for staying, but I feel relieved at the same time. As long as Galen can't tell he's there, it'll be fine.

"Yes, I have the answer. I think Essos has been under our nose the entire time, and with him gone for good, we can move on with our lives." He grabs my arms and leans in to kiss me and I push him back again.

"What do you mean he's been under our noses?" I try to remember to keep breathing.

"Why won't you let me kiss you? I thought we were getting somewhere." Trust Galen to focus on the wrong things.

"Because I can withdraw consent at any time, and I have. You have not earned the right to kiss me or to show up in my apartment in the middle of the night. You need to go." As badly as I want to hear his theory as to why he thinks Essos is under our noses, he's too erratic right now. I keep my voice firm and unwavering.

Galen doesn't like this answer and throws his fist.

I flinch, expecting him to hit me, but instead, he slams it into the wall. "Don't you care about us?!"

I force back the urge to pull at my powers. "Get. Out." I clench my jaw.

"No. You are going to be my *wife*." He grabs my face and pulls me toward him. I lean back, trying to turn my head away, but he kisses me on the mouth. I don't hesitate to bring my knee up between his legs and my arm down on his inner elbows. This surprises him, and he stumbles back as I simultaneously pull back and away from him.

Maybe it's having been with Essos for the last several days. Maybe it's just having been out of Galen's grasp since coming to Solarem. But I've had *enough*. Enough of playing pretend, enough of appeasing the psychopath. Nothing is ever enough for him; there will always be more he wants to take and take and *take*. I won't let him, and I need to stop offering up pieces of myself in the hope that it will change something.

"You never seem to learn. You're never going to, so I'm done playing games. I've made it pretty clear, even beyond my pretty words, that I hate you, Galen. There is no version of this where I submit to you willingly. Get out. Get out, *now*, before I call your father to come collect you."

Hatred burns in Galen's eyes, but the feeling is mutual. Being near him has sent my blood pressure through the roof and, for my own mental health, I need to be away from him. I thought I could continue with the charade but, after these few days of peace and freedom, I don't have it in me to pretend anymore.

"You *bitch*," he snarls.

"If that's the best you've got, you make a pretty pathetic God of War and Suffering. Being married to you would surely make me the Goddess of Suffering." I take in a deep, calming breath. "I'm not going to repeat myself."

I wait for Galen to say something else, to hit me or scream. He stands up tall so that he towers over me, trying to intimidate me, but I won't be cowed.

"If that is how you want it to be, then that is what we'll do. Enjoy your freedom now, because once we're married, you'll have none. I'm going to start with Cat and then move on to Zara, and I'll make you watch, see what hurts you most. And I'll keep doing it until you learn your place. I'll leave, but I'm going to have a word with the Council about moving up the timing of the remaining trials and moving up the wedding. I got away with killing you once, and I'll do it again once I have the crown."

He leaves the threat hanging between us and walks out of the apartment, the door slamming behind him. I sag against the wall. My bravado is gone, exhaustion in its place. I let my body slide down so I can sit on the floor, my legs tucked to my chest.

"Are you all right?" Zara is the first to reach me. Cat hovers across from me.

"As all right as I'm ever going to be."

Essos appears in the doorway to our room. The muscle in his jaw ticks as he clenches and unclenches it. He looks like he's about to punch a hole in the wall himself.

"I'm going to kill him." Essos's words are low and deadly as he tears his gaze from mine to look at the hole in the wall.

"You're going to have to beat me to it," I huff. I press my palm to the wall, and the hole disappears.

I take Essos's outstretched hand and get up. "I want you to keep Zara with you. She's clever and can help your research and offer a different perspective on everything. I can explain away her absence. I can't explain Cat's—he knows I'm overprotective of her to a fault and won't let her pass into the Afterlife with it in turmoil." My insides are still quaking.

"Do I get a say in this?" Zara asks, crossing her arms.

"No," Essos and I say in unison.

"You heard the threats he made. I can at least *pretend* I dismissed you to the Afterlife. He's under the impression I'm punishing you for the Calling. There's a chance he'll figure it out, but it's small. There is too much chaos in the Underworld right now."

"Do *I* get a say in this?" Cat asks, and I shake my head.

"No. I got you both—I got all of us into this mess. I have to clean it up."

"Have you considered, my love, that your desire to shoulder the burden for everything is why we keep winding up in varying messes?"

I try to keep the hurt from my face. Essos is not the first person to say that, and I hate it. I hate it...because they're all right. But I can't change who I am as a person. I made this mess; it's my job to clean it up.

"But it *is* my fault."

"It wasn't a criticism. We're all at fault one way or another," he tells me.

I try to pull the engagement ring off my hand again, and it holds fast to my skin as if adhered to it. I'm about to scream in frustration, even as I feel the tears pricking my eyes. Essos's hands reach out and still mine. I look up into the depths of his blue eyes, allowing myself to get lost.

"Let's go back to bed and figure this out in the morning," Essos continues calmly.

I step into his arms, needing to hear the thump of his heart. To my surprise, it's racing, the stress of having to stand back and watch me confronting Galen probably too much to ask of him.

"Fine, but I've made my decision. I won't change my mind." I dig in my heels, and Cat and Zara huddle close.

"Is it all right if we stay up and just watch TV? I'm a little on edge." Cat slides her hand into Zara's.

"Of course. I'll call Finn in the morning about going back. Clearly, my absence has made Galen unhinged." I lean into Essos's side, and we all go our separate ways.

I'm too afraid to strip again, terrified of Galen returning. Essos pulls me against his chest, and I worry that this might be the last time I see him until this is over. I don't know what Galen knows about where Essos has been, and I don't want to risk my husband's safety for a few hours' worth of carnal pleasure, even if it comes with a level of comfort I need. His life isn't worth that. What Galen said about killing me again makes me worry that he has the dagger, and that my marriage bed with him will also be my deathbed.

I wonder if Essos is thinking the same thing, because his arms tighten around me, pulling me even closer to his side. I slide my fingers under the thin fabric of his shirt, my hands tracing the ridges of his abs.

"I'm not worried." His voice is quiet in the dark. From the living room, I can hear the sounds of *Last God on Olympus,* a survival show where our gods go to Greece and try to convince tourists that gods walk among them. Mortals attribute the actions to clever tricks, never realizing that magic is being done before their eyes. They pose as Greek gods, rip off our lives, and we have a laugh at ourselves.

"That makes one of us," I mutter.

His hands tangle in my curls and he tugs my hair back gently so I look up at him. His kiss is ferocious. If his will was enough to solve our problems, Galen would cease to exist, the memory of him wiped from the history books, and we would never worry again. I open my mouth to Essos, inching my body up close so I don't have to strain my neck. I give myself over to him, forgetting where I end and he begins. The world could be ending, and neither of us would know.

"I'm giving you my word. We will get out of this," he swears.

"How?" I ask, feeling utterly hopeless.

"I know it doesn't look like I'm doing much, but I think I'm close to learning where the dagger is stashed. But even if I can't find the original dagger, there's a second one I can look for. I've had some help. I've wanted to keep you in the dark—"

"I know, so neither of us knows the whole plan. I've seen a heist movie or two."

Essos chuckles. "Finn and I have been looking for the dagger in the Council offices. I've also been checking Galen's homes for it."

I sit up. "They're not warded?"

"He's arrogant. He believes no one would dare cross the God of War. He doesn't realize just how deep my hate for him runs. I was undermining Galen long before you entered the picture. It wasn't until you that my pranks stopped being childish and became something more. It's why I feel responsible. If I hadn't needled him, then maybe he would have left you alone."

"That was never an option for him, but what kinds of things have you done?"

"I've ended wars, stopped conflicts before they arose. He's made assassination attempts on mortal leaders, and I've thwarted them. Some of them I can't tell you about."

"Can't?" I question.

"Can't. There are other lives at stake. After losing you, I'm not going to make that mistake again."

I nod, lowering my head to his chest. I don't want to sleep; I don't want to miss a moment of being in his presence. I thought I had weeks to figure out a plan, but after only days, I realize that I'll never have all the information.

"I swore to protect you with my life, and I failed once. I'm not going to fail again."

With that, Essos wraps his magic around me like a weighted blanket until my breathing evens and I fall asleep.

31

I'm slowly getting ready with Essos, enjoying what we both know could be our last moments together for three months. Even if Galen is wrong about how Essos is coming and going from the house, neither of us is willing to risk it, not when he could harm either of us to hurt the other. I'm scheduled to marry Galen at the end of that time, and either Essos swoops in with a magic solution, or I'm fucked both ways.

His hands trace lazy circles at the hem of my shirt as we stand at the island talking to Zara and Cat. Zara has finally relented and agreed to stay with him.

"Only because my queen commanded it," she says with an eye roll.

I give her a weak smile. "Thank you. I want to send Cat with you too, but..." My words hang in the air. I've made it too clear that Cat is invaluable; returning without her would be suspicious. I regret putting either of them in this situation.

A knock at the door has all of us freezing in place. Essos digs his fingers into my skin as he reaches for his hat and slips it on. I mask his plate and mug and go to the door.

357

Xavier and Finn stand there, both looking grim.

"Aren't you going to invite us in?" Xavier drawls, looking down at me. I press my lips into a line.

"Him, yes. You? No." Finn doesn't make a move to enter the apartment though.

Xavier doesn't listen to my un-invitation; he just pushes his way in. "Catalina," Xavier says, his voice noticeably softer when he greets her.

Finn finally enters, and I close the door behind them and cross my arms.

"What is this about, Xavier?"

He turns to face me, seeming reluctant to take his eyes off Cat. Finn goes to the counter, unable to resist the pile of bacon.

"You're being sanctioned by the Council."

It feels like a physical blow, and I move back to where I was standing to be beside Essos.

"What for?" I demand.

"Where should I start? Stabbing Galen, harboring a fugitive, consorting with the enemy."

I grip the kitchen counter to prevent my knees from giving out. Essos presses a hand to the small of my back, letting me know he's still there. Stabbing Galen, what a fucking joke. I bite my lips, not wanting to reveal why I stabbed him in front of my husband, not while Essos isn't able to react. I wish I had taken the time to tell him exactly what happened before now.

"I don't know what you're talking about," I manage to bite out through gritted teeth. I need to find my mask and pull it back on, be the indomitable queen I know I am.

Xavier lets out a sigh. I don't miss how he makes sure his arm brushes Cat's. "Did you know I was capable of seeing through Essos's trivial little helmet? This little glamor isn't fooling me, brother. If you want to save your wife—if you love her—you will turn yourself in."

Essos rips the hat from his head, revealing himself, and slams it on the counter.

"I will do no such thing. Turning myself in isn't going to help her. Why would Daphne stab Galen when she's been bending over backward to prove to him that she's on his side? Why aren't you doing anything to help her?"

Xavier scoffs. "*I'm* not doing anything to help her? Get a grip, Essos. I'm there in that house, quelling our brother's darker desires. I'm the one who suggests he drink till he's stupid. I'm the one finding willing women to distract him from *your* wife. I'm bound to the Council and its demands. If you didn't want this to be a fucking disaster, you shouldn't have fled the Calling. You should have abdicated when the vote of no confidence was issued and confirmed, and maybe then you could have taken your wife and fled, but your flimsy attempts to duck your responsibilities have only served to anger him more."

"What kind of king are you, Xavier, that you're letting Galen and your wife control you? You became King of the Gods because you have the most power of us all, and yet—" Essos gestures at us all "—here you are playing errand boy for Galen and the Council you allegedly head. If you were really trying to protect Daphne, you wouldn't let such blatant lies stand."

"He provided *proof*. Her soiled bed sheets, the letter opener still coated in his blood. Witnesses to the aftermath. She refused his summons to speak to the Council about it. I've been doing what I can, but you need to face the music, brother. Galen is going to take your place and take your wife. If you turn yourself in, I can spare your life. We can make the transfer of power seamless. We can find a way to spare Daphne, but without your blood, without your abdication, she is the *only* way he can claim the Underworld, and even then, the gates are still coded to your blood. You are the key to ending this."

Essos turns to me, but I refuse to look at him right now.

"Soiled bed sheets?" he asks quietly. Tension lines his shoulders and there's a hard set to his face, like he's trying so hard to not show his emotions that he's overcompensating.

I look at Finn, hurt flashing in my eyes. He knows at least some of the truth about what happened; he should have done more to stop this. "Et tu, Brute?" I grab Essos's hand, giving it a firm squeeze. "What is my punishment?"

"The remaining trials are being moved up, and so is the wedding. The trials will be held once a week. Due to the nature of my trial, Dion will be presenting his trial next. If Galen successfully completes three, then the wedding will occur within a week of the final trial."

I swallow hard, leaning into Essos completely.

"No. Absolutely not. I'll go with you now if you let Daphne go. I can't stay in the shadows. I won't. If he wants my head on a pike, he can have it, but he needs to leave Daphne alone. She and Zara and Cat need to be allowed to go to free. Set them up far away from Galen, and I'll turn myself in." Essos is firm in his demand.

I push him back, meeting his gaze.

"Finally," Xavier mutters.

"No. *No*," I object. "You *can't* do that. Galen won't settle for your head. Only one thing will appease him, and that is *not* an option. Between the two of us, you stand a chance of defeating him. Don't squander it because of me. Our realm, our people, they're suffering, and they need you to keep fighting. I will be fine." It's a false promise but I have to try.

"Daphne." Essos lowers his voice, cupping my face, even as tears start. "I could *taste* your fear last night, it was so potent. You told me what he said during the Calling. I don't know what these soiled sheets have to do with anything yet, but I can guess, and I am *not* going to let you go back into that sort of situation. The world could be damned twice over before I let you get hurt any further."

"It's not your decision to make, Essos. It's mine. When I took the vow to be your wife and become your queen, it meant more than just pledging my soul to you. It meant pledging my soul to the billions of mortals who come into their afterlife looking for peace. If we can't provide that safe space anymore, we're dooming them all. You were there in the Deep. You heard the testimony of those souls. He was using them for slave labor, something you and I vowed never to do. Don't make me choose between you and doing what is right for all the souls in the Underworld."

Essos covers his mouth with his hand in contemplation before rubbing his face. When his forehead touches mine, resting there, I close my eyes so I can commit this feeling to memory. I don't know if this is going to be one of the last times I'm able to touch him like this. Whatever is left of our time, I don't want to waste it fighting.

"Daphne." It's a plea, but more than that, it's confirmation that he hears me and understands me.

I nestle myself into his side so I can look at Xavier. "So, you're saying that I'll be married within a month." My voice sounds so empty, but that's how I feel. Empty. I used all of my passion in my plea to Essos. I need Essos's strength right now. I thought I had time, thought I'd have a plan in place for what to do if we lost, even if that meant going on the run with Essos.

"Yes," Xavier says simply and reaches for the bacon.

Cat swats his hand. "You do *not* get bacon for helping Galen," she snaps.

Xavier's eyes flash. "I am not helping him. I am trying to do what I can from within the Council. It's not my fault that your friend is literally in bed with the most wanted man in the realm. I am not her mother or her father or her husband—it isn't my job to clean up Daphne's mess."

"And I'm not asking you to, Xavier. I'm just asking you to get me more time." I'm begging him, and I hate it.

361

"So you can, what? Find a way to kill the God of War? Not bloody likely. Everything is spiraling out of control without someone actively ruling the Underworld. I'm not going to fuck it up further by taking the God of War out of the mix. The mortal realm is already devolving into chaos thanks to the lack of regulation in the Underworld."

"So, I stab Galen when he tries to *rape* me, and I get sanctioned, but he actually *murders* me in my bed and gets, what, put in time-out? The hypocrisy! The sexism! Look in a fucking *mirror* for more than just your hair once in a while, Xavier, and see who is causing chaos in the realms." Everyone's eyes are on me. I won't look at Essos. Instead, I take in the look on Finn's face, which... which is actually the same rage I expected from Essos.

"I tried," Finn says tightly, looking at Essos. The tension in the air is so thick right now, I'm not sure any of us can move. No one dares to try.

"I know, and I appreciate you, Finn, but I'm tired of being told that I need to do better and stand by my murderer. You claim to be on my side, and yet you victimize me every chance you get." I meet his eyes, then Xavier's. "Both of you have consistently voted against me with the Council, which I don't understand. Don't make me do this, please." My voice breaks. It's the first time I've begged Xavier for anything. His cold blue eyes stare at me, but I don't think he really sees me or understands what I've been through. It's like a cloud has descended over his gaze, and there will be no getting through to him.

I should be able to walk away, but I meant what I said to Essos. I swore an oath to protect the Underworld; I'm not going to defect from that, even if it comes at great personal cost.

"Finn and I will take the three of you back to the house, where you will be sequestered to your room until the Trials and the wedding. If you feel so inclined to attend therapy with your betrothed, you will be permitted to leave for that and *only* that.

You will not be permitted to have anything to do with the running of the Afterlife. Your husband's life has been spared—I suggest not pressing your luck."

In the past, gods might not have been able to die, but that doesn't mean we haven't come up with punishments that make us wish we were dead.

"So, I'm to be a prisoner in my own home." It's not a question, it's a statement. It's a cold hard fact. No training with Kai and Finn, no trips to the library, no anything. I am to languish in my room for a month until I become the property of Galen.

"If that's how you chose to see it. Or you could look at it as a chance to reflect on the decisions that lead to this moment. Pack your things," Xavier hisses at me.

"Brother, don't do this," Essos pleads. "We need time to get out of this."

"Perhaps your wife should have thought about that before attempting to assassinate a prince."

I want to scream. Even Cat recoils from him, disgusted by his behavior. His eyes turn toward her, and he looks apologetic.

Funny how he's apologetic to her, but not to me.

"I think you need to wait outside. When she's ready to leave, she'll come to you." Essos's eyes are hard as rocks. His voice leaves no room for debate.

"Are you kicking me out?" Xavier asks with a laugh.

"Yes, we are," I reply, standing tall. Xavier's eyes flash from Essos to me and back again, incredulous. Twice in the last twelve hours, we've kicked a brother out of our home.

"You're welcome to wait in the lobby," Essos replies. His hand cups the back of my neck, giving me a gentle squeeze.

"Are you kidding me?" he chokes out. I'm not sure why he's surprised, after the shit sandwich he just delivered to us. Did he expect me to ask him to tea? Maybe see if he wanted a breakfast burrito for the road?

"No. Please, don't make me ask you again, brother. Let me say goodbye to my wife before you lock her in a room and throw away the key." I know my husband; he would get down on his knees to beg if he thought it would do any good.

Xavier stares at Essos, pity on his face. "I'll wait on the balcony, not in the lobby. You have ten minutes."

"An hour," I say quickly, and Xavier laughs.

"Always a negotiation with you. Thirty minutes, and I *can't* spare you any more time than that. Catalina, will you join me outside?" He offers her his arm.

She laughs in his face and swings a piece of bacon at him. "You can go fuck yourself six ways to Sunday." She turns to me, dismissing him.

Xavier's cheeks burn red. It's possibly the first time he's ever been outright rejected. He opens his mouth to say something but seems to think better of it and walks out onto the balcony, slamming the sliding glass door shut behind him like a petulant child in time-out. Finn leans against one of the other counters with his arms crossed.

"Are you all right?" Essos asks me quietly, his hands loose against mine.

I look up at him and melt. "No, I'm not. But yes, about that, I am fine. I handled it—I stabbed him, didn't I?" I attempt levity when I know this information is hurting us both. I don't let my mind go to that place where I can taste fear creeping up the back of my throat like a visceral pain. I don't tell Essos that, for a moment, I thought Galen was him.

Essos looks at me like he wants to press, but he doesn't—he sees the boundary I've established and doesn't push it. Maybe later, when this is settled and we're able to look to the future, we can discuss it, but not now, not in front of everyone.

"You were supposed to protect her." Essos sounds pained as he looks at Finn. "What happened?"

"Last night, Galen demanded a meeting with the Council. He said he was barred access to this apartment and claimed he heard Essos's voice within. Galen said Daphne has been unfaithful and that she stabbed him one night after she lured him into bed." Finn's gaze shoots to Essos, then back to me. "He said that after he won the fight with Kai, you brought him to your rooms and you... you...well, how do I put this delicately in front of your husband? You consummated the bond, and the realization that you belonged to Galen drove you to fury, so you stabbed him. He had your lady's maids come forward as witnesses, and they admitted that you called them to your rooms and made them clean up the blood."

Those treacherous *bitches*.

"My wife belongs to no one but herself. Even if they slept together—and I'm not saying I believe that, but even if it were true—it wouldn't mean that he had any more right to her than you or Xavier do." Essos digs his fingers into the tight muscles of my neck.

"True, but he implied that other vows were made that night, and that Daphne had come to regret them, which was why she stabbed him. Without her there to present a defense—"

"How could I present a defense when I didn't even know he was doing this? There was no summons!" I cry, swiping my arm across the counter and sending the plates flying.

Waffles hisses from the couch at the sudden commotion.

"That's not all."

"Oh gods," I moan, burying my head in Essos's chest.

"Octavia backed Galen up. The Council had no choice but to accept her recommendations for sanctions, though Titus did speak up in Daphne's defense."

"Since when is my mother back?" Essos asks tightly, glaring at his best friend.

"Since last night. She said that Galen called for her after Titus showed up, to bear witness to your—" Finn clears his throat, again looking from Essos to me, "—consummation. She said she saw the start of it and then left them to their, uhm, privacy."

"I didn't fuck him, so you can stop with the insinuation that anything Galen said was the truth," I snap. It doesn't matter how much Essos tries to massage the tension from my body, it's here to stay.

"*I* know that. Most of us know that, but there wasn't anything that we could do."

"Clearly, my theory was correct," Cat says, starting to clean up. I wave my hand, and the mess disappears just as she bends for a plate. She sticks out her tongue at me.

"Theory?" Finn asks.

"I think the Goddess Supreme has been playing puppet master, providing Galen with everything he needs to make this happen." Cat shares her theory with a slightly haughty tone. I don't blame her; it's looking more and more likely.

"Then I guess that knowing she's been frolicking in the mortal realms in places with red tide algae would only solidify your claims," Finn says, grabbing a grape and popping it into his mouth with a nonchalance I don't feel.

I am overwhelmed by everything that has happened, and I don't know what to do.

I turn to Essos. "I love you. Don't give up. We can beat him—there's nothing like working under a shorter deadline, right?"

Essos cups my face when I say this, and he shakes his head. "I'll turn myself in. You and Cat and Zara can disappear, and that will be that. If you're safe, it will all have been worth it." It's once last offer, one last hail Mary from my husband in hopes to save me the only sure way he can right now.

I grip his wrists and shake my head, tears strolling. "You can't do that. You're my only hope, Obi-Wan." My voice breaks. The rollercoaster of the last twelve hours might break me.

Essos wipes at each tear, catching them. "No pressure," he says with a laugh.

I kiss him, tasting the salt on his lips. I can't bear to drag out this goodbye, knowing that if I do, I'll never leave him, never leave this place.

I pull away and turn to Finn.

He holds my gaze. "Does it provide a balm to know that there will be no more balls, it will just be the Trials and then the wedding?"

"Only if it means that I don't have to plan the wedding with Posey either." I give Essos's hand one last squeeze before going to Waffles and picking him up. Zara comes to join us, and I hold up my hand. "I still want you to stay with Essos. I need you both working on this. Find the dagger."

I step toward Finn, holding my hand out to Cat, who takes it. On the balcony, Xavier is resting on his forearms, looking out at his city.

"What about Xavier?" Finn asks, glancing at him as well.

"He'll figure it out," I snap, not feeling charitable toward him. I look at Essos, who is trying to stand tall, but I can tell that he'll eventually collapse under the weight of the pressure. "I love you. Be safe."

I keep my eyes on him, knowing that this might be the last time I ever see him. He presses his fingers to his lips, sending me one last kiss even as I disappear.

THERE ARE ONLY a few days before Dion's trial. I do as I'm told, languishing in my room. I demand that Cat and I have adjoining rooms, and that I'm not to be disturbed while on house arrest.

And it works...for about five hours, until someone bangs on the door. Only Waffles lifts his head from his place on my pillow. I haven't seen my dogs since I got back. It hasn't been long enough for me to worry, so for now I'm going to hope that they're just busy doing their jobs patrolling the realm.

Cat and I are sitting at a table I've had set up in this expanded suite. Finn and Helene were kind enough to provide the power it took to create the merged rooms. It's the actual bare minimum of what they could do, given the circumstances. If I'm to be stuck in here until the day I die, then I should at least be comfortable.

Beside me on the floor are the papers that someone *graciously* left for me to read. There has been a lot of discussion about the overwhelming smell of magnolias and the impact it's having on the citizens of Solarem. Sitting right at the top is an article about the Missing Queen along with speculation regarding my whereabouts, since I haven't been spotted at the house, which only serves to confirm that someone here has been reporting on my comings and goings. It makes me all the more glad that Essos was never spotted.

Not a single article mentions what I told Celestina. Instead, my fertility is a hot button, and now I'm being put on another bump watch, as if my role couldn't be any more degraded. I've been reduced to an incubator again, thanks to Posey's comments about my ongoing nausea and rumors of my infatuation with Galen.

We're playing a round of gin rummy, and I'm getting my ass handed to me. I place my cards on the table and get up to open the door.

Once I do, I point to the sign I immaturely posted, *Do not disturb. Also, no boys allowed.* "Can't you read?" I challenge. I'm in sweats and the T-shirt I was wearing when I left Solarem. I cross my arms, glaring at Xavier.

"Perhaps if I was a boy, it would scare me off, but I am a man and a king." He pushes the door open but pauses when he sees Cat.

"Then act like it," I snap. "Your wife has you by the short and curlies, and I don't understand why. You've never had a problem sticking your prick where it doesn't belong. Why change now?"

"*Where* is Zara?" he asks, acknowledging my words with only a steely glare.

I glare right back. "She decided she would rather pass on to the Afterlife than be stuck in such turmoil." I try to sound disappointed and not defiant.

Xavier's eyes roll in disbelief. "Stop playing games, Daphne, and accept that this is your life now."

"No. I won't stop fighting him. Did you know that before he went to the Council, he came to my apartment and told me that he was going to kill me again? I'm sure he has the dagger, and who's to say that he'll be satisfied just being King of the Underworld? Why stop there when your wife is already his biggest ally? Why not shoot to be King of the Gods? You yourself worried that killing gods would create a slippery slope. Well, I hope you have a good grip, because you're on it."

"You're treading dangerous waters, Daphne," Xavier growls.

"I never understood why your bitch of a wife has so much say over what you do. She says, 'Jump,' and you ask, 'How high?' Why is that, Xavier?"

For a moment it's like a cloud descends over his eyes, and he's staring into space. My brow dips low, and I'm about to wave my hand in front of his face, when his gaze clears.

"I just came here to remind you of what you need to do. You're only making this harder on yourself. You should have let Essos surrender. You think you're being noble by sticking around, but you're not. You're spitting in Essos's face, and in the face of everyone who mourned you and has tried to help you. Just remember, you had an out, and you didn't take it. Everything that happens from here on out is on you, and you alone."

"I think you should go, Xavier." Cat reaches for her necklace. She's wearing the charm again, but somehow, she feels changed. My friend has been through so much without complaint. She has been on my side, always, and I thought I knew every part of her. But since we returned from Solarem, I sense something lurking in her that I didn't notice before. It could just be that I'm witnessing how her sleep troubles her firsthand, and how often she zones out, staring into nothingness like she's stuck in a memory. Maybe being a mortal with prolonged exposure is changing her in ways no one anticipated. But something's telling me there's more to it.

Darkness flashes in Cat's eyes, and I think Xavier sees it too, because he takes a step back.

He looks at me, frowning. "Be on your best behavior." Then Xavier is gone, and I'm left with Cat, both of us shaking our heads.

What's to come next is anyone's guess. I just know that whatever it is, I don't have to face it alone.

32

I emerge three days later, an outfit repeater. I'm wearing a long-legged wine-colored romper similar to the one I wore when Luminara convinced me to go on that stupid date.

I open the door and find her standing there, a serene smile on her face.

"I think you've been avoiding me," she says, and I frown at her, reaching up to adjust the onyx and diamond crown on my head. The spikes on top are lethal, and at the very least I'm now armed with one weapon. All pretense of playing the good girl has been dropped.

"You don't have to think it; I'll confirm it for you. Yes, I am avoiding you."

She's blocking my exit by standing right in my doorway, but I step forward anyway, pulling my door closed behind me and leaving Cat inside.

Luminara stumbles back a step or two. "Your betrothed has been attending and making a good faith effort to make your relationship work. Why won't you?" She follows me as I walk down the stairs. The jumpsuit has a layer of chiffon attached at the shoulders which flows behind me like a cape. I'm lucky I didn't get it caught in the door.

"Because I have no interest in making it work." I stop at the landing and turn to her. "I thought I had an ally in you, Luminara. You are the Goddess of Harmony and Communication, and you have let me down. You have harmed me through your so-called 'therapy,' and I won't have any more of it. I refuse to be forced to try to make things work with a madman who saw fit to shove a knife in my heart because I rejected him. You and everyone here are complicit if you think I should accept it and move on."

"I am your ally, your grace."

"Your Majesty," I correct.

"I'm sorry?" She sounds confused.

"You should be. My correct honorific is 'Your Majesty.' If everyone insists on pushing me around and telling me to mind my place, then I will remind everyone that my place is on a throne, as queen. So, you will address me appropriately. The lie is, 'I am your ally, Your Majesty.'"

I don't care if I sound like Posey. If everyone continues to insist on treating me like shit, I will just have to remind them who exactly they're talking to.

"It is not a lie, Your Majesty. Just because my support doesn't take shape the way you expect doesn't mean it's not present."

I purse my lips. "You say trust is the foundation of all good relationships, and the key to making therapy work is trust. Right?"

She nods.

"Well, I don't trust you."

I don't give her a chance to respond. I walk outside to where Dion's trial is being held. The plan had been to host it in Solarem, but since I'm under house arrest, it seems that no one wants to run the risk of me fleeing or rallying my supporters.

The press is seated in a section for them, but Celestina, who has been covering the events of the Trials, is noticeably absent.

My entire back patio is littered with wine barrels, and I should have seen this coming. In the interest of expediting the whole charade, there are no guests milling about. Sybil is there, pointing people in different directions and providing snacks for the Council. Sybil looks tired, haggard even. I grimace. The impact of my actions is too far-reaching, and I hate that I've done this to them. They've been weathering the storm I left in my wake. I press my hand to their shoulder, and they break into a wide grin. Sybil is usually the picture of formality, bowing and using formal titles, but they pull me into a hug, squeezing me.

"I've been trying to keep this place running, but Galen has not made it easy."

I wave my hand, dismissing the explanation. "I'm pretty sure nothing could have stopped Galen from doing what he wanted. How have you been?"

"Awful. I miss Essos. I want things to go back to the way they used to be." They gesture to where they are to set up the livestream.

"I can't say I disagree with you. One way or another, this will all be over soon, and I'll be glad for it." It's the truth. I'm emotionally spent. I don't know if it's from the lack of moving around and being stuck in my room, but I'm exhausted all the time, barely wanting to get out of bed. Every day there are two different trays sent up for every meal, one arriving immediately after the other, always delivered by the same young server who dropped a tray in front of Essos during the Calling. The second tray always has a white lily on it, letting me know it's safe and a reminder that, even in the worst of times, I am never alone. If someone is still trying to poison Cat and me, Estelle has stepped in to take care of that very concern.

Cat has done her best to coax me out of bed with card games

and encouraged me to read my book in different places around the room. She even ventured out one day to the house library and gathered a stack of books featuring Princess Lorelei and her dashing Captain of the Guard, Giancarlo. She's taken to reading the more risqué scenes aloud to get a reaction, and it always works.

"I wish more could be done. I know Luminara mentioned she was going to look for you."

I try to avoid pursing my lips like I've tasted something sour. "She found me. She wants me to try therapy again." I want to ask Sybil how they can be with this woman who is intent on tormenting me in such microaggressive ways. I hardly have a Ph.D in psychology, but I'm pretty sure removing your patient's memories of their murderer to try their hand at dating again falls into the bad-idea category.

"Well, that sounds like a terrible idea. I swear, Your Majesty, I don't know what has gotten into her. During the Calling, she was so happy for Essos that you had returned, and now, sometimes I don't even recognize the woman in my bed." It's the most real Sybil has ever been with me, and damned it if that doesn't make me feel all sorts of shitty for never having a deeper conversation with them. It's another thing I'll add to my list of things to do when this is all over. "What makes her think that Galen will change?"

I shrug. "She's your girlfriend." To spread my own rumor, I change the subject. "Zara has decided to move on to her Afterlife. Too much here is unknown for her, and she was worried about her safety, so I let her go." The way I say it is like it's an afterthought, but Sybil knows us better than that.

They arch an eyebrow but say nothing more about Zara. "I've been demoted to party planner. After the *Council* meeting, Posey went to Solarem with Octavia to plan the wedding, since you made it clear you have no interest in marrying Galen, what with the whole attempted evisceration."

"I was going for castration, but I get your point."

Their words sink in, and I have to mentally rewind the conversation to make sure I caught that.

"Will Posey be here today?" My heart takes off at a gallop.

We have our suspicions about Octavia, nothing confirmed, of course, but still. Knowing that she's back in the picture feels like confirmation enough that Cat is right and Octavia is behind it all. She's showing up so she can watch the endgame unfold.

"Of course, Posey will. She has to oversee it all, blah blah. She's the most important person in the room, blah blah. The Goddess Supreme will not be, however, citing the need to familiarize herself with the latest fashions. She came back for the Council meeting and then left again." Sybil points a man wheeling another barrel of wine to an area that has been stacked with them.

It's not surprising that they've kept Octavia's return on the down-low. There's too much focus on the Trials and talk of expediting the process because my love is *so* great. I saw one headline when we got back about my alleged desperation to give Galen what Callista never could, a baby. I turned the pages of that particular paper into origami beasts that tore each other apart.

"So, what you're saying is, I'll be walking down the aisle looking like a train wreck. Got it. Do you think Galen would take pity on me and just kill me again *before* the wedding?" I see Posey now, arguing with Xavier over who knows what. Helene and Kai are also present but keeping their distance from me, and I wonder if they've been told to do so, or if they're avoiding me. It hurts my chest to think that they might believe I lied about not sleeping with Galen.

"Something tells me that he wants your punishment drawn out for as long as his attention span can handle it."

I grimace. "Always the optimist, Sybil." I squeeze their arm and walk to the staging area, where I'm expected to sit.

No one acknowledges me, and I feel awkward. Should I go to them? I perch on the edge of the chair and startle as shackles snap around my ankles and wrists with just enough give that I can move. For a second, I can't believe what's happening. I'm tied down like an animal, but even an animal doesn't deserve to be treated like this.

I nearly Hulk out of the bondage in rage, but of course the restraints won't budge. Why shouldn't I have a physical reminder of just how trapped I am?

"You're a flight risk, *my love*." The pet name Essos has for me is taunting on Galen's lips. My head snaps in his direction as he emerges from behind me like he was waiting for this moment.

"I hope you choke," I snarl at him, tugging on the chains. I'm satisfied when he takes a step back from me.

"Save the bedroom talk for later. Our wedding will be here before you know it." Galen winks at me, and I have to work not to slump in the chair in defeat.

I no longer have to worry about not having approached the rest of the Council, because they're quickly crowding around and looking down their noses at me.

"Go to hell," I growl at them all.

Galen leans closer, a triumphant smirk on his face. "Do you know how weak harpies are? Your little friend tried to submit that article about me and smear my name in the papers. She didn't realize that *I* am the one who controls the message. It was a valiant attempt to undermine me, but ultimately futile. She sang like the bird she is, after I broke her wings, of course. She begged for me to let her live, but ultimately, her little bird heart gave out. What was her name again? Carla? Cori? *Celestina?*"

My heart is pounding so loudly in my chest that I know he can hear it, but I don't blink. I don't look away from him. I don't so much as *breathe.*

"Is this really necessary?" Finn asks, walking up to us. He casts a critical gaze at the chains around my wrists. The panel on my jumpsuit that makes it look like I'm wearing a dress hides the ones on my ankles.

"We can't have a runaway bride on our hands," Posey answers. She gives me a gloating smile.

"I'm not going anywhere," I try to reason.

"I have to agree; it's not necessary," Helene says, resting a hand on my shoulder. She gives it a squeeze, but nothing on her face betrays the concern she might be feeling.

"I know you're not going anywhere, but you've been colluding with an enemy of the crown. While you were gone, we discovered that your guard dogs were allowing Essos and his supporters access to the house. Of course, after catching them, we put him to death." Posey pauses, and I nearly leap out of my skin. I struggle with the restraints, not caring that my skin is rubbed raw. If she touched any of my dogs, I swear to the gods above and below I will take my time peeling the skin from her body and then shoving it down her throat to choke on. I've been denied access to them, and this must be why.

Posey waves her hand dismissively. "The supporter, not your little mutts. We can't *destroy* such valuable assets. The dryad sang like a *canary.* How many times did you meet with him? You should be glad we don't put your mutts to death for their loyalty to the man, not the crown."

I jerk against the cuffs, pulling so hard I can feel the metal slice into my skin. My safety be damned, if she hurts my dogs, I'm going to fucking feed her alive to the monsters of the Deep, and I'm not talking about the creatures that patrol there, keeping wayward souls in line.

"You wouldn't dare," I challenge, breathing heavily. If looks could kill, I would have incinerated her. My powers are flaring just under my skin, but I won't release them, not yet. I need an ace up my sleeve. If they know I have my powers back, who knows what else they'll do to me?

"Wouldn't I? I have to ensure your cooperation somehow." When it becomes obvious I'm about to break the chair, powers or not, she taps my cheek condescendingly. "Calm your tits; your mutts are fine. I have another way to keep you under control." Posey gestures to someone, and out steps a goon, holding Cat by the upper arm. She has some sort of band around her neck, and I wrinkle my brow. Some of the fight leaves my body as realization grips me.

"What is the meaning of this, Posey?" Xavier asks, deadly calm. He's taken the words out of my mouth, and I tear my eyes from where Cat stands, still in her pajamas, eyes red with tears.

Posey turns to Xavier. "Don't look so shocked, Xavier. You gifted the mortal some jewelry using stones from our home, so I gifted her some of my own. Did you think I wouldn't recognize the stone as the one you found when we were at Lake Solarem? If you want to stick your prick in some bitch, then I'll make sure she's accessorized like a bitch. Any time Daphne even *thinks* about stepping out of line—" Posey pauses again, and I watch in horror as Cat's body seizes, a strong shock running through her system. Posey drags the shock on longer than she needs to, past my screaming for her to stop, tears running down my face at my friend's pain. I struggle to get out of my bindings to get to my friend.

My wrists and ankles are raw and bleeding as I beg. "Stop it, stop it, stop it. I'll do anything you want. Please, please Posey, just leave Cat out of this."

"That is *enough*," Xavier orders, and Posey finally releases Cat.

I'm shaking as Cat crumples to the ground, and I am so

thankful when Finn runs to her and starts gently slapping her face.

"I don't know that it is, husband. You dishonor me by fooling around with a mortal under my very nose. I can tolerate only so much disrespect, and fucking the lowest type of creature is a step too far." Posey's blue eyes cut to me. "So much as a *thought* out of line, Daphne, and your friend suffers. You made us do this with your desire to act out like a child, your desire to fight against the natural order. Essos got into your head and made you think ridiculous things, but you belong with Galen. The Fates *demand* it."

I nod mutely, not looking away from Cat as Finn lifts her unconscious body. His eyes meet mine, sad and angry, and he carries her inside.

"Punish me," I plead, one last effort.

Galen grabs my chin and lifts my face to him so I have to stare into his golden eyes, see the pleasure within them. I never expected this level of torture to come to Cat. I should have made her stay with Essos and Zara. Bringing her back was selfish, so selfish of me.

"That will come later, pet. I promise you that." Galen's voice holds the promise of violence. I can practically see in his eyes the things he wants to do, and I feel the blood drain from my skin.

Kai surprises us all by shoving Galen back, breaking the connection. "She's not yours yet," he says evenly.

Helene's hand on my shoulder tenses. We're both remembering how Galen beat Kai the last time they went toe to toe.

"But she *is* my betrothed," Galen counters.

"Then I will assert my right as a king. You are not to touch her. She is under my protection." Kai is seething. I can practically see the steam coming off his skin. Beyond us, the waves crash violently.

"And what do you plan to do about it, barnacle boy?" Galen says, taking a step toward Kai.

"Fuck around and find out, douchebag." From my vantage point, Kai doubles in size, swelling to his full height.

"Take them out and measure them later, boys, we have a trial to conduct," Posey barks, clapping her hands.

"Way to take a stand, Xavie. Did she take your balls before or after the wedding? Gods," Helene hisses at her twin.

He leans toward her as Posey and Galen stalk off to where Dion has been obliviously setting up his trial. "You say that like she's not going to hurt Cat when I act out too." Xavier doesn't look at me.

"I asked you for one thing, and one thing only—to stay away from Cat because your wife is a psychopath—and you just couldn't do it." I want to rub my eyes but can't lift my hands high enough to brush the tears from my face.

Three weeks from now, this is all going to be over, one way or another. I can feel the static in the air. Things are going to move fast, and there's no way to stop this train.

Dion's trial lasts all day. I zone out, resting my chin on my fist. It's an undignified slouch, but I can't move much more than that. Once I'm free, I'm going to choke Posey with these chains, and it's going to feel amazing. It's the only thing that keeps me going through the day. It's not the first time I've spent a day fantasizing about murder, and I consider that maybe I *would* have made a good bride to the God of War. That is, if the God of War was Essos and not Galen.

Galen is tasked with identifying two hundred different types of wine that have been set before him, various reds and whites and sparkling drinks. For every wrong one, Galen is to drink an entire barrel of the wine. I wish we could enclose him in one of the barrels and drown him in it like the fool he is.

Galen has to correctly identify one hundred and eighty of the wines. I feel hope when he incorrectly identifies a Riesling Spätlese as a Riesling Kabinett. He spirals out of control from there, confusing a malbec for a Syrah and a brut champagne with a prosecco extra-brut. Dion tries to act impartial, but I watch his smile spread as the number of incorrect answers climbs. I catch Dion's eye, and he gives me a wink. Finally, a desperately-needed win.

The trial ends spectacularly with Galen smashing the taster glass when he gets his twenty-first one wrong. He sweeps his arm down the table, knocking over the remaining six glasses. He came so close, and the failure tastes so good to me—like a fine wine.

The Trials are now tied two to two. There's a decent chance I'll still be forced to marry Galen, but if we can best him in the next two, maybe, just maybe, I can get enough public support to reverse the no-confidence vote.

Dion rises to his feet, his tone neutral as he makes his proclamation. "The trial set forth required Galen to correctly identify one hundred and eighty wines of the two hundred available. Galen incorrectly identified twenty-one wines, resulting in an automatic failure. So concludes my trial." Dion seats himself again as Xavier bangs the gavel, and I have hope again that I can survive.

FINN IS SITTING in my room beside Cat when I return. She looks pale and so small in the center of my bed, her eyes closed. A damp towel rests on her forehead.

Finn moves it to her neck. "How did it go?" he whispers.

I walk to Cat and press my palm to her cheek. She doesn't so much as flinch. Feeling the warmth under her skin and seeing the movement of her chest makes me sag with relief.

I turn my back to Finn. "Can you unhook me?"

His fingertips graze the back of my neck as he unhooks the jumpsuit and then unzips it partway. Cat warned me as she strapped me into it that this would not be the type of outfit I would be able to pee in, and she was right. My bladder is ready to burst.

"Are you going to leave me waiting with bated breath?" Finn asks as I walk away from him, sliding the suit off my shoulders.

When I get to the bathroom, I don't know what to do first. A wave of nausea takes hold of me, and I just make it to the toilet in time. My body is finally free to expel the stress of watching Cat be tortured. I should have sent her away with Essos, regardless of what anyone would think.

Stupid. Stupid miscalculation.

Another misstep I can't afford.

If Finn hears me, he doesn't comment when I leave the bathroom, my bathrobe tied tight around my middle. It's a thicker plush one than the silk ones I usually wear. I want comfort right now.

"He lost. But that's the only good news today." I slump into a chair in the corner of the room, not wanting to disturb Cat.

"You look like hell, kid." Finn takes a seat at the table.

I don't look at him, instead gazing out the window and tugging on my lip. "I feel like it." I have to wonder if something more is wrong with me. Would I have any way of knowing if someone's poisoning me again? Staying on alert all the time is wearing on me. Maybe I need to relax a little bit.

"What are you going to do?" Finn asks.

"What *can* I do, Finn? I can do what I'm supposed to do, what I'm told to do—sit and smile. I can lie there and let Galen violate me and pretend to be happy to be there. Maybe if I go through with being with him, I can still find a way to protect the souls of the Afterlife. I turned one nation into trees, maybe I can do that again and again, until I find the dagger or another way to kill him."

Finn reaches forward and squeezes my knee. "It's not going to come to that. There isn't a chance in the Afterlife that Galen wins my trial."

I give him a grim smile in response. "I know it's not. Kai took me under his protection, for whatever that's worth. I'm just being fatalistic. I don't want to get my hopes up again. I feel like an extreme yo-yo. I have hope, and then it's dashed within the same breath. I'm exhausted all the time, and it nauseates me. I don't know how much more of this I can take."

"Even if he wins the next two challenges, we will *not* make you marry him. We won't let it get that far."

"Why should I believe you, Finn? The Council is *packed* with my friends, and you all let this keep happening to me. I refuse to let Cat pay for my actions. Maybe if I stay docile, I can undo the damage Galen's done to the souls in the Underworld, assuming it's reversible. I go back and forth on what the best thing to do is. Should I just roll over? But if I do that, I'm sacrificing everything that I am.

"I wonder if...if I had just rolled over for him from the start, maybe some of this could have been avoided."

"No one is telling you to do that. I promise, we'll figure something out." His hope should be infectious, but instead, it just feels draining.

I love Finn, and I want to believe him, but I can't.

"Don't I get a say?" Cat croaks from the bed.

I smile, glad to hear her voice. "I think we're out of options for now. Until the dagger is found, we have to do as we're told. How are you feeling?" I might have asked Xavier why he lets Posey get away with everything, but I get it now. She must be holding something over his head—something more than just Cat.

"Like a dog with a shock collar. Remind me to never use one on an animal; they're inhumane."

"I'm sure Posey dialed it up extra high. She knows about your flirtation with Xavier." I climb into bed beside her, ready to see to my friend's needs now that she's awake.

Finn rises. "I'll get out of your hair. Ring me if you need anything."

"Find my dogs," I demand. We go from one crisis to another.

"On it," Finn promises with a small bow before leaving. But when he opens the door, Shadow, Dave, and Spot rush in and crowd onto the bed with us, much to Waffles's chagrin. "Already found them. See? I've got you covered. Trust me, Daphne. We won't let you down again."

I'm not sad to watch him go. I need space from the Council, and from everything that is going on, and I can't even look at Cat. I can't see the shock collar sitting around my friend's neck like some fucked-up new accessory. I want to destroy it, but if I do, Posey will know I have my powers, or worse, she'll find a new way to hurt Cat. I still attempt to get rid of the power fueling it, but it's blocked; my magic is unable to penetrate the wards powering it.

A shock collar.

I fight a surge of fury. To do this to Cat...to treat her like an animal... I won't throw an *I told you so* at her or Xavier, but I did tell them. I warned them both that Posey was vindictive. But even I couldn't have foreseen this.

"And where have you been?" I ask the beasts as they lave us with kisses.

Dave presses his forehead to mine, and I see as clear as can be the cages they were put in, separated from each other, left in the dark for days. Bile rises in my throat.

I have a cage I would very much like to put Posey in.

Dave settles himself between Cat and me, licking tears that escaped from my eyes.

Cat frowns, reaching for the hand that is scratching behind Dave's ears. "I'm so sorry," she says, giving my hand a squeeze.

"You have nothing to be sorry for, nothing to feel guilty about. We can both be sorry until we're blue in the face, but the reality is, we're both victims in this cruel game of gods. We're pawns right now, but that's their mistake—treating a queen like a pawn. They forget that I can move any way I want and am more powerful than a king."

"How did today go?" she asks, snuggling closer.

I grab the remote and turn on the TV above my dresser. "The games are now tied, two losses and two wins."

"And if he wins the next challenge?"

It's a fair question.

"I don't know. Really, he should have to win by a majority, but Posey—I mean, 'the Council'—keeps changing the rules."

Which means I need to start playing by my own rules.

33

With the time between trials reduced from one month to one week, I'm getting whiplash from the change in pace. The next week moves quickly, despite my desire to slow it down. The cuts on my wrists are healing nicely, something I don't do for myself. I want whoever was poisoning me to think that my powers are bound, but every day, when it's just Cat and me in my room, I practice shaping my vines and plans into chess pieces that move across the board until I can find some semblance of a strategy to save myself.

I'm seated in front of my vanity as Ellie plaits my hair. Her pretty mouth is set in a frown, and I wonder if she expected the Council to just kill me. If I have to have someone wait on me, I wish it would be Miranda rather than the woman my husband had an affair with, but the mousy blonde has been absent since my return. It occurs to me that she may have shared Celestina's fate if she decided to speak in my defense.

"Disappointed I'm not dead?" I ask as Ellie tugs another strand of hair unnecessarily hard.

"I'm not sure what you mean by that."

"Your Majesty. 'I'm not sure what you mean by that, Your Majesty,' is what you meant to say. After all, I am your queen." I meet her eyes in the mirror and wait for her to respond. Okay, maybe I understand a little better why Posey keeps throwing her title around.

"You never deserved him," she says, ignoring my correction.

"I beg your pardon?" I scoff, watching her. I give her just enough rope...

"You never deserved Essy. You always thought that you were so much better than everyone. You didn't care that picking Galen ruined him. I was there for him when you turned your back on him. He sought comfort in my arms, between my legs."

"That is *enough*." I snap, turning to her and rising. "You are on *very* thin ice speaking to me, *your queen*, this way."

"You never were my queen, and you certainly never were Essos's. He picked you because you were more palatable to his family than a nymph. The time you caught us wasn't the first I was bent over his desk, and it wasn't the last." Fury tinges her cheeks red.

I start laughing in her face. "I'm sorry. You must not know my husband well at all if you expect me to believe that. It's a nice attempt, though. Brownie points for effort." Once, her words would have filled me with doubt, but not now. Not in this century.

I thread my fingers through my hair, shaking out the braid she was crafting. I reach for my crown and set it on my head while I lock eyes with her. I want to do so much worse, but I won't let my emotions get the better of me.

"You're wrong. I promise you, if you saw him now, it would be me he was thinking about." Ellie sounds more and more desperate. She's trying to puff out her chest and make herself sound bigger, meaner.

I lean in close and pat her cheek, savoring how she flinches from the gentle touch. "You keep thinking that if it makes you feel better, but it will be *me* he's inside." My voice is low as I whisper this to her, a ghost of a smile tugging my lips up.

A knock at the door halts any response she might have had. Whoever it is doesn't wait for my permission to enter.

I still as Galen strolls in, surveying my outfit from the bottom up. I'm in black booties that give me an extra four inches of height. Tucked within are black leather pants that fit a little too snuggly around my middle, a surprising amount of bloat there, given my inability to keep anything down. My top is half-bodice, half-coat, with snaps closed down my front. It shows more cleavage than necessary and has tails on either side of me that extend to the floor. The long peasant sleeves cover the ruby engagement ring, which feels heavier day by day. The blood-red color of the coat matches the gold and ruby crown on my head. I wanted some sort of fancy updo, but alas. I have regrets about the cleavage when Galen's eyes linger before eventually meeting my gaze.

"You're looking a little peaky today," he says by way of greeting.

"Such a charmer. Save your sweet words for when we're married," I snap at him.

Galen raises his hands. "I meant no offense. Should we send a healer to look in on you?" His hand reaches out to touch my forehead. I swat it away. He rubs his fingers together, looking surprised by the moisture.

"I'm fine. I'll be better once the Trials are over." I touch my hairline, feeling the beads of sweat. Maybe the coat and leather pants are a touch too much. I do feel warm, but I won't say anything.

From Galen's casual sports attire for today's trial, I can guess what Finn has in store for him. The shorts expose his long, lean legs, which are tanned as if he's spent more time in the sun lately than anywhere else.

He wraps my arm through his, much to my annoyance.

"With any luck, that will be today. If I win, we can be wed tomorrow." Venom laces his words, and I don't miss his meaning. I guess it's been decided that, if he wins today, it's game over.

I have to have faith in Finn.

"You still have one more trial after today. Victory is not guaranteed," I point out.

Galen covers my hand with his and squeezes, crushing the delicate bones. "Daphne, in case you haven't noticed, this is your nightmare, and it is very, very real. I can assure you, whether our wedding is this week or next, we *will* be wed, and I will taste all that you have to offer." He's distracted, murmuring this in my ear, and it's undignified of me, but I use my magic to tug the carpet up enough for him to trip.

Galen releases me to catch his fall, but he's able to right himself before any damage is done. He can't pinpoint that it was me, either because he expects me to be powerless or because it was just a rug.

"You were saying?" I ask serenely, fighting the smile tugging at my lips.

His golden eyes narrow, but he moves on. "I was saying, I can't wait for our wedding night so I can show you what it's like having a real man between your legs."

I resist the urge to roll my eyes lest they get stuck like that. "Try something original instead of your cookie-cutter misogynistic bullshit, Galen. Eventually, your threats lose their bite."

"You're just scared you're going to be mine," Galen blusters.

"I'm positively quaking in my boots," I deadpan. "You seem prepared for a challenge of a physical nature today," I say changing the subject.

"I am afforded a certain level of notice and preparation. Enough so I know if it's a physical or mental event."

We exit the house into the backyard and see that a track has been laid down on my beach, obscuring the sand. It looks like a boardwalk, but the surface is made of the latex rubber material that was used for my high school track in the mortal realm.

Of course, the Messenger God, the God of Speed, would challenge Galen to a race. From the distance, it looks to be an out-and-back course with a sharp turn. I'm not positive about the actual distance, but I'm eager to see how it will go.

"Galen," Finn greets with a smug smile. For Finn, this should be no contest, and I hope that's the case.

"Phineas." Galen frowns. "The first thing I'm going to do when the crown is on my head is ban you from this realm."

"You're awfully confident for a guy who hasn't stretched. Why don't you get started, and I'll escort the queen to her throne?" Finn offers me his arm, and I take it, letting him lead me away from Galen, who grumbles to himself that stretching wastes unnecessary energy.

The shackles are still attached to the throne, and I pretend it doesn't pain me to see them.

"I tried to get them to take them away, but they wouldn't listen." Finn lets go of my arm and places his hand on the small of my back.

I give him a smile and perch myself on the edge of the chair. "And by *they*, you really mean Posey," I correct. "How far is the run?" I divert my attention from the chains as they snap around my wrist and ankles.

"Marathon distance. The track is rigged, so for us it will feel like we're moving, but we'll just be staying in place for your viewing pleasure."

"How delightful, a giant treadmill. What is your record?"

"Probably thirty minutes? If I want to make a show of it, I could do it for an hour. Can't be much more boring than Hel's trial with the bees."

I scowl at him. "Let's see if you can beat your record. I would rather not draw this out or take unnecessary risks."

Finn playfully taps my chin with his fist, and I scowl at him.

"So little faith," he teases.

"It's not that I have no faith in you, Finn. But this is my life, not a time to show off." I reach for his hand, but the chain doesn't extend far enough.

The rattling sound pulls the joking smile from his face. "I'll win. I promise."

Helene approaches us in a simple blue dress, while Kai and Xavier argue by the track.

"Someone looks like she's regretting wearing leather in the sun." Helene makes sure her light dress swishes around her legs. We haven't gotten a chance to speak since I turned tail after Posey's trial. Our heart-to-heart after our big fight feels so long ago.

"I'm quite comfortable, thank you," I say.

"Then do you have a fever?" Helene reaches out and touches my forehead. When she pulls her hand away, her fingertips are damp with my sweat.

She pulls a sea breeze over to cool me, and I'm thankful for it, even if I don't show it. I'll let Posey and Galen think they have me right where they want me. The breeze wraps itself around me, acting as my personal air conditioner, and I wish I had thought of it for myself.

"I'm fine. Can we get this show started?" I demand. "The sooner I'm out of these chains, the better."

"Testy testy," Titus says, approaching us. In his black leather jacket, dark-washed jeans, and white T-shirt, he looks as ready for the beach as I do, and I can appreciate that. His stubble has gotten worse since I saw him last, almost a full-grown beard now.

"It would seem seeing your ex-wife didn't agree with you," I say, wondering where he was during the last trial.

Titus gives me a wolfish smile. "Seeing Octavia was...a delight. We took several hours to get reacquainted, much as I expect you and your husband did while you were away. Or is it ex-husband now? I'm not clear on the rules, since you're not only a reincarnation but betrothed to my other son. How complicated this family tree is." Titus eyes the chains on my wrists.

"Can we get started? A marathon is not a trifling thing!" Posey shouts, clapping. She moves to her throne beside Xavier's, grander than mine, of course. I am delighted to see she is still wearing that awful diadem that Galen "found" for her.

"I'll visit you later," Helene assures me, and goes to sit with the rest of the Council. I should be there beside them, given that, as Queen of the Underworld, I'm a member of the Council too, but both Galen and I were barred due to our vested interest in the Trials. Once the Trials conclude, I imagine I'll have to petition for my reinstatement.

Finn walks to the track like a clown, taking long strides, making a show of stretching and waving to his adoring fans. The Trials are no longer attended by the masses, so it is only the camera he is waving to for those livestreaming. I don't know what tricks Finn has up his sleeve for today, but I'm sure there are plenty.

"The trial today requires that Galen defeat Phineas in a race for a distance of twenty-six-point-two miles. Should Phineas cross the finish line first, it shall be a failure for Galen," Posey announces before sitting down.

We wait for the start, everyone holding their breath. Finn smiles and waves at the camera before the pop and sparkle of fireworks go off overhead.

Finn takes off like a shot, and I can barely see him move. The track flows beneath him like a treadmill, as promised. He goes forward somewhat to make up for the hills and obstacles that he put in place. Some hills are gradual, others sharp, sending the men practically horizontal to climb them. I grip the throne, my hands digging into the surface. There is a screen that shows us their progression, so the home viewers know what they're seeing as well.

Somewhere, I'm sure Essos is watching, his hands curled around his chair as he waits to see what the outcome will be. Slowly and steadily, Finn builds a buffer between himself and Galen. I don't fight my smile. I glance at Dion, who only has eyes for his boyfriend, a mixture of pride and worry on his face. We had faith Kai would win his trial as well. I want to grab Dion's hand and give it a reassuring squeeze.

The breeze around me falters, and I glance at Helene, who is leaning forward and watching Finn. Ever the showboat, Finn makes a dramatic display of yawning and checking his watch as he approaches the sharp turn. He makes it and passes by Galen, who's still running toward the turn, and the camera captures the wink Finn gives him.

I wish he hadn't done that, because Galen's eyes flash red and he starts to close the distance between them until they are neck and neck again. Time flies by as we watch them skitter down hills and avoid potholes and speed bumps and those gods-awful reflector lights that dot the middle of the road. They're so close until Galen steps on one of those, his ankle twisting horribly, throwing off his cadence. They're in the last five miles, and whatever Finn was holding back, it's like he hit the NOS in the *Fast and Furious* movies, because he practically flies.

Finn's feet barely touch the ground. He stays focused on the finish line, which he bursts through with trumpets and confetti and fanfare. Galen is several steps behind, slowing before he even crosses.

"The task was to beat me in a race, and you have failed, Galen," Finn says, sounding satisfied with himself. Finn places his hands on his hips grinning. "Oh, and your nipples are bleeding."

Galen doesn't maintain his composure; he's lost it along with this trial. He slugs Finn, giving him a mean right hook that sends Finn to the ground. Dion is beside him in a flash, and Kai comes up behind Galen, locking his arms back. Kai's fingers interlace behind Galen's neck, leaving him struggling to get out of the grip.

"Someone's a sore loser," I call from my throne, unable to join the fray.

"Calm yourself," Kai's voice is soothing.

Finn gets to his feet, spitting blood at Galen's shoes, a taunting smirk on his face. "Get used to it. You're never going to touch her again." It's the only time a Council member has so blatantly defended me during their trial.

Galen struggles again but goes slack, waiting for Kai to release him from the full-nelson hold.

"Are you calm?" Kai asks, tone even.

"I am," Galen grits out. Kai releases him, and Galen rolls his shoulders. "He cheated."

"I saw no evidence of cheating." Xavier's reply is whiskey smooth, a smirk tilting his lips up.

"You wouldn't, big brother. This whole thing has been a sham," Galen accuses.

"Daphne is right. You *are* a sore loser," Helene says. "I'm going to escort her out of your toxic presence."

"I have to agree. I didn't see any obvious cheating. Do you have evidence to support your claim?" Titus asks, equally smug.

Galen looks at his father and then at the assembled crowd. "Go ahead and gloat, but next week, she becomes my wife." Galen's words are more a threat than anything else.

I feel the shackles fall away as Helene approaches me.

"I'll escort her to her room." Posey takes my arm.

"I think I can find my own way. This is, after all, *my* house."

Helene grips my other arm, and both my sisters-in-law tug me toward them in opposite directions.

"Not likely. You've proven yourself untrustworthy on numerous occasions. If you keep acting out, I'll be forced to punish Catalina for your actions." Posey *tsk*s at me, and I can only take a steadying breath to avoid cleaving her in half. *Someday.* Someday I won't hold back.

Helene backs off, letting me go now that Cat is in play.

Posey looks triumphant, leading me inside. "You ran off before we could pick your wedding dress." Her tone is conversational.

"From what I understand, you and Octavia have that covered."

At the speed Posey walks, the journey to my room feels like it's a full marathon distance. I try to speed up, but she tugs me back, her fingertips digging into my upper arm.

"Well, I have taken into account your requests. You must not worry. The theme will be black and red and all that, though I don't believe that black is an acceptable wedding color."

"Posey, your wedding was a black-tie affair, and your dress code was literally just black and white. You kicked Finn out for wearing a purple pocket square."

"I don't recall that happening." She tuts as we take the stairs.

"Of course, you don't, Pose." I roll my eyes.

"All I'm trying to say is, this wedding is happening. I know you loved Essos at some point, we all did, but he's proven himself to be incompetent. The vote of no confidence was necessary. Accept the wedding, accept your role as wife and not coruler, and prepare that womb for babies." We reach my door, and she pats my abdomen like that's all I'll ever be in life, a baby-maker.

I want to rip off her arm and beat her over the head with the bloody stump. My thoughts have been particularly bloodthirsty lately, and I'm not sure why.

"Delightful," I say through gritted teeth. I don't dare say how much I hate that idea. I want to be a mother, but I want to be a mother with Essos, not Galen.

"Unless Galen fails the next trial, the plan is to proceed with the wedding immediately after."

"He could fail," I point out, not able to hold my tongue. Inside my room, I hear something break, and I look at the door sharply. My eyes narrow on Posey. A slow, painful death it is.

"You should be mindful of what you say. Even if he does fail, we'll push the wedding through. Get used to the idea." She doesn't wait for a response, choosing instead to walk away. I don't get why she's insisting on this sham of a wedding. Unless...

I stare in the direction that Posey just walked, biting my nail. The door swings open as I lean into it, desperate to change into something comfortable and just sit with my friend.

I see Cat breathing heavily over a shattered mug. She's gripping her neck, tears brimming in her blue eyes when she looks up at me. She tries to blink them away, but I can still see the pain in her eyes. Shadow is whimpering at Cat's side, licking her legs.

"I'm okay." She sucks in a shaky breath.

"I should have made you go with Essos, consequences for me be damned. I was selfish, and you're paying for it."

"We can have this conversation a hundred times, and it will change nothing. You, however, should change. You're sweating."

I scowl at her and try to unfasten the clasps on the jacket. When I struggle with the first two, Cat steps forward to help.

"I've got this," I grumble.

"You clearly do not. Besides, it helps me to have something to focus on."

I won't begrudge her this, and I won't tell her she's not strong enough to stick around. She is strong enough, I know she is, but that doesn't mean I want her in danger.

Cat makes quick work of the stupid clasps and, once the jacket is off, I feel like I melt. My posture reverts to one that I perfected over years of hunching over a computer. Cat laughs a little as I slouch, then stretch my shoulders and straighten again.

I toe off the booties through pure strength of will and work on the leather pants. I have to peel them off. Finally, I stand there in my underwear, feeling like I can breathe again.

"Thy cup runneth over," Cat remarks, poking at my breast, which does indeed spill over the cup of my bra. I wince then poke her boob just as hard in retaliation. "Shouldn't you always have perfectly-fitting bras? I feel like that should be a perk of having magic."

"This does fit. It's probably just been crushed in the jacket and got all out of sorts and also, ow, that hurt." I swat at her hand and grab a loose-fitting dress that lets my body expand.

"Do we have a plan of attack?" Cat asks. She keeps waiting for me to conjure this magic plan to get us out of this, and the truth is, I just don't have one. I can't wave my magic wand and fix the mess I've dragged us into. Titus refuses to help, and as we move close to the last challenge, tensions are high. I have support among the Council members, but Posey is relentless. She will not give up on Galen or forcing me under her thumb.

Maybe I've been asking the wrong questions. Why is Posey so invested in making sure Galen wins? Is it just so she'll have someone under her control? He's proven himself unwilling to do the work of a leader. I suppose it could have been Posey's plan all along to make Galen king so there is always chaos for Xavier to swoop in and clean up, making his approval rating higher than anyone else's. Not that approval ratings matter, but Xavier has always had a hard-on for being well-liked.

The bigger mystery is how Posey keeps control over the Council. No one agrees with the decisions that are being made, and yet, her measures keep getting passed. Kai, Helene, Finn, and Dion resent every decision, so how is she getting her plans pushed through?

"We cross our fingers and hope Essos and Zara have better luck than us."

I can see disappointment flicker in Cat's eyes. She hoped I would have the answer, but what I have now are more questions.

34

As we move closer to the final trial, it's harder and harder to sleep. I try not to disturb Cat, who has been sharing my bed.

On the morning of Xavier's trial, it's Cat who cries out, pulling me from the sleep I finally found. She's thrashing in the sheets, screaming, but I can't hear what she's saying. Her words are unintelligible, and it sounds almost like she's speaking another language. I know she took French in school, but it sounds like she's screaming in Italian.

A simple shake of the shoulders doesn't get her to stop, so I roll over and straddle her. I don't know if this is the right move when someone has night terrors, but I give it a try.

Cat's flailing arm backhands me squarely in the mouth, but I don't flinch. *"TROPPO FREDDO,"* she screams, her body trembling under me.

I try shaking her shoulders again. "Cat!" I shout in her face. It still doesn't work. I'm running out of ideas. I call forth cold water in a bubble and hover it over her face, then I release it.

Her eyes shoot open and find me. "*Troppo freddo*," she repeats. "*Che cos'è?!*"

"*Catalina!*"

A fog lifts from her eyes, and she looks so confused.

"You speak Italian?"

She stares at me, and gradually, her eyes focus. "Why am I wet?" she asks, touching the wet strands of hair that are fanned out on her also-wet pillow. I sink back only to realize I've rested my entire weight on her stomach.

I roll off. "I couldn't get you to wake up. You scared the daylights out of me. I had to drop a ball of water on you." Now that she's awake, my tongue probes the cut made by my teeth when she hit me.

"That seems excessive." She seems irritated at being woken up.

I snort, pulling the moisture back into a ball then slowly reducing the size to nothing. "I was sitting on top of you, Cat. You didn't so much as twitch. What was your dream about?" I fold my legs under me, watching her.

She sees that I'm not going to let this go, so she sighs and sits up. I remember the intensity of my dreams about Essos and Galen when I was starting to get my memory back, and how it took me a while to decide to talk about them.

Cat seems reluctant to open up, but I'm patient. A glance out my window shows the morning light just starting to stream in.

The clock is ticking. This is my last morning with Cat for who knows how long. I am under no illusion that Galen will let her stick around. It's a dangerous play, but I need to trust Xavier to keep her safe. If anyone can protect her, it's the King of the Gods, and even though he's done a shit job so far, I know that his interest in her is not platonic. He is her best chance.

Cat looks at the window and seems to have the same realization I do. "It was just a stupid dream. I dreamt I was on the

400

Titanic, and I was drowning. It was the strangest thing. It felt so vivid, like when Essos showed us our memories of the crash. I was unconscious then, but I could still feel the water seeping into my lungs."

"You were an Italian on the *Titanic* in this dream?" I ask.

She tilts her head. "How did you know that?"

"You were screaming in Italian. It took me a minute to place the language." I sigh. "It's not too late; I can pass you into the Afterlife, fuck the consequences for me. I know the Afterlife isn't in the best shape right now, but it *has* to be better than this." It's an empty offer, one she'll never take, and I don't know if I would seriously send her into the Underworld now.

I could always send her to Essos with Finn and fuck the consequences.

Cat grabs my hand, squeezing it. "I'm in this till the end. Ride or die."

"That could be today," I point out. If Galen wins, it's a sure thing there will be no escaping what will happen. Posey's words echo in my ears. Even if he loses today, I need to get used to the idea of marrying Galen. There will be no more stalling. If he wins, they want the wedding held immediately following the trial.

"Then it's today." She shrugs. "I'm not leaving my best friend on the biggest day of her life. This could very well be your wedding day."

I glance at the bag that Posey dropped off last night. I am supposed to wear whatever she brought to the trial so it can segue right into the wedding. I am getting married no matter what.

"I want you to stay close to Xavier. He'll protect you, and so will Finn and Dion. Helene and Kai too." I can trust them to get Cat out and *somewhere* safe. Maybe that trust is misplaced, maybe Xavier hasn't learned his lesson, but I don't have options.

"You need me," she whispers.

"Not more than I need you to stay alive. You can figure something out. When it calms down, I can pass you into the Afterlife."

"Posey sent me a red dress to be your bridesmaid. I'll be there for you."

"When the rain starts to fall?" I ask.

"Always."

We lie back down in bed, not ready to start the day. Shadow snuggles closer to her, and Dave crowds my other side.

I understand now why Essos never wanted the dogs on the bed, because with Waffles feeling left out and settling between us, there is no space for Spot, even if he does still try by settling himself at our feet.

"Do you remember when you started to date that guy from the college Republicans Club and he called out 'Ronald Regan' in the middle of his orgasm?"

Cat snorts and then dissolves to giggles. "I mean, my first mistake was sleeping with someone in the Republicans Club. But also, like, he said the whole freaking name. Who does that?"

I laugh along with her. She had felt conflicted about dating him, but he'd called her out about having drinks with the president of the Democrats Club, saying she was on the newspaper and had to give equal attention to both parties, and she gave in.

"Really, the fault is mine. Friends don't let friends fuck guys with truck nuts," I say with an over-dramatized sigh.

"I mean, I also should have protected you from that frat guy who swindled you into the pity fuck with the news of his dead uncle. I should have warned you he told that story every weekend."

I groan, remembering the unremarkable guy. A week after the unfortunate coupling, I overheard him telling some other girl about it, and I realized I'd been played.

"Do you remember that spring break we went down to LA and

you thought you met John Stamos and told him it was always your dream to fuck Uncle Jesse?" I say, laughing.

"Are we really doing this, going through our lists, on the eve of your wedding?" Cat says with a giggle, but it sobers me immediately.

My wedding. My wedding to a man I don't love. A man who killed me.

"Maybe we should get going. No magic today."

Cat nods in agreement. Whatever I want to do today, we'll do.

I take my time in the shower, shaving my legs and washing my hair, then using a clay mask for my face as well as a hair mask. I'm willing to do anything to stall to keep this day from happening. I emerge in a bathrobe, dreading putting on the dress.

I don't know what it looks like. I don't even know what to expect from the evening. I still have two hours before Xavier's trial, and I don't know how long it's going to take. Helene's was set to take twenty-four hours. With any luck, Xavier's will too. Usually, whoever is hosting the trial is too busy setting up to do anything else, but I need Xavier to talk to me.

I sit at my vanity while Cat does my hair, closing my eyes and savoring how it feels to have her run a brush through it.

"You know, I'm not a professional hairdresser." Cat twists my curls into submission.

I smile, catching her hand. "You mean this wasn't on your presidential résumé?"

"Oh, don't get me wrong, I envisioned a future where I would be braiding the Princess of Wales's hair—well, hopefully the hair of the Queen of England by then." Cat's voice is wistful.

"Something I'm sure not many world leaders have on their bucket lists."

"I bet it's something not even the queen did."

"She didn't strike me as the type to indulge in a French braid," I say. I'm not sure I can imagine the late queen as a mother at all.

"Of course, she didn't—a French braid isn't very British." Cat laughs.

With my hair set, Cat works on my makeup, slowly applying foundation and eyeshadow. I want to be honest and tell her that I'm scared, but it's not fair to burden her.

I want to talk to my husband. I want to close my eyes and wake up from this horrible dream.

I'm applying my mascara while Cat gets dressed in a show-stopping off-the-shoulder red dress. At least Posey listened to me when I said that I wanted red as one of my colors.

"At least the red will cover the bloodstains if we have to go to battle?" Cat offers glibly. She tugs at the shoulders, admiring the look in the mirror.

"Well, that's grim." I scowl.

A light tap at the door draws my attention, and my hope soars that it's Finn or Helene, but Posey walks into the room. She's dressed in white, and I choke on the laugh that bubbles from my chest.

She gives me an assessing stare. "I'm glad you're finally taking this seriously." Her tone is imperious, and I have to remember that I can't turn her into a tree, even if I want to.

"Yes, Posey. Is there something I can do for you?" I try to add pleasantness to my tone, but I'm just exhausted.

"I'm here to escort you to the trial." She's enjoying this; I can hear it in her tone when she speaks. She wants to see me brought low. What did I ever do to her?

I swallow the tears building in my throat.

"I'll get dressed then. Let's get this over with." Dread fills my tone as I finally unzip the large garment bag. The skirt unfurls from it, voluminous and smooth despite being crushed in the bag all week. Black lace vines snake up from the bottom of the dress and wrap around the bodice. The top layer of chiffon is black or grey, something to dull the white. I touch crystal flowers tucked within the vines.

"I have this covered," Posey announces, and the dress vanishes from the bag and appears on my body, my robe cast aside. Under the dress, I feel the boning of a lingerie corset.

"Thank you," I grit out through clenched teeth. The dress is backless, and when I turn and look in the mirror, I see black lace leaves edging the sides that frame my naked spine. The plunging neckline accentuates my cleavage and kind of hurts my breasts, given how tight it is. The long sleeves are thankfully not tight.

Posey opens the door for me to exit, revealing Ellie wearing the same dress as Cat. The key difference is Cat's necklace is the shock collar. Still no Miranda, and I'm afraid to ask at this point.

"Can we take this off her, please, Posey?" I *hate* begging Posey, but for Cat, I'll do whatever I have to.

She frowns, her lips pursing as if she's actually considering my request. "No. If anything, today is the day I'm going to need it most. Let's go." Posey glares at Cat and gives her just a little jolt. Cat's hands clench, but it's over as fast as it started.

I scowl, clenching my own fists, but for a different reason. "One last thing." I reach into the drawer of my vanity and conjure the same spiked crown I wore the night of the Calling Ball. I pull it out like it's been there the whole time and set it on my head.

Posey's blue-green eyes lift to the crown, a scowl twisting her mouth. "I suppose we shall be off then. That is, if you're ready." It's her last attempt at a dig, but I don't let it phase me.

"Let's go. There is nothing quite like rolling squad deep." I give myself one last look in the mirror, my dark brown eyes sad and assessing, seeking holes in my armor. The biggest one yet stands just over my shoulder, her own blonde curls pulled away from her face to showcase the collar on her neck.

I look away and start walking, leading everyone out of my room, and hope that this isn't the end of everything for me.

As we enter my backyard, which is now an arena, I hold my head high, feeling like a dead man walking to the gallows. I still have hope that I can contest this marriage if Galen loses. Fuck Posey and whatever she thinks she can control. She can't do anything about keeping her husband under her control, and he certainly doesn't let her influence how he rules the kingdom. For a goddess, she amounts to nothing more than a trophy wife, and an annoying one at that.

But that nagging part of my mind reminds me that she can do so much. She alone has been the one to keep me locked in this farce.

Maybe she thinks that she can control Galen and the Afterlife, but if she thinks that, she's sorely mistaken. I cannot bend. I cannot break.

The sky is blindingly bright, and I want sunglasses, but I'm sure I wouldn't be allowed such a comfort. Xavier is standing in the middle of the arena with a large beast sitting beside him. Much to Posey's chagrin, I cross to him.

I study the beast. It appears to have feathers all along its back and the tail of a lion. When Xavier tosses a large fish in the air, using magic to send it up, the beast's wings unfurl, and it shoots skyward. One flap of its wings sends a plume of dust into the air. I see its eagle head reach to capture the fish in its beak.

I remember then that Xavier breeds gryphons. Another flap of its wings, and it's soaring higher and higher until it drops the fish only to follow its trajectory, hovering in the air for a moment before diving for it, catching it in its beak again, and swallowing the thing whole. The beast circles as I approach Xavier.

"It's beautiful," I remark, bumping into my brother-in-law. He's still dressed in his usual suit, but the sleeves are reinforced to be protective. Xavier might be hard to kill, but you can still hurt him, and an injury caused by gryphon claws would hurt like a motherfucker.

"*Beautiful* is an insufficient word. Majestic, powerful, breathtaking. They could be our masters, if only they could speak." Xavier never takes his eyes off the animal, tracking it through the sky, where I feel like it's watching us.

"I need a favor." The beast is swooping in for a landing, and Posey and her entourage don't want to get close. Even Cat has stayed with them.

The gryphon lands in front of me, then rolls over with its back legs in the air, waiting for another fish or a belly rub, if I know anything about animal behaviors.

"Always with needing a favor." Xavier drops a fish into its mouth and then does rub the animal's belly. When he pulls away, it rolls around, indulging in a dirt bath.

"I need you to keep Cat close. When this trial is over and I've lost, please, promise me you will keep her close and get her to Essos."

Xavier's gaze doesn't find mine but seeks out Cat where she stands beside his wife.

"I'll try." He's hedging his bets, and I backhand his center, not hard.

"Don't try. Do. You have to. Posey will kill her, and if Posey doesn't kill her, Galen will..." I clear my throat, unable to voice what my betrothed might do. "You've been to war with him. You know how he can be about the spoils, especially if it means punishing me."

It's a confirmation that I know what my life will be like if I marry him. I want to keep Cat out of both of their clutches.

"*I'll try.*" He says it again, but the look in his eyes is all the assurance I need that he will do more than try; he will fight. I squeeze his upper arm in thanks. There are no words that can convey how much it means that he'll do that for me.

Galen walks out, a smirk on his face as he looks at the gryphon. As I pass him to go to the stands, he catches my arm.

"What, no kiss for good luck? You look beautiful, my blushing bride." He leans toward me, and I cover his mouth with my hand.

"It's bad luck to see the bride before the wedding. No need to make it worse. I hope the trial goes well." I hope that the trial goes well for me and that Xavier's gryphon eats his kidney, but I'm not going to say that, not to my groom on our *wedding* day. I tug my arm out of Galen's grip and walk away from him toward my throne. Posey is standing there, holding up one of the chains.

I shake my head. "No. No chains. This ends today." My voice must be commanding enough, because the chains vanish.

I sit and hold my breath, waiting for the event to start. Cat's hand rests on my shoulder, reassurance that she's there even though I want her miles from this. Galen and Xavier shake hands, the gryphon again sitting beside Xavier. It towers over them both, and hope surges in my chest that maybe all is not lost. I should temper my hope, but it wants to run wild with the idea that I can get out of this for real.

If Galen loses, with Titus on site, I will demand that things revert to Essos and I ruling, and that Galen be locked away in some prison he can never escape.

I would settle just for him never being allowed near us again.

Xavier steps forward. "Today is the sixth and final trial. Today, Galen will need to best a gryphon. This does *not* mean kill it." Xavier cuts his brother a look. "Whoever submits first will be the loser. If Galen emerges victorious, then the nuptials of Galen and Daphne shall proceed this evening. Galen is permitted one weapon. You may begin."

Xavier leaves the arena and settles among the Council. Helene gives me a nervous look. She's dressed in the same red gown as Cat, Ellie, and Miranda, who has finally shown up. Kai holds Helene's hand, not looking away from the two opponents in the center of the arena. He thought he could best Galen as well.

Dion and Finn also both keep their gazes on the ring.

A longsword appears in Galen's hand, and he twists it, watching the gryphon rise into the sky, wings beating furiously. It's sizing Galen up, looking for weaknesses he doesn't have. Galen has to wait for the beast to come to him. I'm surprised when Galen sits down and rests the sword in front of him.

The gryphon dives, coming from behind, and Galen spins the sword in his hand. The gryphon dodges to the right as Galen swings left. Galen manages to land a blow across the gryphon's chest as its talons gouge his shoulder. There is so much blood between the two of them that I don't know who is bleeding more.

The gryphon takes back to the skies while Galen struggles to his feet, angry. I can only hope that in his anger, he gets sloppy. But I know that's never the case. With his anger, Galen becomes the sharp edge of a sword, willing to pierce anything that comes his way.

The gryphon manages another pass at Galen, its talons digging in deeper. I watch as it lifts Galen in the air, until Galen wildly swings his sword and clips the gryphon's wing. It drops him, watching him fall to the ground. Xavier trains these beasts to fight, but they're still just animals. The sloppy fury I was hoping for from Galen, I see in the gryphon instead. It hovers in the air, wings beating, and I can tell it's losing strength. It lists to one side, and when Galen hurls his sword at it, it can't dodge.

The sword misses its chest and buries itself in the beast's shoulder. I can't help but watch as it falls to the ground, trying to spin and do anything it can to avoid a rough landing. It sets its back paws on the ground and stumbles, landing on its good wing and leaving the damaged one in the air. Due to where the sword is embedded, it can't fold the wing in without potentially doing more damage.

It rises, letting out a sad caw before lowering its head in submission. Galen doesn't care though; he comes up behind it and grabs the wing, snapping it. We all jump to our feet, even Posey.

"Brother, don't!" Xavier calls, as Galen reaches for his blade. There is desperation in his voice. He had faith in the animal and its abilities. Galen hurting it grievously was never a concern or consideration. "You have won. The trial is over and you are the victor. Release the gryphon."

We all step closer, willing Galen to let the gryphon go. Galen rips the sword free, and the animal screams. The shriek nearly drives me to my knees.

"Let it go, Galen, please. You've proven your point. It's time for us to get married," I say, taking another step closer to him, hoping I can reason with him. The eagle head is leaning back, a keening sound coming from it, its wild bird eyes darting around. I press a hand to the animal's chest and feel its heart beating wildly. I understand the feeling, and that alone is crushing to think about.

I look at Galen, and he holds eye contact with me. He moves so fast, no one registers his movement until it's over. The blade slices through the beast's throat, hot red blood splashing my face and dress. I feel its heartbeat slow and then stop under my hand. I don't try to stop the tears when they start, working their way down my cheeks. One glance at Xavier shows me that I'm not the only one being bombarded by a flurry of emotions. Prevailing on his face is utter despair. His shoulders droop.

Brutal, unnecessary violence is Galen's way. He's going to do this anywhere and everywhere he can; I doubt that he'll be satisfied ruling the Afterlife.

He pushes the body of the gryphon to the ground and grabs

my face, pulling me to him. He kisses me, the metallic taste of the gryphon's blood smearing our lips. I want to cry harder.

I wrench out of his grip and spit on the ground. "I hate you," I seethe, and his eyes brighten. He gets off on the challenge, on the thrill of the chase, and I am the ultimate prize. I can sacrifice my soul submitting to him, or he'll take what he wants from me and ruin me. I lose either way.

"You failed, Galen," Xavier says, but this isn't the voice of a king, of a ruler. It's the voice of a shattered man. Galen looks at his brother before completely disregarding him.

"The wedding will be now." He grabs my wrist and tugs me along behind him, marching me inside, to my end.

35

Galen leaves me to change and have his wounds tended to. I refuse to let anyone clean the blood off me, my voice near feral when I tell Posey to leave me. She drags me into Luminara's office and seals the door shut behind her with magic so I can't escape. I pace while I wait for someone to tell me what comes next. I should be bolstering myself, but I don't know what to prepare for or how to get out of this situation. It was never supposed to get this far. I was never supposed to be stuck having to marry Galen. I knew it was a possibility, but my hope for a reprieve had been too strong.

I can still feel the gryphon's feathers under my hand. I rub my fingers together to try to get the downy softness and the wild beating of the animal's heart out of my mind, but I can't. I am that magnificent creature, who thought I had the upper hand, only to have Galen ruin me. It's going to be my blood splattered every-where next.

Xavier's look of defeat convinced me that there isn't going to be an eleventh-hour save from him either.

I'm alone in the room with only my thoughts and feelings left to remind me of what a failure I've been so far. This room has become my bridal suite and my sentencing chamber.

I can't let this be the end. I will fight Galen with everything I have, even if it kills me. I have my powers, and I have my training.

Sybil appears in front of me with a glass of water that I take and throw against the wall. It's satisfying when the glass shatters, the water dripping down the creamy yellow paint. I don't find the color very soothing anymore.

"You should really—"

"I don't particularly care what I should and shouldn't do, Sybil." I turn away from them.

"You *need* to care. After the wedding, you'll be able to affect real change. You can start to fix the things that are broken. The Inbetween is empty. Even the souls in the Deep are gone."

I freeze and look at them. "Gone? But I turned the souls in the Deep into trees."

"Gone. I don't know where, but as of this morning, they simply weren't there. No trees, no scent of magnolias, just the absence of everything. I have others checking on the rest of the Underworld, but I'm not optimistic. There is something *very* wrong, and you need to marry Galen to fix it. Once you're wed, you should be able to exert more power, assert your right as queen in a way you're not able to now. We can figure out where to go from there. You know I don't suggest this lightly."

"I'm going to be sick," I blurt out, and barely make it to the trash can in time. I fall to my knees, holding the small can in my hands as I empty my already empty stomach.

Sybil's hand is soft on my back. "You have been tasked with protecting this realm and these souls. They need you."

I vomit again, my stomach seizing as it finds nothing to force out. "How can I do this for others when I can't even do it for myself?" I want to cry, and I want my husband. Like a child, I want to kick and scream for the things I can't have.

"That's why you have to." Sybil is emphatic in their plea.

Helene slides into the room, proving anyone can enter, only I can't leave, and pulls me into a tight embrace. I want to fight her for a minute, but I can't. I have no more fight left, and whatever I can scrounge up, I need for what is to come next.

"You look like shit," she tells me bluntly, handing me a conjured napkin. I use it to wipe my face, then toss it toward the trashcan, incinerating it as it makes its way there.

"Have *you* looked in a mirror lately?" I clap back.

Helene only grins, "Glad to see you're still a bitch under that hideous frock."

"You can take the girl away from the bitches, but you can't take the bitchiness away from the girl. Any last-minute ideas to stop this?"

"I can try the bat signal, but I'm not sure it's going to get us anywhere."

Finn is the one who would need to contact Essos anyway. Does he know? Is there someone here who has been reporting to him this whole time? Did he watch the livestream?

"If you see him, if you find a way to get a message to him, tell him that I love him." My voice breaks, because it feels like goodbye.

"Don't pull this shit. You know why I locked you morons in that cabin a million years ago? It's because I knew that, when it came down to it, you were meant to be. There is no one in all of Solarem or on the face of Earth or in the Underworld that can bring my brother to life the way you can, same as he's the only person who can possibly have the patience for you. You bring out the best in each other. Your journey together has been long and hard, but it's not over. So don't you dare give up on him. Not today, not tomorrow, not ever. Because when it came to you, he never gave up. He pushed and pushed and *pushed* to get you back, so push for him. Fight for him."

I don't get a chance to respond, because Posey opens the door, a sick smile on her face. "It's time, Daphne," she tells me, triumph in her voice.

I frown, lifting my chin. Helene is right. I can't give up on Essos. A loss today does not guarantee a loss tomorrow. I have to be more clever, craftier, and, fuck my scruples, I need to do whatever it takes to get Essos back. Today is temporary. What comes next is temporary. My love for Essos is forever.

My entourage, including Elle and Miranda, crowds into the room. Cat's eyes are red-rimmed. This could be one of the last times I see her too. I know I'm making the right decision. Essos will keep her safe.

Calm settles over me. I was given a second chance with this life, and I've done nothing but squander it as a pawn since the ball. I don't believe that Galen will change, but I can have hope that I will still be able to accomplish real change. I will fight Galen as best I can from inside the system, just like Sybil suggested.

I won't fail anyone else.

We walk out, led by Posey, in a single file line.

"I am so sorry, Daphne," Helene says, reaching for me.

"Helene!" Posey scolds, thrusting a bouquet into her hand. There is something off in her tone, not just in how she says it, but in the threat of power behind the words that has Helene lowering her hand and facing forward. Gods forbid Posey gets any more power; it would truly be a reign of hell. I give Helene a small, reluctant smile.

Posey shepherds us forward toward the ballroom. With every step I take, it feels like a little more of the world crumbles around me. I expect to hear some sort of funeral march music playing instead of the joyful sounds of a full orchestra.

There are two servants dressed in full livery standing at the doors to the ballroom. Further inspection reveals they're not actual living creatures but animated plaster that sends a chill skittering down my spine. They pull the doors open for the reveal of the bridal party and myself.

In true Posey fashion, a handful of white doves fly up toward the ceiling before showering the room in feathers as they dissipate. Why she thought exploding doves raining feathers on everyone was a good idea after watching how Galen handled the gryphon, I'll never understand. A fresh wave of nausea rocks me.

Cat stays close in front of me as we walk down the makeshift aisle. There are little to no people here, only the usual suspects. The Council is, of course, in attendance, as is a handful of reporters. They've been Team Galen the whole time, so I'm hardly surprised they're here. Titus is up front, but noticeably absent is Octavia. Good. I couldn't stomach dealing with her too.

The doors close behind me, sealing us all in the ballroom. The altar has been set up just in front of our mantle and fireplace. For the time being, the piano has been removed from the space. This room has been the site of so many highs and lows, it feels fitting that it witness another. Galen stands at the front beside Luminara, who is going to officiate this farce.

Xavier steps up beside me, offering his arm. "Can I give you away?" he asks, and his voice sounds shattered. His eyes flicker to Cat, his message clear. This is how he can stay closest to her. I nod in relief, threading my arm through his. I walk slowly, stalling as we make our way toward the altar. I don't know why I'm delaying the inevitable, but if stalling gives me just a handful of free breaths before I'm shackled to Galen, I'll take them. I may not have faced worse, but for Essos and the souls of the Underworld, I will endure. I will hold my head high. I will bide my time to figure out what is happening, and I will kill Galen.

I don't think anyone in this room is happy except for Galen and Posey. Even Ellie looks disappointed, I suppose because her king of darkness will be a king no longer. Kai, Finn, Dion, and Titus stand on one side of the room while Cat, Helene, Miranda,

Ellie, and Posey stand on the other. For a room this vast, I would have expected guests, but there are none outside the reporters and Council.

I'm halfway to the altar when the doors behind me blow open. My steps falter, and I spin to see who is interrupting the event.

"I have to say, a tie in the Trials doesn't exactly sound like a victory," Essos drawls from the doorway. He looks every bit the king I know he is, and my heart swells to bursting at the sight of him. He's dressed casually, as if expecting a fight. I want to run to him, stand by his side, but Xavier holds on to me. I glare at him and try to pull out of his grip, but he doesn't loosen it, holding me close to his side.

"Don't distract him. Stay out of the fray," Xavier hisses, and I stop fighting. He's right. Essos needs to be focused.

"What is the meaning of this?" Galen demands, advancing on Essos.

Xavier pulls me to one side of the aisle.

"The meaning of this is obvious. You are trying to steal my *wife,* and I'm here to stop you." Essos seems unconcerned. He doesn't even appear to be in a rush.

"You're too late." Galen tries to add a tone of victory, but now he's uncertain, and I get a thrill.

"As a member of the Council, I have the right to provide a trial. I think, given the circumstances of the tie, it's very appropriate." Essos's tone is cool, and he looks marvelous in low-slung jeans and a black T-shirt that stretches over his muscular frame.

"No, you are too close to the situation." Posey's tone is panicked as she crowds closer to us.

"I think that sounds like an excellent idea, son. What is your trial?" Titus asks. The way we are clustered lends an us-versus-them feel to the situation. No one dares to contradict the God Supreme. Without Octavia here, there's no one who could.

"Use the Scepter of the Dead to take a soul from the Afterlife."

Essos makes it sound so simple, so easy to just pluck a soul from the Afterlife. It isn't, which makes the disappearance of the souls all the more troubling.

Galen turns red at the demand, probably knowing that he'd have better luck changing the color of the sun. There will be no winning this trial. There will be no wedding. There will be no crown. Essos knows it, Galen knows it, Posey knows it, and Titus knows it. Without the scepter, it's an impossible task.

"This is *bullshit!*" Galen shouts, and we all face him.

Xavier moves away from me, letting Cat move to my side between us. Her hand slides into mine and squeezes. Nothing like getting an eleventh-hour save after all.

"This is bullshit," Galen repeats.

"What is *bullshit* is you killing my wife and thinking that means you have any sort of claim to her. What is bullshit, *little brother*, is you throwing a temper tantrum because you lost. Fair and square. This is over," Essos seethes, his mouth pinched in a line. He's still standing where he entered, a gulf of space between us. I'm not looking at anyone but him...and that is my mistake. I took my eyes off the venomous snake because I thought it was caught.

"If I can't have her, no one can."

I turn my head just in time to see a knife sailing through the air. It's too long and wide to be *the* dagger, so at worst, this is going to hurt like a bitch.

But Cat doesn't have that train of thought. She just sees the weapon. She sees it sailing through the air, and my best friend places her body between me and the blade. The force of the impact pushes her into me, and I stumble backward, falling to the ground with my friend in my arms.

"No, no, no!" I cry, holding on to her. I don't want to move her too much, because I know that Galen's aim is deadly. I know that the sharp point is pressed into her heart, and with each breath, with each movement, more and more blood is seeping out of her chest. She should die instantly, but she doesn't, so I have hope that he did miss, but when she coughs and blood bubbles out of her mouth, I know it's too late.

I should tear my eyes away, scream for Xavier to do something, *anything*. If I take out the knife, she'll die instantly. The weapon itself is the only reason she's not gone yet. I can't stop crying as the realization hits home. I have no idea what will happen to her soul. When I almost died during the Calling, Essos thought that my soul would be lost, but we have no idea what will happen to Cat.

"Red does hide blood well," she quips, and I press my hands around the blade and her wound. My thoughts are too panicked, too frayed, for me to grab on to any sort of power that could help her. I can cover the wound, I can pack it, but I can't seal it. I can't close the hole in her lung or the possible nick in her heart.

"Cat, you're going to be okay. I'll fix this. Someone here has to be a healer. Someone help me!" I scream, my voice breaking, but everyone is too stunned to move. I look at Essos, begging and pleading with my eyes for him to do *something*. He is the King of the Underworld. he can step in; I just don't understand why he's not. Even Xavier just falls to his knees. I feel hands on my shoulders, holding me as I tap into my power to try to heal her, try something, anything, but my powers don't respond, like even they know it's too late to try. And that's the truth of it. It's too late. Essos and Sybil could heal wounds that aren't mortal wounds like this one. "Please, damn it." My tears are falling on Cat's cheeks, making it look like she's the one crying.

"I remember," she whispers, her eyes on mine, a hand reaching for my face. Her bloodstained fingers graze my cheek, and then it falls limply to her side.

"No, no, no. You can't—" My voice breaks. "Cat, you're my person, my ride or—" I can't finish. I hug her to my chest, and then I scream. The force of my grief causes a concussive force outward, sending people stumbling away as I sink into my grief. Silence falls around me as I hold my best friend's cooling body. Finally, gently, I place Cat's body on the ground. Then I rise to my feet.

"You have taken everything from me." My voice is low and lethal. I realize that Essos has come to me. He doesn't offer me comfort this time, but places something cold and hard in my hand.

"She shouldn't have gotten involved," Galen snarls, like it's Cat's fault for wanting to protect me. He moves toward me, and suddenly power floods my veins, that same power that abandoned me when I needed to save Cat responding tenfold.

I call two large creatures from the ground. My floor shatters as they emerge, made of roots and vines and thorns, and advance on him.

"You shouldn't have magic!" Ellie exclaims.

I remove her mouth, done with hearing her voice. I spare her a glance, just so I can always hold on to that memory. Noticeably absent is Miranda, who was probably smart enough to get the fuck out while she could. Ellie's eyes flash angrily in my direction as she pulls at where her mouth should be. For now, she should feel lucky I don't do worse, but I have bigger fish to fry.

Posey looks furious. "You're spoiling everything! Do you know how hard I have worked for this? And you are *ruining it*," she screeches.

I nearly growl. Enough about the fucking wedding. No one gives a shit anymore.

I ignore her as the root men get larger and larger, growing around Galen until they have most of him covered. He cannot struggle; he is locked into place. I look down at what Essos gave me and smile grimly, then flip the dagger in my hand and advance, my footsteps slow but sure. Galen tries to struggle, but I won't let him, nearly encasing him in roots. It's not sporting of me, to hold him back and make him defenseless, but I. Don't. Care.

He must dig deep into his own well of powers, because he blows through his encasement, sending chips of wood flying around the room. If it hadn't felt like a physical blow for him to do that, I might have reacted fast enough to change the debris into something softer. Instead, I feel it slice my cheeks as he rains wood chips down on the room.

"What have you done, you stupid, good-for-nothing oaf!" Posey screeches, suddenly there, pounding her tiny fists on Galen. He ignores her and pounces on me, grabbing my arm and twisting it.

"You made me do it. Her death is on *you*, Daphne. If you had just been good and done what you were told, your friend would still be alive," Galen shouts, spittle flying in my face.

I can sense Essos behind me, moving to intercede, but I don't need him to save me this time. Kai taught me well, and I'm able to break free of Galen's hold, surprising him. Just for that look, it's all worth it.

I try to strike him with the weapon Essos gave me, but he parries the blow with a weapon of his own. I start to lay a trap, forcing him to chase me. Galen falls for it, thinking he has the upper hand until a vine snakes up between us and blocks him. The surprise has the desired effect, because he stumbles back against a wall. My newly-forged root monsters are there to catch him and hold him fast once more.

That's when I strike, stabbing the dagger into his heart, forcing it in to the hilt. Shock flickers in his eyes, maybe that I had it in me, but he did this. He made me this hateful thing.

"How does it feel, asshole?" I choke out, tears streaming down my face. His hand reaches out to touch my face, brushing away a tear.

"I only wanted to love you." His voice is a whisper, barely audible. My tears are not for him. They are for me, for Cat, for what he took with his dagger. I can finally start to balance the scales.

"Liar," I snarl.

His gold-flecked eyes stay on mine, the light starting to leave them. I didn't have to do this, so up close, so personal. I'm sure Essos would have done it, but I wanted to feel Galen's blood on my own hands.

"Posey," he whispers, and I'm confused why he would call out for her, but it's too late to ask questions. The light is gone, the stone at the end of the dagger bright, swirling now with his soul. That's when I realize that this blade isn't the same one that he used to kill me long ago, and I'm almost disappointed to lose the symmetry of that. It's such a stupid thing to hold on to, but it keeps me from spiraling. This must be the twin blade we read about. Essos must have found it during the time we've been separated.

Hands grab my shoulders and pull me back as Galen's body is released from my root monsters, which cease to exist. His body crumples to the ground, empty of everything that made it sentient. The reality of the last several minutes starts to sink in, and a sob wracks my body.

"It's okay, love. It's over." Essos pulls me to his chest and smooths my hair as I cry over my best friend. I can't handle the amount of blood on my skin, and I want to lie down and scream, but I can't.

"You stupid, *bitch*." Posey's shrill voice breaks through my mental fog. I turn my swollen eyes to her.

"It's over, Posey." My voice is a croak. I slip out of Essos's arms and stumble in my bloody wedding dress toward Cat. I don't care that the tulle rips and gets dirtier.

I failed her.

Xavier stands beside Cat's body, which is now covered by his jacket. He looks as lost as I feel.

"No, you stupid bitch, you ruined *everything*."

My throat starts to close as Posey curls a hand in my direction. I grab at my throat, but I have nothing to grip. There are no hands to pry away from my skin. There is only Posey's fist, too far away from me. Essos jumps to his feet, running to her.

"Release her!" Startled by Essos, Posey does, and I cough. Everything in the room freezes—Titus, Xavier, even me. Only our eyes flick around, looking confused, until Posey moves. Her hand slams across my cheek, and I can't do anything about it. My head doesn't even move.

"Fuck you, you pathetic excuses for gods. Fuck every last one of you for underestimating me." She punches Essos in the face. "For belittling me." She slaps Helene. "For treating me as less than." Titus gets a knee to the balls for that. "Especially you. I can't believe I *slept* with you." Posey spits in Titus's face. "You don't deserve to even *breathe* in my presence, let alone live. I should take the God Killer and slit all of your throats and rule as Queen of Solarem. I may not be the darling that Daphne is, but if I emerge as the sole survivor of a massacre, surely the people will flock to me. They will *have* to love me then!"

Posey produces a dagger similar to the one that still protrudes from Galen's chest. The colors swirling in the stone are different, and there seem to be many shades, many souls trapped within it, undulating in circles.

This is the dagger that was plunged into my heart, and even frozen in place, my heart tries to break away in recognition.

Posey starts speaking in a language so ancient I don't even recognize it, and my grief has to be forgotten, put away in a box, because we need to figure out how Posey has managed to freeze the God Supreme and all his children. My eyes find Essos, and I see fear and understanding settle in them, I want to reach for him, but I can't move.

Posey is raising the dagger over her head, still chanting, when the doors behind me fly open and Estelle and Sybil walk in.

They look different. Gone is Estelle's chef attire, and Sybil's usual braid is loose, their long hair blowing as if in a stray wind. They're both wearing long billowing robes, Estelle's in reds and Sybil's in shades of purple.

"Sister," Estelle and Sybil say in unison. I strain my eyes to look between the three of them. Posey's outfit changes too, from her wedding finery to a similar cloak in shades of green.

"You," is all Posey says through clenched teeth.

"Us," they confirm in unison.

Posey gestures at her siblings. "This is all because that dumbass killed Catalina." Posey seems to deflate.

"What have you done, sister?" Sybil asks, surveying the room. Most of the guests fled when Galen and I started fighting. Only the frozen Council and Titus remain.

"What I had to. What you were too weak, too useless, to do yourselves."

"Our role as Fates is to never interfere," Estelle says vehemently.

"All we do is interfere! What do you think cutting threads and playing matchmaker is? It's interference, you dolts." Posey raises the dagger above her head again. What she's going to do with it, I don't know, but I assume we'll find out shortly.

"No. We plan, we weave, we set fate. Your interference with Xavier and Catalina is unacceptable. Your interference with Galen is unacceptable. Your interference with Daphne and Essos is unacceptable. How did you even get the dagger?" Sybil asks, moving a step closer. Posey scrambles backward, lowering the dagger.

"Who do you think suggested the daggers be made in the first place? Titus and Octavia were always too busy fighting and fucking to have a single other thought. But Octavia remembered they existed, and she saved me a step. I didn't even have to remove mention of them from the books, because as soon as Daphne died, Octavia knew what killed her, and *she* covered my tracks. When the daggers were forged, everyone was too focused on the Scepter of the Dead and what it was capable of to notice them, but these daggers are so much more. Titus has a scar on the palm of his hand from one dagger. It can *scar* the God Supreme. I knew they had to be capable of immortal death. Galen proved me right—the evidence is right there." She points a bony finger at me.

"This madness has to end." Estelle steps closer to Posey.

Posey shakes her head. "Don't you get it? The madness has only just begun."

She says a few more words, and then plunges the dagger into the ground.

36

A concussive force blasts from the impact. We're all unfrozen and thrown outward. Essos catches me, his body curling protectively around mine, softening the impact as we hit the wall. The ceiling rips away, and what feels like a tornado descends upon my home. Wind whips this way and that indiscriminately. Flowers, tables, and other detritus become projectiles to dodge.

I don't hesitate to get up and claw my way toward Posey. She did this. She did *all* of this. It was her actions that set everything into motion.

Posey isn't focusing on anything but her task, because whatever she did by stabbing the dagger into the ground clearly wasn't the end. I can still feel the echo of her slap on my face when I reach her, and I slam my fist into her cheek. She jolts sideways then looks up in surprise, as if she didn't expect me to hit her back.

Chaos reigns. Titus, Sybil, and Estelle are dealing with the cavern growing in my floor, trying to stop it from spreading and swallowing the house whole. Xavier jealously guards Cat's body, keeping her close to his chest and burying his face in her hair. Kai, Helene, Dion, and Finn are trying to counter the wind, but it grows in strength, pulling the walls and floor farther apart. Their efforts to create a secondary boundary around the wind seem futile. Even Luminara is working to contain the damage as best she can by turning flying debris into dust.

"What have you done?" I scream, echoing Posey's earlier outrage. The hand-to-hand fight with Posey is close to how Helene fights—dirty—but she lacks the skills of my sister. Posey grabs my hair, but I give her a solid punch in the nose and revel in a sick sense of satisfaction when the cartilage breaks under my blow.

We're still facing off as she tries to justify her actions. "I have made the world right for *me*, for *my* purposes. The people will *finally* love me. They will *finally* appreciate me and all I have done. I have so many ideas for making Solarem better, for making the people happy, and Xavier never wanted to hear them! He never listened to my suggestions on population control, or how we could effectively eliminate those social do-good programs you were always introducing. Sometimes the weak are meant to die.

"Xavier never wanted more power, would never listen when I told him to take more responsibility from Essos. Instead, he gave him *more*. I chose the wrong prince, and as I saw it happening, I thought if you broke up, I could rectify that situation, but not even him cheating on you was enough to keep you apart!" Posey maneuvers behind me and grabs me so her arm is folded across my chest, the dagger at my throat. "No, no, princeling." She turns us so I can see Essos advancing.

He slows. "Release her, Posey." Essos keeps his voice calm. When he takes another step toward me, the edge of the dagger presses into my throat.

"Essos, take the dagger and kill her. We know that the dagger traps souls, and you'll get me back, but not if you don't *kill her*. I will find you again in my next life, I swear it," I grind out through tears.

Posey laughs behind me, this horrible giggle, high-pitched and maniacal. "I wouldn't do that," she warns, and Essos's gaze shifts to where Finn is moving toward the dagger still in Galen's chest. "This stone is still full of human souls. It is *occupado,* my friend. Daphne's soul will never make it in, and neither will the soul of your babe."

Essos and I both freeze. It feels like the whole room is suspended, and I wonder if she's worked her magic and frozen everyone again. Essos's face becomes unreadable stone, and he stands up straighter, a hardness in his eyes.

"Let her go," he says, his voice soft.

"Give me the scepter," she counters, holding out her hand.

I shake my head, feeling the sharp edge of the knife nick my skin. A warm trickle of blood makes its way down my neck.

"Don't, Essos. Don't do it." I grab her wrist and try to twist it, but her powers are unlike anything I've faced before, and she freezes my whole body again. She moves the dagger from my throat and presses the blade to my lower abdomen.

"Even if you have no shred of survival instinct, think of the child that quickens in your womb. I'd estimate conception right around the end of the Calling, but who knows who the father might be?"

"I have to. I won't let her harm you or our child," Essos says to me, the Scepter of the Dead appearing in his hand, called from wherever it was hidden. He holds it out to Posey, his blue eyes trained on the blade at my belly. I can't even digest the fact that I might be pregnant right now. Essos *cannot* hand over the scepter.

"Essos. If you hand it over, what will stop her from killing me anyway?"

"You have my word," she says with a laugh. I can picture her manic face in my mind's eye.

"Why, Posey? Why are you doing this?" I ask as she grabs the scepter from Essos's outstretched hand.

She brings the blade forward and nicks his wrist before stepping away. "Because Solarem deserves better than this pantheon of fools. Titus and Octavia should never have ruled over everything, and neither should their children." She pushes me toward Essos, and he catches me and holds me close. He shoves me behind him, eyes flicking to where Kai is approaching Posey from behind. Posey smirks, flicking her wrist, and Kai disappears, an octopus appearing in his place. Helene runs forward and scoops up her husband. His tentacles wrap around his wife, clinging to her so she can be hands-free.

Posey slips the dagger into a notch in the top of the scepter's skull. As the pieces fuse together, a brilliant light illuminates the room, showing just how much bloodshed there has been. The bottom half of the scepter falls away, revealing a third sharpened blade I'm not sure any of us knew was there.

"Do *not* do this, Posey," Titus says with alarm. "I remember now. You did such a great job shielding our memories of you. It was so clever, I'm impressed."

Her eyes flash to him. "Then you remember how you belittled me and my pleas. You remember how I asked, nay, *begged* you for a greater purpose than to sit in a cavern with my siblings, weaving time and the epic lives of others."

"There is no greater power, Posey. Don't you see? You are Fate itself. You're unstoppable," Titus tells her, his hands outstretched in an appeasing manner, as if she'll just change her mind and give him the blade. I think he might actually believe that she will, and for a moment, it looks like that's what she's going to do. Posey lowers her hands in seeming defeat before she looks back up at Titus.

"I know." And she swipes the blade across his throat.

This time, Helene and octopus Kai are showered with the

429

blood of Helene's father. Titus looks shocked as the blood pours from his throat and stains his white shirt red. He gurgles as he tries to breathe, and I fight the urge to be sick. The iron scent of his blood makes me grip Essos tightly. Helene screams, running to her father as he collapses.

Essos and I are frozen as Xavier finally folds Cat's hands over her chest and rises.

"Enough, Posey." Xavier holds up a hand and pulls lightning from the sky. Thunder rolls and rain falls, washing away the blood of my friend, my tormenter, and my father-in-law. Xavier's hair, normally styled back, hangs limply around his face. His features are etched in stone as he stares down his wife. That same devastation when the gryphon died is visible in his blue eyes, only they're threaded through with golden bolts of lightning, not unlike Cat's necklace.

"No, Xavier. You had your chance." Posey's eyes are wild as her hair falls out of its intricate updo.

He doesn't hesitate, hurling the bolt at her. She barely dodges it, the lightning grazing her skin. A blackened streak appears before her skin heals back to her usual ivory complexion.

"You need to submit," he growls.

"I have never submitted to you. I just let you think I did. I saved you from an unhappy life, and this is the thanks I get? Lightning bolts? You're an ungrateful little boy! You *never* would have been happy with Catalina as your bride. My sisters might have thought you a match, but you would never have been content with only one woman in your bed. I should know. I let you get away with everything! You stuck your little prick into anything that moved, and you got the 'oohs and ahhs' I wasn't willing to fake. She would never have let you do that."

Xavier throws another bolt from the sky, and Posey skitters back just enough for it to burn through my floor and churn up the ground underneath. She smiles and doesn't hesitate to again plunge the dagger, now coated with traces of our blood, into the ground below.

Essos folds in half, clutching his midsection. I catch him, wrapping an arm around him as he groans.

"What did you do, Posey?" I scream as the storm howls.

"You're just going to have to wait and see." Her tone suggests that we're not going to like it.

She disappears in a pouf of green smoke.

I flinch, expecting something more to happen, but instead of some sort of explosion, in her absence, everything calms. The world seems to return to normal, the wind dying down and the ground stilling.

Essos straightens up, but he's visibly in pain from whatever Posey just did. The strain on his face and the slight hunch of his shoulders give him away. I rest my hand on his back, hoping to lend him strength, and he pulls my body against his and squeezes me.

"You shouldn't have backed down," I scold as he pulls back and cups my face.

"Daphne, you're pregnant. I would have given her my life if it meant your safety, and I don't regret that." His thumbs gently push my chin upward so he can look at where she nicked me with her knife.

"I'm fine," I assure him. Then I gasp. "Your father."

We turn to where Kai has reverted to his normal form. His hands rest on his wife's shoulders, and everyone is clustered around Titus's still body except Ellie, who seems to have disappeared when Posey did.

Good. I hope her mouth is still sealed shut.

"He's gone," Sybil announces calmly as the remaining two Fates approach.

We're all silent. Titus was so much larger than life. It's hard to believe that he could not be here any longer. There's no stone to store his soul in and bring him back. Nothing can undo the blade across his throat.

Helene's strangled cry is the only sound in the room as this sinks in.

"But we can still save her," Estelle says, gesturing at Cat.

"How?" Essos, Xavier, and I all demand at the same time.

"Do it," I then say without hesitation. They can explain as they get started.

"Posey locked her in a loop. She's been dying in the mortal realm and returning to the mortal realm over and over and over, without ever entering the Underworld," Sybil explains as they kneel beside my friend.

I want to reach out to Cat, to hold her hand while they do this, but Essos prevents me from going to her side. He's not wrong to do so—who knows what effect the Fates' magic will have on Cat, let alone a baby. I cling to him, remembering the *Titanic* dream she had.

"Dying in our realm released her from that loop," Estelle finishes.

Both Estelle and Sybil lay their hands on Cat's still body, and Xavier reaches out and takes my hand. I give Xavier the lifeline he needs and squeeze his.

"How do you know this?" Essos asks, holding me tighter.

"You mean if she had passed on to her Afterlife...?" I let my question hang. Our questions come at the same time.

"We are Fate itself. It's how Posey knew that Daphne was pregnant even before she did. Posey was our sister." There is bitterness in Estelle's voice as she explains.

"Cat would have started to loop again," Sybil tells me, not bothering to look at me.

"What did Posey mean about me and Catalina?" Xavier asks, eyes intent on them.

They ignore him as they start to chant under their breaths.

Light emanates from their hands, red from Estelle and purple from Sybil.

The knife slides from Cat's chest and clatters to the ground, allowing her wound to close.

There is a long pause as we all wait to see what will happen. It stretches longer and longer and *longer*, and with each second, with each hiccupping sob from Helene, my hope starts to diminish, until I feel Xavier's hand go slack in mine.

It didn't work. Of course, it didn't work.

My knees start to give out, but Essos is there, holding me, standing for both of us. I want to crawl back to Catalina and apologize for all the wrongs I've done her.

Then it happens.

Cat takes a deep breath in and sits up. She's visibly confused.

"What happened? Where's Galen? Is it my turn to kick him in the family jewels?" Her brain catches up, her hand flying to where her wound should be, only to find her skin healed.

I pull out of Essos's grasp and drop to my knees beside her. I hug her to me, a sob breaking free. I'm grateful for the space that Xavier gives us. Her arms fold around me as I cry into her shoulder.

Estelle speaks. "We had meant for Catalina to become Queen of the Gods, but our sister intervened." She looks at Cat. "Before Solarem was established, Posey put your soul in the mortal realm and rewove you out of our tapestry for Solarem. She wiped all three of us from the memories of Titus and Octavia and inserted herself in your place, dooming you to a life of reincarnation."

Cat pulls away and meets my gaze. At this point, words are barely registering for me. Catalina was meant to be queen? Catalina was meant to be *here*? Does that mean...

"I'm sorry. Are you trying to say I'm a *goddess*?" she asks, her tone skeptical. She pushes to her feet, and Essos helps me up. She looks at Xavier uncertainly, her hand going to the necklace he gave her.

"The Goddess of Motherhood and Fertility, to be exact. I would wager that you have a tremendous amount to do with this particular situation." Estelle gestures at my stomach. "That charm you wear around your neck further weakened Posey's magic. Returning to your intended state is likely why you were so ill lately. During the Calling, you were in a sort of stasis, and once it concluded, Fate tried to get its hooks back into you. Without us there to guide it, it tried to correct to what was written in the stars." Estelle reaches for the necklace and runs her thumb over the smooth lapis lazuli surface. Gently, she drops it, then reaches for the offensive collar and tugs it off in one easy move.

"This...situation?" Cat asks, as if realizing she missed a lot. Her eyes keep glazing over, and I recognize the look. Memories are surfacing. How many lives did she live? How many times did she die?

What circumstances of life put us together as roommates, goddesses reincarnated as mortals? Is Fate something larger than three women and the webs they weave?

"I'm knocked up, according to Posey, but that could just be her trying to mess with us," I reason.

"It's true," Helene says. "When we sparred a few months ago and I healed you, something felt different. I chalked it up to you being in a different form, having been mortal, but pregnancy makes sense."

My cheeks burn. "If that's the case, I was *barely* pregnant," I point out.

Essos cradles me to him. Since we found out, he's refused to be more than an arm's length away from me, and I can already tell we're going to react to this situation very differently.

Even as my heart tries to run away with dreams of tiny fingers and toes and Essos stroking my swollen belly, I'm afraid to hope.

I've been disappointed too many times. The memory of meeting my mortal birth parents and seeing that exact image flashes in my mind. Was it a premonition of what was to come? Of what will be in a few short months?

Essos and I lock gazes, and an entire conversation passes between us. We share the excitement that this is real, the fear of what it means to be pregnant with Posey on the rampage with the blades, and the uncertainty about what just happened in this room. But most important is the shared joy that this thing we wanted more than anything in the world is happening now.

That this hope has taken root in my womb at both the worst possible time and the time we needed it most is probably the most apropos thing.

They say it always happens when you stop trying.

A nervous laugh claws its way up my throat, and I let my elation free. Essos gives me an uncertain smile, like he's not sure if it's mania taking root, but we both break into grins, and I kiss him, finally able to enjoy this news for the first time since hearing it.

Both of our faces are tracked with tears. Essos crushes me to his chest, and I breathe him in, able to relax into the comfort that we're *finally* together. No threat of Galen is hanging over our heads.

I bury thoughts of my tormentor immediately. I'm not going to let what happened taint my happy memories of this moment.

"Fates," Essos curses. "I blasted my pregnant wife." He runs his hands through his hair, as his gaze does another visual scan of me. As if the events he's thinking about didn't happen a month ago.

"That's sort of how this thing happens, but if you need me to explain the birds and the bees..." Cat says, with a nervous chuckle.

"It's the truth. Posey wasn't manipulating you about that,

though many of her actions were intended to compel you," Sybil states. Their voice is different; there's a dreamy quality to it.

"Not to interrupt, and really, mazel tov on the baby, but what the *fuck* just happened? What did Posey do?" Finn asks. Dion is right behind him, looking just as ashen as the rest of us.

Essos squeezes my arms then rubs my back. "I have a guess, but it's too outrageous to consider."

"What?" Xavier asks, his voice ragged.

"I think she's raising the dead."

37

The room explodes.

"How is that possible?" Xavier asks, fury tainting his words.

"The scepter. Whatever she was chanting must have unlocked other powers it had when combined with the dagger. They were created the same way, at the same time. I don't know. I'm on just as uncertain footing as you. In case you didn't notice, I never raised the dead," Essos defends peevishly.

"Did you forget about Tiffany?" Xavier points out.

"That's not the same thing, and you know it," Essos argues. "That was a one-time exception—it's not like I made a habit of it. Don't be an asshole for the sake of being an asshole."

Cat gets off the ground, still looking a little dazed as she fingers the hole in her dress. My gaze keeps being drawn to the long tear.

"Can it bring Daddy back?" Helene asks, looking up from her father's corpse. Kai helps her rise as well.

I don't see it happen, but Finn is quick with a sheet from the altar to cover Titus, and another for Galen.

"I don't think so," Essos hedges carefully.

"So, what, that stupid knife can bring Daphne back, but not Daddy? You just don't want to because you hate him." Her accusation rings in the room.

Essos slides a hand up my shoulder and tugs me even closer to him. If he could fuse me to his side, I think he would.

"It's not that simple, Hel," Essos says, looking torn between staying close to me and comforting his sister. "The dagger..." He takes a deep breath. "The dagger was left in Daphne's chest long enough for her soul to transfer into the stone as she..." Essos looks at me like he needs visual confirmation I'm here and safe. "As she died. It's too late for dad. Posey said that the stone could only hold so much. It currently holds the souls of almost everyone in the Underworld, purged and primed, for what I don't know. My guess is that the soul of a god and all the mortals in the Underworld are too much. Sybil told me the Underworld has been emptied. My guess is Posey's been orchestrating this for a while," Essos muses.

"Wait, you had time to stop and talk to Sybil before interrupting my wedding to your brother?" I ask, turning to face him.

Surprise flashes over his face, then he gives me a devilishly handsome grin. "It was all about the timing, my love."

"Have your little lovers' spat later," Xavier says. "We have much larger issues at hand. Posey murdered our father, our brother is dead, and my wife is a Fate and ran off after raising the dead. Sybil and Estelle are also Fates, and Cat is..." He looks at Cat.

She raises her eyes to his. "Cat is tired," she proclaims, squeezing my hand.

"I think we all need sleep," I say, but I know none of us will be able to sleep. It's late afternoon, maybe even evening, but we're all wired.

"I have to agree with Daphne. We need to regroup," Kai pipes up.

"I know I'm new to the whole goddess thing, but if Posey is

raising the dead, where is she doing that?" Cat asks. Her arms fold over her chest, her thumb catching the tear in her dress. Essos and I exchange a look, and he nods at the fireplace mantle behind the altar, where a TV appears. When it turns on, the screen is split with Solarem news coverage on the left and the news in New York City on the right.

They both look fairly innocuous, until the newscaster in New York cuts to coverage in Italy. A foreign correspondent is gesturing wildly, but the volume isn't on, so I nudge Essos, and we hear the voice filter into the room.

"—it sort of just appeared in the sky. No one knows how or what it is, but from what I can see, it appears to be some sort of city in the far distance. European powers are currently scrambling jets to try to get a closer look and figure out how these people have evaded notice. Have they always been here? Are aliens finally making contact? No one knows what to think, and really, Robyn, I'm just baffled."

I cut the volume and sag against Essos.

The video pans to show Solarem, which looks like a city floating on a cloud. It's barely visible from afar, but as the camera zooms in, I can make out the skyline of Solarem City. From Solarem we can't see the mortal realm, but we know it's there, somewhere beyond our borders.

"She broke the barrier," Sybil says, disbelief in their voice.

"Come again?" I ask, my voice sounding weary. I'm suddenly bone-tired and want to sink into a hot, hot bath, though I would settle for sitting.

"The barrier between realms. She broke it," Estelle explains.

"Is that better than raising the dead?" Cat asks, reaching for the bright side.

"I need a drink," I mutter, looking at Dion, who is squeezing Finn's hand. He looks so lost, so young. Dion shakes his head, denying me.

439

Essos kisses my temple.

"They think we're aliens." Helene sounds tremendously offended. It's better than the all-encompassing grief of before.

"I need to go to Solarem. We need to protect it." Xavier has found his voice, and he's found a task he can throw himself into.

"Aren't we exposed here?" Cat asks.

"Not strictly. We're on the California coast, and the house is actually *in* California. I suspect it's why your friend Steve was able to find it. Mortals could always see the house here, but if they ever try to come near, the road gets longer and longer, and they never actually get here," Essos explains.

"Will it work the same for Solarem?" Cat asks, looking to Xavier.

His expression softens but he's still worried, still angry. "We don't know. Maybe? Maybe they'll just never reach it, but we can't be certain. We haven't tested the theory."

"Uh, guys, volume?" Finn asks, motioning at the TV.

The volume rises, and we watch, slack-jawed, as skeletons and corpses move behind the newscaster. The poor man turns, dumbfounded, probably feeling like he's an extra in some movie where the world ends...and then one ambles too close to him and bites him.

The zombie apocalypse has begun.

38

No one can decide what to do, so we split up. Most go to Solarem to possibly defend it from attack, but also to do research. Since the veil between the two realms has never been broken like this, no one knows if human weapons can reach us.

I've never been happier that my house is in California.

Right now, two genies have gotten out of the bottle, and we're going to need every god, goddess, and being we know to fix this mess. Cat looks torn between staying with me or going with Xavier, their connection stronger now that they no longer have to deny something's there.

I can tell he wants her to go with him, but I'm certain he won't say it, because she'll be a distraction. Xavier has always been one to chase tail, but now I wonder if that was the Fates at work, pushing him away from Posey.

"I'm going to stay," she announces, tearing her gaze from Xavier. He nods, his only acknowledgment.

"You're always welcome here," I assure her, pulling her into another hug.

"Thanks. Now...where is Zara?" She turns to Essos.

"Safe. She's actually in the stables. I thought it was the best place for her until after whatever was going to happen... happened. I told her to stay there no matter what she heard."

"What do we do with the bodies and this?" Finn asks, holding up the dagger he removed from Galen.

"Keep it safe for now. You never know when the God of War might come in handy," Essos says. A chill runs up my spine, and Essos squeezes my side in reassurance.

I watch the TV. The reporters who are safe in their buildings are so confused, not sure what to cover or what to do. My eyes drift to the other screen with the news reports in Solarem...and my blood runs cold. The volume rises at my command, and Posey's voice filters into the room. She looks beaten and bloody. I get a sick satisfaction at seeing her broken nose. I have a feeling it's the only satisfaction I'm going to get from her being on screen.

"I cannot in good conscience stand by while the gods do whatever they want. Essos has raised the dead in retaliation for Galen winning Daphne's hand. When it became obvious she couldn't have both of them to herself, she *killed* Galen using an ancient dagger given to her by Essos. Xavier just stood by and watched, unwilling to defend his brother, and now the humans can see us! Worse—" Posey sniffles "—she killed the God Supreme, and when I tried to fight back, to stop her, she *beat* me. Know that I will do everything in my power to rectify this situation."

Octavia steps out of the background and hooks an arm around Posey's shoulders. There is a shocked murmur from the reporters. She looks every bit the ice bitch I always knew she was. Her white skin looks pale against the mourning-black dress she's already wearing, as if she anticipated this. Octavia looks at the crowd with tears in her eyes, but I can't listen to any more bullshit, so I kill the sound again. When I look at my husband, my heart breaks at the disappointment on his face.

His father is dead, and his mother is siding against her living children. Even if they didn't have the best relationship, he always had hope for things to get better.

"*Now* can I have that drink?" I ask, as silence around the room greets me.

"I guess I'll have extra rooms made up." Essos looks at everyone, but Xavier shakes his head.

"We're sticking to the plan. I'm going up there. I won't let that bitch take my kingdom."

"You have my support," Kai says, placing a hand on Xavier's shoulder.

"We should go," Helene says.

"*We* should go," I say, turning to Essos.

His response is swift and emphatic. "No. We need to stay. We have troubles in our own realm to address. We cannot face the humans and the shit that Posey is pulling and deal with what is wrong in our kingdom. And I want my wife back for one night. One night for us to recuperate, so I can make love to you properly, and then tomorrow, we will make pancakes and we will start to plan and plot how to fix this. Please, Daphne. I don't ask much from you."

"*Awk*ward," Finn mumbles into Dion's shoulder, looking away from us.

I can't argue with Essos. It's true—he never asks anything of me, but I get the feeling he'll be asking for a lot in the coming months.

"Fine." I turn to my family, the ones leaving me behind. "May the Fates protect you."

"Fuck the Fates," Xavier snarls, and leaves first, with the rest of the Council leaving shortly after.

For now, the Fates and Cat remain.

"I will get Zara and bring her back to her room in the house before taking inventory of what my sister has done," Sybil hedges.

"Yes, please. Thank you." I can't even imagine what these recent events looked like to Zara.

Estelle goes with her sibling to collect my friend.

The room feels empty now.

"How are you feeling?" I ask Cat as Essos gets to work to put the house in as much order as he can. He starts with the hole in the roof, while I walk with Cat.

"I'm feeling a lot of things that I don't know how to process. Magic 8 Ball answer? Ask again later."

"It's an adjustment, but it doesn't change anything between us. I'm here for you regardless," I say, squeezing her arm. I perhaps understand what she is feeling better than most. There aren't many of us in the "Surprise! You're a Goddess!" Club.

"Thanks," she says quietly. I can practically see the gears turning in her head. "Should I be apologizing too?" she asks as we get to the top of the stairs.

I feel somewhat more winded. Little changes in my body and how I've been feeling make more sense now.

"What for?"

Essos is trailing us slowly. He goes into my old room to rescue Waffles and the dogs, who greet him with glee. I turn Cat toward a different wing of the house, and she lets me lead her. It's the more private wing that contains Helene, Xavier, and Finn's rooms, but most importantly, the suite Essos and I share.

If Cat is staying here long-term, she and Zara will need rooms that suit them better than the spaces they occupied during the Calling and Trials. As they grow into their roles, so too should their rooms.

"I can't imagine now is a convenient time to be pregnant?" she offers sheepishly.

I snort, my hand reaching for the not-yet bump.

"No, but it's a blessing all the same. We had..." I pause, considering how to say it, "...losses before. This is something we wanted. It just means I have to be more careful. Between taking down Posey and stopping the zombie apocalypse, I'll need to see a healer."

Cat snorts. I approach a filigreed door and push it open. She walks in and finds it looking suspiciously like her room at her parents' house. It's more spacious than before. The room has converted itself into a suite, so her bedroom is separate from a sitting area and her bathroom. I tried to make it homey, something she'll feel safe in. My magic is part of the house, so now that my powers are restored, making alterations within it is something I can do with half a thought.

Without the looming presence of Galen and Posey, my magic feels freer.

"What is this?"

"I figure you need some comfort, something that feels like home. Shadow?" I call, and the dog comes running. I lift my hand, palm up, and she sits immediately, waiting for her command. "You are responsible for guarding Cat. You have done so already, but this is now an order." Shadow seems to nod, and then I lower my hand and she jumps onto the bed.

Essos and I wish Cat a good night and close the door behind us. Essos threads his fingers through mine and pulls me toward our room. Our real room. I had avoided this long hallway since getting my memories back. There was too much here, too much history to face without Essos by my side.

I'm silent as Essos twists the knob and opens the door. I expect the room to smell stale from months of disuse. I don't know if he even used the space after I died. The idea of that toad Ellie being in our room tries to surface, but I won't let it ruin this night.

Our bed is made with the same lush red comforter that

Essos and I spent many nights under, snuggled together. Burning candles fill the air with the sweet scents of a bakery. The curtains are pulled back, showing the sun setting over the beach.

My stomach churns at the memory of Galen standing over me, of the knife. Essos wraps his arms over my shoulders, pulling my back to his chest, as if reading my thoughts.

"He can't get you anymore. You're safe," he whispers. My safety in general isn't a certainty, but I *am* safe from Galen now. The tears start slowly, and then the waterworks don't stop. My knees buckle, but Essos holds me firmly against him.

For the first time since Galen put it on my finger, I'm able to rip the engagement ring off my hand. I don't give it a second thought as I cast it into the cold fireplace. Immediately, the flames roar to life, and I know I have Essos to thank for that.

"Get me out of this dress," I beg. I can feel Essos's magic tugging at it, but the dress won't budge, one long-lasting effect of Posey's magic, meant to punish me. A pair of scissors appear in Essos hands, and he very gently cuts the fabric behind my neck and down the back. Carefully, his hands slide along my shoulders under the lace. They're warm, guiding the fabric and sleeves down my arms. I finish tugging the sleeves down and let the dress drop from my hips. Essos hugs me from behind again, one arm folding around my natural waist, the other crossing my breasts. The hand on my waist drifts lower, to my abdomen.

"Let's get you cleaned up, my love." He leads me into the bathroom where our tub is already full of piping hot water, steam rising off it. Just as we did with the one in our apartment in Solarem, we had it custom-made to fit both of us. I want to get in, but the thought of sitting in a tub filled with blood makes a shudder run through me. I slip into the Tuscan-inspired glass shower stall first and turn on the water, not bothering to wait for it to warm up. Essos follows me, his body bare. I shiver in his arms, but he stays silent, taking a fresh loofah and scrubbing my neck and back.

There is nothing sexier than having your lover wash your hair. His fingers dig into my scalp, massaging away the tension headache that was forming. I turn to face him as I rinse out the shampoo.

"How are you?" I ask, my hand touching his face. His brother and father just died, and I killed one of them.

"Scared, happy that I have you back, devastated. Sorry, I'm not scared. I'm terrified." He pushes my wet hair out of my face.

"I'm sorry," I say. I'm sorry for so many reasons.

"What for, my love? What could you possibly be sorry for?" He cups my face, brushing the water off my cheeks with the pads of his thumbs. I'm not sure if it's water from the shower or my tears.

"I killed your brother. I'm pregnant at the most inconvenient of times."

A small smile tugs on his lips. "Good riddance to Galen. I am not going to lie to you and say that I'm not utterly terrified of what we're facing now, because I am, but I was able to survive losing you. We were brought back together again—I got you back, and I'm certain we can face anything as long as we do it together." His lips are soft when they brush mine. "Besides, it took two of us for this to happen. I can't let you take all the credit."

I let him lead me to the tub. Knowing that hot baths are now on my No list, I lower the temperature of the water. Finally, I'm able to sink into the warmth and let the tension seep out of my body. It soothes me, the feeling of Essos's arms around me, the press of being skin to skin with him. I need more from him though. I turn in the tub, not caring as water splashes over the sides.

Confusion flashes over Essos's face until I press my lips against his and straddle him. He grabs my hips, hands sliding up my back to my shoulders. Essos keeps our bodies pressed against each other until I grind my hips against him, feeling him harden in response. Our kisses are full of the intimacy we have shared for centuries. We know exactly which buttons to press, the right flicks of the tongue that elicit moans of pleasure.

"I thought I was going to lose you today," I tell him, moving my lips down his neck.

"I wouldn't let that happen. He could have won every trial, and I still wouldn't have let that happen. You belong to no one but yourself...except right now. Right now, you belong to me, and me alone."

"I have always belonged to you," I assure him, our eyes locked. I lift my hips and Essos positions himself at my entrance. I want to go slow, but he thrusts up, sheathing himself inside me, and I cry out from the instant fullness of him. I make sure he knows how much I need him, how grateful I am to have him back to be able to start rebuilding our lives together.

We make love in the tub until the water goes cold around us. Bundled up in our warm towels, we move to our bed.

I reach for Essos's towel, and he watches me with hooded eyes.

"Wife," he warns.

"Husband."

He doesn't object as I pull the towel off him and drop it on the floor. Essos presses a kiss to my neck, nipping when I take his erection into my hand. The weight of him in my palm has me shivering with delight. Essos doesn't rush me as I run my hand slowly down the length of him.

"I'm trying to be patient here," he scolds, slipping his hand into my hair. Essos tilts my head back, giving him better access to my neck.

"Why?"

Essos growls, tearing off my towel and baring me to him. This time, he drinks in the sight of me, finally clean of the night's events.

There's a tense pause as anticipation builds, and I wait for him to do something. When he doesn't, I pump his cock again.

This seems to snap the tether he has on his control, because he lifts me and throws me down onto the bed. I laugh, but he swallows the sound as his mouth covers mine in a decadent kiss.

He's plundering my mouth as he places his cock over my clit, rubbing himself over that sensitive bundle of nerves. It's enough for me to arch my back and moan in pleasure. I'm offering my breasts and my body to him, and he takes all of it.

He waits until I'm panting and begging under him before he finally sets himself to enter me. This time, he doesn't do it in one quick thrust. He works his way in slowly with micro-movements until I'm sobbing for release.

With one hand braced on the bed, Essos uses his other to grip my face. "Look at me my love, and remember who you belong to."

"You. Now *fuck me*, Essos, like you told everyone you would."

He slams home until I'm so full of him and love for him that I don't know where I end and he begins.

Begging is the theme of the night, because I need him to move. I need to feel every last sensation he has to give to me.

Essos and I move together until the pressure builds and builds and I am nothing more than starlight and an explosion of feeling. My powers reach out, filling all the broken places of our hearts and our home until Essos is falling the same way I am, and, for a moment, we can forget that anything exists beyond this bedroom.

Essos collapses beside me once the aftershocks of pleasure have been wrung from us both. I'm breathless and panting as he gets up to clean us both before sliding into boxers and curling his body around mine. His hand tangles in my hair, pulling gently at the damp curls as I stroke his chest.

"You can't keep me from this fight," I say, knowing he's already thinking it.

"I can't say I wouldn't dream of it, because I absolutely would, but I know you won't back down."

"Not with what Posey has done. I didn't think she was capable of such manipulation. I thought your mother was behind it."

Essos's hand stills. "I think that's the problem. We perpetually dismissed and underestimated Posey. I'm not saying that she was justified. But we need to assume she'll continue to move us around the board like chess pieces," he says.

"She was a pain in the ass. I just don't understand. Why me?" I bemoan.

"Probably because I wouldn't give her the time of day. This was before us, when she was still being courted by Xavier, but now I wonder if it was Cat he was supposed to be courting. Anyway, she came on strong, said she understood I was going to be taking on such a difficult job, figured I would want some stress relief."

I prop myself up on my elbow to watch his face as he tells me this. His eyes stay true on mine, regardless of my bare body. "I declined, and I saved you from a runaway chariot. The rest is history."

I fall back onto the bed at the thought of all the changes that have been made. "Not to speak ill of the dead, but Galen really fucked us over. The last I was able to look at our numbers, we were speeding toward the red. He was embezzling funds. I fear this is just the beginning of the deception."

Essos rolls on top of me, settling his weight over me. "We can worry about that all tomorrow. Why don't I let you worry about fixing that mess, and I'll worry about Posey and the zombies and returning all those souls to their afterlives?"

"You're funny. I've been pregnant for five minutes, and you're already sidelining me."

"Of course, I am. You would be foolish to think I won't. You would be furious with me for not even trying. If I'm going to receive your ire, then I would rather it be because I'm being over-protective. I'm going to do everything in my power to keep you safe. I deserve several centuries of exactly that." A quick kiss. "Now sleep. We had a big day."

Essos leaves no space for argument, pulling the covers up around us and holding me close. I nestle into his arms, my head on his chest. But it's still a long time before I'm able to succumb to the darkness of sleep.

39

The news in the morning isn't much better. The *Solarem Times* discusses the incompetence of the royal family. There is no confidence in Xavier and Essos. The only one who seems to be escaping the ire of the citizens is Helene. I'm grateful that she and Kai still hold their trust. It gives me hope that we'll come out of this on top.

Essos drops a plate of pancakes in front of me with a kiss pressed to my temple before he sits beside me.

"I made breakfast," he says brightly. "It didn't seem right to ask a Fate to keep cooking for us."

"You're going to need us for a lot more than that." Sybil walks in with Zara behind them. I jump up and hug Zara, crying, thankful that she's safe. When Cat comes in, the three of us cling to each other.

"Posey is bent on destroying everyone. The Afterlife is now being overwhelmed by those killed by zombies, and there's an incredible amount of support for her in Solarem." Estelle takes a seat beside Sybil.

"We need to retrieve the scepter, and we need to get the souls back from the mortal realm and into the Underworld," I say.

"Thanks, Captain Obvious." Zara rolls her eyes.

I forgive her the snark, since we're all dealing with a lot of stress that no one knows what to do with. "That's *Queen* Obvious, thank you very much." I take a huge bite of pancake.

Essos rubs my back, winking at me. "We've faced worse odds."

"When? *When* have we faced worse odds, because the answer is never." I force a laugh. I don't know if it's the morning sickness or nausea over what we have to do, but I feel sick.

Essos's hand reaches forward, brushing my abdomen before settling on my thigh. "I don't know, but we *will* do this. I'm not going to give up on getting peace and quiet back. I have the ulti-mate gift, which I'm working to protect. Trust me. Posey might think she's motivated, but she's not."

"She's also killable," Estelle says.

"Are you okay with that?" I ask, frowning. "Killing your sister?"

"She stopped being our sister when she enchanted us. When she stuck me as a cook. Not that I resent you all, but honestly, I used to weave the most beautiful lives. She took everything from us. Even before her latest moves, the human world was in chaos. Without the intervention of the Fates, things have been happening in a way they shouldn't have. With our help, you can defeat her, but it comes at a price."

"Everything has a price," Essos grumbles.

"Are you willing to pay it, King of the Dead?" Sybil asks, eyeing us both.

Essos and I look at each other. Are we?

"Anything is negotiable," Essos drawls. He marks that I've stopped eating and rubs my back.

"To kill a Fate will throw the world balance out of equilibrium. We need a replacement." Estelle purses her lips.

I turn to look at the woman who was living her great life as a cook. Whatever magic Posey was using was ancient and powerful. She was able to banish a goddess to live in a loop in the mortal realms. She forced her great siblings into small roles and toyed with their memories. Who knows what else she has done?

"Add it to the list. Estelle, I need your help in Solarem. I think you and Gisella should be able to find any texts that might possibly be hidden by your sister's magic." I turn to Sybil. "I'm sorry to do this to you. I don't want to force you into a smaller role than you have, because you're a Fate and deserve the utmost respect, but Galen and Posey wreaked havoc on the Afterlife. We need to fix it, and we need to fix it fast. You have the experience and the information we need to make that happen, or I wouldn't ask."

Sybil places a hand on my forearm. The siblings share a look, and I have no doubt that they're communicating silently. "Of course, any assistance you require, Your Majesty."

I fight the urge to roll my eyes. "Pretty sure Fate ranks higher, but whatever you want. Cat, take time to digest everything. Zara, I want you to stay with her. Essos and I have damage control to do."

Essos nods. He doesn't contradict me or my orders.

"I'm fine to jump in and help," Cat says, and I look at her.

"I don't doubt you, but I also don't want to overwhelm you. Take a week—just a week—and relax, please. We need to figure out exactly what your situation is. This is going to be a marathon battle. If you want to do something right now, you can visit the house library and learn more about anything and everything."

"You're giving me homework, Your Majesty?" There's an edge to her tone.

"Yes. I am." We lock eyes, and she looks away first.

Cat rises with grace. "Then as my queen commands, I think I'll head to the library with Zara." She doesn't give me a chance to apologize before she strides out, followed by a slightly smirking Zara.

The Fates are not far behind, ready to tackle their new tasks.

There is a tense moment in the room as the stark reality sinks in. Nothing is the same.

I turn to Essos. "We should visit the Underworld today, see if we can find out what Galen has done. We need to show our faces, reassure our employees that we're back and will sort things out."

"I can go to the Underworld and you can look into the paperwork," he suggests, putting a piece of bacon on my plate as if I can be bribed. As if we didn't talk about him doing this very thing last night.

"Essos..." I warn.

"Yes, love?"

"We're in this together. That's what we took vows for. You wanted my blood keyed to the kingdom so that we would be equals. Me being pregnant doesn't change that."

I think perhaps seeing the vitriol in the papers has changed that for him. Some of the things being printed about me in the *Solarem Sun* turned my cheeks pink. Someone offered an expose about my sex life with Galen and how I was planning a coup for not only the Underworld but for all of Solarem.

The so-called evidence is damning. Years of correspondence related to Xavier's lack of attention to Solarem social projects that I worked on, comments made about how, if Xavier wasn't interested in ruling, he should leave it to those of us who are.

Quotes from old friends and employees filled an entire page across from an in-memoriam article listing those who died because of my actions. I understand Essos's protectiveness, but I'm not going to be locked away in my own home any longer.

"No, being pregnant doesn't change that, but it does change

what you should do. First and foremost, we need to get a healer to check you out, and then—"

Essos never finishes his sentence because Xavier appears in our dining room, looking worse for wear.

"She locked me out of my fucking house, my office, everything. That *bitch*." Xavier is still dressed in his clothes from last night; Cat's blood is right there on the white of his dress shirt, and whatever appetite I had left flees.

"Posey?" Essos asks for clarification, even though it's obvious.

The blank glare from his brother confirms that was a stupid question. "Certainly not our mother, who has forsaken her children in favor of that two-faced whore."

"You're always welcome to stay here," I offer. "After all, my husband decided this is the Hotel California."

Essos twists to face me. "You *are* allowed to leave. I just want it to be safer when you do so, and for you to wait until *after* a healer has looked you over."

Xavier glances skeptically between the two of us. "As tempting as your offer is to stay here with a different sort of marital strife happening between these walls. I'll pass. I need you to let me into your apartment in Solarem."

"Which one?" Essos asks, then blanches when my head snaps toward him.

Xavier shakes his head. "I meant the apartment the two of you shared, not your den of sin."

Wow. Okay, clearly, we will be having words about *that* later. I have to assume it's the apartment where Essos took Ellie, and I'm grateful he didn't bring her into our space, but the idea that he has this whole place that's his and that I don't know anything about doesn't sit well with me. Especially when paired with the fact that he took her there.

"Of course, you can stay in our apartment." I push up out of my chair to move toward Xavier. "We can take you straight there. I assume since your wife is trying to lead a revolt against you, you don't want to be seen on the streets."

Essos beats me to it, running to his brother's side. "You sit and relax, maybe see if Sybil can find you some of the actual reports on the number of souls Posey stole from the Underworld."

"Essos," I warn again. "Don't do this." I could transport myself, but that's not the point.

"I'll be back. I'll even bring some of those cream puffs you like." He doesn't even hesitate. "I love you."

His promise still rings in the air when he and Xavier disappear.

40

My anger is palpable, and as I pace around in the ruins of my living room, I think of all the clever ways I'm going to make Essos rue the day he decided not to listen to me. We're supposed to be partners. We're supposed to make decisions together, and him leaving with Xavier feels like a decision we did *not* make together.

I'm still pondering my options, including making Essos sleep in a guest room—which would only serve to punish *me*—when Miranda runs into the room. She's rather put together, given how disastrous the evening was for the rest of us.

"Where in all of the Underworld have you been?" I demand, turning on her.

Her nervousness is gone, replaced with a certain shift of her eyes. "Would you believe me if I told you?"

I study her. She's wearing skinny jeans and a blazer that just barely covers her breasts. The creamy white skin of her chest is on display, and I wonder just how much I don't know about this girl.

"Would you tell me the full story?"

"Yes, but I need you to come with me." She casts another furtive glance around the room and relaxes when she sees that I'm alone.

I cross my arms, skeptical. "Why should I trust you?" She's never given me any reason to do so.

"Because Celestina is my best friend, and I think she's still alive. I figure, since you nearly got her killed, it's the least you can do."

GUILT WINS ME OVER. The reporter didn't deserve her fate for taking the tip I gave her and running with it. If there's a chance Galen was lying and made her a prisoner somewhere, I have to take it.

If Essos gets home before I'm back and finds me gone, he's going to be livid, and worse, worried. So, I do what any responsible wife would do. I leave him a note and take backup.

With Dave by my side, I transport us and Miranda to where she thinks Celestina is being held. It's in the Deep, a location a little too clever for my liking, holding the woman there under my nose.

The silence of the Deep is more bone-chilling than the fighting was. Not even the wind blows through as we walk through this section of the Afterlife. The soul trees I made are gone, sucked into the dagger by Posey. There is so much that is fucked up about this situation, and not even knowing where to start fixing it is problematic. When I became queen, I swore to serve the souls of the Underworld, and I've done nothing but fail. Maybe the *Solarem Sun* had it right when they called me the Queen of Failure.

Another secret under my nose. It makes me wonder who, exactly, Cassius was talking about when he warned me.

"Start from the beginning," I command as we walk. I keep my voice low, as if I might disturb someone. Truthfully, I'm a little afraid of disturbing the eerie silence. My footsteps sound too loud to my ears.

Miranda copies my tone, her voice hushed as she stays by my side, Dave between us. "Celestina and I met at Solarem University. She's always been a reporter, and I was her inside source. When she found out that Posey was looking for loyal lady's maids, I put my hat in the ring."

"And you were chosen just like that?" I raise a disbelieving eyebrow.

"No. You know Posey. I had a leg up because I knew someone who helped me get in. I just had to agree to tell Posey everything. You want to know who was leaking story after story about what was happening inside the house? It was me. I was the inside source. After Posey's trial, Celestina told me that she had some scoop from you and wanted my corroboration, but I warned her that Posey wouldn't want anything negative printed about Galen."

"Do you know if they were having an affair?" Not that I care, but I wondered.

"Galen and Posey? No, she had her sights on someone else—someone who doesn't return her affections. But still not the point. The *point* is, Celestina's in there."

Miranda stops walking and gestures at a cave. It's been a long time since I was able to tour the Underworld. I don't remember this cave being part of it. I don't know when this cave appeared in our realm, but I wish Essos were here with me to investigate.

"Lead the way," I tell her, waving her on.

I've seen horror movies. I'm not walking into the scary cave with an unknown at my back. I'm not sure I can trust Miranda. I'm glad she's not dead, but she's done nothing to prove I have any reason to trust her—if anything, she's proven that I *can't* trust her.

"I can't go in. It's warded. As a goddess and Queen of the Underworld, you can. Isn't that what you love to tell everyone, that your blood makes you queen?"

She's baiting me, and I lift my chin. Around me, it feels like the temperature has dropped. Dave is growling.

"It does, but if you think I'm dumb enough to walk into a cave..."

Then it happens.

A pained voice calls out to us from the depths of the darkness. "Please...help me..."

I know that voice. The smugness is gone. Instead, there is only desperation in it. Celestina.

Fuck.

My gaze flicks to Miranda. "If I die again, I'm going to be really, *really* pissed." I look down at Dave and wish that I had brought Spot and Shadow too, but it looks like it's going to be just the two of us.

I conjure a blade. I don't know if this will work, but it has to be better than trying nothing. Miranda takes a cautious step back.

"What are you..."

"This isn't for you." I slide the blade along my palm, wincing as the sharp edge cuts into my skin. Yeah, Essos is going to be super pissed about this too. I hold my hand out and wait for her to take it. "Tell me, where have you been all this time?"

Miranda flinches, her eyes wide, before she speaks. "Busy, trying to clean up your messes."

I expect her to keep balking at my offered hand, but eventually, she does slide her hand into mine. The shock from our touch surprises me, and her critical gaze does nothing to assuage my concerns that I can't trust her.

Blowing out a resigned puff of air, I gesture for Miranda to lead the way into the cavern, a little surprised when nothing stops us. All the hairs on my arms stand on end as my eyes adjust to the darkness. Magic so potent I can smell it fills the air. Miranda drops my hand and steps farther into the cavern until she's out of sight. Dave positions himself between me and the vast emptiness before us. His growling grows in volume before he barks.

"Miranda?" I call, stepping farther in, but Dave's reaction gives me pause. I may not know Miranda well, but I still don't want her to die in here.

"How nice of you to finally join me, Daphne. I've been looking forward to this heart-to-heart for a long time."

I've cursed that voice many times.

When a glowing orb appears, I wince at the brightness. I don't want to stick around to hear what this woman has to say, but when I try to transport Dave and me out, I can't.

"You're not going anywhere anytime soon, little queen. Not until we've had a talk."

Dave's barking stops as I glare at the woman before me. As she stands in front of me, I'm not imagining that she's getting taller— I'm watching it happen Her features change from the soft-faced innocent who helped clean the blood from my bedroom into sharp cheekbones that are all too familiar. The blonde hair that had been flowing around her shoulders pulls up and away from her face into a severe bun, and she looks just as glorious as she has since the dawn of time. She practically shines in a beige sheath dress.

It's the eyes that seal the deal, as they change from deep cerulean to familiar ice blue.

My stomach bottoms out as I realize what I've done. What a colossal mistake I've made.

Octavia.

The Goddess Supreme.

My mother-in-law.

I'm caught in her snare, and all I can think is how Essos was right.

ACKNOWLEDGMENTS

It is thanks to the support of so many people that this book is out in the wild.

I would be remiss if I didn't thank you, my readers, for your continued love of Daphne and Essos's story. Your reactions and theories and enjoyment makes every late night and hair pulling moment worth it.

To my husband, Michael, for being the best cheerleader I could have ever asked for. On days when I can't believe in myself, you believe in me enough for both of us. Even as I worked through two vacations

To my sisters, Jennifer and Danielle, your enthusiasm is *everything*.

To Tracy, Hannah, and Katie for helping keep me sane as I second guessed myself at each turn.

I cannot thank Tashya and Amanda enough for helping make this story the absolute best it can be. Your comments and feedback kept my spirits up.

COMING SOON

The stunning conclusion arrives Spring 2023!

THE ROYAL GAUNTLET

Pre-order here now!

About the Author

Nicole Sanchez has been writing stories on any scrap of paper she could get her hands since before middle school. She lives in New Jersey with her high school sweetheart and love of her life along with their two quirky cats. When she isn't writing or wielding the Force, she can be found traveling the world with her husband or training for her next RunDisney Event.

For more books and updates:

Newsletter

Website

Facebook Reader Group

ALSO BY NICOLE SANCHEZ

Love in the Big Apple Series:

Central Park Collision

Las Vegas Luck

Madison Avenue Mediator

Game of Gods Series:

The King's Game

The Queen's Gamble

The Royal Gauntlet